Elizabeth Coleman is the author of four published plays, including the smash hits *Secret Bridesmaids' Business* and *It's My Party (And I'll Die If I Want To)* (published by Currency Press). Her theatre writing has also appeared in several anthologies. As a screenwriter Elizabeth adapted *Secret Bridesmaids' Business* into an award-winning ABC telemovie and has written for many of Australia's most popular dramas, including *Miss Fisher's Murder Mysteries*, *SeaChange* and *Bed of Roses*, which she co-created with Jutta Goetze. Elizabeth's prose has appeared in *Dear Jack* (published by Random House), *New Idea*, *The Sun-Herald* and *The Newcastle Herald*. *Losing the Plot* is her first novel.

Losing
the
Plot

elizabeth coleman

ALLEN&UNWIN
SYDNEY · MELBOURNE · AUCKLAND · LONDON

First published in 2019

Allen & Unwin
83 Alexander Street
Crows Nest NSW 2065
Australia
Phone: (61 2) 8425 0100
Email: info@allenandunwin.com
Web: www.allenandunwin.com

 A catalogue record for this
book is available from the
National Library of Australia

ISBN 978 1 76063 343 1

Set in 12/16.2 pt Minion Pro by Bookhouse, Sydney
Printed and bound in Australia by Griffin Press

10 9 8 7 6 5 4 3 2 1

 The paper in this book is FSC® certified.
FSC® promotes environmentally responsible,
socially beneficial and economically viable
management of the world's forests.

For Alan, just because

'No one can make you feel inferior without your consent.'

Eleanor Roosevelt

Chapter 1

VANESSA

The End.

Vanessa paused and frowned at her laptop as dawn broke outside the kitchen window. Was it cheating to write the last two words first? Not according to Natalie.

'It'll help give you the confidence that you *can* actually finish,' she'd said. 'And then your novel won't just become an abandoned displacement activity so you can avoid processing your pain.'

Natalie was a counsellor, she knew about this kind of stuff, and her advice was proffered with a perfectly judged balance of professionalism and personal warmth. Vanessa could still picture her supportive smile and feel the gentle squeeze of her hand.

Bitch. Whore. Husband stealer.

But still. She'd be cutting her nose off to spite her face if she didn't take advantage of Natalie's expertise. Although look how that had turned out the first time.

'I'm leaving you for Natalie.' The End.

She should have known there was something wrong when Craig suggested they talk their feelings through with a counsellor, but she

1

was so excited when he used the words 'talk' and 'feelings' in the same sentence that she somehow missed the signals. Craig was a man of few words, who was always loath to discuss his emotions unless they related to sport. In front of the footy with his mates he'd weep with joy over a 'screamer' and wallow in unbridled sentimentality about players' retirements and knee replacements, but when relationship issues came into play, it was like a door slammed shut. Vanessa sometimes wondered if putting on a pair of footy shorts and kicking a ball around the kitchen might get her more of a reaction? The thought tickled her, but she'd never do it. Mainly because she knew it was juvenile. And there was cellulite to consider too.

But then they'd sat in Natalie's office and something about the counsellor's empathic gaze and toned biceps opened a floodgate, and an ocean of emotions spilled out of Craig.

'I'm sorry, Ness,' he mumbled at the end of a lengthy monologue, 'but I need someone I can communicate with.'

Oh.

'Well, if that doesn't take the cake!' she wanted to yell when she could eventually think again. 'It might have been handy to tell me this before, and then maybe I wouldn't have wasted the past ten years respecting your need for silence.' But instead she was silent. Shock will do that to you.

Vanessa heard herself exhale. Eight months later, Craig's absence was still the primary presence in the house, and right now she could feel him in every corner of the tired old kitchen. They'd been planning to renovate when they bought this 1960s bungalow in multicultural Preston in Melbourne's north eight years ago. Grand dreams of granite benchtops and open-plan family living! All come to nothing, because Craig was too busy building other people's houses—and maybe his heart was never really in it anyway? It was ironic that there was so much building going on all around them—in the past few years, three neighbours had sold to developers who'd promptly demolished their houses and stuck up apartment blocks. The feel of the quiet street where everyone once knew each other was changing, and Vanessa wondered who'd succumb next. At least Mrs Bianchi next door, who'd been in Australia since 1972 but still had only a rudimentary grasp of English, was clinging on.

Daisy nudged Vanessa's leg for a pat, and she reached under the table to scratch her beloved labradoodle's head. Daisy met her gaze as if to say, 'It's okay, we'll get through this together,' and Vanessa's eyes misted over. Funny how a dog can do that to you. Through the window she could hear little mynas tweeting on telegraph poles and her heart ached for the smog on their tiny lungs, but the sun was rising over the backyard and she could spot the first daffodils popping up, so that was something. Vanessa wasn't much of a gardener but she loved daffodils. But, then, who didn't? Spring. New beginnings.

She turned back to her laptop. *The End*. That's how it had felt when Craig left. And now here she was, on the brink of forty, which she was contemplating celebrating by sticking her head in a bucket. No, not really.

Well, possibly.

She regarded her rounded tummy under her dressing-gown. At size 12 she was one size smaller than the average Australian woman, so how come the clothes she bought were almost always labelled 'large'? It was a conspiracy against womankind and she knew it, but it still made her feel like an elephant. Especially when she compared herself to Natalie, whose tummy was as flat and taut as a drum. Natalie was a fitness junkie. Which seemed at odds with being a relationship counsellor, but why should it? Just because she spent all day sitting in a chair listening to people complain and cry, it didn't mean she was sedentary by nature. Far from it! Sitting was just what Natalie did when she wasn't working out, her glossy dark ponytail swinging from side to side as she attended boot camp in the park each morning, optimising her own wellbeing so she could be there completely for her clients. With compassion in her heart and Nikes on her feet, Natalie was Craig's dream girl. And the fact that her eyes were beady and a bit too close together was clearly an irrelevancy to him. Sitting here in front of her laptop, Vanessa couldn't help thinking that Craig and Natalie were living a grand love affair in real life, while she would have to suffice with fiction.

She was going to call her novel *Lost and Found Heart*. It would tell the tale of Georgie Sinclair, a feisty New York cardiac nurse who is assisting in a heart transplant operation when she discovers that the donor heart belongs to her fiancé, who has just been killed in a car crash. Georgie faints in the operating theatre, incurring the wrath of the arrogant but brilliant transplant surgeon, Dr Magnus Maddison. It's the first of many clashes between them, but as the tale unfolds and Georgie's heart heals, she and Magnus surrender to their sexual chemistry and fall deeply in love. Dr Magnus Maddison is an alpha male who intuits Georgie's emotional needs and will never fall out of love with her. But how do you *fall out* of love, anyway? 'Oops, I fell.' Like love was a hammock. Vanessa thought that falling out of love was just an excuse for people who'd stopped trying. But Magnus would never stop trying—not that he'd need to try, because he and Georgie were perfect for one another.

Vanessa was suddenly gripped by panic. She was a dental assistant, for goodness' sake. For twenty-three years she'd been sterilising orthodontic pliers and ingesting humanity's fetid breath. That might qualify her to scribble a handbook on flossing etiquette, but a romance novel? Who was she kidding? But then she rallied as her mind flew back to the 1994 Lower Plenty High School speech night, and holding her breath as she watched Mrs Flannery the English teacher waddle up to the microphone. The mic made that awful high-pitched sound and Mrs Flannery reeled back, wincing.

But then she regrouped and announced: 'The year ten English prize is awarded to Vanessa Spriggs.'

Vanessa remembered her face flaming with pride and embarrassment as Mrs Flannery told the assembled parents, 'Vanessa has done wonderful work on our English texts all year, but it's her creative writing that shows particular promise.'

Applause!

Vanessa pondered the screen. Should she put a full stop after *The End*? She turned to a pile of medical-themed romances by her favourite author, Charlotte Lancaster, but a quick flick-through revealed that none of them ended with *The End*. So where did that leave Natalie's advice to start with *The End*?

Brrrrring!

It was 6.30 am already?! Vanessa jumped to her feet in frustration and flicked off the oven alarm. All she'd written were two redundant words and she'd have to get the kids out of bed soon. Her heart lurched as she plugged in the iron and grabbed a couple of crumpled school shirts from a washing basket. Her oldest son Jackson was now nudging thirteen, and the sensitive little boy she'd adored had morphed into a smelly stranger who got up to God knows what in his bedroom—although judging by his crusty sheets, she could guess. She was just glad he didn't share a room with his rambunctious younger brother Lachie, who'd just turned ten. Of course, it was inevitable that puberty would snatch Lachie too, but there was no need to give it a head start.

Once again, she was struck by how sad it was that the boys no longer had their dad at home to help them navigate that stuff. How had it come to this? They said in retrospect you could see the signs but, in all honesty, she hadn't. She'd always assumed she and Craig would live happily ever after, even when they weren't. It had never occurred to her that she'd become a single mum with hairy ankles and a hole in her heart where her husband had been.

Heart!

Inspiration zapped like a thunderbolt. She had the last sentence of her book! She hurried back to the table and planted herself in front of her laptop, typing rapidly with three fingers:

Magnus drew her into his arms. He put his hand over her heart and gently lay her hand on his own. 'You hear that?' he said. 'Two hearts beating as one.'

Vanessa sat back and beamed with pride. For the first time in eight months, she felt a flicker of optimism.

Which meant that Natalie was right. Damn.

Chapter 2

Georgie handed Magnus a needle and suture thread, and she felt a shock of electricity as their hands touched through their sterile gloves. Those same manly hands that sent electricity pulsing through her fingers had just placed a new heart into the chest of her critically ill sister—

'Give it back!'

'Get off me!'

'Mum! Lachie stole my phone!'

Oh great, the boys were at it again. Vanessa tried to ignore the fracas coming from Lachie's bedroom.

'Tell him to give it back!'

'Shut up, you loser!'

'*You're* the loser!'

'M-u-u-u-u-m!'

Vanessa didn't budge, because quite frankly her bum would have to be on fire to make her leave the computer right now. Almost a year to the day since typing *The End,* she was tapping towards the finish line! She could scarcely believe it. Somehow she'd dragged herself out of bed at 4.30 am for three hundred and sixty-eight days in a row. She'd stuck it out through all the doubts, until the ideas had started flowing and Dr Magnus Maddison and sassy nurse Georgie Sinclair came alive and somehow made everything else make sense. It was as if creating a fictional world had helped her to see the real one more clearly.

In hindsight, Craig wasn't solely at fault for their marriage failure—not that anyone ever is. Vanessa could see now that she'd tried too hard not to rock the boat. She should have demanded Craig's attention and engaged in some air-clearing argy-bargy, but conflict had always made her toes curl. She sometimes wondered if things would be different if she and Craig had been one of those couples who revelled in volatile screaming matches followed by passionate make-up sex. Maybe, but that was so not her. She was a 'people pleaser' through and through—although, ironically, she hadn't pleased Craig . . .

Her eyes fell on a vase of perky daffodils that she'd picked this morning. Another spring. Another new beginning. Maybe it was time to actually forgive Craig and Natalie instead of just pretending to for the boys' sake. It had been twenty months now, and they'd all moved on. Vanessa was in love again—with Dr Magnus Maddison. Was that wrong?

Their gazes locked above their surgical masks. Magnus's eyes were unfathomable pools, as deep and dark as the night itself, and yet there was a vulnerability in them that she hadn't seen before. Were they shining with the hint of a tear?

The daffodils were vibrating in time with Vanessa's tapping, which she chose to take as a happy omen, even though she knew it was really due to the wonky table that had a coaster under one leg to stop its wobble. Which wasn't working.

'Mum, he won't give it back!'

Jackson appeared in the kitchen doorway with Lachie right behind him.

'Dibber-dobber!'

Vanessa dragged her eyes away from the screen and turned to her sons. They'd both been blessed with Craig's height and thick mop of honey-brown hair, but while Lachie also shared his broad shoulders and perpetual tan, Jackson was a skinny kid whose complexion was cut from the same freckled cloth as Vanessa's. The genetic short straw, in her opinion.

'Lachie, give it back. You should be doing your Desert Animals project, anyway.'

But Lachie's thumbs kept tapping away with the astonishing dexterity of a digital native.

'Just let me exterminate the Ender Dragon—'

'It's my phone!'

Vanessa snuck a quick peek at her screen. Should she change 'shining' to 'glistening'? Yes, glistening with the hint of a tear sounded better.

Meanwhile Jackson lunged for the iPhone and Lachie lost control of his game. He thumped his brother. Jackson thumped him back, and it was a tangle of freckled arms and fists.

'I was about to kill the Ender Dragon!'

'It's my phone and I want to kill a Wither!'

'That's enough!' Vanessa whipped the phone out of Lachie's hands. 'There must be someone you can murder together.' She pointed to the living room. 'This iPhone is confiscated. I want you both on the Xbox now.'

'But Mum . . .'

'It's not fair . . .'

She raised her hand. 'No arguments. It's *Call of Duty* or bed.'

Jackson and Lachie loped off grumpily, and Vanessa experienced a bleak moment. What kind of mother orders her sons to play a violent warfare game? The kind who thinks that if she doesn't get some peace, she might kill them.

She hadn't always been so permissive. She used to fret about the boys playing violent games, but Natalie had thoughtfully assuaged her fears.

'You really don't need to worry. Young minds can differentiate between fantasy and reality, and believe it or not Xbox controllers are good for their dexterity and hand–eye coordination.'

Of course, Vanessa could have said, 'You know where you can stick your advice, you scum-sucking husband-stealer?' But let's face it, Natalie was telling her what she wanted to hear, because the Xbox kept the boys busy and freed her up to write her book. She just hoped that *Lost and Found Heart* would sell enough copies to pay for their therapy if they needed it later. Or their bail, maybe. Which wouldn't be as funny as it seemed right now if it actually came to pass.

Peace at last, she thought as machine-gun fire rang out from the living room. She attacked her keyboard with gusto:

As Georgie watched his skilful hands sewing up the long thin wound running down her sister's chest, she prayed with all her heart that Holly would make it through the critical post-operative period . . .

Daisy put her head on Vanessa's lap as if to cheer her on, and Vanessa's heart overflowed. Daisy had been with her every step of the way, offering support from under the table at all times of night and day. Vanessa was planning to include her in the acknowledgements, but would readers think she was a bit odd for thanking her dog? Oh, who cared? Hadn't Elizabeth Barrett Browning written a beautiful poem for her cocker spaniel? Vanessa was sixteen when she first read 'To Flush, My Dog' at Mrs Flannery's suggestion, and it still made her sigh.

But of thee it shall be said
This dog watched beside a bed
Day and night unweary,—
Watched within a curtained room,
Where no sunbeam brake the gloom
Round the sick and dreary.

Sublime.

Unfortunately, Daisy chose that moment to emit a particularly malodorous fart. Vanessa winced. She was sure Flush wouldn't have done that.

⁓

It was 3 am, and Vanessa could feel her heart beating fast as her fingers flew towards the finish:

And so the danger was over. 'Thank you for saving Holly's life,' whispered Georgie. 'When I think of what you've done for her . . .'

Magnus smiled down at her with a slightly mocking air. 'Silly girl. I saved your sister's life for you.'

Georgie gasped. A lock of hair fell free from her surgical cap, and Magnus wrapped it skilfully around his surgeon's fingers. 'I know you think you're invisible but, to me, you're the brightest star in the sky and the only sunshine I ever see.'

Tears welled in Vanessa's eyes, blurring her view of the screen. She dabbed them away with a Chux Super Wipe.

Magnus drew her into his arms. He put his hand over her heart and gently lay her hand on his own. 'You hear that?' he said. 'Two hearts beating as one.'

Flouting convention, Vanessa typed *The End*. Then she let her tears fall. She'd actually done it. She couldn't believe it.

The clock ticked loudly in the empty kitchen.

And then the back door flew open and her mum Joy entered in a flurry of joie de vivre and Beyoncé's Midnight Heat perfume.

Vanessa beamed at her. 'Mum! I just finished the novel.'

'Finished? Oh, Nessie!' Joy clattered across the kitchen and threw her arms around her daughter. 'I'm so proud of you!'

'Thanks!'

Joy squeezed her tight and Vanessa saw her mum's fulsome under-arms dimple. A crisp September night like this would have warranted sleeves for anyone else, and Vanessa thought that Joy's 'body contour' cocktail frock could probably stand some rethinking—but so what? Why should her mum start dressing like a senior when she still had all her sexpot credentials? At sixty-three, Joy remained a heart-breaker, which was a bit of a worry for most of her boyfriends, who already had compromised cardiac function.

Joy winked. 'Charlotte Lancaster had better watch out, you'll be pushing her off the bestseller lists.'

'Oh, I reckon there's room for both of us.'

They laughed together, and Vanessa felt a rush of gratitude; she owed this achievement to her mum. When Joy moved in after Craig left—to help with the mortgage—she'd given Vanessa a copy of Charlotte Lancaster's first novel, *Intensive Caring*, a love story between an orphaned intensive care nurse and an emotionally distant emergency physician. 'You'll love it, Nessie,' Joy had promised, and Vanessa had loved it so much that she'd devoured the rest of Charlotte's novels and felt inspired to finally repay Mrs Flannery's faith in her and attempt one of her own.

'Charlotte would never think of this heart transplant story,' Joy declared with unabashed bias. 'It's awesome.'

'*Mum.*'

Vanessa stuck out her palm. She loathed the ubiquitous 'awesome' so much that she fined herself and her family if they used it.

But Joy just laughed and pushed her hand away. 'I'm not giving you a dollar when the context was so supportive.'

Which was a fair point, Vanessa had to concede.

Joy tossed her tote bag down on the table and kicked off her six-inch heels, and Vanessa felt a twinge of annoyance. Her mum was always leaving stuff lying around and she seemed to think that magic fairies flew in and picked it up. Vanessa wondered what would happen if she waited for Joy to retrieve those shoes, but every polar bear in the Arctic would be extinct by then.

Joy zeroed in on Vanessa's manuscript and stopped in shock when she saw the cover page.

'What's this? *Lost and Found Heart* by *Mia Fontaine*?'

Oops, thought Vanessa, here goes.

'Who's Mia Fontaine?'

'I've decided to use a pseudonym. It's got a ring to it, don't you reckon?'

Frankly Vanessa was surprised that a pseudonym hadn't occurred to her all along. It was one thing to want her novel to be famous, but when she'd started thinking about *herself* being famous, raw panic had kicked in. She knew that probably made her a freak in this post-Kardashian, social media-obsessed world, where everyone was supposed to be chasing fame and shyness was seriously out of fashion, but if Elena Ferrante could choose anonymity, why not Vanessa?

Joy looked appalled, and Vanessa found herself transfixed by the scarlet lipstick caught in the little spidery lines above her mum's mouth.

'But, Nessie, you're hiding your light under a bushel.'

Frankly, that's where Vanessa preferred to keep it.

'Mum, even Agatha Christie wrote romance novels under a pseudonym. *The Rose and the Yew Tree* by Mary Westmacott. Ring a bell?'

Joy looked blank. It hadn't rung a bell with Vanessa either, and she thought that was probably the whole point.

She'd hated being the centre of attention for as long as she could remember, which was strange when you thought about it, because both her parents were the kind of people who hoovered up all the attention in any room they entered. But, then, maybe that was exactly why she shied away from too many eyes?

She wondered how poor J.K. Rowling coped with life in the public gaze. The billions of dollars probably helped. Billions! Imagine that. What if 'Mia Fontaine' became the second author after J.K. Rowling to make a billion dollars? Somebody had to be second, surely? Vanessa imagined spending her Rowling-esque royalties. She'd give most of it away to worthy projects like Bill and Melinda Gates did—nobody needs a billion bucks—but she'd still be able to buy an amazing home (or three!) for herself and Joy, and give her boys the best education that money could buy. She had a sudden flash of Jackson making a graduation speech as school captain of Geelong Grammar. It would be so insightful it would go viral. She'd be in the front row wearing a fabulous dress, and her handsome husband would squeeze her hand and whisper, 'This is *your* doing.'

'But, Nessie,' Joy intruded, 'you deserve the accolades.'

'Mum, you know I prefer to keep a low profile.'

'So do I,' said Joy as she adjusted the black lacy bra that was carefully positioned to peek out from her miniscule cocktail frock. 'But sometimes attention comes with the territory.'

Before the Mia Fontaine issue could escalate, Vanessa changed the subject.

'How was your night with Barry?'

Joy stretched luxuriantly, and Vanessa heard a succession of cracking sounds.

'*Fabulous.* He's a master at dancing his fingers over a clitoris—I think it's because he plays the piano.'

'I'm glad he doesn't play bongos, then.'

'Oh, Nessie!'

They both cracked up, but then a shadow fell over Joy's face, erasing her twinkle.

'Of course, he wasn't a patch on your daddy.'

And there it was, exposed like an open wound in the kitchen: the gaping hole in Joy Spriggs's heart. Everything still began and ended with Vanessa's father, Jack Spriggs, whom they'd both adored. Vanessa could still remember her mum launching herself into Jack's arms the second he arrived home from one of his frequent work trips. They'd disappear into their bedroom, and young Vanessa would hear the urgent rhythm of mattress springs and her mum giggling for what seemed like hours. And, afterwards, her daddy would always find the time to make *her* feel special too. Even now she felt a pull in the pit of her tummy as she recalled Jack holding a tiny teapot in his manly hands while the two of them took morning tea in her 'palace', which was actually one of those little kids' tents from Kmart.

'May I pour you more tea, Your Highness?' he'd ask.

'Yes, you may.'

And Jack would wink because they both knew something Joy didn't—there was Coke in the teapot! (After years of managing dental practices Joy had banned Coke from the house.) They'd drink their contraband together and then Jack would tickle her toes while Vanessa giggled her head off.

And now, all these years later, she realised with a sudden start that she'd modelled Dr Magnus Maddison's looks on Jack: tall and charismatic, his thick dark hair spiked with silver, and the kind of smile that made you feel like everyone else was invisible. Wow. It showed how vivid her dad still was in her subconscious, even though he'd died a long time ago. Killed in a car crash one hot January night in 1995 and, decades on, Joy was still searching for a Grand Passion to fill the void he'd left behind.

'Your daddy was my knight in shining armour.'

'Oh, Mum . . .'

Vanessa hugged her. In some ways, she knew how Joy felt. After a year spent intimately entwined with Dr Magnus Maddison, she doubted she'd ever find a man who could live up to *him,* but at least her dad had once existed.

They clung to each other as the clock ticked, and then Joy wiped her eyes. She smiled through her tears and Vanessa watched as her mum's natural effervescence fizzed back up to her surface.

'But enough about *me.* Are you going to send your book off now?'

'Now? At three in the morning?' (As if that hadn't occurred to her already.)

'Why not? There's no time like the present.' Patience had never been Joy's strong suit. 'Get your opus out there, Nessie. You just need to dash off a covering letter.'

As it happened, Vanessa had done that a month ago. Patience wasn't her strong suit either. She brought the draft email up on her screen.

'Here's one that I prepared earlier.'

Joy laughed, and Vanessa felt alight with excitement. This was so surreal; she was about to send her very own novel to Charlotte

16

Lancaster's publishers, Wax! She did a quick check for typos—she'd already proofed everything she'd written up to yesterday—and after making a couple of minor corrections, she attached the manuscript to her email. The moment felt epic.

'Wait, I want to take a photo.'

Joy began searching for her phone, chucking the contents of her tote bag all over the table. Vanessa made a mental note to pick up the 'Spicy Nights Enhance Her Pleasure' oil before the boys saw it. She suspended her finger over the trackpad as Joy finally unearthed her phone and put it in camera mode.

'Ready? Smile!'

If there was ever a redundant exhortation! Vanessa was smiling so widely that she thought her face might explode. Joy snapped a pic as Vanessa clicked on send, and *Lost and Found Heart* winged its way through cyberspace to Wax.

Vanessa was officially an author!

⁓

She was still in a haze of happiness the next morning when she drove to her job at the Smile Clinic in Reservoir, a neighbouring suburb to Preston's north. Vanessa caught the train most days to avoid emitting greenhouse gases, but today she was doing the grocery shopping after work so she needed the convenience of her Corolla. Luckily, it was a quick trip—she was travelling against most of the traffic that was heading into the city.

As she walked into the clinic, she was greeted with cheers from her best friend Kiri Naawaina, a strapping Maori beauty.

'It's Vanissa Rooney, world-famous novelist!'

Vanessa was touched by this act of support from Kiri, who made no secret of the fact that she found romantic fiction 'complete crep'. Kiri's husband, mild-mannered dentist Anthony Altieri, who was at least half a head shorter than his wife, appeared and whistled through his teeth. Vanessa took a playful bow. Even though she was a bit over dental nursing—let's face it, there are only so many times you can sterilise a periodontal pocket probe before you want to stab yourself with it—she loved working at this cosy little clinic with Kiri and Anthony, who'd become family friends. Anthony and Craig had bonded over their mutual love of the Collingwood Magpies footy club, and Kiri and Anthony's son Sam was even in Jackson's soccer team, the Redbacks. It was all so idyllic, a happy foursome (or eightsome, if you counted the kids). But after Craig left, Kiri declared that she'd always thought he was a bit of a dickhid. And, clearly, she still did.

'Craig can get stuffed,' she said, just before she admitted the first patient. 'I bet that dickhid's never written so much as a postcard.'

'I saw him write a shopping list once.'

Kiri snorted with laughter. As a fresh dumpee, it had been empowering to know that Kiri thought Craig was a dickhid, but now it almost didn't matter, because dickhid or not, Craig couldn't hold a candle to Vanessa's fictional hero. She was on cloud nine as she settled the first patient into the chair.

It was only later, when she was polishing some orthodontic pliers, that the emptiness hit. Dr Magnus Maddison was gone, and she missed him already.

Chapter 3

Vanessa knew it could be months before she heard back from Wax, but in the six weeks since she'd submitted her manuscript she'd still found herself checking her email at least once every half-hour. Even if she subtracted eight hours a day for sleeping (if only!) that still added up to checking her email 1344 times. Frankly, it was doing her head in, so last week she'd tried to distract herself by going to a Melbourne Cup party with Kiri. She'd bought a fascinator and even indulged in a spray tan, which looked fabulous until it rained, and she and Kiri were reduced to fits of giggles by the brown stripes running down her legs. The bubbles flowed freely and Vanessa was having so much fun that she almost forgot about the race, but she bought sweep tickets in the nick of time and scored second prize. She arrived home sixty-eight dollars richer and high on life—until Lachie revealed that he'd left her laptop on the tram.

#$@&%#?>*!

Her blood still ran cold at the memory.

'Sorry, Mum.'

'Please tell me you didn't.'

'It was Jackson's fault.'

'I wasn't even on the tram!'

Jackson thumped Lachie and Vanessa felt like joining in. This couldn't be happening! Her novel was on that laptop—a whole year's worth of blood, sweat and tears, and a whole lifetime's worth of dreams. But she comforted herself with the fact that she could retrieve her manuscript from her sent box—except it turned out that she couldn't, because Jackson had tried to spare her from spam by reprogramming her email and trash to empty itself every week. So all was lost. She didn't even have a back-up copy of her novel, because ten days ago Joy had accidentally put her back-up drive out with the rubbish.

#$@&%#?>*!

It was so typical. Her mum dumped *OK* and *Who* magazines all over the house without a thought, and then once in a blue moon she made a performance out of picking them up and dumping them in the recycling bin. Bravo, Joy. But how about checking to see if anything was caught inside them? Argh! Vanessa suspected that her mum was secretly relieved about Lachie losing the laptop, because it took the heat off her.

'It's all right, Nessie,' Joy said soothingly. 'We'll ring lost property at the tram depot. I'm sure they'll have it.'

But they didn't. Vanessa rang twice a day for a week, but no one had handed in the laptop. In desperation, she made a flyer and stuck it up at every stop on the number 11 West Preston tram route—*Great Sentimental Value, Reward Offered*—although God knows where the reward money would come from. But that didn't matter in the end, because her only response was a couple of cringe-worthy calls from creeps—the laptop resolutely refused to be found. Vanessa was disconsolate.

'It's okay,' Joy said, in an attempt to gee her up. 'Wax has still got a copy, and they'll be in contact soon.'

But when?

With the boys leaving for the weekend with Craig at any minute, Vanessa was anticipating another forty-eight hours of relentlessly checking her email, which was bound to be fruitless because, let's face it, Wax wouldn't get back to her on the weekend. She wished her mum was at home to distract her, but Joy had just left for a romantic getaway with her latest squeeze, Gordon.

As Vanessa flung the boys' clothes into their backpacks she heard the front door open and Craig's deep voice call out a greeting. Kiri thought that Vanessa should demand Craig's key back or, at the very least, change the locks, but Vanessa wasn't prepared to treat him like a common criminal, as much as she might fantasise about it sometimes. Craig was Jackson and Lachie's dad, after all. She heard the boys greet him, but at least there was blessed silence from Daisy, who didn't even bother getting up off the floor for Craig anymore. Vanessa couldn't help feeling victorious about that, and it made her adore Daisy even more.

Craig's voice rumbled something indistinct and Jackson and Lachie mumbled back. In spite of herself, Vanessa patted down her recalcitrant hair. There was a fine line between curls and frizz, and as far as she was concerned, hers crossed it way too often. Natalie's hair was glossy and lustrous and worthy of a shampoo commercial. Vanessa had spent a lot of time trying not to imagine how it must look splayed over a pillow. Craig probably buried his face in it. And then her mind flew unbidden back to a time when Craig used to playfully pull at her reddish-blonde waves and call her his 'curly girlie'. Her heart seized. So much water under the bridge since she was that twenty-one-year-old dental assistant shyly affixing a bib to Craig, a cheeky chippie of twenty-three who'd just presented for a wisdom tooth extraction . . . She grabbed her iPhone to distract herself, and suddenly there it was in her inbox:

Sender: amy.dunphy@wax.com.au
Subject: Lost and Found Heart

Oh my God. Oh my God. Vanessa darted a look towards the door and steeled herself to keep reading, hardly daring to breathe:

Dear Ms Rooney,

Re: Lost and Found Heart by Mia Fontaine

Thank you for submitting your manuscript *Lost and Found Heart* to Wax Publishing. Unfortunately, it is not suitable for us at this time, but we wish you all the best with your writing career.

Regards,
Amy Dunphy
Commissioning Editor

Oh . . .

Vanessa sank onto Jackson's bed. It was only with the hope suddenly sucked out of her that she realised how much she'd been holding inside. But had she seriously believed that *Lost and Found Heart* would be snapped up by a major publishing house? That her silly story would sell a million copies and she'd be the new Charlotte Lancaster? And as for J.K. Rowling, let's not even go there. Amy Dunphy probably read the first paragraph and said to her colleagues, 'Hey, get a load of this. For a novelist, "Mia Fontaine" makes a great dental assistant.' And then they all sniggered. 'No wonder she used a pseudonym—I wouldn't cop to this crap either.' Amy had probably tossed the manuscript over her shoulder—that's if she'd even bothered to print it out. Or maybe she'd put it straight through the shredder? Vanessa wouldn't blame her—that's where it belonged. She'd been fooling herself all these years. And what did

Mrs Flannery know, really? She was just a not particularly good English teacher at a not particularly good high school, whereas writing was Amy Dunphy's business.

Vanessa's cheeks burned at her self-delusion, and before she could pull herself together, Craig and the boys appeared in the doorway.

'G'day, Ness.'

'Hi, Craig.'

'What's wrong?' asked Jackson. 'You look weird.'

'Nothing's wro—'

But Jackson had already grabbed her phone. Please God, don't let him read that email aloud in front of Craig!

'*Dear Ms Rooney,*' he read aloud in front of Craig. '*Thank you for submitting your manuscript* Lost and Found Heart *to Wax Publishing. Unfortunately, it is not suitable for us at this time* . . . Bastards!'

'It's no big deal,' Vanessa cried shrilly.

'Arseholes!'

'Wankers!'

'Boys!' Vanessa didn't want Craig to think that standards had slipped since he left the house. 'I appreciate your support, but there's no need for that kind of language.'

'Your mum's right,' agreed Craig, dripping with his newfound emotional wisdom. 'She's not swearing, and she's the one who's been rejected.'

For someone who'd refused to wear patterns throughout their marriage, Craig now showed a fondness for paisley shirts. Mauve? Really?

He smiled at Vanessa sympathetically. (His teeth looked whiter. Was he bleaching them?) 'Are you okay?'

'Of course! I'm fine.'

She grabbed her phone back and deleted the email from both her inbox and trash lest anyone feel tempted to read it aloud again.

'Are you *sure* you're okay?'

Jackson touched her arm awkwardly and she saw a glimmer of the sweet little boy who used to be so concerned for her feelings. He was still in there somewhere. She felt herself melt.

'I'm sure, sweetheart.'

'Those people at Wax are morons,' he raged. 'Just send it to another publisher—or you could publish it yourself online.'

Vanessa knew she should consider those options, but she couldn't quite face the thought right now. Her confidence had just plummeted, and she'd need a bucket with a very long rope to retrieve it.

'I might leave things where they are for now.' She tried to sound upbeat. 'It was a fun experiment, but maybe I need to give writing some thought.'

Craig nodded, and she noticed his broad shoulders straining under the paisley. He should have bought a size bigger, but then Natalie probably bought it for him. That must be how she spent her time when she wasn't schooling him in the art of emotional support.

'Good for you, Ness. A lot of people would just keep chasing that pipe dream and wasting their time, but you're prepared to accept your limitations. I admire you.'

Dickhid.

Chapter 4

DAVE

Dave Rendall LLB was on the phone to a stroppy client in his office in High Street, Preston, next door to the two-dollar shop that was currently groaning with light-up bunny ears and 'Hoppy Easter' bunting. He was glad that Christos Pappas had called him instead of coming in—it had spared him the bloke's world championship halitosis and body odour that suggested he hadn't showered since the twentieth century. Dave would have been worried that Christos was living rough if it wasn't for his pristine wife Maria, who must have had her olfactory receptor cells surgically removed.

'It's a joke,' Christos was complaining sourly. 'I just did the pre-settlement inspection and the place was a bloody disgrace.'

Dave made a mental note to be too busy if Christos ever needed conveyancing again. As a rule, he tried to prioritise Preston's Greek, Italian, Chinese and Vietnamese residents, who were under increasing threat from Anglo hipsters with their micro-breweries and turmeric lattes but, for Christos, he was willing to make an exception.

'What, have they left rubbish lying around?'

'No, but they haven't polished the skirting boards.'

'Polished the skirting boards?'

Christos snorted. 'They must live like pigs.'

Dave thought this was a bit rich coming from a bloke whose stench could wilt a geranium at twenty paces.

'I'm not going to settle unless they pay for a professional cleaner.'

'They've already paid for a cleaner as per the contract. If you want it cleaned again, you'll have to do that at your own expense.'

'I'm not paying for their filth!'

As Christos ranted, Dave's eyes roamed around his office, a fetching shade of seventies grey, and came to rest on his twelve-year-old daughter Nickie, who was pretending to do her homework while covertly Snapchatting under his desk. He felt a perverse pride at her subterfuge skills, although he supposed they couldn't be that great if he'd noticed.

Christos coughed into the phone and Dave symbolically reeled from the stench.

'I'm advising you as your solicitor that this is an unreasonable request.'

'I'm the client—I know how it works. You have to follow my instructions.'

'Okay, no problem. I'll ring the vendor's solicitor and make the latest in a series of capricious and unwarranted demands then, shall I?'

'Yeah, you do that, smartarse.' Christos hung up.

'Love you too,' Dave cooed.

Nickie giggled. She clicked out of Snapchat and slipped her phone into her pocket, probably feeling as proud of her subterfuge skills as Dave did.

'Dad! Did he hear you?'

'The point is, did you? If you've overheard a confidential solicitor/client conference, I'll have to kill you.' Dave grabbed a couple of weapons from his desk. 'Death by stapler or bulldog clip?'

Nickie graced him with a long-suffering smile and rolled her eyes for good measure. He wanted to spray something on her so she'd stay like this, a little girl who thought she was grown up, as opposed to an actual grown-up. Not that Nickie was little in a technical sense—she was a tall and skinny string bean, all gangly limbs, just like her dad. Dave had always been delighted that she was swimming in his gene pool, but he wasn't dumb enough to assume that Nickie felt the same. He was sure she'd much rather take after her knockout mum Evanthe, but what girl wouldn't?

Dave could still remember the first time he'd met Evanthe, when she'd brought her *yiayia* in on a probate matter. He thought she was the most glorious, exotic creature he'd ever laid eyes on, and it seemed she saw something in him too, because within weeks they were making the kind of passionate love that made his past encounters seem merely polite. The next thing he knew he was the ecstatic groom at his own big fat Greek wedding. And then Nickie came along and his heart exploded with a primal love that he'd never known existed. He'd die for this kid—even when she was trying to con him.

'How's the homework going?'

'Good.'

'Are you sure?'

'Yeah.'

'Really?'

'Dad! Where's the trust?'

Dave snatched up her exercise book and scanned it. 'This page is looking a bit bare. Are you certain you haven't had any phone-related distractions?'

'Well, since you're asking, it *is* pretty hard to concentrate when you're yelling at some client over the phone.'

Dave hid a smile. She was good. Maybe she'd follow him into law?

His office door abruptly opened and he felt himself tense. Ms Izetbegovic appeared. She looked irritated, but considering that irritation was her default mode, he would have been more surprised if she didn't.

'Yes, Ms Izetbegovic?'

Ms Izetbegovic had been Dave's PA for fifteen incredibly long years. She'd migrated to Australia soon after the Bosnian War—which surely couldn't be a coincidence? Not that she'd ever alluded to the war; she never alluded to anything much. She was his sole employee, yet Dave felt like he didn't know her any better now than he had fifteen years ago. He sometimes wondered if he'd doomed their relationship on that very first morning, when he'd struggled to pronounce her surname properly. Anxious not to offend, he'd asked if he could address her by her Christian name instead, but when that turned out to be Trklja, it had only compounded the problem. So, while she was on her first lunchbreak, he called the Croatian consulate.

'Could you please tell me how to pronounce I-Z-E-T-B-E-G-O-V-I-C?'

But he must have left it too late, because Ms Izetbegovic had seemed unmoved by his perfect pronunciation. To this day her manner towards him was curt, and she was lackadaisical about her duties, to say the least. Dave suspected her poor work perform- ance was probably due to traumas she'd suffered at the hands of Slobodan Milosevic. 'Would *you* find office files important if you'd endured the siege of Sarajevo?' he used to counter when Evanthe insisted that Ms Izetbegovic was 'having a lend'. She urged Dave to sack her, but he worried that Ms Izetbegovic wouldn't find another employer who'd make allowances for her post-traumatic stress disorder. Not that she'd ever told him she had PTSD, but Dave knew from painful experience what war zones could do to people.

When he was tiny, his father Graham had returned from Vietnam shell-shocked and withdrawn. He could still picture Graham in his brown leather chair with a rip on the arm, staring at *Cheers* and laughing in the places he was supposed to laugh, but half a second too late. Dave always suspected that if they took the laugh track away, his dad wouldn't know when to laugh at all. Graham was sacked by a series of employers who didn't understand PTSD—not that anyone really did back then—and Dave refused to make that same mistake. He wasn't an idiot; of course, it had occurred to him that Ms Izetbegovic might just be a horrible human being, but he didn't feel comfortable making that call. She was always so immaculately presented. What horrors was she trying to paint out of her past when she applied her eye shadow so perfectly?

'The old lady's here,' she announced now with conspicuous apathy.

Dave drew a blank. 'Which old lady?'

'Mrs Legsley.'

'Mrs Legsley? I don't know a Mrs Legsley.'

Ms Izetbegovic looked at him like he was a flea buzzing around her face.

'Yes, you do. Little. Stupid. Mrs Legsley.'

'You mean Mrs Hipsley?'

'Yes. Hipsley, Legsley.' Ms Izetbegovic exhaled impatiently, already bored by the conversation.

'But I wasn't expecting her until tomorrow.'

If Ms Izetbegovic's eyes could talk, they would have said: 'And I care because?'

Dave sighed. This wasn't what he'd planned for his afternoon, but Mrs Hipsley must have got her days confused, and he could catch up on his other work tonight.

'All right, send her in.'

Mrs Izetbegovic nodded dismissively, but before retreating her gaze shifted to Nickie, and her features softened.

'Nickie, *mijelnik*, are you hungry? Thirsty? Would you like some biscuits? Hot chocolate? Tea, maybe?'

Not for the first time, Dave was struck by Ms Izetbegovic's transformation around his daughter. It was like all her hard edges melted. Was it because she didn't have kids of her own? Or had she lost a child—or more than one—to the war? Dear God. Dave had a sudden flash of Ms Izetbegovic in a headscarf faced with a Sophie's Choice situation.

Meanwhile, Nickie was smiling politely. 'No, thank you, Ms Izet ... Iz ... I'm fine.'

Mrs Izetbegovic regarded her fondly. 'Well, you let me know if you change your mind.'

Nickie nodded. Mrs Izetbegovic gave her another beatific smile and turned to go. Dave seized his chance.

'Ms Izetbegovic? I'm sure Mrs Hipsley would like a cup of tea.'

She tsked in irritation and Dave quickly retracted his request. 'You're busy. I'll do it.'

And so, five minutes later, Dave presented Mrs Hipsley with a cup of Earl Grey and two Scotch Finger biscuits. 'There you go.'

'Thank you, David,' Mrs Hipsley said in the little birdlike voice that matched her little birdlike body. She was perched on his couch in front of a half-constructed Tudor-style doll's house on the coffee table. Dave stepped around a pile of Amnesty International magazines displaced to the floor and took *The Atlas of Human Rights* by Andrew Fagan off the couch so he could sit beside her. He glanced back at Nickie, who finally had her nose buried in her books. He'd confiscated her mobile phone and she'd been forced to forgo Snapchat for improper fractions. Poor kid. Maybe he'd buy her an ice cream later. Or a bottle of Scotch. Just kidding.

Dave turned his attention back to Mrs Hipsley. 'Now, where were we?'

'What's that, David?'

She'd forgotten to turn on her hearing aids again.

'I said, what were we up to?' he shouted.

'The window in the downstairs bedroom.'

'Right ...'

Dave slipped on his glasses and spread out the elaborate instructions. He was helping Mrs Hispley construct the doll's house for her next-door neighbour, a young Sudanese woman called Zafeera, whom Mrs Hipsley had apparently taken under her wing. According to Mrs Hipsley, Zafeera had twin daughters who were 'the sweetest little poppets you could ever see'. Dave was dubious about the relevance of a Tudor-style doll's house to Sudanese kids, but Mrs Hispley's heart was nowhere if not in the right place.

Obviously, he should say no to stuff like this. He was flat-out with his conveyancing and probate matters and his weekly volunteering gig on an after-hours legal advice line, but he couldn't seem to turn away the elderly locals who came to him with miniscule matters on a miniscule budget. He'd first met Mrs Hipsley when someone stole her wheelie bin. Earth-shattering stuff. But she was a retired factory worker and you'd need to be a NASA engineer to understand these doll's house instructions. He frowned at the indecipherable diagrams.

'No, I think this window's for the other bedroom . . . No, wait. Is it?'

Mrs Hipsley just smiled at him trustingly. She had complete faith that he would conquer this task, and Dave found that oddly touching.

'It might take us a while,' he shouted, 'but it's going to be awesome.'

Mrs Hipsley smiled, then she turned to Nickie with a grandmotherly twinkle. 'Maybe your daddy will get you one, Nickie?'

'I hope so!' Nickie yelled politely.

Dave felt a rush of pride. What a sweet kid—a doll's house was the last thing she'd ever covet. 'Actually,' he shouted, 'Nickie's not really into doll's houses. She's always been more sporty, haven't you, sweetie?'

Mrs Hipsley winked at Nickie. 'Oh, all children are naughty.'

'No, *sporty*. Nickie's a bit of a soccer star.'

'D-a-a-a-a-d.'

'Well, you are,' Dave boomed. 'She's just started in a new team, and there are only three girls.'

'Well, that's marvellous.'

'Yeah, we're really proud.'

'Dad's the coach,' Nickie screamed.

'Yeah, the other bloke left and I put my hand up. The truth is, I couldn't coach a budgie out of its cage, but it seemed like a good opportunity to follow Nickie around and annoy her.'

Nickie gave a long-suffering sigh. 'We're called the Redbacks,' she told Mrs Hipsley.

'The Get Backs?'

'No, the Redbacks,' Dave yelled. 'Like the spider.'

'Oh.' Mrs Hipsley smiled at Nickie. 'You like spiders? Well, that probably goes with being sporty. No wonder your daddy's so proud of you.'

Chapter 5

VANESSA

Anthony's four-wheel drive pulled up across the road from Readings, the iconic bookstore in Carlton, a suburb nudging the CBD that was home to Melbourne Uni, umpteen Italian restaurants and at least one infamous gangland killing (although the less said about that the better). Readings usually attracted the so-called 'inner-city elite', but today there was a broader sub-section of the community gathering—and Vanessa couldn't wait to join it. Anthony's car had barely stopped when she unclicked her seatbelt.

'I have to wee. I'll meet you on the line in two minutes, Kiri. Thanks for the lift, Anthony.'

'No worries,' said Anthony, who always switched from boss into buddy at 6 pm. He flicked some fluff off his dentist's uniform. 'Have fun.'

'Thanks.'

'I'll get us a good spot,' Kiri promised.

Vanessa sprinted off, weaving her way through studiously scruffy outdoor diners and past Cinema Nova, pausing only to buy a *Big Issue*. She could never walk past a *Big Issue* seller—she'd even been known to buy the same issue two or three times, which made her feel good about her compassionate nature but not her financial management. As she slipped the magazine into her bag and hurried onwards towards the ladies' toilets in Lygon Court, her heart was racing so fast that she wondered if it would get there before her. Charlotte Lancaster was right across the road in Readings and, frankly, her timing couldn't be better. Events of the past five months had squashed Vanessa's dreams to a pulp, and she was counting on Charlotte to re-ignite her inspiration.

No pressure!

It still seemed so weird . . . They said that truth was stranger than fiction, but what if you didn't know whether something was truth or fiction in the first place? A few days after Wax editor Amy Dunphy rejected *Lost and Found Heart*, Vanessa had picked her ego up off the floor. So she'd had one knockback; was she really going to fall at the first hurdle? What kind of message would that be sending the boys? *If at first you don't succeed, give up, it's not worth the bother . . .* So she'd decided to try another publisher; after all, she was hardly the first author to face rejection. Margaret Mitchell's *Gone with the Wind*—thirty-eight rejection slips! J.K. Rowling's *Harry Potter and the Philosopher's Stone*—twelve! (Again with the J.K. Rowling.) Vanessa knew she'd never forgive herself if she gave up this easily. So she emailed Amy Dunphy and asked her to email the copy of *Lost and Found Heart* Vanessa had sent. But when she received Amy's reply, you could have knocked her over with bellybutton lint.

Dear Ms Rooney,

Thank you for your email, but I regret to say that I'm not aware of any manuscript entitled *Lost and Found Heart* having been submitted to myself or any other Wax employee via email or otherwise, and I'm afraid I have no record of any previous correspondence with you. Perhaps you've mistaken Wax for another publishing house? I'm sorry I can't be of more help, and I wish you the best of luck with your endeavours.

Regards,
Amy Dunphy
Commissioning Editor

Vanessa was completely stonkered. Either (a) Amy Dunphy had the shortest memory in living history, (b) there'd been some kind of dreadful mistake, or (c) she was lying—but why? Vanessa begged Amy to check her trash, but Amy said there was nothing there, and after deleting her own emails with Wax and having lost her laptop and back-up drive, Vanessa couldn't prove a thing. It was devastating. She'd even half wondered if she was going mad and she'd imagined writing *Lost and Found Heart*. Joy and the boys assured her the book was real, but by then it had disappeared into the mist like a ghost ship. It was a ghost novel and, after several fruitless phone calls to Wax, she'd been forced to give up on *Lost and Found Heart* for good.

She'd attempted to move on by signing up for a botanic art course, but botanic art didn't float her boat and she abandoned it halfway through a watercolour of an *Acacia pycnantha*. Then she tried photography and Thai cooking, but the same thing happened. It seemed like the more she tried to distance herself from romance writing the more she missed it, and then Kiri surprised her with tickets to see Charlotte Lancaster at Readings tonight—an act of true friendship on Kiri's part, considering her scorn for romance. Vanessa was convinced that hearing Charlotte read from her new novel, *Love Transplant*, would give her the confidence to start a new novel of her own.

She flushed the toilet and pulled up her old cotton undies, grimacing at the fraying elastic. Joy said it was dangerous for Vanessa's self-esteem to wear undies that screamed a non-existent sex life—she should be wearing skimpy thongs to attract the passion she wanted. Which is all very well, Vanessa thought, but I don't like the feeling of being sliced in half by dental floss. Did thongs feel like dental floss to other women, or was that just due to her profession? She'd always found skimpy lingerie uncomfortable. Craig used to say that comfort was more important and she was sexy just the way she was, but then one day she'd seen black lacy thongs hanging on Craig and Natalie's line, and she'd felt like the unsexiest woman in the world.

Better not to think about it.

She washed her hands and stuck them in the vertical dryer, and it almost sucked her watch off. She checked the time. Charlotte was starting in six minutes—it was lucky Kiri was saving a spot. But when Vanessa emerged from Lygon Court, Kiri was still in the car.

In a panic, Vanessa stepped out onto the road, straight into the path of a cyclist who seemed to be attempting some kind of speed record. What was it with those lycra-clad guys with their grim intensity and their dead eyes? He swerved to avoid her, hurling abuse. If she was somebody else she would have hurled abuse back, but she wasn't, so she didn't. She could feel red blotches popping up on her neck and cursed the way they always betrayed her feelings.

She made it to the other side of the road and took her place at the end of the line. A gaggle of elderly ladies gathered behind her, chatting excitedly among themselves. Vanessa gave them a distracted smile and turned to peer through the bookshop's window, hoping to catch a pre-emptive glimpse of Charlotte.

Chapter 6

DAVE

Dave pulled his 2006 Volvo station wagon into a loading zone outside Readings. The car was caked with dried mud from a camping weekend a month ago, and some clown had scratched *Wash me!* on the rear windscreen—not exactly original, but it had still given Dave a chuckle. He and Nickie were dropping Mrs Hipsley off at the bookshop to meet the other members of her romance readers' book club. Apparently one of their favourite authors, Charlotte something-or-other was appearing, and judging by the line outside it was generating a lot of excitement.

As Dave alighted from the car he regarded Readings with affection. It was great to know there were still some stores that thrived by selling actual books. Dave had a Kindle and he listened to audio books now and then, but it wasn't the same. He knew he could never relinquish the evocative smell of paper or the thrill of turning an actual page. And imagine a world without bookcases. It didn't bear thinking about. But Dave was quietly confident that, for Nickie's generation, 'old school' books would become retro cool in the style of vinyl records. Could be a way off, though. Nickie declined his offer to buy her a book, preferring to stay in the car and check out her friends' 'Insta' stories.

Dave helped Mrs Hipsley out of the Volvo and guided her over to her mates at the end of the line.

'Rosalie!' they all twittered, throwing curious looks at him. A younger woman in front of them glanced around briefly, and Dave was struck by her slate-blue eyes and dainty upturned nose.

'This is my solicitor, David,' Mrs Hipsley announced. 'David, this is Myra and Gwen and Joan and Pat.'

'Oh, David!'

'David, we've heard all about you!'

'David, hello!'

'So you're David?'

'It would appear so.'

They all giggled appreciatively.

'Are you a fan of Charlotte Lancaster?' asked Myra, a plump lady whose pink scalp was peeking out from beneath her thinning hair.

'Can't say I'm familiar with her oeuvre.'

The ladies all competed to fill him in, talking over the top of each other. It seemed that Charlotte Lancaster wrote turgid tales about feisty nurses and doctors with jaws like Chesty Bond. As the ladies bickered about their favourite fictional doctors, all of whom sounded like the same ill-conceived cardboard cut-out to Dave, he couldn't resist teasing: 'So you like the look of his scalpel, do you?'

Mrs Hipsley's girlfriends shrieked with laughter and Dave chuckled obligingly. He'd always been a bit of a magnet for post-menopausal women, which was nice, but not quite as gratifying as being a magnet for pre-menopausal ones.

'Rosalie,' yelled Myra, 'David's teasing us about our stories!'

'Oh, I don't think romance is David's thing,' Mrs Hipsley said with a twinkle. 'Is it, David?'

Not according to Evanthe, no.

Dave felt that kick in his guts all over again. He wondered how long it would come as a shock to him that he was no longer married. He suddenly found himself back on that horrendous night when Evanthe had returned from her girls' weekend away and catalogued his failures.

'I don't feel treasured or cherished or adored,' she'd said.

Dave was baffled. 'But I asked you to marry me. I want to spend the rest of my life with you.'

'Yes, but—'

'And don't I always put you first?'

'Yes, but—'

'And haven't I've always been faithful?'

'Yes, but—'

'And don't I try to be a good dad?'

'Yes, but—'

'And shouldn't a husband be judged by his actions?'

'Yes, but . . .' Her voice trailed off unexpectedly, and she suddenly looked weary and sad.

Dave was gripped by fear, so he went on the attack. 'That's a lot of buts, Evanthe. But what? But my actions aren't good enough? But you've fallen out of love with me?'

A small tic in her cheek betrayed her—she *had* fallen out of love with him. Dave felt as though she'd punched the air right out of his lungs.

'I'm sorry, David, but I need romance.'

'And you got *me*? Ripped off.'

Back at Readings, Dave pushed thoughts of his romantic deficiencies away and forced himself back to the present. 'As long as it's *your* thing, that's the important thing,' he said.

'I wish you men would give it a chance,' Myra sighed. 'Romance is so uplifting.'

'I'm sure it is, but I'm more uplifted by real-life stories. War crimes, genocide, that kind of stuff.'

The old ladies shrieked again. Cheeky boy. Mrs Hipsley seemed gratified that Dave was such a hit. She gazed up at him with a proprietorial air and wrapped her little fingers around his arm.

Dave gently disentangled himself. 'Well, Nickie's waiting, so I'll be off. Enjoy the reading, Mrs Hipsley.'

'What was that, David?'

'I said maybe you should turn your hearing aids on!' Dave boomed.

Mrs Hipsley obliged.

'That's better. Now if a handsome doctor wants to whisper sweet nothings into your ear, at least you'll hear something.'

The old dears seemed to find that devastatingly witty.

'And you young ladies enjoy it too,' he added.

Dave turned to leave, but he'd only taken a couple of steps when something stopped him in his tracks. The woman in front of them with the blue eyes had tucked her dress into her undies. A string of elastic was trailing down her shapely left thigh, and the bottom curve of her bum was exposed. Dave hesitated. Would he look like a perv if he told her? He glanced around for rescue, but no one else appeared to have noticed, and surely she'd rather know sooner than later . . .

'Um, excuse me,' he murmured, but she didn't hear him. He was forced to tap her on the shoulder. 'Excuse me?'

Chapter 7

VANESSA

Vanessa turned to see the tall gangly guy with the puppy dog eyes who'd arrived with the tiny old lady. She'd been surprised to see a man at a Charlotte Lancaster reading, but good for him. He was probably gay, although he didn't look it—she'd never seen a gay guy in a suit that old.

'Yes?' she said.

'I just noticed you've . . . um . . . you've got your . . .'

The guy kept his eyes on her face, but now he was pointing downwards. Vanessa followed his finger . . . to her bum. Oh my God. She reached down to feel her dimpled flesh and nearly died. Not only was her dress tucked into her undies, but the elastic had fallen away and her bare bum was on display. Vanessa could feel her face burning, but she tried to retain some semblance of dignity as she scrambled to untuck her dress.

'Oh! Thank you.'

The gangly guy nodded. She couldn't be sure, but she suspected he was even more embarrassed than she was.

'Right,' he said. 'Well . . .'

Well, what? Why was he still standing there? He hovered uncertainly for a moment and then he left. Thank goodness.

Vanessa backed up against the Readings window. Had everyone in the queue seen? The passers-by? The outdoor diners? She pictured them all nudging each other and asking, 'Was that a bum or a bowl of pink jelly?' Although the thought was kind of amusing, it didn't stop it from being mortifying. And now Kiri was crossing the road to join her. Finally.

'Kiri. About time! Where the hell have you been?!'

Kiri reeled back. 'Chill, Niss. What's up *your* nose?'

Vanessa checked herself. It wasn't Kiri's fault, although it would have been nice if her friend had been here to warn her about her wardrobe malfunction. 'Sorry, I'm just being impatient.'

But Kiri had already shrugged it off. Up ahead, the line started moving into the bookshop, and Vanessa's embarrassment was replaced by a thrill of anticipation. She was just moments away from seeing Charlotte Lancaster in the flesh.

⁓

Vanessa and Kiri were squashed at the rear of the personal development section, but if Vanessa leaned to the left she could get a clear view of Charlotte, who was even more gorgeous than she'd imagined. How could someone be so beautiful *and* so talented? I bow before you, Vanessa thought.

'Thank you all for coming,' the author was saying in her transpacific accent. 'Can everyone fit? I'm so humbled by the turnout . . .'

Charlotte turned to smile at the guy beside her who'd been introduced as Wax's publisher, Alan McManus, and then the young woman on her other side, commissioning editor Amy Dunphy. Yes, that Amy Dunphy. Vanessa wondered what Amy would say if she stood up and asked, 'Why did you lie about not receiving my novel?

Was it so unspeakably bad that you had to erase it from your mind?'
Not that she'd have the guts to do that—but maybe she'd try to pluck
up the courage to corner Amy later?

'Would you like a sneak peek at the cover?' Charlotte was asking
her fans.

'Yes, please!'

'Absolutely!'

'Show us!'

And such.

'Amy, if you'll do the honours?'

Amy pulled a sheet off an easel to reveal a poster-sized version
of *Love Transplant*, which featured an illustration of a petite blonde
nurse and a tall dark doctor getting hot and heavy in surgical scrubs.
The doctor was untying the nurse's surgical gown, exposing a creamy
shoulder. The crowd gasped approvingly and applauded. Vanessa
nudged Kiri, who was playing Sudoku on her phone.

'Fabulous cover.'

Kiri lifted her eyes just long enough to clock the poster and
snort with laughter. It made Vanessa laugh too, and before she knew
it they were both in the grip of the giggles. She forced herself to get it
together—where was her respect? This was the woman whose work
had inspired Vanessa to try to live her own writing dream.

Charlotte Lancaster. Author. Celebrity. Celebrity author. Vanessa
knew her fairytale journey by heart. After arriving in Melbourne
from her native New York at the age of sixteen when her high-flying
father Chip was appointed CEO of a multinational mining company,
Charlotte attended PLC and then enrolled in a nursing degree.
But she was soon discovered by a modelling scout and plucked
out of university. For the next few years her face graced countless
magazine covers, but Charlotte found that lifestyle unfulfilling
and she decided to follow her true dream instead: writing. Eight
novels later she was a fixture on the bestseller lists and regularly

snapped at A-list events with her husband, renowned barrister Marcus Stafford—a man so impossibly handsome he could have modelled for one of her covers.

Vanessa watched Charlotte smooth her auburn tresses while she waited for the fawning to subside. Her whole body seemed a hymn to personal maintenance. How on earth did she find the time for those immaculate toenails, fingernails, eyebrows, etc.? Not having kids probably helped. Vanessa made a mental note to put Jackson and Lachie up for adoption—but not before they'd put the bins out.

'Just to set the scene, *Love Transplant* begins during a heart transplant operation in a major New York hospital.'

Vanessa raised her eyebrows. Great minds think alike.

'Our heroine, Angelique, is a ballsy cardiac nurse from Brooklyn. Tragically, during the heart transplant she discovers that the donor heart belongs to her new husband, who's just been killed in an auto accident.' The audience gasped. Vanessa gaped. 'When Angelique hears this tragic news, she faints in the middle of the operation, and the brilliant but arrogant transplant surgeon, Dr Rufus Rowntree, is furious . . .'

Was she really hearing this? Vanessa nudged Kiri. 'It's the same as mine,' she whispered.

'What?'

'Charlotte's story is exactly the same as mine.'

Kiri looked up from her Sudoku. 'What? The same? But how?'

'I have no idea.'

'He threatens to have Angelique sacked, but she doesn't tell him about her husband's death because she prides herself on her professionalism, and she doesn't want pity. It's their first clash, and they'll clash a lot more, but . . . I think you can probably guess how it ends.'

'With plagiarism?' Kiri muttered.

Vanessa shushed her as Charlotte picked up a copy of *Love Transplant*.

'I thought I'd read from a passage quite early in the story. Rufus is visiting a cemetery to lay flowers on his mother's grave, when he finds Angelique sitting alone by her husband's tombstone . . .'

Vanessa had the exact same sequence in *Lost and Found Heart*!

'Rufus reads the inscription on the tombstone and realises why Angelique fainted during the heart transplant. It's a humbling moment for the arrogant surgeon.'

What on earth?! Vanessa felt like everything was swirling out of control. 'What's going on?' she muttered to no one in particular.

'Shhh!' hissed the balding old lady who'd been standing behind Vanessa in the queue with her friends.

Vanessa smiled apologetically but, as Charlotte started reading the passage, she found herself mouthing along in a whisper:

'You should have told me about your husband,' said Rufus. 'I would have gone easier on you.'

'I don't want any special favours from you,' declared Angelique, meeting his mysterious eyes. They were like two dark pools of fathomless depth . . .'

Some adjectives had been changed and the sentences subtly rearranged, but there was no denying that *Love Transplant* was uncannily familiar. Vanessa felt white-hot rage fill her chest. Amy Dunphy must have lied. How else could Charlotte have got hold of her novel? And did they think she was so stupid that she wouldn't even recognise her own story?

In spite of her grief over Alexander, she was stunned to feel a surge of longing for this arrogant man she barely knew. She shivered as a chilly breeze blew through the cemetery, and

Rufus removed his Armani jacket and wrapped it around her shoulders . . .

In Vanessa's book Magnus was wearing Country Road, but that was purely academic.

She turned to Kiri, incensed. 'I'm going to punch her lights out!' she hissed, echoing a favourite phrase of Lachie's. She pictured herself pelting Charlotte with blows, and quickly felt like an idiot. She needed to get a grip—rational, intelligent adults knew that appearances could be deceptive and things weren't always what they seemed. Especially *this*. After all, why would a bestselling author like Charlotte Lancaster plagiarise the rejected novel of a dental assistant? Vanessa's cheeks burned with the absurdity and hubris of it, and her indignation shrivelled to nothing. 'No, it must be a coincidence,' she said to Kiri.

'It had better be!' Kiri declared.

⁓

As Vanessa and Kiri neared the head of the book-signing queue, Kiri kept poking her in the ribs. 'You have to say something.'

'Shhh. It's just a fluke.'

'Huh, pretty weird fluke.'

'I was wrong,' Vanessa whispered urgently. 'Please don't make a scene, Kiri. I'm begging you. Please?'

Kiri huffed, but she clamped her mouth shut.

'Thank you.'

'Next?'

The fan in front of them moved away from the table, and there was Charlotte in all her glory.

Wow.

She was only a metre away and she was smiling at Vanessa as if they were the only two people in the world.

'Hi,' said Charlotte. 'Thanks for coming.'

Shyness suddenly overwhelmed Vanessa and she fumbled with her copies of *Love Transplant*, dropping them to the floor. 'Sorry,' she squeaked. She picked them up and awkwardly proffered them to Charlotte. 'Um, could you make one out to Vanessa, and one to Joy?'

'Of course, to Vanessa and Joy.' Charlotte leaned around to smile at Kiri, who was still hovering behind Vanessa. 'I'm not really that scary, am I, Joy?'

Amy Dunphy, who was sitting beside Charlotte, giggled.

Kiri poked Vanessa in the ribs.

Vanessa ignored her.

Kiri poked harder.

Vanessa discreetly poked her back.

Then Kiri shoved Vanessa, so Vanessa shoved Kiri and Kiri stumbled backwards, collecting the tiny elderly lady who'd arrived with the gangly guy who'd seen Vanessa's bum.

'Shit, sorry.'

'Watch what you're doing!' the tiny lady's bald mate snapped. 'Her bones are like chalk.'

'I'm sorry,' Vanessa said. She hoped they hadn't done the poor old thing irreparable damage. 'Are you all right?'

The tiny lady nodded, but she looked a bit shaky.

'Vanessa? Joy?'

Vanessa turned. Charlotte was holding out the autographed books.

'Thank you.'

As Vanessa took the books, her chipped nails made fleeting contact with Charlotte's French-polished cuticles. And then it was over.

Or was it? As she stepped away from the desk, her worst-case scenario unfolded.

'Do you have proof that you wrote this?' demanded Kiri, who'd clearly decided she *would* make a scene.

A shocked silence descended. Vanessa willed the ground to swallow her up, but it refused to cooperate.

'Vanissa wrote a book called *Lost and Found Heart* that's exactly the same.' Kiri gave Vanessa a shove. 'Go on, tell her.'

There was no point denying it—and what kind of idiot wouldn't want to address this? (The kind of idiot who would have just walked away if Kiri hadn't intervened, Vanessa confessed to herself.)

'Um, it's true. I mean, I wrote it under the name Mia Fontaine, but I sent it to Wax from my email address—and I got a rejection email from you,' she said, turning to Amy. 'But then I sent you another email asking for a copy and you told me you'd never received it.'

'Which was a blatant lie,' Kiri interjected.

The bald lady, who'd clearly been listening in, cried, 'The hide. Those girls are accusing Charlotte and Wax of plagiarism.'

Vanessa heard gasps of shock spread down the line like wildfire. She winced. Was this going to get ugly?

Charlotte, meanwhile, seemed mystified. 'I'm sorry. I'm not sure what you're referring to.'

'Me neither,' said Amy. Her left eyelid was twitching, but maybe it did that all the time? 'I've never heard of a document called . . . what was it called?'

'*Lost and Found Heart.*'

'No, I'm sorry. I don't know what you're talking about.'

'So now you've forgotten about the email you sent telling Vanissa that you'd forgotten about the other email?' Kiri snorted. 'Are you sure you haven't got early-onset Alzheimer's?'

The old ladies seemed incensed.

'Now they're making jokes about Alzheimer's!'

Bloody hell. Vanessa tried to ignore the escalating umbrage and steer things back on point. 'The thing is, our stories are almost identical.'

She could feel the other fans' glares burning into her, but Charlotte's gaze seemed compassionate.

'I'm flattered that you connect so strongly with my work, but I think you might be a bit confused.'

Vanessa *did* feel a bit confused suddenly. 'But I wrote that story first . . . I mean, I think I did.'

Kiri grabbed *Love Transplant* from her hands and ripped out a page, provoking more indignation. She scribbled down a number and thrust it at Charlotte.

'Vanissa's number. You'd better get your lawyer to get in touch, 'cause you're in big trouble.'

'No, you're not! I'm so sorry. Kiri, stop,' Vanessa implored as the crowd grew so irate that she was glad there were no pitchforks handy.

'That's enough, please,' Charlotte said. 'Vanessa clearly believes this is true. It may not make any sense to the rest of us, but we don't know what else is going on in this lady's life—so perhaps a bit of compassion might be called for?'

The crowd fell into a chastened silence, except for the tiny elderly lady who exclaimed in a remorseful trill, 'Charlotte's right, we should have a heart—the poor girl must be sick in the head.'

⟶

Vanessa and Kiri sat on the crowded train, knee to knee with an immaculate middle-aged woman and a lumpy man in a high-vis vest who reeked of BO and bitterness. An hour had passed since The Incident, but Vanessa still felt raw with humiliation.

'I can't believe I just made a fool of myself in front of Charlotte Lancaster,' she whispered.

'*You* made a fool of yourself?' Kiri scoffed. 'She stole your book.'

'No, she didn't,' Vanessa protested. 'She just came up with the same idea as me. I should be flattered.'

'Flattered? Are you insane?!'

The pristine lady stared past them and Vanessa could tell that she was pretending not to listen.

'You need to get your book and reread it fast.'

'I can't. I haven't got a copy, remember? And it's not like Amy Dunphy will give me one.'

'Huh, Amy Dunphy's a filthy liar.'

The lumpy man unzipped his high-vis vest, revealing a grubby navy blue shirt with *Pappas Plumbing* embroidered on it. Eau de Stale Sweat wafted in Vanessa and Kiri's direction. Vanessa tried not to gag. She threw Kiri a 'please don't tell him to have a shower' look, just as her phone started ringing.

She fumbled around in her handbag. 'This will be home. I hope the boys aren't playing up on Mum.'

'Isn't it usually the other way around?'

'Yeah.' Vanessa grinned. She unearthed her phone and frowned at the screen. 'It says *No Caller ID*.'

'Don't answer. It will just be someone wanting money.'

Kiri was probably right. Everyone knew that No Caller IDs were usually people you didn't want to talk to—but what if the kids had been injured or run away? It could be a hospital. Or JB Hi-Fi.

'Hello?' Vanessa tried to keep her voice down so she wouldn't be one of those annoying people who inflict their phone conversation on the whole carriage.

She was expecting the wretched cheer of a charity caller but instead heard a honey-smooth transpacific lilt. 'Vanessa?'

Vanessa's heart skipped a beat. It couldn't be.

'Yes, this is she . . .'

'Hi, Vanessa, it's Charlotte Lancaster.'

'Oh, Charlotte, hi!' Vanessa squealed loudly, and everyone turned to stare at the annoying person who was inflicting her phone conversation on the whole carriage.

Kiri narrowed her eyes. 'Don't let her con you.'

But Vanessa wasn't listening to Kiri anymore.

'Um, how are you?' she asked Charlotte.

'Okay, I guess. I just wanted to touch base because I felt badly about that misunderstanding.'

'Oh, the thing at Readings? That's okay, it was my mistake. I'm sorry for making a scene.'

Kiri put her hands around Vanessa's neck and mimed strangling her, and Vanessa was glad she and Charlotte weren't on Facetime.

'No, I'm sorry you were embarrassed. My readers are like family to me, and I hate to think of you being upset. I'd love to invite you over for lunch. How's tomorrow?'

'Lunch? Tomorrow?'

Kiri threw her hands in the air.

'Yes. Say, twelve-thirty at my place?'

'You're not falling for this?' Kiri hissed.

Vanessa turned her back on Kiri. 'I'd love to!'

Chapter 8

Vanessa crunched her Corolla into reverse and slid into a space just vacated by a late model Land Rover. Phew. The dashboard clock showed 12.31 pm and here she was, right outside Charlotte Lancaster's huge double-storey Victorian terrace in Middle Park that fronted onto Port Phillip Bay. Vanessa didn't often cross the Yarra River, which divided Melbourne like the proverbial train tracks, and she couldn't help noticing that the soft autumnal light was casting the south in a golden glow that only added to its glamour. But then she reminded herself that in recent years the inner north had acquired a hipster-ish glamour of its own, even boasting the highest proportion of Greens voters in all of Australia. And quite probably the highest proportion of beanies.

But why was she debating demographics? Because she was too scared to get out of the car, that's why. She was freaking out. She needed to calm down, to be mindful for a moment, but mindful of what? Of how much she was freaking out? It was a funny thought but it would hardly help, and the clock had just ticked to 12.32. She grabbed her home-baked hot cross buns and climbed out, comforting herself that at least she looked okay—but then a sea of joggers passed and she suddenly felt like a dickhid. She should have bought Lululemon activewear and jogged to Charlotte's gate with a hint of sweat on her forehead and her hair pulled through a baseball cap in a jaunty ponytail, wearing a pair of purple Converse trainers. She could have greeted Charlotte with a casual, 'Hi, I hope you don't mind me coming straight from my workout?' instead of, 'Hi, I hope you can't tell this dress is a Calvin Klein rip-off from Zara? And even though I bought it especially, I've changed at least seven times, and I've spent forty-five minutes straightening my hair and plucking my eyebrows and please don't look at my upper lip because I did a home wax and the redness hasn't quite abated. But hey, at least my heinous mo is gone!'

Not that she'd say that, but that wasn't the point.

As she walked up to Charlotte's gate, her shyness morphed into panic. Or maybe her panic morphed into shyness—it was academic at this point. She couldn't go through with this. She'd make an idiot of herself. She wished she could ring her mum for a confidence boost, but Joy was away with her new boyfriend Bob and didn't even know about last night's dramatic events. Vanessa didn't want to disturb her, so she resisted the urge to take out her phone.

This lunch date seemed so surreal—almost as surreal as the similarity between their two novels. Of course, she'd been suspicious at first; you'd have to be a dope not to be. But on reflection she'd realised how easily situations like this can arise. She just wished Kiri could see that too, but Kiri still thought she was being gullible, to put it kindly.

'Your stories are identical. If you refuse to believe that she plagiarised you, then how do you explain it?'

It was a valid question, there was no doubt about it—but Vanessa had realised overnight that the Emotionally Distant Cardiac Surgeon Transplants Heart of Feisty Cardiac Nurse's Tragically Killed Fiancé/ Husband idea must somehow be in the fictional zeitgeist. Didn't they say that there are only seven ideas, and every creative work is a regurgitation of one of them? She'd googled 'movies with the same story' and come up with *Antz* and *A Bug's Life* in 1998 and *Finding Nemo* and *Shark Tale* in 2004, just for starters. Lately there'd been more films about Winston Churchill and Dunkirk than you could poke a stick at, and look at *Snow White and the Huntsman* and *Mirror Mirror* back in 2012. At the time, Vanessa had preferred *Snow White and the Huntsman,* largely because she was a fan of Angelina Jolie's work with UNICEF. Which, when you think about it, didn't have a lot to do with the movie.

But anyway.

She plucked up courage and pressed the intercom. Within moments she was buzzed into a courtyard scattered with artfully selected succulents, and Charlotte appeared at the front door.

'Vanessa. Hi.' She was wearing orange Converse trainers and Lululemon activewear that hugged her long, slender legs, and her hair was gathered up in a ponytail with just the right amount of wispiness. 'Sorry for the outfit. I'm just back from yoga.'

'Don't be silly,' squeaked Vanessa, who was sure she must look and sound like Minnie Mouse. She shyly presented Charlotte with the hot cross buns. 'These are for you. I know it's not quite Easter yet . . .'

'That's so sweet! You baked them yourself? Thank you.'

Charlotte leaned in to kiss her, but Vanessa proffered the wrong cheek and their heads butted. Vanessa was mortified but she couldn't help seeing the funny side. They shared a stilted little laugh.

'That was awkward! I'm so glad you could make it. Come in.'

Charlotte led her inside. Even in trainers she was much taller than Vanessa and she somehow seemed to glide. Vanessa reproached herself—why couldn't she glide? She felt herself morph from Minnie Mouse into Quasimodo, all unsightly hump, dragging her ill-shod clubfoot behind her. Charlotte led her past huge vases of exotic blooms and out to a large, light-filled kitchen that Vanessa remembered seeing in *Home Beautiful* last year. Charlotte had been pictured zesting a lime at the marble benchtop while her gorgeous husband Marcus Stafford prepared a kale and freekeh salad:

For all their terrace's space and grandeur, Charlotte and Marcus both gravitate to the kitchen, which they consider the heart of their home.

Vanessa wondered nervously if she'd meet Marcus. She'd seen him on *Q&A* last month, enthralling the audience with erudite points about intellectual property law, and now here she was in his house. What would she say to a man like him? Come to think of it, what would she say to Charlotte?

'Um, can I give you a hand with lunch?' It was the most sparkling repartee she could manage.

Charlotte smiled as she put the hot cross buns down on the bench. 'Thanks, but can I make a confession? I'm so exhausted from the book tour that Dad's sent his corporate chef over.'

Holy cow.

Right on cue, a guy with a Clark Gable haircut, a Ned Kelly beard, tattoos and an intense expression emerged from the pantry with a mortar and pestle. Charlotte introduced him as Atticus Jax, former sous chef at Moses. Vanessa was impressed, even though she'd never heard of Moses. Not that she was about to tell Charlotte that—nor Atticus, who was looking at her like he already suspected.

'You like seafood?' Atticus asked in a tone that suggested there was only one correct answer.

Vanessa nodded obediently.

'Cool. I'm starting with Clyde River rock oysters with grilled sea foam.'

'Yum!' said Charlotte.

'Delicious!' agreed Vanessa.

How the hell do you grill foam? She didn't like to ask.

Leaving Atticus to his artistry, Charlotte led Vanessa out to a striking living room decorated with bold modern pieces that somehow complemented the terrace's period features. She poured Vanessa a generous glass of prosecco and, fifteen minutes later, Vanessa found herself confiding about Craig's betrayal.

'Arsehole.' Charlotte said, her eyes blazing with indignation. 'His loss.' She raised her glass of prosecco. 'Here's to all the fabulous men you'll be fighting off with sticks.'

'I'll use the sticks to form an orderly queue,' Vanessa quipped, miming directions with a stick. 'You stand there and you lot line up behind him—you'll all get your turn.'

Charlotte laughed and Vanessa felt a delighted rush. Charlotte couldn't be more supportive. She swished her prosecco around in her mouth, feeling it softly fizz. She'd have to stop after this glass, but the bubbles had helped to ease her shyness. Who said you shouldn't use alcohol as a crutch? They obviously weren't having lunch with their idol! But she was shaken out of her reverie when she saw a shadow pass across Charlotte's face.

'My marriage is over too.'

Vanessa was staggered. 'What? No. Really?'

Charlotte nodded. Her smile looked strained. 'We haven't announced it yet. I need to get my head around things first. So many broken dreams . . .'

Vanessa felt empathy in her every pore. 'Oh, Charlotte, I'm sorry.'

Charlotte smiled wanly. 'It's such a relief to confide in a girlfriend who's been there.'

A girlfriend? Already? Did Charlotte mean that? But why wouldn't she? Vanessa flashed forward to a future in which they were insep-arable . . . but how would she juggle Charlotte and Kiri? Kiri would probably never warm to Charlotte, and she'd hate to hurt Kiri's feelings—not that Charlotte would ever usurp her, but still.

'I guess all we can do is put one foot in front of the other, right?'

Vanessa nodded. Charlotte was too much of a class act to elaborate, but it seemed pretty clear that Marcus Stafford had done a Craig.

'Marcus is a bastard. And what a fool.'

For a man with such a renowned intellect, he'd just acted like someone with shit for brains.

'Thanks for being in my corner.'

'Of course.'

Conquering her last shred of shyness, Vanessa gave Charlotte a hug. Charlotte leaned into her, and as Vanessa inhaled her subtly smoky perfume she could scarcely believe that Charlotte Lancaster was clinging to her for comfort. All her fantasies were coming true. Oh, except for the one about getting her novel published. A sensible little voice inside her head said, 'How come Charlotte hasn't brought up *Lost and Found Heart*? Isn't that rather an odd omission?' 'Shut up,' Vanessa said back to it.

Out in the hall the front door opened, and a deep male voice rang out.

'Honey?'

'In here, Dad.' Charlotte pulled away from Vanessa and dabbed at her eyes. 'Dad's joining us for lunch. I hope that's okay?'

Vanessa nodded, suddenly intimidated all over again. Chip Lancaster—corporate titan and two-time winner of the Sydney to Hobart yacht race in his world-class maxi *Charlanne*, named for Charlotte and her mother—was here. And Vanessa had just managed to relax. She grabbed the prosecco bottle. Stuff it—she'd get the tram home.

'You're not getting the damned tram,' Chip insisted with a twinkle as he topped up her bubbles. 'My driver will take you home.'

'Oh no, it's fine.'

'Just go with it,' Charlotte advised. 'There's no point trying to say no to Dad.'

Vanessa giggled. 'All right, then. Thank you, Mr Lancaster.'

'Hey, it's Chip, remember?'

'Okay, Chip.'

She giggled again, because why not? It was such an American name, Chip, she mused. Was it short for something? Vanessa couldn't think what it might be short for, but did people actually christen their children Chip? It was like christening your kid Biscuit.

'Actually,' Charlotte said to Chip teasingly, 'has anyone *ever* said no to you?'

Probably not, Vanessa thought. Chip was short and stout with a sallow complexion, but he had the air of a man who always got his own way. Her father Jack had been the same—although Jack was demonstrably more handsome. She felt a wistful tug as she watched Charlotte squeeze Chip's pudgy hand. Charlotte was a self-confessed Daddy's Girl, although Vanessa knew from interviews that she was also close to her mum Annie, a former air hostess who'd met Chip in the first-class section of a Pan Am flight. Chip and Annie had fallen in love, and Chip had made the wrenching decision to leave his first wife, Ros, who'd worked as a cleaner to put him through university. Apparently it was a very painful time for all of them, but Vanessa was willing to bet that Ros had copped the bulk of the pain.

Chip smiled across the table at her with his perfect porcelain veneers. 'Can I ask you something, Ness?'

'Of course.'

'The dentist takes the impression of a patient's teeth, but you actually make the mouth mould, right?'

'Uh, yeah, that's right.'

'And what's the process?'

To Vanessa's surprise, Chip sounded genuinely interested. Dentistry talk usually made people's eyes glaze over—especially hers. She explained the mouth mould process step by step, and then Chip asked how she educated patients about gingivitis and what periodontal scaler she generally used for cleaning teeth.

Eventually curiosity got the better of her. 'How do you know so much about dental assisting?'

'I make it my business to know about things that matter. It's an established fact that dental health is closely aligned with cardiac health, so in my eyes that makes you a lifesaver.'

In normal circumstances that would have struck Vanessa as gilding the lily, but after four and a half glasses of prosecco, she was humbled by her own healing powers. The sensible little voice inside her head said, 'He's just flattering you,' but Vanessa shot back, 'Since when is flattery a crime?'

'Dad's right,' Charlotte chimed in. 'Being a dental assistant is so much more worthwhile than being a vacuous romance writer like me.'

Was that meant to be an opening? Should she take it? The sensible little voice said, 'Do it, dumbo.' So she repressed a burp and bit the bullet. 'Yeah, dental assisting's great, but to be honest I found it much more rewarding writing *Lost and Found Heart.*'

And there it was, the elephant in the room, dunking its long and leathery trunk into Atticus Jax's smoked eel with white chocolate and caviar.

A nonplussed silence briefly descended, and Vanessa felt irrationally guilty for killing the vibe.

Charlotte and Chip exchanged a look and then Chip turned to her sympathetically. 'I have to say I feel for you, Ness. Charlotte told me what happened, and it's a damned shame. But I guess once something's in the zeitgeist, it's just a matter of luck who gets their version out there first.'

'Absolutely,' Charlotte agreed. 'And the cards could have fallen the other way if I'd submitted *Love Transplant* first—although obviously your manuscript never arrived at Wax.'

'It did arrive, and Amy Dunphy wrote back to me. And I know two people can have a similar idea, but page for page, nearly word for word? Don't you think that's weird?'

'It's incredibly weird.'

'It's much worse than just weird,' Chip said, refilling Vanessa's already full glass. 'It sucks, if you'll forgive my French. It's lousy luck for a delightful young lady who clearly doesn't deserve it.'

Wow, he was being so understanding. 'Der!' said the sensible little voice. 'He's got an ulterior motive.' 'I thought I told you to shut up,' Vanessa snapped back.

'You know what, Ness? I'd like to help you. How does twenty grand sound?'

'Twenty grand? What do you mean?'

Charlotte smiled. 'It's the least we can do.'

Chip reached down and pulled a large envelope from his Armani satchel. 'It's not fair that you won't be able to get your own book out into the market, so we think you deserve some compensation.' He held out the envelope. 'Go on, take it.'

With trembling fingers, Vanessa took the envelope and pulled out a piece of paper on a prestigious legal firm's letterhead.

What?

'It's a contract?' she asked.

'Just a formality,' Chip assured her.

'It's no biggie,' seconded Charlotte, but Vanessa noticed she was gripping her father's arm with white knuckles. What exactly was going on here? She looked down at the page and, skipping the preliminaries, focused on the nitty-gritty:

Ms Rooney agrees to relinquish *all* printed copies of her unpublished novel *Lost and Found Heart* to Ms Lancaster, including any research materials and notes prepared in connection with the novel, and further agrees to delete any and every electronic copy of same novel off any and every computer/laptop/mobile device in her own or anyone else's possession, including every copy that is relegated to Trash after said initial deletion. Ms Rooney also agrees to relinquish the computer(s)/laptop(s)/mobile device(s) on which her novel was written to Ms Lancaster. Subject to Ms Lancaster and her representatives being satisfied that no printed or electronic copy of *Lost and Found Heart* remains in Ms Rooney's or anyone else's possession, Ms Lancaster shall pay Ms Rooney twenty thousand dollars ($20,000) plus the reasonable cost of a new laptop computer of Ms Rooney's choosing within seven (7) working days.

Vanessa felt sick in the stomach as she read on:

Ms Rooney further agrees never to speak or to communicate to any other person or persons publicly or privately of this Agreement. Any breach of this clause will be grounds for legal action.

Vanessa looked back up at the Lancasters wordlessly.

Chip produced a pen from his pocket. 'Like I said, it's just a formality.'

'But if it's an innocent mistake, why are you trying to pay me off?'

'It's not a payment, it's a gift,' said Charlotte, but she was tapping her nails on the table.

Vanessa bit her lip. So much for their burgeoning friendship.

'And why do you want all my copies of *Lost and Found Heart*?' she asked, making a mental note not to reveal that she didn't have any.

'Oh, that? That's just to avoid confusion in the marketplace.'

Confusion in the marketplace! Did he think she came down in the last shower? Vanessa felt fury bloom inside her.

'We need to make sure that your novel isn't out there so—'

'So you can hide the fact that your daughter *did* steal it—and that's why you're trying to pay me off.'

'Go, girlfriend,' said the sensible little voice.

'Dad, do something!' Charlotte squealed.

'Shut up, Charlotte! No one's trying to pay you off, Ness.'

But Vanessa wasn't buying it anymore. Incandescent with rage, she waved the contract. 'You might think I'm just a dumb little dental assistant, but you're wrong. I'm keeping this—'

Quick as a flash Chip leaped forward to rip the contract out of her hands, but Vanessa refused to let it go. They tussled and the contract was ripped in two, leaving Vanessa with the top right-hand corner. She jumped up from the table, pushing her chair back so fast that it toppled over.

'This is evidence. I'll see you in court!'

Vanessa stormed off, colliding with Atticus Jax in the doorway and knocking his free trade chocolate soufflé to the floor.

Chapter 9

Kiri thrust a glass of house chardonnay at Vanessa. 'Get that into you.'

Two hours had passed since Vanessa's run-in with Charlotte and Chip, and she and Kiri had snatched the last table at the nearby Beach Hotel, which was heaving with Friday night revellers. Now that she'd faced the awful truth, Vanessa was kicking herself for losing her evidence. It was lucky that Lachie and Joy weren't here, or she would've been tempted to kick them too. Kiri proffered a plate of croquettes with aioli, but Vanessa had lost her appetite. The weirdest thing was how hurt she felt by the Lancasters, even though she barely knew them. I'd never do that to you, she thought, so why are you doing it to me?

'It's my fault,' she said aloud. 'I shouldn't have let Lachie borrow my laptop—he loses everything. And I should've made sure my back-up drive was kept far away from Mum's mess. I haven't got a leg to stand on.' She hiccupped.

'You can't give up. You've got this.' Kiri waved the small triangular piece of the contract.

'That's nothing, Kiri.' Vanessa hiccupped again. 'It's just got the date, the page number and half the legal firm's logo—it could be anything.'

'Maybe, but you've still got the photo Joy took when you sent the manuscript—it's dated.'

'Yeah, but it doesn't prove that the manuscript arrived at Wax. I'm stuffed. I have to be realistic.'

Kiri threw her hands in the air.

'I've got no choice!' Vanessa cried raggedly.

A woman at the next table turned. Her face looked like it had been sandblasted and then snap-frozen, but if she could have moved her forehead Vanessa was sure she would have raised her eyebrows.

Kiri eyeballed her. 'Have you got a problem, apart from your discount plastic surgeon?'

'Kiri, be quiet.'

Sandblasted Face turned back to her waxy-looking friend and Vanessa and Kiri dissolved into giggles, but Vanessa's were complicated by hiccups. She started coughing so much that she almost threw up. Kiri slapped her back and handed her a glass of water.

'Thanks,' Vanessa said when she could talk again. 'Maybe if I was rich I could pursue it just to embarrass Charlotte, but I don't know if I could cope with the public exposure, anyway. And those Lancasters don't take any prisoners. I felt like saying to them—'

'That's your whole problem,' Kiri interrupted, and Vanessa watched her best friend transform into the mature human being she actually was beneath her bluster. 'Seriously, Niss, I worry about you. You do this with Craig and Natalie too. You're always telling me: *I felt like saying* or *I wanted to say*—well, why don't you just say it?'

Vanessa was stumped. Why *didn't* she say what she wanted to say? Because she was a people pleaser—hello! And a coward, probably. She downed her chardonnay in one gulp.

'I take your point, but I just have to suck this up. What's that saying? "Grant me the courage to change the things I can change, the serenity to accept the things I can't change and the wisdom to know the difference."'

Kiri switched back to bolshy mode. 'Serinity is for dickhids.'

'Well, that's me, a serene dickhid.' Vanessa raised her glass but it was empty. She regarded it sadly. 'My shout.' But as she was rummaging around for her purse, she heard a voice call through the din.

'Nessie!'

Vanessa turned to see her mum squeezing through a group of middle-aged blokes in suits, her breasts squashed up against their torsos in the human crush.

'Mum!' She turned to Kiri. 'Did you call her? Thank you,' she hiccupped, suddenly weepy.

'Oh, Nessie, that thieving cow!' Joy said as she reached their table. 'Are you all right?'

Joy was wearing her favourite dress in a red jersey that accentuated the line where her Spanx ended and her tummy escaped with an almost audible sigh of relief.

At the next table, Sandblasted Face nudged her waxy friend and snickered.

Vanessa felt a surge of rage. 'What's so funny?' she demanded.

She leaped to her feet but felt herself fall to the floor.

'Nessie!'

'Niss! Are you okay?'

'I'm good,' she said, but she couldn't quite seem to lift herself up. After a couple of attempts she surrendered to gravity, lying on the sticky carpet like one of those white body outlines. Joy turned to the blokes in suits.

'Can someone help us?'

From what Vanessa could see from the floor, they all shoved each other out of the way in a competition to be the most courteous.

Someone who smelled like beer and cashews plucked her up off the floor and plonked her back in her chair. Vanessa could tell he was hoping to chat up Joy, but after a cursory thank you Joy turned all her attention back to Vanessa.

'Are you sure you're all right?'

Vanessa nodded through a hiccup.

'She's a bit under the weather,' Kiri said.

'Who could blame her?' Joy pulled Vanessa against her leathery décolletage. 'Don't worry, Nessie. We'll make Charlotte Lancaster pay.'

Vanessa snorted humourlessly into Joy's cleavage. She hiccupped again and almost choked. Joy was squeezing her tight.

'Mum . . . I can't . . . breathe.'

Joy released her grip.

'Niss hasn't got any evidence,' Kiri bemoaned.

'Maybe *she* hasn't . . .' Joy winked, suddenly assuming the air of a magician about to produce one hell of a rabbit. 'But I have.'

What?!

Joy reached into her handbag.

'Ta-da!'

'Oh my God, my back-up drive!' Vanessa couldn't believe her eyes. She grabbed it like it was a priceless treasure, which it pretty much was at this point. 'So it didn't get thrown out?'

'No, I found it hidden between Jane Austen and Nora Roberts just before Bob and I left. I was going to surprise you when I got back.'

'Oh, Mum!'

'This is excellent!' Kiri declared. We'll take that bitch for every penny.'

'We'll do more than that,' Joy said. 'By the time we've finished with her, she'll be burning her own books to keep herself warm.'

'Yeah!'

Vanessa tried to match their excitement, but her ebullience was already fizzling into fear. It was one thing to want to sue Charlotte when she knew she couldn't, but now she actually had the evidence, it was a different prospect altogether. The idea of conflict with anyone made her gizzards curdle—let alone conflict with an adored celebrity like Charlotte Lancaster. Could she cope with the kind of public slanging match that suing Charlotte would bring? The very thought made her weak with panic. And, besides, she couldn't afford a lawyer.

But Kiri and Joy weren't about to let her off the hook.

'You have to at least get some legal advice.'

'Your mum's right—and hey, I just remembered, the Redbacks' new coach is a lawyer. Dave Rendall. Have you met him yet?'

'No, Craig's been taking Jackson to training. But I know that Jackson really likes him.'

'Yeah, the kids love him—he seems like a great guy. Why don't you talk to him in the morning? Maybe he'll give you some cheap advice.'

Vanessa didn't want to let Kiri and Joy down. And it was only advice.

'Let's do it.' she said, removing her elbow from the aioli.

Chapter 10

It was drizzling at the Jeffrey G. Kennett Oval, and Vanessa flicked her umbrella open as she scanned the playing field for Jackson. On the sidelines, the coach/lawyer Dave Rendall was running along with his back to her, his hoodie raised against the rain. He was super-tall and his nylon tracksuit pants didn't quite reach his ankles. What kind of lawyer couldn't afford a tracksuit that fit? Vanessa wondered. But that probably wasn't fair—some people didn't care about clothes, and who was to say it hadn't shrunk in the wash? And, anyway, Dave Rendall's legal skills were almost irrelevant. Overnight, Vanessa's fear of suing Charlotte had escalated into sheer terror. There was no way she could go through with it, but she knew that Kiri would kill her if she didn't at least broach the subject. She glanced at the Redbacks coach again. Something about his ungainly limbs gave her a strange sense of déjà vu, but there was no time to contemplate that because Daisy was straining at her leash and barking at an errant seagull.

Vanessa winced. 'Daisy, no.'

Daisy obediently stopped barking and trotted by her side, ecstatic about the prosaic outing. Vanessa wished she could share her labradoodle's joie de vivre, but her head was throbbing and her mouth tasted like the bottom of a kitty litter tray. She was seven minutes late for Jackson's first game of the season because she hadn't heard her alarm—or maybe she hadn't set it; she was so drunk last night that she couldn't remember. She felt a pang of maternal guilt, but at least the statistics were on her side. Jackson had scored a total of five goals in three years—he was hardly likely to have kicked his sixth goal in the past seven minutes.

'Mum!' Lachie was haring towards her. 'Jackson just kicked a goal!'

You're kidding.

'Come and check it out! Natalie filmed it.'

'Did she? Cool! Natalie thinks of everything.'

Gosh, that was skirting a bit close to sarcasm—it was lucky that Lachie was too young for subtext. Pang of Maternal Guilt #2.

'Yeah! Come on.'

Vanessa followed Lachie over to Craig and Natalie, who were sitting on camp chairs with takeaway lattes. Craig's arm was slung around Natalie's shoulders, and her silken mane tumbled like liquid chocolate over his tanned pecs. Vanessa wondered if they were judging her for her tardiness, but of course not!

'Don't beat yourself up for being late,' Natalie offered kindly, even though Vanessa hadn't brought it up. 'I can see you're exhausted.'

'Nat's right,' agreed Craig. 'You look terrible.'

Before Vanessa could protest, Craig leaped to his feet and proffered his chair. Her nerves were on edge and a tiny piece of croissant wedged in his teeth made her want to seize the chair and hit him over the head with it, but she was too desperate to sit down.

'Thanks, Craig.'

She sat.

'Would you like to see Jackson's goal?' Natalie asked.

'Yeah, Natalie, that would be great, because we all know that I'm a negligent mum who gets pissed and turns up late, but luckily your perfection makes up for it.'

But, of course, that was just what she *wanted* to say.

'I'd love to. Thanks, Natalie.'

Natalie passed her iPhone over. 'And you'll be pleased to know that we cheered extra loud on your behalf.'

Get stuffed, you dickhid, thought Vanessa. She dutifully watched Jackson's triumph on Natalie's phone but, as soon as she could, she escaped to join Kiri, who was rostered on at the kiosk.

'What a pair of wenkers,' Kiri scoffed as she watched Craig and Natalie open a packet of baked kale chips.

'At least they arrived on time.'

'Yeah, because they've got nothing else in their sad little lives.'

Vanessa chortled, even though they both knew that wasn't true. Kiri handed her a sausage roll slathered in sauce. It was nectar to Vanessa's hangover, and they chatted happily through the rest of the game while Lachie and Kiri's daughter Emily played with Daisy in the rain. With just two minutes left on the clock the Roos scored another goal, sending them into the lead and the Redbacks into a tailspin. Kiri guffawed as Dave Rendall leaped up and down on the boundary like an overstretched pogo stick. He turned and, for the first time, Vanessa got a full view of his face. Oh God, it couldn't be. But it was. The Redbacks' coach was the guy who'd seen her bum hanging out of her undies on Lygon Street!

'Oh my God, it's him,' she gasped to Kiri, who was locking up the kiosk.

'What?'

'The coach. It's him.'

'Who?'

'The guy. Remember how I told you a guy saw my bare bum outside Readings? It was him.'

Kiri looked astonished. 'Dave?'

'Yeah.'

'Really?'

'Yeah.'

Kiri erupted into laughter and, despite her mortification, Vanessa couldn't resist joining in. Suddenly cheers rang out as the Redbacks evened the score thanks to a nifty goal by a super-tall girl, who Kiri said was Dave's daughter, Nickie.

'Well done, sweetie!' Dave called.

Nickie threw him what looked like a pained glance. 'Don't call me sweetie at soccer,' she snapped back.

'Sorry, sweetie—oops . . . mate.'

Vanessa felt for Dave—it was hard for parents to do the right thing sometimes.

The other Redbacks all gave Nickie triumphant high fives—except for Jackson, who seemed to make a point of being churlish. Vanessa frowned. Where were his manners?

The ref blew his whistle. It was a draw. Vanessa and Kiri headed onto the muddy oval with the other parents. Vanessa threw a hoodie over Jackson's shoulders as Daisy barked happily at their ankles.

'Well done, sweetheart! I'm sorry I missed your goal.'

'What?' said Jackson. He was looking over at Dave Rendall, who was hugging Nickie.

Vanessa's cheeks burned at Dave's proximity. She tried to slink away, but Kiri grabbed her.

'Kiri! I can't talk to him about legal issues. He's seen my booty.'

They both chortled at the term.

'No, come on, Niss. You don't have to worry—he's a man.'

Vanessa looked blank.

Kiri rolled her eyes. 'Hello? Men never remember anything.'

Kiri had a valid point, so Vanessa allowed herself to be dragged over to Dave Rendall, who seemed as friendly as his puppy dog eyes had suggested—not that she could see them now, because she was studiously staring at her feet.

'Anyway, to cut to the chase,' Kiri was saying, 'Vanissa's got a legal problem.'

'A legal problem?' Vanessa heard Dave Rendall ask.

Reluctantly, she looked up, but she kept her gaze fixed on his left earlobe.

'Yeah. The thing is, I need an opinion, but I can probably only pay you, um, fifty dollars?'

'Haven't you heard about the Redbacks family discount? One hundred per cent off.'

What a nice guy. Vanessa finally met his eyes. He showed no hint of recognition, and she felt herself relax.

'Thank you, that's really kind of you.'

'But seriously, Dave, this whole situation is an outrageous miscarriage of justice,' Kiri said gravely. 'Niss has been appallingly treated, and they can't be allowed to get away with it.' She nudged Vanessa. 'Go on. Tell him.'

As Vanessa hesitated, Dave seemed to form his face into a question mark.

'It's kind of . . . It's hard to explain. I'd rather show you, if you don't mind. Do you think you could come to my place for half an hour?'

The poor man probably had far better things to do, but he didn't look horrified, so that was something.

'You won't regret it,' Kiri assured him. 'It's just a bugger that Niss has got no money, 'cause this could be huge.'

'Huge?' Dave looked to Vanessa for confirmation.

'It could be big,' she agreed anxiously.

'Well, sounds like I'd better come then. Out of curiosity, if nothing else.'

Vanessa smiled gratefully. Thank goodness he hadn't recognised her.

⁓

Barely an hour later, Dave was sitting at her wonky kitchen table. He smiled as Vanessa handed him a cup of English breakfast tea.

'Beauty. This'll hit the spot.'

Dave was going to read aloud from *Lost and Found Heart* while Vanessa read the same chapter from *Love Transplant*, and she was hoping he'd tell her what she wanted to hear: 'I'm sorry, but you've got no case. Don't waste your money or your time on something that you haven't got a hope in hell of winning.'

That would be ideal, because then she could chicken out of this and blame Dave. Well, not blame him exactly, but defer to his legal assessment. How could Kiri and Joy argue with that?

She slipped on a pair of oven mitts. Lachie was over at Kiri's place and Jackson and Nickie were in Jackson's room playing Scrabble. The Scrabble was Dave's idea, and Vanessa thought it was a stroke of genius—Jackson couldn't seem to form any verbal words around Nickie, but he might do better with a Scrabble board. She just hoped that everything was going okay; when their visitors had first arrived, Jackson had just stared mutely at his feet.

'I'm sorry,' she'd said to Dave. 'He's not normally rude like this.'

'It's okay, he's just shy.'

Tell me about it. Vanessa often fretted about passing her shyness down to Jackson like some kind of defective gene. How would he fare in this screen-obsessed world of relentless self-promotion? The meek weren't going to inherit the earth in its current form, that was for sure.

But anyhoo.

She removed some hot cross buns from the oven.

'They smell great.'

Dave's legs were folded sideways under the table and his mud-splattered nylon tracksuit pants were riding halfway up to his knees, while Daisy lay draped over his feet. She'd taken an instant liking to Dave, and Vanessa wondered if she was responding to his rangy limbs—maybe she thought he was an Irish wolfhound? This notion made Vanessa smile, and she liked Dave even more; there was no one's judgement she trusted like Daisy's. Still, it was only polite to check that the guy was okay with his feet being used as a pillow.

'Is Daisy bothering you?'

Dave shook his head with a grin. 'She's better than ugg boots, aren't you, mate?' He reached down to scratch Daisy's head.

What a sweet man, thought Vanessa, but she couldn't help noticing a recalcitrant eyebrow sticking out at a perpendicular angle, and was that a toothpaste stain on his sleeve? She felt a twinge of disappointment. Dave didn't look anything like the lawyers she saw every night on the news, striding down William Street in their wigs with their black robes billowing in the wind and their air of being in charge of the world—although, to be fair, he obviously knew a hell of a lot about conveyancing. She'd googled him and seen a plethora of five-star reviews:

Great guy and very efficient. He negotiated a longer settlement on my new apartment with a minimum of fuss. Brendon Luno

If we ever sell this place, we'll definitely get Dave to do our conveyancing again! Tori Hayden

There was plenty of that kind of thing. So what did it matter that he didn't wear robes? And he was giving up his time on a Sunday, so the least she could do was not take up too much of it. She joined him at the table.

'So, should we start?'

'You bet. How about the opening of chapter five?'

Chapter 11

DAVE

'*She moaned,*' Dave read aloud with unalloyed amusement, '*urging his mouth to take its fill as his fingers, so skilled in surgery, danced teasingly over her silken skin . . .*'

This was brilliant! Who'd have thought Vanessa's novel would turn out to be a biting satire on those God-awful bodice rippers that Mrs Hipsley and her mates liked so much? But, then, she *had* been in that line outside Readings—she must have gone to that Charlotte Lancaster thing for research. Dave had recognised Vanessa instantly as the cute woman who'd tucked her undies into her skirt. What were the odds? He'd wondered briefly if he should acknowledge the incident, but maybe she'd forgotten all about it and he'd sound like a perv who'd been obsessing? And this wasn't the kind of case you'd take to a bloke who'd seen your arse protruding from your pants. Thank goodness she hadn't recognised him.

He continued: '*Their eyes locked as though fused by electricity. In that moment she knew that desire was her illness, and he was her only cure.*'

Dave dissolved into chuckles. 'This is hilarious!'

'Thanks.'

Vanessa smiled, but Dave saw something pass over her face and he realised that she was disconcerted. Oh no—her book was supposed to be serious! Why hadn't he guessed? He felt like an oaf, but he couldn't say he felt surprised. He'd always excelled at misreading attractive women, and now he was misreading their writing too, it seemed.

'Oh, it's serious? I'm sorry.'

'That's okay.'

'I thought—'

'No, it's fine. There *are* some funny bits—it's just that this wasn't meant to be one of them.'

She gave him a goofy little smile, and Dave wanted to scoop her up and put her inside his jacket pocket where he could keep her warm and safe—although if she was into this kind of crap, she'd probably prefer that he threw her over a stallion and cantered off into the sunset. He suddenly felt the pall of defeat, even though he wasn't exactly sure what he'd been hoping to win.

'Really, it's fine,' she said again, and he half wondered if she'd read his mind. 'Kiri thinks that romance is only fit for dunny paper, so I'm immune.'

They laughed, and Dave found himself wondering if she was single. Jackson's father Craig—a bit of a nob in Dave's opinion—seemed to be with that dark-haired woman at the soccer, which suggested that Vanessa was single. But how could someone so cute be unattached? Surely some bloke must have snapped her up. Dave started searching the kitchen for signs.

'Dave?' She was looking at him expectantly.

'Right,' he said, pulling himself together. 'Will we both read now?'

They read the rest of the chapter in unison, and Dave was gobsmacked by the astonishing similarities between the two stories—it really did seem that only the odd word and phrase had been altered. But he was soon distracted by a more immediate problem.

Vanessa's voice was soft and appealing, and with laughter no longer an option he was starting to feel something even more mortifying.

'*With one flick, Magnus/Rufus released the ties of her surgical/ surgery gown and it fell to the floor/ground,*' they read together. '*He cupped/held her breasts in his hands, gently/tenderly caressing her erect nipples until she was awash/ached with desire.*'

Dave's eyes zeroed in on Vanessa's soft breasts. He forced himself to look away.

'*Breathless with her need/hunger for him, Georgie's/Angelique's hand/fingers sought and found his throbbing manhood . . .*'

Dave willed his own manhood not to throb.

'*Magnus/Rufus let out a ragged/hoarse gasp, and she could feel his whole body rigid/taut with desire. "I want/must have you* now," *he groaned hungrily*—'

'Dad?'

Dave slammed the manuscript upside down with a flustered cough as Nickie and Jackson appeared. He felt like one of those bumbling dads in a second-rate sitcom.

'Hey, sweetie. What's up?' He quickly rephrased that. 'What's going on?'

'Can I play *Grand Theft Auto* with Jackson?'

'*Grand Theft Auto*?' Dave frowned.

'Yeah. It's harmless.'

'It's educational,' Jackson chimed in.

'So's Scrabble, mate.'

Privately, Dave suspected that Evanthe might steal his testicles if he allowed their daughter to play *Grand Theft Auto*.

'But Scrabble's boring!'

'Boring's nine points. See? It's fun.'

Nickie rolled her eyes, but Vanessa laughed, and Dave felt an unexpected glow of pleasure.

'Please, Dad? Jackson's allowed.'

'It's good for their hand–eye coordination,' Vanessa said.

Dave thought that Vanessa sounded like she was trying to convince herself, but he acquiesced, and the kids headed into the living room to commit car theft and murder.

The interruption had proven a blessing—it gave Dave the chance to let professionalism resume the reins. It was clear that Charlotte Lancaster had got hold of Vanessa's novel and copied it almost verbatim, and Dave's finely tuned sense of social justice was outraged. How could a woman as wealthy and privileged as Charlotte Lancaster steal a year from the life of a financially strapped single mum whose bum looked just as good in jeans as it did hanging out of her undies? Dave was incensed by the arrogance of it. He turned back to her with what he hoped was gravitas.

'I think you have a very strong case for suing Charlotte Lancaster and Wax Publishing for breach of copyright.'

'Really? I do?'

'Yes, I believe you do.'

He thought she'd be jubilant but instead she looked petrified. Dave could relate. This case would be way out of his comfort zone and he wondered if he'd be the right bloke for the job. Intellectual property, or IP, wasn't in his wheelhouse—although of course the pivotal courtroom theatrics would fall to somebody else.

'As your lawyer I'd do all the legwork and research, but I'd need to brief an intellectual property barrister to start the litigation proceedings. You look a bit worried. Are you okay?'

She was silent for a second, but then she nodded.

'Yeah, I am. You know what? I was kind of hoping you'd say I had no case so I could chicken out of this, but now I feel so mad that I just want to shout from the rooftops, "You stole from me!"' Her face was crimson with righteous indignation and Dave felt bizarrely proud, even though he barely knew her from a bar of soap. 'Well, maybe not shout it from the rooftops—hopefully we can keep things quiet—but you know what I mean.'

'I do.'

But then her brow crinkled. 'I don't know if I can afford a barrister, though. How much can you get for a ten-year-old boy on the black market?'

'Not enough,' Dave quipped. 'But sometimes barristers will take on a case for no win, no fee.'

'But why would anyone do that for me?'

Good question, thought Dave. But this case was bound to generate publicity, and wasn't there always some show pony barrister who wanted to get their face on the telly? Not that he'd know how to find one. He was suddenly gripped by nerves, but his crisis of confidence was cut short by a husky female voice from the doorway, and he turned to see an over-tanned sexagenarian in an under-sized nightie. He blinked. He was back in that sitcom.

'Mum,' said Vanessa.

Mum? thought Dave.

'Dave, this is my mum Joy and her boyfriend Bob. Mum, this is Dave, the lawyer who's Jackson's coach.'

'Good to meet you, hon,' Joy said warmly.

Dave and Bob shook hands. Bob was obviously one of those old alpha blokes who saw a handshake as a competition, because he almost crushed Dave's digits.

Joy gave Dave a wink. 'We skipped the soccer so we could have a sleep-in, if you know what I mean.'

Dave winked back. 'I know what you mean.'

Joy gave a bawdy chuckle. She was clearly a good sort in all senses of the expression. She started waving the *Sunday Age*. 'Nessie, you won't believe what I've just read—an interview with Angela Madden.'

'Angela Madden? Really? What did she say?'

Vanessa was clearly intrigued but Dave had no idea who they were talking about.

Joy slipped on a pair of glasses with sparkly things on the frames. 'Listen to this: *"Maintaining a dignified silence gets wearing," said the petite brunette, reaching for another wallaby blood pikelet. "The truth is, I'm devastated that Ned left me for Charlotte Lancaster, and I know Marcus Stafford is devastated too. He thought he was married for keeps and he's very bitter about Charlotte's betrayal."'*

Dave's jaw dropped. 'Hang on a sec—Marcus Stafford? You mean the barrister?'

'Yes! The dreamboat barrister!'

Dave was intrigued. So Charlotte Lancaster used to be married to Marcus Stafford . . . What were the odds? Stafford was an IP whiz and brilliant courtroom operator who breathed the kind of rarefied legal air that Dave had only dreamed about. He turned to gauge Vanessa's reaction, but her face had turned pink with something that seemed to be indignation.

'Charlotte left Marcus?'

'Yes. So she lied to you about that too.'

'What a lousy, rotten—' But she stopped. 'Although I suppose technically she never said those exact—'

But she didn't finish because Joy put a hand out to silence her.

'My Nessie's a people pleaser, Dave, in case you haven't gathered. She needs a lawyer with a killer instinct, and no offence, hon, but you don't seem like a killer.'

'I'm a killer!' Dave insisted politely, and in that moment he almost felt like one. A Machiavellian idea was forming . . . 'Hell hath no fury like a barrister scorned. If Stafford's really that bitter about his ex-wife, maybe he'd act for you no win, no fee?'

Their faces lit up. Vanessa seemed to grab at the idea like a lifeline. 'Oh my God. Do you think he would?'

'Why not? I'll call the Bar Association tomorrow and double-check, but I don't think there'd be any rule banning a barrister from acting against a former spouse as long as there are no material conflicts.'

'Really?'

'Really.'

Bob hugged Joy. Joy hugged Vanessa. Dave wished that Vanessa would hug *him*, but she beamed at him—that would have to do.

'So we're on?'

'We're on.' Dave confirmed, feeling pumped and daunted in equal measure. 'I'll see if I can get an appointment with Marcus Stafford.'

Chapter 12

VANESSA

Vicki Wong had been a patient at the Smile Clinic for six years, but she still hadn't conquered her phobia of dentists.

'Not long now,' Vanessa said soothingly through the plastic visor that covered her face from forehead to chin. The visor was one of Anthony's recent additions—he was always upgrading the equipment to maximise sterility. He said he liked to be on the cutting edge of dental innovations, but Kiri just accused him of being a germ freak.

As Anthony used an A6 instrument to spread Vicki's composite filling, Vanessa held the suction hose in Vicki's mouth to suck up her oral excretions. She snuck a peek at her watch. Dave would be here in ten minutes to pick her up for their appointment with Marcus Stafford, who'd miraculously agreed to see them at twenty-four hours' notice. Vanessa knew she should be thrilled, but she was petrified. She'd barely slept a wink last night, and she'd even contemplated pulling the plug, but Jackson and Lachie had urged her to 'stick it up' Charlotte, and she wanted her boys to think she was a 'badass', to borrow their terminology. Besides, if she didn't pursue it Kiri would kill her, and she couldn't rob four children of their mothers.

'All good,' said Anthony as he finished spreading Vicki's filling. He gave Vanessa the A6 and she handed him the curing light. It beeped loudly, emitting a blue glow, and Vicki's whole body went rigid with fear. 'This is just to set the filling, remember?' Anthony reassured her. 'We're almost there.'

Vicki nodded but her toes were curled tightly in her Kathmandu sandals.

Vanessa patted her shoulder. 'You're doing well.'

Vanessa had learned long ago that you could never predict which patients would be phobic but, even so, Vicki was a surprise. She was a skydiver who'd run marathons all over the world and she'd even climbed Mt Everest, but the minute she climbed into the dental chair she dissolved into a quivering wreck.

The filling set, Vanessa took the curing light while Anthony unscrewed the matrix band from Vicki's tooth. She gripped the chair with white knuckles.

'Almost done,' Vanessa reassured her, even as her own stomach curdled with nerves. Would Marcus Stafford dismiss her as a fantasist? After all, Charlotte's former husband would know Charlotte's talents better than anyone. She imagined the dashing barrister glaring at her with contempt: 'I can't believe you have the temerity to waste my time with this baseless fabrication. Get out of my chambers before I sue *you*.'

'Bite silk?'

Vanessa nodded distractedly and wheeled her stool over to get the bite silk, and then Anthony asked Vicki to bite down on it. The filling was too high so Anthony had to drill it down, but fortunately it was soon over.

'All done.' Anthony smiled and wheeled away to check her X-rays.

'You're a legend,' Vanessa told Vicki.

As she removed Vicki's bib she could hear Dave out in reception, having a joke with Kiri. He had a funny honking laugh that made her smile, and she found herself relaxing a bit.

'All okay?'

Vicki nodded shakily. 'I think so.'

Vanessa handed her a cup. 'Here, have a rinse.'

But as Vicki swilled the rinse solution around in her mouth, Anthony looked up from her X-rays. 'Well, the good news is you only need three more fillings.'

Vicki promptly spat rinse solution all over Vanessa's visor.

'I'm sorry.'

'It's fine.'

Vanessa waved Vicki's apologies away as liquid poured down in front of her face. It was like looking through the windscreen in a car wash.

'That would have gone right in your eyes before,' Anthony pointed out with satisfaction. 'That full-face visor's a keeper.'

'Yeah.' She removed the visor to wipe it down.

'I'm so sorry,' Vicki repeated.

'Don't be silly, it's fine.'

'I just wasn't expecting three more fillings.'

Vicki was trembling like jelly as she got up from the chair, and Vanessa impulsively put an arm around her and guided her out to reception.

Dave was hovering at Kiri's desk, and she was relieved to see he was wearing a new suit and that the trousers reached almost all the way to his ankles. He turned with a smile, but his face dropped when he saw Vicki, and Vicki abruptly pulled out out of Vanessa's embrace.

'Hello, David.'

'Hi, Vicki.'

Kiri smiled at them. 'Are you two mates?'

Vicki hesitated. 'Not exactly. We have a mutual acquaintance.'

Dave made a strangled sound that seemed to be halfway between a laugh and a snort.

There's a story there, Vanessa thought, and aren't I dying to hear it? Kiri had always accused her of being a busybody, but since writing her novel she'd joked, 'No, I'm a student of human behaviour—it's an essential component of the writer's toolkit.'

'How do you know Vicki?' she heard herself ask as soon as she and Dave were outside.

Dave gave an odd grimace. 'She's my wife's lover.'

Vanessa gaped.

Dave clarified. 'I mean my *ex*-wife.'

'Oh.'

'David.'

Vanessa turned to see a woman alighting from a nearby BMW. Dave stiffened and Vanessa gleaned that this was a 'speak of the devil' situation. This stunning creature with the halo of dark curls was the ex-wife? Wow.

'Evanthe. I thought you were still at that conference in San Francisco?'

'I caught an earlier flight.'

'Right . . .'

Dave nodded and then they all stood in an uneasy silence. Evanthe seemed like she was surprised to see Dave, but was the kind of person who thought that showing surprise somehow diminished her. A control freak, in other words.

She spoke first—but then control freaks always do, don't they? 'I'm here to pick up Vicki.'

'Yeah, I figured. This is Vanessa Rooney, a client of mine. She works at the Smile Clinic.'

Evanthe suddenly seemed interested. 'You're Vanessa from the dentist? Vicki says you're lovely.'

'Does she? That's nice. She's lovely too.'

'She's got such a phobia.'

'I know, but she did really well today.'

'She did?'

'Yeah, she was great.'

'Great.'

Silence descended again. They all turned to stare at the door of the Smile Clinic, like people in a lift looking up at the numbers in order to avoid looking at each other.

Vanessa could almost taste the relief when Vicki emerged. She seemed taken aback to see the three of them standing there chatting—not that they *were* chatting, but hey.

'Welcome home, babe,' she said when she'd collected herself. She and Evanthe exchanged a kiss, and Dave squirmed visibly. 'You've met Vanessa?'

'Yeah, just now.'

'Small world, isn't it?' Vanessa ventured chirpily.

They all nodded and then everyone fell silent again.

Awkward.

~

Vanessa's foot was resting on an empty chip packet on Dave's car floor. 'Evanthe said I wasn't romantic enough,' he was explaining, 'but if you could spend four days at a spa resort or have a new mower, wouldn't you pick the mower?'

'Of course I'd pick the mower,' Vanessa chortled. 'Good one.'

'I'm serious. Evanthe's a keen gardener.'

She regarded him quizzically—he *was* serious! But there were four days at a spa resort on offer. Surely he got that?

'I don't get it. It's the same with chocolates and flowers—they don't last, you can't use them, so what's the point?'

'Isn't the point that there is no point?'

Dave chuckled then. 'I don't get your point.'

Vanessa laughed. It seemed that Dave was seriously romance-challenged, but she liked the way he made fun of himself in the face of painful circumstances. Poor thing. She knew how horrendous it felt to be in his shoes. Except for the gay part. She suddenly felt very glad that Natalie wasn't Nate.

'I'm sorry, Dave. You must have been through hell.'

He tried to shrug it off with a smile but she could see the pain in his eyes. 'What about you? What's your story?'

Vanessa waited for her requisite wave of embarrassment, but for some reason it didn't arrive.

'Craig left me for our marriage counsellor.'

'Your marriage counsellor?'

'Yeah. Natalie. He was taken with her cognitive therapy.'

'Oh, is that what they're calling it these days?'

They chuckled together, and Vanessa realised she was having fun.

'So tell me,' Dave asked, 'how did a dental nurse come to write a novel? Or should I say, why is a novelist a dental nurse?'

Good question.

'I wanted to be a writer when I was at school, but my mum and dad didn't think I'd be able to make a living and, then, just after I finished year ten . . . my dad was killed in a car crash.'

'Oh? I'm really sorry to hear that.'

Dave met her eyes sympathetically and Vanessa could tell he was one of those people who wasn't frightened of other people's grief. She felt emboldened to continue.

'Thank you. Anyway, I started year eleven, but I couldn't focus, and I was really worried about my mum—she was such a mess. And then a vacancy came up at the dental practice where she worked, so . . .' She shrugged. 'Sliding doors and all that stuff.'

Dave nodded his understanding and Vanessa thought how easy he was to be with. But as they stopped at traffic lights, she noticed that he still had a Peter Jackson label sewn on his suit sleeve. What if Marcus Stafford saw it and sneered? She knew from interviews that Marcus had his suits made by a bespoke tailor who worked out of a cobbled laneway in Fitzroy. She didn't want to be rude, and in normal circumstances she wouldn't say anything, but Dave's sartorial error might put them at a disadvantage.

'Er, your suit . . .'

'Good, isn't it? Nickie picked it. She's been hassling me to get a new one for years, and I raised the white flag yesterday.'

'I like it, but see that label? You're supposed to take that off before you wear it.'

'Am I?'

'Yeah.'

Dave shrugged, unperturbed, but Vanessa whipped out her nail scissors and snipped off the label. Up close, Dave's eyelashes were long and thick and actually quite gorgeous. It was just a shame about that single eyebrow that stuck out at a perpendicular angle—she was itching to snip that off too.

'Thanks.' He grinned. 'You've just saved me from a wardrobe malfunction.'

'Oh, I've had far worse wardrobe malfunctions, believe me.'

'I do.'

He gave her a cheeky look and Vanessa stared at him in horror.

'Oh my God. You recognised me!'

'You recognised *me*?'

'Why didn't you say something?' she demanded.

'What did you want me to say?' asked Dave. "It's great to make your acquaintance, Vanessa, but me and your arse have already met"?'

Vanessa erupted into giggles. She was glad it was Dave who'd spotted her dimpled bum—it could have been so much worse.

'Thanks for telling me, by the way.'

'I had no choice—I was with elderly ladies with heart conditions.'

Vanessa's giggles intensified. 'Stop the car, I can't go on. You've seen my bum.'

'Hey, my wife left me for a woman—I think I've won.'

Their eyes met again, and Vanessa was surprised to feel a stirring that she hadn't felt for a long time. Gosh, where had that come from? She turned to look out the window at the magnificent Royal Exhibition Building, the first structure in Australia to receive a World Heritage listing. All around it, burnished autumn leaves were carpeting the Carlton Gardens. She and Dave drove on in a flustered silence that lasted until the Volvo was crawling through city traffic and she could feel herself starting to freak out. They were turning into a car park across the road from Marcus Stafford's chambers when she finally spoke.

'Oh God, I'm petrified.' Vanessa was hoping for some kind of reassurance, but then she noticed that Dave was tapping his fingers on the steering wheel.

'Me too. I'm shitting myself.' He smiled as if he was joking, but she could sense his anxiety underneath. It was endearing, in a worrying kind of way.

Chapter 13

Vanessa was busting. She tried to focus on a floral arrangement half the size of a small sedan that was sitting on the coffee table, but it was hard not to jiggle her legs up and down. 'I'm busting,' she whispered. 'I always need to wee when I'm nervous.'

'Wee into the vase, no one will notice.'

Vanessa tried to laugh but she thought she might vomit. She patted her hair down for the fiftieth time and tried to will the blotches on her neck away.

'It's okay,' Dave reassured her. 'I'm all over this . . . Um, who are we? Why are we here? Just kidding.'

She gave him a playful poke and he dropped his briefcase. It flew open, disgorging its contents onto the floor.

'Shit! I'm sorry.'

Her manuscript had slipped out of its bulldog clip and the pages were scattered everywhere.

'It's fine, don't worry.'

Vanessa bent down to help Dave pick up the papers. As they reached for the same page their fingers touched, and she felt herself blush. Dave seemed to be blushing too—his ears were suddenly bright pink. They laughed bashfully as they shoved the pages back into his briefcase and scrambled up onto their chairs. Vanessa felt discombobulated, but in a good way. She'd liked Dave from the moment Kiri had introduced them, but she'd never expected to *like* him. Their eyes met again, and she looked away shyly—just as a deep voice spoke from behind them.

'Vanessa Rooney? David Rendall?'

Vanessa turned. And almost fell off her chair again.

Marcus Stafford was standing before them like some kind of absurdly handsome apparition, and she wondered irrationally if he was real. She'd always known he was astonishingly attractive, but somehow seeing him in the flesh reduced her to a gibbering mess.

'Marcus Stafford. Good to meet you.'

His smile exuded so much charisma that you could slice it and put it in sandwich bags. Vanessa opened her mouth but couldn't form words. And then she realised what was happening—it was as though she'd just come face to face with Dr Magnus Maddison. Which wasn't possible, of course, but Marcus was the spitting image of her fictional dream man, right down to his class I occlusion (or perfect teeth, in layman's terms).

'Good to meet you too,' Dave screeched, then cleared his throat.

'Thanks for coming.' Marcus shook Vanessa's hand and she almost swooned at his touch. Why, oh why, had she ever washed up without gloves? Her paw must feel like a wizened claw. 'Come on in.'

Dave nervously rushed straight past her, but Marcus stood back to guide her into his chambers with his hand lightly touching the small of her back. Vanessa felt like she was wearing crinolines. She knew that made her a flawed feminist, but frankly she didn't give a rat's. It was so nice to feel like a *lady*.

Marcus directed them to plush leather chairs. His chambers were sleek and modern with piles of important-looking papers stacked on the desk and under a window that overlooked a city skyline littered with cranes. A floor-to-ceiling bookshelf was filled with hardcover legal tomes, and on the walls were photos of Marcus with various dignitaries and celebrities—but no sign of Charlotte, Vanessa noticed. She pictured Marcus tossing Charlotte's photos onto a bonfire, tears running down his chiselled cheeks as he stood alone in the darkness . . . But hang on—he was asking if they wanted coffee or tea.

'Can I have a double decaf chai latte with soy?' Dave quipped, but his tone was strained and, although Marcus chuckled politely, the joke fell flat. 'Just kidding,' said Dave, red-faced. 'I'm fine.'

Vanessa felt for him. 'I'm fine too, thank you,' she managed. It was a pretty paltry effort, but at least she'd strung a few words together now.

Marcus took a seat behind his desk. 'Okay, then.' He leaned back, exuding an air of unhurried confidence as he studied them with his azure-blue eyes. Vanessa could tell he was curious, and why wouldn't he be? For all his politeness, he was probably thinking that she was delusional. She felt a sudden urge to cry, 'Forget the whole thing,' and run from the room.

'So, you believe you have grounds for a breach-of-copyright suit against Charlotte Lancaster?'

'That's right,' Dave confirmed. 'I think it's a cut-and-dried case of . . .' He fumbled around in his briefcase. 'Sorry. I dropped my briefcase and everything got out of order.'

'It was my fault,' Vanessa felt compelled to confess. 'I poked him.' Why should Dave be the only one with egg on his face?

'Vanessa, why don't you tell me exactly what happened?'

Marcus sounded genuinely interested, and Vanessa felt her pounding heart settle. She told him everything—from the day she first started writing *Lost and Found Heart* right up to Charlotte and Chip Lancaster's attempt to pay her off.

Marcus listened intently and, when she'd concluded, Dave showed him a few passages from Charlotte's novel and Vanessa's manuscript, which he'd managed to scramble back into order. As Marcus flicked through the two stories, Vanessa was struck by a gleam in his eyes. Was it anger on her behalf or glee at his ex-wife's expense? Either way, who could blame him? A small tic pulsed in his left cheek as he tossed both stories down on the desk.

'This is egregious,' he declared masterfully. His voice had the timbre of Russell Crowe's but came in an infinitely sexier package. 'You're a dental assistant on a modest wage.'

'Anthony would pay me more if he could.'

'But you're trying to raise two kids on your own.'

'My ex-husband gives me child support, but—'

'But your finances aren't what they could have been, are they? That book should have been a ticket to a better life for you and your kids.'

He was right. He'd just articulated what she'd been thinking but hadn't dared to say aloud. They were so in sync! Vanessa couldn't help noticing that, even furrowed with indignation, Marcus' eyebrows were perfectly aligned.

'I'm glad you agree,' Dave chimed in. 'I've advised Vanessa that we can seek orders for Charlotte's novel to be withdrawn from publication and all the remaining copies destroyed.'

'We can do a lot better than that. Vanessa, in my view you're entitled to an account of the profits the defendants have made from the copyright infringement—meaning that, if we're successful, the court will award you all the profits that both Charl—I mean Ms Lancaster and Wax have made from *Love Transplant*. I've done some cursory research and, while it hasn't sold as well as some of her other books, that would still be a sizeable sum—at least a couple of hundred thousand dollars.'

Vanessa nearly flipped out. 'A couple of hundred thousand dollars?'

'Better than a poke in the eye with a blunt stick, eh?' Dave grinned.

'Indeed. That's if the court accepts our argument, of course—but I believe it will.'

'Excellent! So you'll take the brief?' Dave asked, or something like that. It was hard to focus on Dave right now, because Marcus was focused on *her* again. For the first time, Vanessa noticed purple smudges under his eyes, and she wondered if he'd been lying awake, grieving for Charlotte. She imagined the moonlight glowing through his bedroom window, casting silver light on his broad, bare chest— but she forced herself back to the present.

'You deserve to be compensated for the year you spent writing this book and the several decades you would have spent enjoying the fruits of that labour, and I think I can make that happen. If we win, you pay me. If we lose, you don't. Fair?'

'You mean, you *will* do it for no win, no fee?'

Marcus nodded and Vanessa felt a ridiculous urge to reach out and touch his stubble. She imagined Charlotte running her fingers over that manly jaw . . . but Charlotte had broken Marcus's heart. Would pursuing this case take too great a personal toll on him?

'I'm not saying it won't be awkward,' Marcus conceded, as though he'd read her mind, 'but regardless of my ex-wife's involvement, this is the most outrageous case of breach of copyright I've ever encountered.'

Wow.

'You'll need to keep the back-up drive stored safely in your office,' he instructed Dave. 'The document's dated, so it's our only evidence that Vanessa wrote her novel before Charlotte published *Love Transplant*. At this point we don't have proof of the email trail between Vanessa and Wax, so obviously you'll need to issue interlocutory applications for Wax's records.'

'Uh, yeah, obviously.' Dave made a note with a chewed biro.

'And, Vanessa, I'd like you to keep a USB copy at home.'

Vanessa nodded. She was glad that she was sitting down because she thought her knees might just have melted. Marcus was so commanding.

Dave pulled Joy's photo out of his briefcase. 'We do have this dated photo of Vanessa sending her manuscript to Wax.'

Marcus glanced at it for a millisecond then tossed it down. 'It's taken from behind the laptop. She could be sending anything to anyone.'

'Yeah, I know, but I thought I should mention it. And you don't think our witness accounts will fly?'

'Vanessa's mother and friends? Charlotte's legal team will eat them alive.'

'Of course.' Dave looked embarrassed. He pulled out the small triangular piece of the contract that Vanessa had wrested from Chip. 'And I guess this . . . No, of course not,' he said—or something similar; Vanessa found that Dave was growing a bit blurry in the face of Marcus's magnetism.

'Obviously your first step is to issue a writ in the Federal Court. I'll draft the statement of claim for you. Charlotte's a celebrity, so the media will be all over this—we'll use the twenty-four-hour news cycle to our advantage.'

Oh God. The twenty-four-hour news cycle.

Vanessa felt all her panic return and squeeze her in its sickly clutches. Surely there must be another way.

'Couldn't we try to keep things under the radar?' she suggested.

Marcus stood and walked around to lean against her side of the desk. He was so close that their legs were almost touching.

'It's a strategic advantage. The media glare will reflect so negatively on Charlotte and Wax that they'll just want to make it go away.'

They won't be the only ones, thought Vanessa.

'Could we use the name Mia Fontaine, so nobody knows it's me?'

Marcus shook his head. 'I'm afraid not. All the court documents will have to be lodged in your real name.'

Oh. For a second Vanessa wondered if she might actually vomit on his carpet. She steeled herself to ask another question that she'd rather not know the answer to. 'And do you think it could get ugly?'

'Yes. There's a strong chance that things will be quite unpleasant for a while, but I don't want you to worry—I think we can pressure them into settling quickly. Will you trust me, Vanessa?'

Up close he smelled like cinnamon and the sea. Their eyes locked and Vanessa realised that she'd never felt so safe. She nodded.

'Thank you. I won't let you down.'

Marcus put his hand lightly on her shoulder and a bolt of electricity shot straight from her clavicle to her groin. Meanwhile Dave's lips seemed to be moving. Vanessa assumed he must be saying something, but she couldn't hear a word.

⁓

Late that night she lay in bed, bathing in memories of Marcus. His heart-stopping smile, the thrill of his touch, his self-assurance and certainty. Maybe she *could* actually win the case? The whole thing still terrified her, but now there was another feeling—a secret joy she hugged to her chest. She'd been too quick to dismiss poor Mrs Flannery; after all, one of Australia's leading intellectual property authorities had just confirmed that her novel was good enough to be stolen!

All evening her mind had been racing with ideas for her next book, *Child's Play*, the story of a spirited nanny who clashes with a brooding widower with a dark secret. She knew that *Child's Play* owed a lot to *Jane Eyre* but, from what Vanessa could gather, you were allowed to copy a famous story as long as you called it a 'reimagining'.

But, then, did that mean Charlotte Lancaster had 'reimagined' *Lost and Found Heart*? The thought changed everything. Vanessa decided to come up with another story, something one hundred per cent original. She'd already done it once, hadn't she?

Chapter 14

MARCUS

Marcus reached across the table. A crumb had found its way onto her cheek and he gently brushed it away. 'A crumb.'

'Thank you, darling.'

She smiled. His heart swelled as he took in her sweet face, but then he made the fatal error of allowing his eyes to drop to her sundress—polyester and sleeveless, hardly appropriate for Melbourne in May. It puckered around her waist and the putrescent floral pattern was faded from a surplus of washes. He felt a familiar flash of irritation. Why wouldn't she wear the dresses he bought her? Why wouldn't she let him pay for a haircut, some half-decent shoes? But they'd had that discussion so many times.

'You should save your money for more important things, darling. And I like what I like.'

'Yes, but what you like is cheap mass-produced trash and along with your Strine and your limited grasp of world events it screams your lowly position on the totem pole—and you wonder why I don't introduce you to my friends.' All this roiling around in his head as he smiled and acquiesced. 'Fair enough, Mum.'

Shirley was visiting from Kalgoorlie and she was in awe of Marcus's shiny new apartment, or 'unit' as she called it. She was deferential to every fitting and eyed the oven with particular trepidation, as though it would yell, 'Imposter!' if she dared approach it. Not that Marcus wanted Shirley to master the Miele anyway. He'd had enough of her pedestrian fare to last him a lifetime, and he was now quite a handy cook himself. Tonight he'd thrown together a carbonara that would have done Antonio Carluccio proud.

'This is delicious, darling. And what a view to enjoy it with.'

He watched his mother gaze out the floor-to-ceiling windows at twilight over the Royal Botanic Gardens and wondered what she really thought of Melbourne's stark trees and grey skies, at such odds with the relentless colour of Kal.

'I think this unit is perfect for you.'

It would do. He'd acquired this place after Chip had bought him out of the Middle Park terrace for more than his half was worth—which showed how much Lotts wanted him out of her life. It was typical that Chip had paid him when Lotts (he really must drop his pet nickname for her; hereafter he would think of her only as Charlotte) was entirely capable of buying him out herself, courtesy of her potboilers—and in truth there would have been some poetic justice in that. But that was never going to happen, because Charlotte was the most entitled brat he'd ever met—which was one of the things he'd always found most attractive about her.

He topped up Shirley's pinot gris, trying not to notice the snow storm of salt she was raining down on her fettucine.

Charlotte Lancaster, breacher of copyright, plagiarist, thief. Of course she'd lost her ability to write after she left him for that so-called 'tech entrepreneur' Ned Kasch—that was hardly a surprise. Marcus's mind flew back to Lotts (*Charlotte*) sitting in bed beside him, wearing nothing but one of his old T-shirts, as she tapped away at her MacBook Air. If she was working on a sex scene he'd murmur, 'We really should subject that scenario to scrutiny . . .' And later she'd lie with her head against his chest and he'd think, She's beautiful, she's rich, she's famous, and everyone knows that she's mine.

But it turned out that Ned Kasch knew something he didn't, because for the last year of their marriage Lotts had been sleeping with Kasch and, like the most dim-witted of husbands, Marcus hadn't suspected a thing. Then one night when they were brushing their teeth, she spat into the sink and informed him that she wanted out. What pedestrian phrasing had she used?

'You and I are on different paths.'

'I think you'll find we're both in the bathroom.'

'That just illustrates my point!' she'd snapped with a pent-up resentment that surprised him. 'You're such a condescending smart-arse, and I'm sick of being judged and found wanting.'

Apparently, Ned made her feel 'adored and affirmed', because clearly Ned was a limpet with no life of his own.

'You'll fall to pieces without me,' he'd predicted.

'I'll *fly* without you.'

And now she'd copied an amateurish potboiler written by a dental assistant. Ha!

'That's a cheeky smile,' Shirley commented as she twisted the lid on the cheese. 'What's so funny?'

Marcus suppressed a wince. He'd asked her to buy parmesan and she'd come back with a pre-packaged tube with holes on top like cleaning powder. No doubt it tasted like cleaning powder too—not that he planned to find out.

'Oh, I was just thinking about something that happened at work.'

After a few weeks' preparation, Dave Rendall had issued the writ on Lotts—*Charlotte*—and Wax this afternoon. It was only a matter of time before some court clerk leaked it for a quick buck, and Marcus's neural pathways tingled in anticipation of Charlotte's public disgrace. It was nothing less than she deserved. And when she made a settlement offer to stem the PR haemorrhage, Marcus was going to screw her. Not that he could share any of this with Shirley, who just wanted him to forget Charlotte and her betrayal. But Marcus hadn't inherited his mother's gift for forgiveness, and that was fine with him.

Shirley yanked too hard and the lid flew off, spilling chemically processed parmesan all over the floor.

'Oh no, your beautiful carpet.' She was already pushing her chair back.

'Don't worry, I'll do it. Sit down, Mum.'

Marcus went to his broom cupboard and grabbed his dustbuster. He sucked the cheese up with the lint and the dust, where it belonged.

'Thank you, darling,' Shirley said, looking pleasantly lost. She was never quite sure what to do with herself when somebody else was cleaning up.

Marcus put away the dustbuster and topped up her wine again. She was certainly getting through it tonight, but why not? She never indulged at home because of Kevin Stafford, Drunken Prick.

His mind flew back to that stiflingly hot day when he was twelve, in that shitty old house in Kalgoorlie, watching Shirley vacuum around his father Kevin's feet because Kevin was too pissed and too lazy to lift them off the ground. And this after Shirley had already been out cleaning all day to provide for Marcus and his brothers, because Kevin's only career was the booze. Something inside twelve-year-old Marcus snapped and he grabbed his father's stinking feet and yanked them off the ground—only to receive a cuff on the ear which made Shirley cry, defeating the whole object of the exercise.

'I hate him,' he spat to his brothers Shane and Todd later.

'What did you expect? You moved his feet.'

'You're just up yourself, Marcus.'

And that was it. Lying on his bottom bunk that night, staring up at Todd's bedsprings, he'd made a vow: 'I'm going to get out of this dump and I'm never coming back.'

And he'd been true to his word. He'd studied hard and excelled at school and he was accepted into law at Melbourne University. He could still recall having to temper his elation when he'd climbed on board a crowded bus for the three-day journey. Shirley was there to see him off, one hand waving in the searing air while the other wiped tears from her eyes.

'It's okay, Mum, I'll be back for a visit soon.'

No, I won't.

At uni he'd quickly discovered a talent for reinvention. It was like Kalgoorlie was an ugly coat that he'd shrugged off his shoulders and left discarded in the dirt behind him. And as much as possible he kept his promise to himself of never going back. Kevin and his brothers were on to him.

'He's too good for us now.'

'He's a Melbourne yuppie.'

'He doesn't want to know about us.'

But Shirley accepted his every excuse.

'Of course, darling, you're very busy.'

'Well, you've got a lot on your plate.'

'I know you'd come home for Christmas if you could.'

No, I wouldn't.

He and Charlotte had even eloped to Rome so his family couldn't come to their wedding. He'd felt a pang of guilt about Shirley, but the one time she and Kevin had mixed with Chip and Annie at a Thanksgiving dinner, it had been excruciating. Kevin got pissed, naturally, and Marcus's cheeks burned at the shocked reactions quickly stifled, the polite but bemused conversation, the discreet looks flying between Annie and Chip. ('How could Marcus have come from *them*?') It was unendurable. So he adopted the

Lancasters; they felt like the right fit in a way his own family never had. But, of course, he and Lotts (*Charlotte*) hadn't abandoned Shirley. Charlotte thought Shirley was 'cute' and treated her like an old doll that you'd glance at affectionately in passing, but Marcus was much more hands-on. He phoned Shirley regularly and sent her money when she'd accept it. He'd even offered to buy her a house of her own so she could leave his father, but she always dismissed his offers.

'Better the devil you know,' she'd say, and then, with a hopeful catch in her voice, 'Do you think you might come for a visit soon?'

No.

But he comforted himself that at least he'd tried to make amends since his break-up. This was the third time he'd flown Shirley to Melbourne in the past several months. He watched her suck spaghetti up into her mouth like a retractable cord on a vacuum cleaner. She was the dearest, most decent person he knew, and he felt eternally grateful that she'd always put him and his brothers first. It was time to do the same for her—but he'd prefer to do it in private.

'How was your big dinner last night?'

Marcus brought himself back into the moment. Last night he'd attended a Victorian Bar Association event feting Graham Goetze, a fellow IP silk and 'frenemy' from his uni days. Marcus had taken his new girlfriend, model and Instagram 'influencer' Ivy Jones, whose personality was proving less pleasing than her face.

'It was terrific. I was so happy for Graham.'

Which was certainly true on some level. The Bar Association had honoured Graham with a humanitarian award for pro bono work he'd done defending some Papua New Guinean villagers against a multinational that had swooped in and stolen their primitive proto-type for a water filter—Efoki Village vs Attwood Industries. Graham had won the villagers millions of dollars in compensation, which was now being put to good use in development and education projects.

Unlike himself, the years hadn't been kind to Graham. He was short and stout with enormous ears, but as he'd made his acceptance speech, the respect in the room had been palpable. It was unsettling. Marcus was accustomed to admiration for his linguistic acrobatics, but this was different—Graham had earned his peers' esteem for placing the greater good above the dollar. Their eyes met during the warm applause, and Graham's humble expression read, 'Yeah, suck this up, you shallow show pony.' It rankled. Just because Marcus had made career choices that garnered him a profile, it didn't make him a show pony. But the moment had only added to the general malaise Marcus had been feeling over the past several months—a malaise that even sleeping with a succession of stunning women couldn't seem to lift. The only bright spot in proceedings was the envious glances he'd attracted when he crossed the room with Ivy. Take that, Graham!

Shirley was smiling at him proudly. 'You should get an award too. It's wonderful that he did that work for the villagers, but I bet he hasn't represented a *Home and Away* star and a famous talkback radio host.'

Christ, he *was* shallow. Even at uni, Graham had been drawn to the underdog, but Marcus was different—he was drawn to winners. There was nothing intrinsically wrong with that, so why was he feeling like a moral vacuum? But then he remembered his newest client and he brightened. After all, who was Vanessa Rooney if not an underdog?

Chapter 15

VANESSA

Vanessa gazed at Marcus's animated face as he posed on the red carpet at the Human Rights Arts and Film Festival opening with his gorgeous girlfriend, Ivy Jones. He was throwing his head back in amusement as though someone had just said something funny, but it seemed pretty clear that Ivy hadn't cracked the joke—she was posing with a sultry expression and her lips pouted in the ubiquitous 'duck face'. Why did girls always feel compelled to stick out their lips like that? Did boys do it too? Vanessa had a mental image of Jackson and Lachie posting duck-face selfies and it disturbed her.

She felt a nudge in her ribs from Joy.

'Now there's a man who could drive his sports car straight to a woman's G spot.'

Vanessa laughed. 'Yeah.'

She zoomed in even closer, until Marcus's face took up her whole laptop screen.

'But, seriously, it's positively eerie,' Joy said. 'I don't know why I didn't notice before, but it's like looking at Dr Magnus Maddison made flesh.'

'I know. It's such a coincidence.'

Joy shook her head. 'I'm with Oprah on this one, Nessie—I don't believe in coincidences. This must be the universe's doing.'

'The universe?'

'It's kismet. That's why you wrote *Lost and Found Heart* in the first place—so Charlotte would plagiarise you and then you and Marcus would meet and fall in love. I think the universe has been planning this all along.'

'Mum, I think the universe has got better things to think about— and I haven't got a hope in hell. He's got a girlfriend.'

'Oh, you can get rid of her.'

'As if! Look at Ivy Jones and look at me.'

Joy focused on the laptop screen and then turned back to regard Vanessa. 'You've got something she hasn't—a beautiful heart.'

'She might have a beautiful heart.'

'No, she's got a beautiful arse, but not a beautiful heart.' They chuckled, but Joy soon grew earnest again. 'Nessie, if you believe it, you can make it happen. You just have to visualise Marcus in your bed and he'll come—in more ways than one.' She winked and Vanessa cringed.

'Mum!'

'I'm just saying, I want you to have the once-in-a-lifetime love that I had with your daddy.'

'I know.' Vanessa patted her mother's arm. She could already feel the mood shifting. Jack's birthday was only a few days away, and it was always a difficult time for Joy. Her mum's smile was starting to wobble.

'He would have been sixty-seven on Thursday. Can you believe it?'

Yes. No. I don't know.

Vanessa's mind flew back to that muggy night in January 1995, when her Aunty Julie had gently shaken her awake. Why was Aunty Julie here? Why was she crying? Dazed with sleep but filled with dread, Vanessa followed Aunty Julie out to the living room and found her mum catatonic on the couch. Joy reached for Vanessa but couldn't speak, and it was left to Aunty Julie to tell her that Jack had been killed in a car crash. Vanessa yelled at her aunty and called her a liar—shoving past her to pace around the room as if she could somehow outrun the news. But then her legs buckled beneath her and Aunty Julie had to break her fall. Vanessa crumpled onto the couch beside Joy and sobbed in a ball.

Even lost in the wilds of her own grief, her mum had been so protective. Joy banned Vanessa from watching the news or reading the paper or listening to the radio—the internet was still a few years away. A sense of awful secrecy had shrouded the accident, and Joy's friends would stop mid-whisper when Vanessa entered the room. It made her wonder what they thought she couldn't bear? Had her father's death been even worse than a 'routine' car crash? Had he been decapitated? Incinerated? Had his legs been ripped from his body? Had he been dragged along the road by another car, screaming and keening in agony? For years afterwards, Vanessa had nightmares about her father in each of these states and worse, and she'd wake up sobbing. But she didn't ask Joy about it because she sensed that, in protecting her, Joy was protecting herself too.

Eventually the nightmares went away, but never the questions. And now, twenty-four years later, she heard herself asking, 'Mum, what happened to Dad on the night he died?' She saw Joy flinch, but there was no turning back. 'I'm a grown-up now. I can take it.'

Joy was silent for a moment, then said, 'You know what happened. Your father's car hit a tree and he was . . . killed.'

The last word said with a quiver.

'But how?' The question was so hard to ask. 'Was he . . . decapitated?'

'Decapitated? Dear God, no!' Joy wrapped her arms around her daughter, and Vanessa caught a whiff of her freshly applied fake tan. 'My poor Nessie. Why would you think a thing like that?'

'I don't know. I just always felt like there was something even more terrible you were protecting me from. Was there?'

'No, of course not.'

Vanessa breathed decades of relief.

'My darling girl, I'm sorry you've been thinking such awful thoughts.' Joy dabbed at her teary eyes. 'Now I'm going to have streaks in my tan.'

'I'm sorry,' Vanessa said.

'Don't be silly. But let's talk about something happier, like you and Marcus.' Joy turned back to the laptop. 'I'll do another google search.'

'Mum, there *is* no me and Marcus.'

But in spite of her protests, dreams of Marcus intruded. Vanessa imagined him making love to her all night and then making pancakes for the boys at breakfast. As he skilfully flipped the pancakes the boys would say, 'You're wicked, Marcus!' And he'd say, 'Your mum's the wicked one,' and he'd give her a secret smile that said, 'Everything I did to you last night, I'm going to do again tonight.' And while they were eating their pancakes Daisy would run off with his barrister's wig, but Marcus would just laugh fondly and scratch Daisy's woolly head before popping the wig back into his briefcase and giving Vanessa a lingering goodbye kiss. Vanessa completely lost herself in the fantasy. She was composing a love note to slip into Marcus's lunchbox when her worst fears suddenly came to pass.

'It's hit the press!' Joy exclaimed.

'What?'

'You're in Buzzfeed.'

What?! Vanessa's tummy twisted with panic. Dave had only issued the writ today. Surely the media couldn't have got hold of it already? But there it was in the Buzzfeed newsfeed:

WRITING WRONGS?

Celebrity author Charlotte Lancaster has been slapped with a breach of copyright suit by a suburban dental nurse. Vanessa Clooney, 49, claims that Ms Lancaster's latest bestselling novel, *Love Transplant*, was plagiarised from her own unpublished work, *Lost and Found Heart* . . .

Vanessa was utterly horrified. 'I'm not forty-*nine*!'

'And Vanessa *Clooney*. We wish. Now there's one of the very few men who could hold a candle to your daddy or Marcus Stafford.'

'Mum, can't you see how awful this is? What if it goes viral?'

But Joy waved her concerns away. 'Oh, Nessie. It's the last item—you have to scroll down to even see it.'

Vanessa didn't feel comforted. She'd never been one to stick her head above the parapet, and now she felt like she was dancing on the parapet naked.

Joy patted her knee. 'These sites get refreshed all the time; this will be chip wrapping by tomorrow morning, in a digital sense. And don't forget that Charlotte's the famous one—it's her they'll be chasing.'

'Yeah, you're right. Phew.'

Vanessa started to relax. Then her mobile rang and she jumped.

'Who's going to ring me at eleven o'clock?' She checked the screen. 'No Caller ID. Kiri says if it's No Caller ID—'

But Joy had already grabbed the phone. 'Hello?' she said in her husky phone voice. 'Vanessa Rooney's line . . . Oh, really?' She suddenly perked up. 'Of course, she's right here. I'll put her on.' She held out the phone and whispered, 'Now, Nessie, everything's going to be fine.'

'Who is it?'

'It's *A Current Affair*.'

⁓

Lachie turned his back on the swing and folded his arms in defiance. 'I'm not doing it,' he said, glowering.

They were in All Nations Park in Northcote on a day that had started out unseasonably warm for May but now, in typical Melbourne fashion, was turning Arctic.

Vanessa cringed with embarrassment as *A Current Affair* reporter Zac Woollcot put a matey hand on Lachie's shoulder.

'Buddy, it's TV, we need some action—you get that, right?'

Zac was a blandly good-looking guy in his twenties who seemed to have majored in insincerity at journalism school. Vanessa was surprised by how short he was. Someone had once told her that most of the men on TV were diminutive, and she found herself wondering if it was 'small man syndrome' that compelled them to want to be larger than life. Zac was certainly not backward in coming forward.

'So how about it, eh, mate? You're a smart kid, you know what we need.'

'I said no.'

Lachie had dug in his heels and Vanessa knew there'd be no wriggle room.

'Couldn't we just walk around the park with Daisy?' she suggested.

'I need colour and movement.'

'We could walk fast.'

Vanessa detected a tic of impatience behind Zac's empty eyes. Nearby a sloppy cameraman was checking Facebook and a boom operator yawned, revealing a mouthful of blueberry muffin.

Oh God, what was she doing here? She forced herself to remember Marcus's wise counsel over the phone.

'I can understand why you don't like the idea,' he'd said in his deep, sexy voice, 'but there's nothing the Australian public loves more than an underdog. And a high-profile interview like this could well prompt Charlotte to make a settlement offer.'

It was a compelling argument made by a particularly compelling man, so Vanessa caved, but she did make one request. 'Could we have our faces pixilated?'

Marcus laughed, and she wasn't sure whether to be thrilled or embarrassed.

'Sure, if you want to look shifty. Disguising your identity implies that you've got something to hide, which is the opposite of what we're aiming for.' He was right, of course; he was always right. 'Think of it as short-term pain for long-term gain.'

He sounded so confident, so masterful and totally beautiful, that Vanessa would have walked into fire. And so here she was in the park, which felt about as comfortable as a fire would have. Zac Woollcot was now looking at his watch, and she wondered if he wanted to say, 'Hurry up, I've got other people to exploit today.' She felt her pulse quicken with the pressure and turned back to Lachie. 'Please, sweetheart? The sooner we do this, the sooner we'll get it over with.'

'I said no!'

'But, Lachie . . .'

'No!'

'I'll do it,' Jackson mumbled.

Vanessa was astonished and a little alarmed. 'It's all right, sweet-heart, you don't have to—'

'That's the way, mate,' Zac cut across her. 'Hop on, eh?'

'But Jackson's almost thirteen.'

'Get on the one behind your mum, the background looks better.'

Jackson hurled himself down on the swing, his freckled face puce with mortification.

Vanessa cringed. 'You don't have to do this,' she told him.

'Can we just get it over with?' he snarled.

'The kid's making sense. And, Mum, why don't you give him a push?'

A bridge too far. 'Push him? Are you kidding?'

Zac's laugh had a jagged edge. 'I'd love to stay here all day and argue, but we need to get this story to air tonight.'

'But I don't want Jackson to look—'

'Mum! Just do it.'

'Yeah, just do it, Mum!' Lachie yelled, and she could have cheerfully throttled him.

'Oh, all right.'

Vanessa reluctantly stood behind Jackson and started pushing him on the swing. He was a lot heavier than the last time she'd pushed him, but so was she, probably. They both looked like idiots and they both knew it.

'That's great, Mum. Now, Larry—'

'It's Lachie.'

'Yeah, Lachie. You play with the dog behind them.'

Lachie and Daisy started frolicking.

Jackson looked pained. 'Can I get off now?'

'We're not shooting yet. I want you all to relax and have a laugh—you know, like you're enjoying a fun family day at the park.'

Vanessa and Jackson tried to oblige, but who were they kidding? Some passers-by stopped to watch and openly snickered. Vanessa couldn't see Jackson's face, but the back of his head looked like it wanted to die.

'Can I get off yet?' he begged again.

'No, we'll need to do a few takes.'

Zac positioned himself in front of Jackson. The cameraman started filming and Zac launched into his patronising on-air patter. As Vanessa pushed Jackson like a twit she reminded herself that this was a necessary evil. Marcus was right: the people of Australia loved an underdog, and Charlotte would be shamed into settling. She felt her spirits lift. It was a brilliant tactical move, when you thought about it.

What could possibly go wrong?

Chapter 16

'I'm just saying,' said Craig, who'd turned up unannounced soon after *A Current Affair* finished, 'that I feel it's misleading for you to call yourself a struggling single mum when I live up to my full responsibilities as a father and I never miss any maintenance payments.'

He sounded like he'd learned his speech off by heart. No doubt Natalie had devised the most non-threatening phrasing so Craig could make his displeasure felt without putting Vanessa on the defensive. But of course, that was Natalie's field of expertise. Along with stealing other people's husbands.

Craig paused for effect and Vanessa caught a waft of aftershave, something he used to abhor. She wasn't sure she was up to this right now. The story was already going viral. Joy had three hundred and seventeen new Facebook comments and the phone hadn't stopped ringing. It seemed like the whole world wanted to talk to her, but she just wanted to run away. Thank goodness she could draw some comfort from Daisy, whose warm woolly body was pressed up against her leg.

'You've maligned me,' Craig continued self-righteously. 'I'm concerned that my reputation has been damaged with my friends, my colleagues and the wider community.' And then he improvised, 'And what the fuck was Jackson doing on that swing?'

Vanessa wanted to burst into tears.

'I'm sorry, Craig. I didn't describe myself that way, Zac Woollcot did. And he wanted one of the boys on the swing—he wouldn't let it go.'

'But Jackson? The kid's in high school.'

'I know.'

Vanessa was riven with guilt. In retrospect, she should never have caved to Zac Woollcot's demands, but she'd been so eager to get the whole thing over with that she'd failed her oldest son. The online bullying had already started and, although Jackson was insisting he didn't care, she could tell the poor kid was dying inside. And now Craig thought that she'd publicly branded him a deadbeat dad, which maybe she had, but not deliberately because, for all his faults, Craig was a devoted father adored by his sons. In spite of Natalie, he didn't deserve this. Suddenly it all felt too much and her eyes welled. She bent down to pat Daisy and collect herself, but when she straightened Craig was looking at her like her old Craig, and her heart wept for what they'd lost.

'It's okay, I know you wouldn't have done it deliberately,' he said with genuine kindness. 'And everyone knows those TV arseholes manipulate people.' His eyes were soft and understanding.

No, don't be nice, thought Vanessa. You've gone and I've mourned you—don't make me go back there. But looking into the eyes she used to consider home, she couldn't conceal her fear and uncertainty.

'It's just . . . it's all so overwhelming . . .'

Craig nodded, and the next thing she knew he'd pulled her into his arms and she was resting against his broad chest. They stood in silence for a moment. It felt so familiar and so lovely. Maybe he was still her Craig after all? Maybe he'd realised his mistake?

'I know it's overwhelming for you,' he said gently. 'The truth is, we're both worried that you're in over your head.'

We? Both? It was a punch to the gut. Vanessa broke free of his embrace. She should have known the old Craig was gone for good—there was only new Craig, the dickhid wenker.

'Natalie's concerned. Rightly or wrongly, we live in a celebrity culture. Charlotte Lancaster's rich and famous, and you're a dental assistant—who's going to believe you?'

Not you obviously, thought Vanessa.

'And the reality is, you don't know anything about suing people. We're worried you'll come off second-best.'

Vanessa wanted to kick him, but instead she heard herself reassure him. 'It's okay, Craig. My lawyers think this will force Charlotte to make a settlement offer. It could all be over by tomorrow night.'

Craig looked surprised. 'Really? But why would she settle?'

You mean other than because I wrote the story?!

'Because of the negative publicity.'

'Oh, right.' Craig nodded. 'I s'pose she'd want that to go away, even if she didn't copy your novel.' Then he added quickly, 'But I'm sure she did. Natalie and I both believe there's no way that you've imagined this.'

Daisy, who was immaculately house-trained, weed all over his shoes.

⁓

Vanessa felt so grateful for Daisy's support that she let her sleep under the doona that night. As Daisy snored in flutters beside her, Vanessa stared up at the ceiling. If Charlotte made an offer tomorrow, the first thing she'd do would be to buy a new bed that she'd never shared with Craig.

'How much will we get?' Lachie had asked that evening. 'Fifty or sixty million?'

The boys had already spent the money on drones and robots.

Vanessa laughed. 'A lot less than that. And, hey, it's the principle that counts, remember? Standing up for what's right is much more important than money.'

The boys seemed dubious about that and, frankly, so was she. Two hundred thousand bucks would make a massive dent in her mortgage, and right now that seemed more important than almost anything. But would this whole nightmare really be sorted so easily? The sensible little voice inside her head was demanding to be heard. 'Charlotte won't just give up at the first hurdle,' it said. 'Oh, what do you know?' Vanessa snapped back, but she found herself catastrophising. What if Charlotte didn't make an offer? What if she and Chip were enraged? Chip was a man who didn't like to lose. What if he hired someone to break Vanessa's legs or, even worse, to bump her off? Dear God, if Chip took out a hit on her, what would happen to her boys? As she pictured Natalie raising Jackson and Lachie, a primal rage rose inside her and she thought to herself that this was how poor Princess Diana would have felt if she'd known that William and Harry were going to end up with Camilla.

She was being ridiculous and she knew it, but somehow the knowledge didn't help. She'd worked herself into a state. Her shoulders were bunched up around her ears and as hard as she tried to slow her breathing it was coming out in shallow rasps. She looked at Daisy's snout peeking out from under the doona and wished that Marcus were there instead. Marcus Stafford was the only person who could soothe her fears and make her believe it would all be okay. If only she could hear his voice. She stared at her phone on the bedside table and willed it to ring—and it did! Vanessa scrambled for the phone so fast that she knocked it to the floor. She scooped it up, her eyes darting hopefully to the screen, but the caller was Dave.

Bummer.

Dave was lovely, but she couldn't face a chat right now. She let the call ring out and a couple of minutes later her phone chirped with a text:

> Hi, just tried to call and check you're okay. Don't worry, expecting a call tomorrow offering lots of $. Dave. PS. Was it Jackson's idea to go on the swing?

Vanessa felt reassured. Of course Charlotte would settle. Dave had put a smiley face emoji at the end of his message, which made Vanessa smile in spite of herself. It occurred to her that that's what Dave was—a human smiley face emoji.

Chapter 17

DAVE

When the horror had unfolded on *A Current Affair*, Dave and Nickie were eating dinner on their laps in his living room, which somehow managed to be messy and spartan all at once. Dave had bought this two-storey townhouse in Thornbury, one suburb south of Preston, off the plan when he and Evanthe split. If he'd bought it ten years earlier he would have paid a third of the price, but gentrification had cycled northwards and Thornbury was now on the right side of the Tofu Curtain, depending on your perspective. Shell-shocked by his marriage break-up, Dave had clutched at what seemed like an easy option, and it was only after he moved into his shiny new home that he realised he found the place a bit soulless. He'd been meaning to do something about that but hadn't got around to it yet.

On the TV, Vanessa was inexplicably pushing Jackson on a swing while a smarmy young git addressed the camera: '*She's the struggling single mum and suburban dental nurse who's sinking her teeth into celebrity author Charlotte Lancaster, claiming that Ms Lancaster's best-selling novel* Love Transplant *was copied from a novel* she *wrote . . .*'

'You hear that?' Dave had quipped. *'Dental nurse? Sinking her teeth? This guy's puntastic.'*

Nickie had rolled her eyes, which was probably what he deserved.

The camera moved in close on poor Vanessa, whose face wore the expression of a hostage in an Isis video. Dave's heart went out to her. Being patronised in front of the Australian viewing public by this supercilious little nob was a pretty unpalatable pill to swallow—but at least it should prompt a settlement offer from Charlotte Lancaster's lawyer, Mike Schwartz. He wondered what time Schwartz would call him the next morning. Nine o'clock? No, he'd probably play it cooler than that. Nine-thirty, maybe. Whenever it was, Dave hoped Ms Izetbegovic would be polite, although he knew she wouldn't.

On the TV, Lachie was roughhousing in the background with Daisy, who seemed to be enjoying herself way more than everyone else.

Dave would have to make sure that he played it cool too. He'd act like two hundred thousand dollars was nothing special—he'd take it to his client and get back to Mike, blahdy blah. He felt thrilled that he'd be the one to tell Vanessa. Maybe he'd find the guts to ask her out and joke that it was her shout? But he shouldn't get ahead of himself. There was always a possibility that Mike wouldn't ring. Where would that leave Vanessa—and him? If the case proceeded to court, he wasn't sure what he was supposed to do next. It was one thing to be in demand for meat-and-potatoes legal matters, but IP litigation was in another stratosphere altogether. Dave felt a small tug of anxiety.

Meanwhile, Nickie's fork had stopped halfway to her lips and peas were dropping onto her lap.

'Why is Jackson on that swing? He looks like a spaz.'

'Hey, we don't use terms like that,' Dave had chided gently, but Nickie was right. What thirteen-year-old boy lets his mum push him on a swing? The poor kid *did* look intellectually challenged—although Dave supposed it was a means to an end. At least this whole matter should be wrapped up within twenty-four hours . . .

But after the story went to air there'd been radio silence from Charlotte's side for three days—until this moment, when Dave found himself staring at a sealed envelope from Michael Schwartz and Associates that Ms Izetbegovic had just tossed onto his desk. He'd been hoping for the phone to ring all morning and practising his authoritative but reasonable voice. He wasn't expecting this. Ms Izetbegovic was already halfway back to the door.

'Ms Izetbegovic? Was this hand-delivered?'

Her lip twitched with irritation. She pointed to the envelope. 'Stamp. Postmark.'

'Oh yeah, of course.' Dave could see perfectly well that the envelope had arrived by post. He had no idea why he'd even asked the question—some kind of absurd stalling tactic, presumably. 'Thank you, Ms Izetbegovic.'

She nodded curtly and headed back to reception.

Dave regarded the envelope. According to Stafford, a settlement offer was generally broached by phone, but no doubt there were exceptions. He allowed himself a small moment of pride. Here he was, holding an envelope that could make the cutest woman in Melbourne hundreds of thousands of bucks. With Stafford's guidance, he, David Rendall LLB, had issued a writ against a famous novelist and a renowned international publishing house, and now they'd responded directly to him. Sure, it wasn't the human rights law that he'd dreamed of practising, but Vanessa was an especially appealing human and she had rights—hopefully at least two hundred thousand of them.

He made a little drum roll on his desk with pencils and ripped the envelope open. It was Charlotte and Wax's response to Vanessa's breach of copyright claim—no surprises there . . . but hang on.

Dave's eyes widened with dismay as he pored over the forensically detailed pages. Surely they wouldn't have the gall? But it seemed they did. Dave felt a thud of panic and his thoughts flew to Vanessa—not that they really needed to fly, because they were always hovering around her anyway. He leaped up from his desk and headed out to reception, where Ms Izetbegovic was filing her nails.

'I'll be out for a while, Ms Izetbegovic.'

She barely acknowledged that he'd spoken. Out of habit, Dave rummaged around in his pockets for change and deposited $3.15 into a life-sized Seeing Eye Dog collection box near the door. Then he strode outside, jumped into the Volvo and drove to the Smile Clinic, with his stomach churning.

When he walked in, Kiri greeted him with a bright smile. 'Dave Rendall. What brings you here?'

Why couldn't Ms Izetbegovic be more like Kiri? For one wild moment, Dave wondered if her husband Anthony would consider swapping. But Kiri was looking with bated breath at the envelope in his hand.

'Have you got news? Has that bitch offered Niss a million bucks?'

Dave hesitated, and Kiri seemed to read the answer on his face. 'She hasn't, has she?'

'I should tell Vanessa first,' Dave said glumly. 'Is she around?'

'She's just drying a mouth mould. I'll go and get her.'

Kiri marched out the back. Alone in reception, Dave breathed into his hand and sniffed. He was glad he'd thought to freshen his breath with a Mentos from an old pack in his glove box. He straightened his jacket.

'Dave?'

He turned and there she was, lifting a plastic visor from her face to reveal those beautiful blue eyes. Her forehead was crinkled with trepidation. Dave wished it was in his power to reassure her, but he was here to do the opposite. Kiri was right behind Vanessa, and even Anthony had appeared mid-extraction. Dave could glimpse a patient lying prone in a chair out the back.

'Hi, Vanessa. G'day, Anthony.'

'G'day, mate,' said Anthony through his sterile mask.

'Well?' Kiri demanded impatiently. 'Tell us what's going on.'

Dave gave Vanessa his full attention. 'It's not good news, unfortunately. I got this in the mail this morning.' He waved the envelope.

'She's not offering to settle?'

'No, she's not.'

'She wants to go to court?'

'Yes, she does.'

Vanessa's face crumpled. Dave hated to be the bearer of such bad tidings, and it was about to get worse.

'There's something else, isn't there?' Kiri said shrewdly.

'Yeah.' Dave nodded unhappily. He paused, trying to soften the blow. 'She's actually filed a counterclaim. She's suing you for defamation.'

Chapter 18

VANESSA

An empty juice bottle hurtled through the air and hit Charlotte Lancaster on the nose.

'Score!' cried Jackson.

'Bravo!' cheered Joy.

'Bullseye!' exclaimed Joy's boyfriend Bob.

But Vanessa couldn't share in their jubilation. Her insides were stretched too tight; and, besides, she'd be the one who'd have to clean the sticky juice drops off the screen.

'Shhh!' she said. 'I want to hear this.'

Which couldn't be further from the truth really, but forewarned is forearmed, and tonight Charlotte was telling 'her side of the story' on *A Current Affair*. She was sitting on St Kilda Pier with Zac Woollcot, draped in a soft cashmere wrap and looking dewy and vulnerable. Vanessa wondered why the TV camera wasn't adding five kilos, like it had to her. Charlotte looked slender and appealingly fragile, while Vanessa had come across like a robust milkmaid who could toss a cow over her shoulder and burp it.

'Good-looking bird,' Bob said appreciatively.

Joy sniffed and pulled out of his arms. 'She's nothing but a thief, and she hasn't got two brain cells to rub together, not like Nessie.'

Bob chuckled and pulled Joy back into his arms. 'Nessie knows I don't mean any offence. Don't you, love?'

'Of course.'

Vanessa turned back to the TV. It was a windy day, and as kite surfers launched themselves into the air from choppy grey waves behind them, Zac Woollcot was feeling Charlotte's pain.

'What went through your head when you heard that Vanessa Rooney was suing you for breach of copyright?' he asked sensitively.

Charlotte shook her head in distress. 'I was devastated . . . completely confused.'

'Bitch!'

'Liar!'

'Hag!'

'Shhh!'

'Did you know that Miss Rooney is a dental assistant who's never written a book before, but she's read all of your best-selling novels?' Zac asked provocatively, but Charlotte refused to rise to the bait. He wanted her to go low, but she was going to go higher than Michelle Obama.

'So I believe. All I can tell you is, there's no truth to her claims.'

'What would you say to her if you could speak to her right now?' asked Zac with a spectacular lack of originality. He really was a little worm, Vanessa decided, as if she hadn't known that already.

Charlotte paused. 'I guess I'd say what I've been forced to say to friends on occasion: there's no shame in mental illness, and help is available.'

'Mental illness?'

Vanessa felt the blood drain from her face. Not only did she look like a front-row forward, now her mental health was in question.

Jackson grabbed the remote and changed channels. 'She's a loser, Mum. She's a lying old bag.'

'She's a filthy dirty old slag!' said Lachie.

Joy reached over to pat her knee. 'Don't worry, Nessie. With the twenty-four-hour news cycle, it'll all be forgotten by tomorrow morning.'

Vanessa had a feeling she'd heard that before.

Her mobile rang on the coffee table, and Jackson scooped it up.

'Oh God, that's probably a psychiatric hospital wanting to send a padded van,' she tried to joke. 'Ignore it.' But even as she grabbed a cushion and hid her face, she felt a tug of guilt. 'Obviously I shouldn't joke about mental illness, it's no laughing matter—but I still don't want to talk.'

'It's okay, Mum,' Jackson said from the other side of the cushion. 'It's just Dad.'

Fabulous!

Vanessa lowered the cushion. 'Oh, really? Great. Thanks, sweetheart.' She steeled herself and answered the call. 'Hi, Craig.'

'Vanessa, it's Natalie,' came a warm, solicitous voice.

'Oh, Natalie,' Vanessa replied like a strangled chook.

'How *are* you?'

'Oh, you know,' Vanessa replied vaguely. She couldn't think of what else to say but that was okay, because Natalie was more than on top of the conversation.

'Craig and I just saw the story on *A Current Affair*. I can only imagine that it's raised some issues for you. Maybe you'd benefit from talking things through?'

Yeah? Maybe I'd benefit from killing *you*!

'Thank you, Natalie, but—'

'I wish I could help you, but it wouldn't be appropriate for me to treat you. I could recommend another counsellor, though, or I know a couple of very user-friendly psychiatrists.'

'User-friendly psychiatrists?'

Joy snatched the phone out of Vanessa's hand. 'Natalie, this is Joy. Thank you for your kind offer, but Nessie does not need a psychiatrist. If I were you I'd look a lot closer to home—it's Craig who needs psychiatric help because of some very poor life choices. Goodbye.'

She pressed end and flung the phone down with a flourish.

'Mum!' Vanessa laughed.

Joy winked and Bob made a meowing noise, but Jackson and Lachie weren't amused.

'What's so funny?'

'Dad doesn't need a psychiatrist,' Lachie told Joy heatedly.

'No, of course he doesn't,' said Vanessa. Oops, another bad mother moment. 'Nan was just joking—weren't you, Mum?'

'Yes, I was just joking,' Joy assured the boys. Then she whispered into Bob's ear, 'Not.'

'Meow,' Bob said again, pulling Joy into a kiss.

The boys seemed appeased, but the humour had already evaporated for Vanessa. What if everyone who'd seen *A Current Affair* thought the same thing that Natalie did? Her heart hung heavy with a sense of dread. This was just the beginning.

Chapter 19

MARCUS

Implying that Vanessa was mentally unstable was the most tired trick in the book, but then Lotts—*Charlotte*—had never been much of a creative thinker, despite what her slavering fans believed. Marcus shook his head at the TV contemptuously. This whole puff piece was a masterclass in banality. Now Charlotte was strolling along the St Kilda foreshore hand in hand with that so-called 'tech entrepreneur', Ned Kasch. Marcus snorted as he took in Ned's man bun and beard, and his low-crotched, skinny-legged jeans. The guy looked like he'd modelled his entire presentation on a Hipsters R Us catalogue—clearly, he didn't have an original thought in his repertoire, either.

He downed a Scotch and considered turning off the TV, but now Charlotte and Ned were perched on a bluestone fence, engaging earnestly with the pubescent *A Current Affair* hack.

'Ned's been such a support to me,' his wife said, squeezing her lover's limp hand. 'I don't know what I'd do without him.'

'You'll never have to find out,' Ned simpered.

'Good!' Charlotte said, and she kissed him.

Marcus made a dry-retching motion to disguise a genuine stab of pain.

'You guys are so in love,' observed the infant 'journalist' who was already excelling at mediocrity. 'Ned, what's it like for you to see Charlotte accused of something like this?'

'What can I say, Zac? It's tough. Charlie's so talented and so successful—why would she need to plagiarise anyone?'

Marcus raised his glass to Charlotte. 'I can think of a reason, Lotts.'

She turned to look directly into the camera, almost as though she'd heard him.

'I didn't know what love was till I met Ned.'

Okay, that hurt. Bitch. So now everyone in Australia thought that Charlotte Lancaster had never loved Marcus Stafford. Well, the morons who watched *A Current Affair*, anyway. He grabbed the remote.

'You're much hotter than him.'

He turned. Ivy was walking up behind him, wearing nothing but sexily tousled hair and his court robes. She put her arms around his waist, wrapping a long slender leg around his.

He smiled. 'You think?'

'I think,' she whispered into his ear.

Marcus turned to prove her correct with a steamy and lingering kiss. Then he gently disengaged and turned off the TV.

'Do you want to eat here, or should we go out?'

He was halfway to the kitchen before he realised that she hadn't responded. He turned back to see that she was planted on the spot, looking peeved.

'What about me?'

Marcus was briefly confused.

'Do you think I'm more beautiful than Charlotte?'

He hid a prick of annoyance. Had she only offered him that compliment in order to elicit one for herself?

'You're okay,' he teased her. 'Fair to middling.'

Ivy pouted her full lips playfully. With her dark bob and brown doe eyes, she could give a younger Audrey Tautou a run for her money. She walked over and put her hands around his neck, pretending to strangle him. 'Tell me the truth!'

The truth? thought Marcus. The truth is I've never felt quite so bleak as I do in this moment, and I have no idea why. He felt an unexpected rush of yearning for his mum, who'd gone back to Kalgoorlie the day before. Was life always destined to be like this?

'You're more beautiful than anyone I've ever seen,' he said.

'Just as well,' Ivy purred.

Chapter 20

DAVE

'It could be worse,' Dave tried to console Vanessa as they parked around the corner from Marcus's chambers. 'Anyone who's ever met you knows that you're not delusional.'

She pulled a funny face. 'Yeah, but the problem is, there are so many more people who *haven't* met me.'

Dave laughed more loudly than her little jest warranted, but he liked how she made fun of herself. Vanessa was awesome. She must have faults, obviously, but he hadn't spotted any yet. He wondered what they might be. Was she messy? That was okay, so was he. Was she inconsiderate? Lazy? Selfish? They all seemed very unlikely. He climbed from the Volvo, allowing himself a moment of smugness at finding a park in a city street that was congested with cars and buses and courier vans. Well-dressed pedestrians were weaving their way along the footpath as Important People in business suits (trousers *and* skirts), strode past en route to Somewhere Important. It made High Street, Preston, seem like a country town, and he quickly felt his smugness shrivel.

'Dave?' Vanessa brought him back to earth. 'What happens next? I mean, now that we have to go to court.'

'Your guess is as good as mine.' She looked alarmed and he said hastily, 'Just kidding. Now I have to prepare a defence to their counterclaim and lodge it with the court, apparently. But this stuff is Stafford's bread and butter. I'm sure he'll help me out.'

Her smile brightened then. 'Yeah, you're right. Marcus will look after everything.'

Her face suddenly went bright pink. Must be nerves, Dave thought. Or was she having a hot flush? But wasn't that supposed to be menopause? Vanessa was way too young for menopause. Just looking at her, you could see how fecund she was, how ripe and—

'We'd better hurry,' she said. 'We don't want to be late.'

'Yeah,' said Dave, thanking God that she wasn't telepathic.

'Marcus's time is valuable.'

Yeah, extremely valuable, thought Dave. Valuable to the tune of a thousand bucks an hour. It made his own fees seem puny and inconsequential; but, let's face it, so were his cases—a fact that couldn't have escaped Stafford's attention. Dave felt intimidation clutch at his guts. Get a grip, Rendall. Who was Marcus Stafford anyway? Just a better-looking bloke with a better degree and a better job and a better bank account who commanded more respect in a day than Dave would likely accumulate in a lifetime. Apart from that he had nothing going for him! Dave chuckled inside, but his grip still tightened on his battered briefcase.

'Dave. G'day.'

He turned to see Chris Tatarka, the head solicitor at NorMel Community Legal Centre, where Dave volunteered one night a week. Chris was a big bear of a bloke with a mop of grey curly hair and a rebellious disposition, and just seeing him somehow made Dave feel better.

'Chris, g'day! Vanessa, this is Chris Tatarka. Chris, this is my client, Vanessa Rooney.' He felt irrationally proud, as if he was introducing his fiancée. Settle down, Dave.

'Hi,' said Vanessa, smiling.

Chris grinned. 'G'day.' He turned back to Dave. 'I've got a DUI in the Mag. What about you?'

'Meeting with Marcus Stafford on an IP matter.'

Chris whistled through his teeth, mock impressed. 'Well, excuse-fucking-me.'

Dave laughed. Chris sprinkled 'fucks' around like salt and pepper and, as far as legal advocates went, it was hard to believe that he and Stafford occupied the same universe. Chris was a social justice warrior who'd somehow kept the flame alive well into his fifties. He kept threatening to leave NorMel and move into corporate law so he could finally make some dough, but everyone knew he'd never go through with it.

'What can I tell you?' Dave joked. 'I'm hanging with the big boys now.'

Chris laughed and fell into step with them, and Dave felt himself relax. He didn't know much about criminal matters when he started volunteering on Chris's advice line, but he'd quickly caught on. Why shouldn't it be the same with IP litigation? He felt a new spring in his step as they turned into the epicentre of Melbourne's legal precinct, William Street.

'Holy fuck!' Chris exclaimed.

A phalanx of photographers and TV crews were waiting outside Stafford's chambers, and someone had already spotted them. They were swarming towards Vanessa en masse.

'There she is!'

'That's her, over there!'

'Look, it's Vanessa Rooney!'

'Fucking hell—I'll catch you later,' said Chris as the vultures pushed past him, thrusting cameras and microphones at their prey.

'Vanessa, Charlotte Lancaster claims that you have mental health issues!'

'Is it true that you're mentally ill?'

'Are you a fantasist?'

'Give us a smile!'

Vanessa blanched in terror and stared at the ground as they jostled around her. Dave was splenetic. What a pack of mongrels! And now passers-by were stopping to stare and film. What was this, feeding time at the zoo? Dave leaped in front of Vanessa with his arms outstretched.

'Hey, that's enough!'

They ignored him, pushing and shoving to get closer.

'Do you have a comment, Vanessa?'

'Have you sought help for your mental health issues?'

'No comment!' Dave yelled into the fray. 'Leave her alone!'

But a photographer thrust past him, knocking Dave backwards into an overflowing garbage bin.

'Hey!' he yelled again, but no one was listening. The media beast had engulfed Vanessa, and Dave could only see the top of her head. As he scrambled out of the bin and tried to push his way back to her, an authoritative voice cut through the chaos.

'That's enough!'

Dave turned. It was Stafford in his full court get-up.

'I'll thank you to back off and give my client some space.'

The vultures miraculously quietened. As Stafford headed for Vanessa they parted like the Red Sea. Dave blinked in astonishment. The bloke was a media whisperer.

Marcus put his arm around Vanessa, and from what Dave could see from the back of the scrum, she looked incredibly relieved.

'Mr Stafford, does your client have mental health issues?'

'What do you say to your ex-wife's claims that—'

'I said *enough*.' Stafford silenced them with a raised hand. Dave peered over a passer-by's head to see the barrister looking straight down the barrel of a TV camera while Vanessa blinked up at him.

'Vanessa Rooney is a writer of prodigious talent whose copyright has been shamelessly breached, and this desperate smear campaign insults the intelligence of the many people who know her for the talent she is.'

He paused for a second or two as cameras whirred and clicked and bystanders held up phones—but before anyone could bark more questions, he cut them off at the knees.

'Thank you, but that's it for today. I appreciate you've all got jobs to do, but so do we. So, if you don't mind, we have a defence to prepare.'

With his arm still around Vanessa, Stafford started guiding her to his chambers. The journos threw out a few half-hearted questions but soon dispersed, and the passers-by moved on to something else. There was no doubt that Stafford was an impressive operator, and Dave felt his nerves come rushing back. Relax, he's just a bloke in a silly wig. Yeah, keep telling yourself that, Dave.

As he hurried after Stafford and Vanessa, a TV cameraman pushed past him and stomped heavily on his foot.

'Ow, shit! Jesus, mate!' said Dave, hopping up and down in pain, but the TV cameraman just kept going.

Arsehole, thought Dave. He turned to see Vanessa and Stafford disappearing into the building without a backwards glance.

Chapter 21

VANESSA

Vanessa's cheeks were shining pink, and it had nothing to do with the heat coming from the bolognaise sauce she was stirring on the stovetop.

'It was amazing, Mum. It sounds so cheesy, but he rescued me.'

'Of course he did,' said Joy, who was sitting at the table with a glass of bubbles. 'He's your knight in shining armour.'

'No, he's Ivy Jones's knight in shining armour. I just borrowed him for the afternoon.'

Her senses still tingled when she thought of Marcus sweeping her into the building and to the safety of the empty lift. It was only when the doors slid closed that he'd released her from his arms.

'Are you okay?'

Vanessa nodded shakily.

'I know you don't like this kind of exposure, but it will be worth it, I promise.'

Their lift swept upwards, but then suddenly Marcus groaned and pressed the emergency stop button.

'Marcus?'

Vanessa looked into his eyes and caught her breath as she saw the same burning desire that Dr Magnus Maddison felt for Georgie Sinclair.

'You're driving me crazy,' Marcus rasped. 'I can't think straight.' He pinned her against the wall and a shudder of longing convulsed her body. 'I have to have you now.'

And he ravished her in the lift.

Yeah, right!

What actually happened was he took her up to his chambers, offered her a chair and said, 'Would you like a coffee?' And then Dave turned up and she was briefly taken aback, because she'd forgotten that he was there too.

'Oh. Dave.'

'Sorry,' he said. 'Had a bit of trouble fighting my way through the vultures.'

'No problem,' said Marcus.

Vanessa noticed that Dave was limping. 'Are you okay?'

'I'm fine. Some wanker just stood on my foot.'

'Oh, you poor thing.'

'Take a seat,' Marcus said, and Vanessa wondered if he'd forgotten that Dave was coming too. 'I was just about to call to see where you were.'

Okay, maybe not.

Dave sat in one of Marcus's low chairs with his knobbly knees in the air and his trousers riding up to reveal pilled black socks. Vanessa saw a dusty boot print on top of his shoe. As he scrabbled around in his briefcase self-consciously, she wanted to pat his arm and say, 'You're flustered. It's okay, just take a few deep breaths.' She was floating on air because she and Marcus were in this together. Even though that media pack would have once been her worst nightmare, now it just seemed an irritant. It was astonishing what a difference one man could make. So what if a fan of Charlotte's had bailed her up this afternoon and accused her of lying? Or that the *Daily Mail* website had published a picture of her with her eyes half closed and her mouth wide open next to a photo of Charlotte looking stunning with the caption: *Who would* you *believe?* Somehow it was bearable, because she and Marcus were a team.

And didn't they say that these kinds of intense situations led to love? She was trying so hard to keep her feet on the ground and accept that she wasn't his type—Ivy Jones, hello!—but what if Marcus was feeling it too? She imagined doing an interview together in future, hand in hand and radiating a loved-up vibe that would bring a smile to the sourest observer's lips.

'We tried to keep our relationship strictly professional,' she'd tell the interviewer, and then Marcus would hold up her left hand with the dazzling diamond and say with a laugh, 'Obviously we didn't try hard enough.' Yes, all the excruciating humiliation was worth it. The universe could throw whatever crap it wanted at her, because it was Marcus and Vanessa against the world.

Oh, and Dave of course.

Joy joined her at the stovetop. For a second Vanessa wondered if her mum wanted to help with the cooking—but she should have known better. Joy dipped a teaspoon in the sauce and tasted. 'That could do with a bit more salt.'

Grrr! Vanessa thought.

'Forget about Ivy Jones,' said Joy. 'She's an obstacle you can get around. You just have to believe that Marcus is yours, and he will be.'

'Mum, it's not that simple,' Vanessa told her, trying to hide her frustration.

Joy fixed her with an intense look. When she spoke again her tone was evangelical. 'But it's worth it, because Marcus is just like your daddy—living proof that you shouldn't listen to all those judgy women and so-called "relationship experts" who try to tell you that knights in shining armour don't really exist.'

Joy paused to sip her bubbles and Vanessa noticed her hand was shaking. This was so much more than her mother's opinion—it was her mission statement.

'Just because they don't have the courage to hold out for the perfect man, they'll tell you that *you're* the one with the problem. But you and I both know they're wrong.'

Their eyes met.

'You're right, Mum,' Vanessa said, her heart swirling with hope.

'Woof!'

Daisy pawed at her leg, reminding her it was time for dinner. As she went to the fridge and took out Daisy's chicken and vegie roll, the front door opened and slammed shut and the whole house shook. Vanessa winced. The boys were obviously home from swimming.

'Is it true that girls are quieter?'

'You were much quieter,' Joy confirmed. Then she added cheekily: 'Your daddy and me were the noisy ones.'

Wasn't that the truth.

'We're in here!' Vanessa called.

As she started cutting up Daisy's dinner Lachie appeared in the kitchen doorway, his damp hair sticking up in cute little spikes.

'I'm starving. What's for dinner?'

'Will this do?'

Vanessa held up the dog roll, but Lachie barely acknowledged her feeble joke. He sniffed and looked into the pan with disgust.

'Spaghetti bolognaise *again*?'

'We haven't had it for at least ten days. How was swimming? And school? And where's my kiss?'

Lachie gave her a cursory peck on the cheek. 'It sucked.'

'Which? Swimming or school?'

'Both.'

'Why?'

Lachie's face contorted as he struggled not to respond honestly. 'Dunno. I'm starving. Can I have a packet of chips?'

'No, you can have a banana. It must have sucked for some reason.'

Lachie looked like he was holding in a secret that was in danger of making him burst, but all he said was: 'Nuh.'

Vanessa frowned.

'Hey,' said Joy from the table, 'how about giving your nan some of that sugar?'

She tapped her cheek. Lachie kissed Joy too and she slapped him on the bum and it evolved into a playful tussle.

But Vanessa was feeling a little unsettled as she put Daisy's bowl on the floor. Why had school and swimming sucked? And, more importantly, why wouldn't Lachie tell her why? Lachie was a voluble chatterbox who couldn't resist sharing exactly what was on his mind whether other people wanted to hear it or not. Vanessa had always treasured this quality in her youngest son and hoped that he would retain it as he entered his teens, when everyone knew that boys became notoriously non-verbal.

'Why did swimming and school suck?' she persisted.

'Can I have a chocolate biscuit?'

'No, you can have a banana or nothing, dinner's in fifteen minutes.' She looked around in search of her oldest son. 'Where's Jackson?'

'I think he's tired,' said Lachie, who was one of the least gifted liars in the world. 'He wanted to go straight to bed.'

Vanessa and Joy exchanged a look and Vanessa headed for the door.

Joy pushed her chair away from the table. 'I'll put the pasta on.'

'Thanks, Mum.'

Vanessa strode to Jackson's bedroom with Daisy at her heels.

She stopped at the door and knocked. 'Jackson? Sweetheart? Are you all right?'

'Yeah,' called Jackson from inside, adding a loud yawn for good measure. 'I'm just not hungry. Think I'll go straight to bed. 'Night.'

Not hungry? This was a kid who ate half a loaf of bread within ten minutes of coming home from school and then hassled her about dinner.

'Is something wrong?'

'No, everything's sweet. See you tomorrow.'

'Jackson . . .' Vanessa tried to open the door but there was something pushed up against it. Her pulse started to race. 'Jackson! I want you to get this thing away from the door and open it right now.'

'I want to sleep.'

'I don't believe you. Open the door.'

Daisy picked up on the stress in Vanessa's voice and started barking. Lachie and Joy appeared from the kitchen, drawn by the kerfuffle.

'Open this door now!'

'You'd better open it—Mum's going mental for real now,' Lachie called to his brother.

There was silence for a few beats and then they all heard something heavy being dragged away from the door. Vanessa burst through in time to see Jackson jumping back into bed and pulling his Collingwood doona up over his head.

'Sweetheart, what's wrong?'

'Nothing,' he said from under the doona. ''Night.'

''Night,' Lachie replied unhelpfully.

Vanessa tried to pull back the doona but Jackson clung to it. Daisy leaped onto the bed and tried to lick his face.

'Daisy, get off me!'

What was going on? Vanessa exchanged an anxious look with Joy and then reached over and yanked the doona free, finally revealing Jackson. He tried to turn his face to the window, but she pulled him back around, then gasped. Jackson's left eye was black and swollen, and there were purple bruises on his arms. Her baby!

'Jackson! What happened?'

'I fell over.'

'No, you didn't. You don't get a black eye like that from falling over.'

'I did,' the poor kid insisted.

Vanessa turned to Lachie. 'Lachie?'

Lachie looked like he was about to burst.

'You shut up,' Jackson warned, but he was too late. The dam broke.

'A kid in year eight said you were a psycho, so Jackson pulverised him,' Lachie said in a rush.

'What?!'

'That's crap! I just tripped.'

'Everyone's been bullying him on the bus. They reckon you're mental. Jackson's been, like, spewing every morning before school, and when Ryan Derrickson said you were a psycho, he lost it and punched his lights out.'

'Shut up!'

'And then all these other kids started beating up Jackson too, and they were saying, "Rooney's mum's a psycho!" and Hamish Mushin Snapchatted that video of Jackson on the swing and he wrote: *Little Jackson Rooney just shit his pants.*'

A wave of guilt washed over Vanessa and threatened to knock her off her feet. She sank down onto the bed. 'Oh, sweetheart . . .'

'It's okay,' Jackson mumbled.

'It's not okay. I'm so sorry I didn't know any of this.' She hugged Jackson tight, ignoring his protests, and held out her hand to Lachie. 'Lachie? Is this happening to you too?'

'Some kids try,' said Lachie, puffing up his chest, 'but I just say, "My mum's going to get fifty million bucks, so you can get stuffed!"'

Vanessa felt a surge of relief. Lachie was much more resilient than Jackson but, even so, the fact that he'd been forced to fend off bullies made her feel wretched.

'I want to have a talk with Jackson,' she said, giving Lachie a kiss. 'I'll be out in a minute, okay?'

'Okay.'

Joy took Lachie's hand. 'Come on, gorgeous, I reckon you can have that packet of chips after all.' She winked.

'Yes!'

'And Daisy, I've got a treat for you too,' said Joy, and Daisy trotted after them eagerly. Joy pulled the door closed, leaving Vanessa and Jackson alone.

Where to start? Vanessa wondered.

'You've been vomiting before you go to school?'

'Only once or twice,' Jackson said unconvincingly. 'It doesn't matter.'

'It does!' Vanessa took his hand and, thank heavens, he let her hold it. 'Yours and Lachie's happiness is the most important thing in the world to me.'

But it occurred to her with a stab of shame that she hadn't been behaving that way. She'd been so preoccupied with her silly fantasies about Marcus Stafford that she hadn't even noticed her kids were suffering. A good mother would have been on to it, but Vanessa had taken her eye off the ball.

This couldn't go on.

Chapter 22

MARCUS

Marcus was accustomed to masking his feelings with a tactical smile, but he found himself overtly alarmed.

'You want to *what*?' he asked.

Vanessa shifted uncomfortably. Her large blue eyes were apologetic. 'I'm sorry for wasting your valuable time, but I want to call off the case.'

She was biting her lip and there was something strangely endearing about that, although it didn't make her announcement any less concerning. Where had this come from? Why now, when Marcus had Charlotte squirming on a hook?

'But why would you do that?'

Vanessa hesitated, and he saw her eyes moisten. 'I know we thought the media exposure would be one of our most effective tools, but the whole country thinks I'm a loony—I mean, mentally ill—not that there's anything wrong with that if I was, but I'm not. And my boys are paying too high a price.' She actually started crying then. 'I'm sorry . . .'

'No, don't be.' Marcus leaped to his feet. He went to sit beside her and pulled a handkerchief from his pocket. He vaguely wondered how long it had been there; he always used tissues. He gave it to her.

'Thank you.'

She blew her nose and then dabbed at her tears. Marcus could sense that this was no premeditated performance intended to melt his heart or put him at a disadvantage. Vanessa Rooney was devoid of womanly guile, and he found himself disarmed.

'What do you mean, your boys are paying too high a price?'

She lifted his hanky away from her nose, revealing a quaint smattering of freckles that he'd somehow missed before.

'They're being bullied. Especially Jackson, my oldest.'

Marcus framed his face sympathetically and made an all-purpose 'tsk' sound.

'He's very sensitive, and he's so stressed that he's been vomiting before school, and I didn't notice because I was too busy thinking about, um, the case. And now he's got a black eye and God knows what emotional injuries, and it's all because of me.'

Marcus took a moment. It was vital that he couch things in terms she'd find ethically acceptable, but he knew from many years of experience that even the noblest of intentions crumbled in the face of the dollar.

'I'm sorry to hear that, Vanessa. Boys can be brutes. But you have to remember that while the bullying will be temporary, the benefits you'll be able to bring to their lives from winning this case will be permanent. You stand to be awarded a lot of money.'

'I don't care about that,' Vanessa replied, giving a very credible impression of someone who actually didn't. 'I mean, of course I'd like the money. Who wouldn't? But not at the expense of my kids' emotional health.'

Marcus refrained from pointing out that with money like that she could afford the best child psychiatrists, so surely a bit of emotional damage was worth sustaining in the short-term?

'Dave hasn't lodged our defence to Charlotte's counterclaim yet,' she continued, 'so I think it's best that I pull out now, before we're in too deep.'

Her voice was quavering but her tone was unwavering. She meant this. She was prepared to throw away hundreds of thousands of dollars for her sons' sake, and Marcus found himself robbed of the deadliest weapon in his arsenal. He was suddenly acutely aware of her soft breasts rising and falling beneath her mass-produced jumper, and her shapely thighs pressed against the chair. There was a wayward thread on the knee of her jeans, and he had to resist a sudden and startling impulse to bite it off with his teeth.

'Vanessa, I hear what you're saying, but if you pull out now there's a very good chance the court will order you to pay Charlotte's legal costs.'

That clearly rattled her, but she rallied. 'Well, I guess that's a chance I'll have to take.'

If there was one thing that Marcus never misplaced, it was his vocabulary, but suddenly he couldn't locate so much as a word. He watched mutely as she picked up a large cooler bag off the floor and lifted it onto his desk. Her face was aflame.

'I feel terrible about wasting your time, and I'm sorry I can't afford to pay you yet. I know how busy you are, and a man living on his own . . .' As she started unzipping the bag, her voice climbed a few octaves with embarrassment. 'I hope you won't think this is silly, but I've made you some comfort meals for the cold weather.'

While Marcus watched, dumbstruck, she pulled out plastic containers full of food.

'This is osso bucco, and this is spaghetti bolognaise. These are my salmon patties—they're the boys' favourite. And this is lasagne and this one's a chicken and spinach—' She suddenly stopped mid-sentence. 'I'm sorry, this is dumb. You don't want these.'

'Yes, I do,' he assured her, and he realised he wanted them very much. 'I don't know what to say. Thank you. This is the most thoughtful thing a client has ever done for me.'

And it was, indubitably. The most thoughtful, the most stupefyingly unsophisticated and the most utterly charming thing he could remember. He smiled into Vanessa's eyes. There was a single tear caught in an eyelash and he found himself transfixed.

'You're welcome.' She blushed. 'I was cooking for the boys anyway. They love their food.'

Her boys again. Clearly Vanessa Rooney's world began and ended with her sons. Marcus wondered how it would feel to bathe in the glow of Vanessa's love.

'You can keep the cooler bag; we've got too many. My mum buys a new one for her bubbles every time she goes to Coles. I'm like, "Mum, you've already got about seven of these—where am I supposed to store them?" And she's like, "Oh, I didn't realise I had that many," and, anyway . . .' She trailed off self-consciously. She was delightful.

Marcus grabbed a permanent marker from his pencil holder and scrawled *Property of Marcus Stafford—Hands Off!* with a skull-and-crossbones on the back of an affidavit. He taped it to the cooler bag.

'Now nobody else will dare to touch this before I take it home.'

Vanessa giggled and it gratified him.

'I'm going to put this in the fridge, and then why don't I grab us a coffee?'

'That would be lovely, thanks. I might go to the, um . . . ?'

'Down the corridor, second door on the left.'

'Thanks.'

Marcus used his time in the kitchen to regain his equilibrium. This case had seemed like a lay-down misère, even with Graham Goetze,

Champion of Efoki Villagers, acting as Charlotte's counsel. Marcus was sure Graham must have taken the case to get under his skin—not quite so saintly after all! But on the upside, Graham's involvement would add to the piquancy of his win. The only thing he hadn't factored in was a client who was prepared to forfeit public vindication and a bucketful of money in favour of her sons' wellbeing. Vanessa Rooney, an unanticipated and surprisingly attractive stumbling block. But there was no way he'd allow her to drop the case.

He'd just arrived back with the coffees when she returned from the bathroom. Her nose was still red and shiny—she hadn't bothered to reapply her makeup, and he found that strangely enchanting. She smiled shyly and held out his hanky, a scrunched-up snotty ball.

'I'm sure you'll be wanting this back now,' she joked.

He laughed and her cheeks flushed pink.

'Just kidding. I'll take it home and wash it first.'

'Keep it,' he said with a smile. 'It's yours.' And he wrapped his hand around hers and gently closed it around the hanky.

She gave a tiny jump at his touch, and the pinkness spread to her ears.

Marcus leaned in close. 'Vanessa, I'm sorry your boys are being bullied, but aren't your boys the very reason you should stick with this litigation? You've been grossly wronged, and I'd argue that you owe it to your sons to model courage in the face of adversity. Surely it's best for them if you stand strong and prove your integrity?'

She looked tortured, which only added to her beguiling air of vulnerability.

'I'd love to do that,' she said eventually, 'but it kills me seeing Jackson so upset. It's not fair that he has to defend me—and what about the long-term effects?'

'I understand,' said Marcus understandingly. His eyes drifted down to the soft curve of her hips. 'But what if I could divert the negative attention away from you and onto Charlotte?'

She brightened briefly but then looked dubious. 'That'd be amazing—but how?'

'I have my means. Rendall's almost finished drafting our defence, so why don't I release the hounds on her in the meantime?'

Vanessa was starting to look hopeful now, and it lit up her whole face. 'What kinds of hounds are you referring to?'

'Hairy hounds with very big teeth. If I can guarantee that Charlotte will bear the brunt of the storm and you and your boys will be yesterday's news, will you proceed with the case?'

She hesitated a moment, then raised her chin. 'Yes. I will.'

Marcus resisted an urge to kiss her. 'Consider it done.'

Chapter 23

DAVE

As the Redbacks jogged around the freezing oval, Dave was squinting at Vanessa's phone.

'Can you believe it?' she said jubilantly. 'It just popped up five minutes ago.' She read aloud: *'In a damaging new twist in the breach of copyright scandal engulfing bestselling novelist Charlotte Lancaster, the* HuffPost *has learned that in 1997 Ms Lancaster was expelled from the exclusive Manhattan Young Ladies Academy for copying another student's essay.'*

Dave whistled through his teeth. 'You're kidding? This is excellent.'

'Yeah, and it gets better: *Former classmate Melissa Chastain confirmed that Ms Lancaster copied her essay. She told the* HuffPost, *"Charlotte was notorious for stealing everything, including other people's boyfriends."'*

'Excellent,' Dave repeated. 'I'm not sure the boyfriends are relevant, but—'

'Shhh, there's more.'

'What, steak knives?' he quipped, but Vanessa wasn't listening.

'The HuffPost *has also learned that Ms Lancaster was twice arrested for shoplifting at the exclusive Bergdorf Goodman department store in Midtown Manhattan. It's believed her father, prominent mining executive Chip Lancaster, intervened to avoid a conviction being recorded.*'

Dave's eyes widened. This was manna from heaven for them. But how had the *HuffPost* got hold of it?

'Marcus leaked this to take the attention off me and the boys,' Vanessa explained.

Dave was taken aback. 'I didn't think a barrister was allowed to do that.'

'Well, he didn't do it himself; somebody else did.'

'On his behalf?'

'You're missing the point: it's all true, and it's great for our case, isn't it?'

Dave couldn't help but agree, and somehow that cheered him and depressed him all at once. 'Yeah, it is. You're right. I'm still not certain it's ethical, but Stafford sure knows how to pack a punch.'

'Yeah, he's incredible.'

Dave regarded Vanessa's pretty face, all pink and vibrant beneath her striped beanie. It was great to see her so stoked about Stafford's efforts, and he wanted her to feel proud of him too. 'I've finished drafting the defence,' he announced, feeling like a kid trying to get a favourite teacher's attention. He may as well have been waving his hand in the air. 'Miss Rooney, pick me!'

'You have? That's great! Thanks so much. Was it a lot of work?'

'Oh, you know—once I'd done the research and figured out what I was actually doing . . .' Stop it, Dave, you sound like a goose. He tried to replicate Stafford's swagger. 'Yeah, it was pretty time-consuming, but I think I've come up with a bulletproof document.' But had he? What would Stafford think of his work? Would Stafford have to rewrite the whole thing? Dave hoped that he hadn't embarrassed himself.

The Redbacks ran past, emitting little clouds of condensation. Even though winter was in full swing, they all insisted on wearing shorts to training, and their legs looked like twenty-two purple toothpicks. Dave was often reminded of his mum saying to him as a kid, 'You're making me cold just looking at you.'

'Dad,' called Nickie, 'how many more times around the oval?'

'Keep going till I come up with something else.'

Nickie groaned and rolled her eyes at Tom McDonald, who was jogging beside her. Tom was the alpha male of the Redbacks. He was loud and cocky and, from what Dave could see, he didn't have a reflective bone in his body, so he was probably destined to go far. Jackson was bringing up the rear, and Dave wondered whether he should mention the shiner.

'I guess you've noticed Jackson's black eye.' Vanessa grimaced, making the decision for him.

'Bit hard to miss.'

'He got into a fight sticking up for me.'

She obviously felt guilty about it so he tried to reassure her. 'If it's any consolation, a shiner's a status symbol at his age, so right now Jackson's the coolest kid on the team.'

Vanessa brightened. 'Really?'

'Yeah, really. I had a black eye myself when I was twelve, and suddenly my mates thought I was Muhammad Ali. I never had the guts to admit that I'd got it trying to open a jar of peanut butter.'

She laughed, and a wave of happiness washed over him. And he realised that he'd like to make Vanessa laugh like this every day and to wake up beside her every morning after making love to her all night. Well, maybe not all night, that was a bit over the top, but at least for an hour or so on Fridays and Saturdays. Dave reminded himself that dating a client was unethical, but if Stafford could discreetly leak to the media, why couldn't he and Vanessa discreetly fall in love and get married? But he was getting way ahead of himself—the first step was to ask her out.

He felt a stab of shyness, and suddenly he was that pimply, lanky fourteen-year-old boy again, already at least three heads taller than everyone else and the object of giggles behind girls' hands. But he knew Vanessa wasn't like those girls—he was willing to bet that bitchiness had bypassed her even in puberty. But where would he take her? And when should he ask her? Now?

'Hey, Niss. Dave. You have to check this out.' Kiri was striding over to join them, waving her mobile phone in the air. 'Jeez, how freaking cold is it? You guys have got this one in the bag. Charlotte Lancaster was expelled for—'

'Expelled for copying, I know.' Vanessa beamed. 'Isn't that awesome?' But then her brow creased. 'Damn, I just said *awesome*—I owe myself a dollar.'

The moment was lost, so Dave left Vanessa and Kiri gossiping and turned his attention back to training. When he'd volunteered for this role, he'd had no idea how to coach. To be honest, he'd assumed that would rule him out, but it seemed the Redbacks, perpetual wooden spooners, were desperate. A brief period of panic had ensued before he'd decided just to follow his instincts and get to know the kids, and now he was fond of all of them, even the ones he didn't like. After their first win he'd been surprised to feel the stirrings of a dormant killer instinct—and now, ten weeks later, with the semi-finals in the Redbacks' sights, this innocuous kids' soccer comp had assumed the stakes of *The Hunger Games*.

He was en route to the car with Nickie after training, when his mobile rang. Dave checked the screen. It was Stafford. He let it ring a couple more times and then answered 'nonchalantly'.

'Marcus. G'day.'

Nothing to see here, folks, just two colleagues chewing the fat.

'Hi, Dave, how are you?' Stafford asked, but the question was obviously rhetorical because he didn't wait for an answer. 'I just wanted to let you know that you've done a terrific job with the defence.'

'Yeah?' Dave replied 'casually' as he jumped up and down and pumped his fist in the air Rocky-style, earning another eye roll from Nickie. 'Good, I'm glad it works.'

'Yeah, me too. I've just made a few very minor changes and tossed it back to you, but it's ready to lodge tomorrow.'

'Sweet,' said Dave. He was chuffed by Stafford's praise, but did the bloke have to sound quite so surprised?

'And as soon as we've got that lodged with the court, you can start making discovery of all the relevant documents.'

'You bet,' said Dave, already feeling his confidence fizzle. He refrained from asking the question on the tip of his tongue: Exactly which documents were relevant?

Chapter 24

MARCUS

'You're contemptible,' Charlotte spat as she slipped off the Prada coat he'd bought her in Florence two winters ago and flung it over his ottoman. A small pulse throbbed in her neck. 'You know I was in crisis when I copied that essay and swiped those handbags from Bergdorf Goodman.'

'Do I?'

Marcus regarded her coolly. Rage suited her, but then most things did. Lotts—*Charlotte*—was nothing if not predictable, and he'd been expecting this 'surprise' visit. When he'd buzzed her up to the apartment, she'd swept inside with all of her requisite entitlement, and he'd watched her eyes scan the place (in search of Ivy?) before coming to rest on his half-finished meal.

'I'm sorry to interrupt your . . .'

'Salmon patties.'

He may as well have said 'yak's testicles'.

'Salmon *patties*? Whatever. We need to talk.'

'Fine,' he'd said coolly. 'Take a seat.'

'I don't want to sit,' she'd snapped.

And so here they were, standing beside his gas log fireplace, framed by the city lights through the window. Conversing like the mature adults they weren't.

'Where's your compassion?' She was trying a different tack now: injured waif. That suited her too. 'It was a terrible time for me. My grammy had died—I wasn't coping. I told you that.'

'You told me a lot of things.'

She 'humbly' copped that on the chin.

'Okay, I probably deserve that. But you've leaked this stuff completely out of context. What are people going to think?'

'I imagine they'll think, correctly, that you steal other people's work.'

She met his eyes defiantly. 'I didn't steal Vanessa Rooney's novel.'

'We both know you did, and we both know why. Poor baby, what a shame your daddy couldn't buy you some talent.'

She raised her hand to slap him but obviously thought better of it. She took a step back, trying 'calm and rational Charlotte' on for size. 'But don't you think this is all getting out of hand? Your claim, my counterclaim, your defence to my counterclaim. Why perpetuate the unpleasantness? Let's call things off before everyone loses.'

'I don't think I'll be doing that, Charlotte.'

And now the injured waif was back.

'Charlotte? What happened to Lotts?'

'Good question.'

She looked crushed then. It was quite convincing. No doubt she'd practised in front of a mirror—but, then, that was her favourite place to be.

'I know things haven't worked out for us, but I never thought you'd do something like this to me.'

'I never thought *you'd* do what you did to *me*.'

And then she hung her head in shame, or some fabrication of it. Poor little Charlotte, so misunderstood. She looked glorious, of course. Everything about Charlotte's body was put together perfectly, as though the universe had been stirring up trouble, to borrow from Raymond Chandler's oeuvre. She was wearing high-heeled black suede boots and a woollen dress with a long zipper down the back, and Marcus toyed with the idea of reaching out and unzipping it.

She looked up again, her eyes now soft and entreating. 'Marcus, what would you say if I told you that I'd made a huge mistake?'

He ignored the sudden leap of his heart. 'I'd say you're trying to play me again.'

'I'm not,' she murmured, fixing him with a gaze that had always set his pulse racing. 'I've been thinking a lot about things, and I'm hoping it's not too late for us. I don't want to have an ugly, drawn-out fight with you.'

'Because I'll win.'

'No, because I still love you.'

She was good. He almost believed her.

'But I thought you didn't know what love was until you met the limpet?'

It was a childish riposte, but he didn't care. She bit her lip appealingly. 'That was TV. You know what it's like. I was just telling them what they wanted to hear.'

'Just like you're telling me now.'

'So you *do* want to hear it?' She moved close, reaching up and lacing her fingers around his neck. Her familiar smoky perfume almost caused a Pavlovian response. Down, boy. She stood up on tiptoes and whispered, 'Let's make love, not war, Marky.'

She was trying to manipulate him with sex, of course, but better that than other tactics. Marcus prided himself on being able to think with two organs at once, so he knew he could turn the tables on her. He could make love to her right here and then murmur into her perfect ear, 'I'll see you in court.'

She smiled and moved her face even closer. She was irresistible and she knew it. Marcus moved his face down to meet hers . . . closer and closer . . . Their lips were almost touching when he realised with a sudden burst of clarity that he couldn't be bothered. It was a watershed moment that spelled freedom. He whispered against her lips, 'Go home to the limpet,' and stepped away.

Charlotte stood frozen with astonishment. For the first time her injured expression seemed genuine.

Marcus sauntered to the door and opened it. 'If you don't mind, I'd like to get back to my salmon patties. Goodbye, Charlotte.'

Chapter 25

VANESSA

Vanessa was holding a bottle of tomato sauce and peering at the list of ingredients. 'My God, this sauce is thirty per cent sugar.'

She put it back on the shelf. She'd have to buy organic tomato sauce, although that would still have sugar—but not as much, presumably, and the sugar itself would be organic. Could organic sugar still give you cancer?

'That's how I like to think of myself,' said Joy, interrupting her ruminations. 'Thirty per cent sugar.'

Vanessa chuckled at her mum's joke, and felt a rush of joie de vivre. Life was good. Marcus's leak had done the trick and in the past few weeks she'd slipped back into anonymity. She was even starting to get some ideas for her new book, which was exciting, because before the leak she'd been so stressed that she was stumped. But, most importantly, the bullies had moved on from Jackson, and he was back to his normal monosyllabic and smelly self.

Thank goodness!

Joy reached past Vanessa to grab some Weight Watchers salad dressing, her curves on full display in thigh-high boots and a fitted mini with a low-cut neckline that defied the icy air of July. Vanessa was wearing her sensible tunic and work slacks under her winter coat with her comfy surgical shoes, a godsend at the end of a long day's standing over the dental chair. Her hair was in need of a wash, so she'd scraped it back into a ponytail, and every time she passed a mirror she thought it looked like a fountain of frizz exploding from the hair elastic.

'Thanks for helping with the groceries, Mum.'

Joy smiled but her voice took on a shrill edge. 'Well, it's not like I've got anything else to do. I'm a single girl again.'

Vanessa was so surprised that she almost steered her trolley into an elderly shopper. 'Mum, no. That's terrible. What happened?'

'Bob wasn't the man I thought he was.'

'What do you mean? I thought things were going so well for you two.'

'So did I, but remember how yesterday was my birthday?'

'Of course.' How could she forget? For the ninth time in a row the boys had been told to pretend that Joy was turning fifty-five and Vanessa had wondered how long it would be before Lachie's compulsion towards honesty made him refuse to cooperate. 'Bob turned up with flowers and took you out to dinner.'

Joy sighed. 'I honoured our dinner date because I was trying to give him a second chance, but I couldn't get past what he'd done.'

Vanessa was mystified. 'What did he do?'

'Well, it was more what he didn't do. He didn't ring me.'

'What do you mean?'

'I mean he didn't ring me to wish me a happy birthday before he picked me up for dinner.'

Vanessa was perplexed. That was it? 'Maybe he was busy.'

'Too busy to ring the woman who should be the most important person in his life on her one special day?'

'But he took you out to a nice restaurant. And maybe he had other things going on.'

'More important things than me?' Joy said petulantly as a woman stopped beside them to reach for gherkins. '*I* have to be the thing, Nessie. Your father used to wake me up singing "Happy Birthday" into my ear and then he'd make passionate love to me and chuck a sickie and we'd go on a romantic picnic and make love again under the trees.'

The women with the gherkins, looking enthralled, pretended to survey the pickled beetroot. Vanessa took her mum's arm and pushed their trolley into the next aisle.

'But, Mum, Bob's not Dad.'

'And that's the whole point,' Joy said defensively. Vanessa could tell that she was feeling judged. 'You think it isn't hard for me to hold out for another prince? But your father always made me feel like a princess, God rest his beautiful, sexy soul.'

'Oh, Mum . . .'

Vanessa's heart ached for Joy's loss, but she couldn't help feeling for Bob too. She'd never especially warmed to the guy, but there was no doubting his devotion to Joy. 'But I've seen you and Bob together at close quarters for months now, and—'

'Of course you have,' Joy snapped. 'Because I moved out of my flat to help with your mortgage and forfeited all my privacy in the process!'

Vanessa winced. Joy was right. The move couldn't have been easy for her, and it was no wonder she resented it now and then.

But Joy was already looking contrite. 'I'm sorry, Nessie.'

'No, don't be. I understand we must drive you nuts sometimes, and I do really appreciate what you've done.'

'I know.'

They shared a warm and fuzzy moment.

'And you know what, Mum? It's *your* love life. It's none of my business.' And it wasn't, when she thought about it. Who was Vanessa to criticise Joy for her refusal to settle for second-best? She should be applauding her for her courage. 'I'm sure you'll find another prince one day.'

'I hope so.' Joy seamlessly switched gears back to wicked. 'I think we both know that you've found yours.'

Vanessa's insides turned to custard at Marcus's very mention. 'Mum, how many times do I have to tell you? Marcus isn't my prince.'

'He could be if you play your cards right. When did you last speak to him?'

'At eleven twenty-three on Monday morning.'

'But it's two minutes past five on Thursday evening!'

'I know that, Mum.'

'Ring him up now.'

'What?'

'Ring him up now and say you want to get together tomorrow to clarify certain aspects of the case.'

'What aspects of the case?'

'Who cares? That's not the point. Out of sight, out of mind, Nessie. You need to remind him of what a fabulous woman you are before the weekend comes, and then absence will make his heart grow fonder.'

Vanesa resisted pointing out that Joy had just argued with contradictory clichés. Maybe she *should* ring Marcus? But did she dare? Joy twinkled at her. 'Even a knight in shining armour needs a little encouragement. And wouldn't you like to see him?'

YES!

Vanessa pulled out her mobile and stared at it nervously. 'What should I say?'

'Just say that you want to clarify certain aspects of the case, so you're hoping you can drop by his chambers tomorrow.'

'Right. I want to clarify certain aspects . . .'

She brought up Marcus's name in her contacts list but couldn't summon the courage to take the next step.

'Just do it, Nessie, don't think about it.'

It was good advice. She grimaced nervously and pressed his number. He answered on the second ring.

'Marcus Stafford.'

That sexy voice!

'Hi, Marcus, it's Vanessa,' she squeaked. 'Um, Vanessa Rooney.'

'Vanessa, hi.' He sounded like he was smiling, but maybe that was wishful thinking? 'You don't need to tell me your last name. What can I do for you?'

How about marry me?

'I, uh, I was wondering if I could drop by your chambers tomorrow? I'd like to clarify certain aspects of the case.'

Joy winked and held up crossed fingers.

'Oh? What aspects of the case aren't you clear on?'

'Umm, certain aspects . . .' Vanessa replied vaguely, casting a 'help me' look at Joy. Luckily a tinny voice came over the PA and announced that avocadoes were on special, giving her a little time to regroup. 'I'd rather discuss it in person.'

'I'm afraid I'm in court all day tomorrow.'

'Oh.' Bummer. That's if it was true. Maybe court was just an excuse? Suddenly she felt like a total fool. 'Of course, that's fine. Well, sorry to disturb you. Bye, then.'

To her surprise, Marcus jumped in. 'Wait,' he said. 'I've been derelict in my duties. I should have been keeping you more up to speed. Why don't you drop over to my place tonight?'

Vanessa almost suffered a coronary.

'Drop over to your place tonight? Sure, why not?'

Joy started dancing an elated little jig right there in the frozen foods aisle.

'Let me give you my address,' he said.

As Vanessa jotted down Marcus' address on the back of a box of fish fingers, a passing septuagenarian grabbed Joy and twirled her around, but Vanessa barely registered—she'd just caught sight of herself in the freezer door. In her dowdy uniform and sensible shoes with the frizzy fountain on her head, she looked like an extra who'd just been cast in a movie as Frumpy Woman #1. Normally that thought would have amused her, but not in the current circumstances.

'How about a couple of hours?' Marcus suggested.

'A couple of hours?' Vanessa freaked. 'Er, could we make it three hours?'

'Sure. I'll see you at eight o'clock, then. Would you like to stay for dinner?'

Vanessa emitted a squeal and tried to transform it into a cough.

'Hmm, yeah, dinner would be awesome.'

And no, she wasn't going to fine herself for awesome. It would be awesome—so there.

'Terrific,' said Marcus. 'I'll see you then.'

'Yeah, see you then.'

Vanessa pressed end and leaned against the freezer for ballast. Her heart was performing a gymnastics routine in her chest and her legs felt like mashed potato. Meanwhile Joy was panting, and Vanessa couldn't tell whether it was because of her little jig or the excitement of the phone call.

'Oh, Nessie . . . I told you he wants you.'

And for the first time Vanessa allowed herself to believe that he actually might.

Joy's eyes were filling with emotional tears. 'He's going to be such a wonderful lover. I bet you'll go off like a firecracker.'

Vanessa allowed herself to indulge in that blissful thought for a moment before panic kicked in and wrecked everything. Who were they kidding? Marcus wouldn't touch her looking like this, and she only had three hours.

'Mum, look at me! What am I going to do?'

Joy looked her up and down and grimaced. 'Thank goodness for late-night shopping.'

⁓

Vanessa lay prostrate on a table as a beauty therapist called Aleesha stirred hot wax with what looked like a paddle-pop stick. Aleesha had rectangular eyebrows and long jet-black hair parted in the middle Kardashian-style, and she was wearing so much make-up that it looked like she'd need a trowel to remove it. Kim Kardashian had a lot to answer for, Vanessa mused. Her vacuous impact was everywhere and enriching her by the moment. She'd even released a pool float in the shape of her bum! Vanessa had no idea if Kim had intended that as a joke, but Vanessa certainly found it funny. She'd been planning to buy one for Kiri as a gag until she discovered they were one hundred and twenty-eight dollars. In your dreams, Kim!

Aleesha spread warm wax on Vanessa's inner thighs with the paddle-pop stick and applied a white strip.

'Relax.'

Vanessa tensed. Aleesha waited a beat and then ripped her pubic hair out by the roots.

'Ow!' Vanessa screamed. Her eyes watered as Aleesha regarded the hair collected on the strip with what seemed like repugnance. 'Thanks again . . . for fitting me in,' Vanessa gasped.

'I've got another client waiting. I didn't realise you'd take this long.' She glanced down at Vanessa's pubic area accusingly and Vanessa felt like a beast from the Borneo jungle.

'It's been . . . a while.'

Aleesha nodded. Clearly. As she applied more wax, Vanessa glanced at the clock on the wall. She was due at Marcus's place in two and a half hours.

'I'm sorry, I don't mean to be rude, but could you hurry?'

'There's a limit to what I can do with this,' Aleesha replied tersely. 'Relax.'

Vanessa stiffened like a corpse with rigor mortis. Aleesha ripped back the strip.

'Owww!'

'If you leave it too long this is going to happen,' Aleesha said as she tossed the hairy strip into the bin and then repeated the intensely painful process three or four more times. Then she stopped and started looking for something, and Vanessa wondered if it was pruning shears. But instead she picked up a small pair of tweezers and started plucking out recalcitrant hairs. Vanessa winced at all the pinching, but eventually it was over, thank goodness, and Aleesha was rubbing aloe vera on Vanessa's burning inner thighs. It was hard to know which of them was the most relieved.

As Vanessa watched Aleesha leave the room with a toss of her long black mane, she noticed that her bum was nothing like Kim Kardashian's. Hopefully she'd keep it that way. Vanessa had heard about girls undergoing dodgy surgery called a Brazilian Butt Lift to make their bums look like Kim's. Madness.

She stood up to get dressed and noticed in the mirror that her upper thighs were covered in angry red spots. She looked like a plucked chook. But all she could do was hope it would settle in time, because right now she was late for the hairdresser.

⌐

'I love it.' Vanessa beamed at her reflection in the mirror and tilted her head from side to side. 'I don't look like me at all.'

'That was the whole point,' said Jaymes, a senior stylist at DisTressed. Miraculously, he'd had a cancellation and he'd shampooed and blow-dried Vanessa's frizz into submission so that she now had a shiny curtain of glossy straight hair falling past her shoulders.

Yes!

Jaymes whipped the cloak away with a flourish and brushed her shoulders free of loose hairs.

'Spray?'

'Maybe just a bit. Something light?'

'You got it.'

Vanessa glanced anxiously at the clock as Jaymes picked up an industrial-sized can of hairspray. He sprayed it all over her head for what seemed like hours—but maybe that was just because Marcus was expecting her in seventy-eight minutes and she still hadn't bought her outfit. Vanessa suddenly realised that she was glad for all this running around—it distracted her from feeling too nervous about what might actually happen this evening. She felt a delicious little shudder through her plucked chook region.

'Flyaway hair like yours needs all the help it can get,' Jaymes declared. He'd finished with the hairspray now and her hair looked like a coagulated helmet. He led her to the front counter, grabbing a few products en route. 'I think you need Artemis Moisture Complex shampoo and Artemis Moisture Plus conditioner. And you should give your hair an intensive moisturising treatment with Artemis Lush Tresses at least once a week.'

'Oh, um, okay.'

Vanessa already had shampoo at home, but God knows it wasn't working, and she and Jaymes had hit it off so well that she didn't want to rock the boat. He put the products on the counter and gestured to the radiantly pretty receptionist, who had green hair and a ring through her nasal septum.

'Astrid will look after you. Did you guys meet? Vanessa's on her way to a hook-up with a hot guy.'

'Awesome.'

You'll have to take a dollar off the bill for that, Vanessa thought.

'Great to meet you, Vanessa.' Jaymes kissed her cheek. 'Have an awesome time.'

Make that two dollars.

Jaymes headed off to greet his next client, leaving Vanessa and Astrid alone.

'Jaymes is, like, such an artist,' Astrid said. 'He's taken at least ten years off you.'

Vanessa wondered how old she'd looked before. 'Thank you but, um, I'm in a bit of a hurry.'

'Cool.'

As Astrid popped Vanessa's products into a bag and added it up on the register, Vanessa found herself riveted by the receptionist's septum ring. She hoped her boys would never pierce their septums and sully their beautiful faces. She reassured herself that Jackson was unlikely to do anything like that but, as for Lachie, it was anyone's guess.

Astrid looked up from the register. 'Jaymes is a senior stylist so he's a hundred and eighty,' she said. 'And the shampoo is fifty, the conditioner is forty-five and the moisturising treatment is forty-eight . . . so that'll be three hundred and twenty-three dollars.'

Vanessa's mouth popped open and shut like a goldfish.

⁓

What the hell was wrong with this zipper? Vanessa could feel her stress levels escalate as she yanked at a recalcitrant zip on a little black dress in the Zara change room. It was caught on something—a wayward thread. Oh, great. She slipped off the dress and bit off the thread and then put the dress back on and finally managed to pull up the zipper, but she'd wasted forty or fifty seconds, which was time she could ill afford.

'Calm down,' she told herself in a soothing voice. 'If you have a heart attack, you'll never get there.' It was an amusing thought in some ways. She imagined the headlines: CHARLOTTE'S ACCUSER FOUND DEAD IN CHANGE ROOM. THE ONE ENDING SHE COULDN'T HAVE WRITTEN. That kind of thing. But the door was locked. Who would find her? And would they carry her body through the store past horrified shoppers? Surely not. But she was getting distracted— another thing she didn't have time for.

She checked herself in the mirror. The dress was reduced from two hundred and ninety-nine to one hundred and thirty dollars, so no complaints there. It showed a bit more cleavage than she was normally comfortable with, especially in the freezing Melbourne winter, but it was a good fit—although her tummy *was* sticking out a bit (just for a change). She stood in profile. Whatever happened to 'slimming black'? If only she could wear Spanx with it, but that would be way be too risky. Imagine what Marcus would think of Spanx! Her face flamed at the thought, but reality check—this was probably just a work dinner and Marcus wouldn't even see her undies. The thought was supposed to reassure her, but instead it made her feel crestfallen.

But not crestfallen enough to buy Spanx.

⁓

Vanessa hobbled across the floor to Myer's intimate apparel department in sky-high shoes that looked fantastic but were already cutting her heels in half. She would have loved to put bandaids on her ankles, but she could hardly turn up at Marcus's place like that and, besides, there was no time to buy some. It was 7.19 pm.

Argh!

She grabbed a pair of sheer black pantyhose and limped on gamely towards a sales rack of lingerie, rifling through until she found a size 12D black lace bra with matching undies. The undies were so tiny that they looked like a lacy pocket handkerchief. Should she buy size 14 instead? They'd certainly be more comfy, but comfort wasn't the issue here—if it was, nobody would ever buy sexy lingerie. She stuck with the size 12s and raced to the sales counter.

'Hello,' the saleslady said with a smile. 'How are—'

'I'm in a hurry,' Vanessa snapped.

The saleslady pursed her lips and nodded.

Vanessa felt contrite. What was she always drumming into the boys? There was no excuse for rudeness. 'I'm sorry, thank you for asking. I'm fine, but I'm in a bit of a hurry.'

'Of course.' The saleslady smiled. She took the lingerie and examined it in a leisurely fashion. 'This is pretty, isn't it? And twenty-five per cent off, what a bargain.'

Vanessa's whole body twitched with impatience as the woman rang up her purchases. She threw the correct cash onto the counter and yanked the lingerie out of the saleslady's hands.

'Thank you, I don't need a bag—I'm going to wear them.'

'I haven't taken—' the saleslady called after her, but Vanessa had no time to stay and hear the end of the sentence.

She entered the change room at 7.36 pm and disrobed to find that she still looked like a plucked chook. She slipped on the pocket-handkerchief undies (which were even smaller than she'd thought), pulled on the black pantyhose and threw on her new bra—a perfect fit, thank goodness. Then she slipped the little black dress back over her head, not worrying too much about messing her hair because Jaymes had applied so much spray that it wouldn't budge in an unprecedented weather event. With shaking fingers, she quickly made up her face and slathered her neck in liquid makeup in the vain hope of covering her nervous blotches. Then she looked at her phone again. It was 7.53 pm.

She shoved her surgical shoes and uniform into the Zara bag, threw on her coat and hobbled out of the change room.

Chapter 26

As the lift shot skywards towards Marcus's apartment, Vanessa gasped for breath. She was still puffed from running three blocks because she couldn't find a parking spot any closer, and it seemed she might have that heart attack after all.

Ping! The lift arrived at Marcus's floor much sooner than she would have liked. Vanessa stepped out, fighting for air and feigning a nonchalant smile, two feats that were tricky to achieve simultaneously. Then she saw Marcus waiting across the corridor, and her heart almost *did* stop. He was looking like a total dreamboat (as Joy would say), in Levi's and a white cotton T-shirt.

He smiled warmly. 'Vanessa, hi.'

'Hi . . . Marcus . . .' she panted.

He was dressed so casually that she suddenly felt ridiculous. What was she doing in this ludicrous cocktail outfit? She must look so needy and desperate.

'You look amazing.'

!!!!!!

He sounded like he actually meant it. Vanessa would have blushed if her face could have gone any redder than it probably was already.

'Thanks,' she rasped, patting at beads of sweat on her forehead. 'Are you okay?'

'I'm . . . fine . . . It's just . . . unseasonably warm.'

Marcus nodded as though that made sense, even though the temperature was about three degrees below average.

'Well, come in.'

Vanessa was glad that Marcus lived right across from the lift because she couldn't have made it down the corridor without limping. Her heels were rubbed raw after all that running in her new shoes and every step she took was excruciating.

Marcus stood back chivalrously. 'After you.'

She attempted a casual stroll past him into an ultra-modern apartment with panoramic views of the Royal Botanic Gardens and the city's neon nightscape. She stopped at the window to rest her heels and replenish her lungs.

'Wow . . . what an . . . amazing view.'

But frankly a vista of an abattoir would have looked stunning to her right now. Marcus joined her at the window and her whole body tingled at his proximity. She tried to still her jagged breath.

'Are you sure you're okay?' he asked quizzically.

Vanessa nodded.

'Can I get you a drink? What would you like?'

'Um, I think I might . . . start with a glass of water.'

Marcus headed into his immaculate kitchen, the kind that TV real estate shows refer to as a 'chef's kitchen', as if a mere mortal grilling cheese on toast would somehow be an affront to the oven. He poured her a glass of water from a crystal jug and brought it over.

'Thank you.'

Vanessa felt an electrical charge when their fingers touched. She drained the glass while Marcus went back to the kitchen. He opened the fridge and pulled out a bottle of Moët.

Moët!

'Maybe when you've finished your water—oh, you already have.'

'I was thirsty,' Vanessa said shrilly. 'I'd love a glass.'

Marcus reached for a couple of champagne flutes and brought them over with the bottle. Vanessa was getting her breath back now, which was freeing her up to start fretting. What was she doing, assuming that this was a 'date'? The poor man had only asked her here because she'd requested clarification on the case, and it just happened to be convenient for him to do it at home. The Moët didn't signify anything—it was probably just like cordial to him. And he was wearing jeans and a T-shirt, which proved that tonight meant nothing special. It made her own fevered anticipation seem frankly pathetic.

Marcus opened the Moët with a pop, poured her a glass and gave it to her.

'Thank you.'

'You're welcome.'

He poured his own glass of bubbles and regarded her with an enigmatic smile. No doubt he was thinking, *Oh God, the poor woman thinks this a date. How can I let her down gently?* Vanessa felt a compulsion to let him know that she wasn't a total desperado. Even though she was.

'Can we discuss the case?' she asked abruptly.

Marcus looked taken aback, but he nodded. 'Of course, that's why we're here. Take a seat.'

She sank into the plush surface of his leather lounge, and he gestured towards her pointy heels.

'Feel free to take off your shoes if you'd like.'

Alleluia.

Vanessa kicked off her sadistic heels. She was glad that she'd resisted the urge to take them off when she was running here so she could keep the soles of her feet pristine.

Marcus sat down beside her. 'So, you were saying there are some aspects of the case that you'd like clarified?'

Joy and her brilliant ideas. Where was her mum now that Vanessa had to clarify which aspects of the case she wanted clarified? She'd only had a few minutes to think this through between ripping out and blow-drying bodily hairs.

'Um, yes, that's right . . . I was just wondering what the status is with the, er, interlocutory applications.'

Thank goodness she'd googled 'interlocutory'.

'Well, now that your defence to the counterclaim has been lodged, Rendall's about to start making the interlocutory applications for discovery of the relevant documents. But there's sometimes a degree of stalling from opposing counsel, so he'll have to keep the pressure on.'

Vanessa nodded intelligently, even though her brain felt like a scoop of ice cream that had just been dropped into lemonade.

'Actually, Rendall left a message about wanting a meeting and court's been adjourned tomorrow because the judge is ill. Why don't I call him and see if we can all meet at his office and chew through everything together?'

'Okay . . . great.'

Vanessa hid a pang of disappointment. Of course he'd want to involve Dave in their conversation, because he couldn't get her out of here fast enough. Who could blame him? Her besottedness was so transparent. He must think she was an idiot. She should leave now before she made even more of a fool of herself—but wait, Marcus was leaning forward and gazing into her eyes.

'You look worried,' he said gently. 'You don't need to be. I'm going to win this for you, I promise.'

There was dark stubble on his tanned cheeks and she wanted to reach out and touch it with her fingertips. She knew she should say something, but she was so flustered she couldn't speak. She looked away shyly and eventually managed a reedy-thin, 'I know you will.'

'Good.' He raised his glass. 'Here's to justice being served.'

'To justice.'

They clinked champagne flutes and sipped, and then Marcus put his flute down on the coffee table. His tanned biceps were perfectly outlined by his T-shirt sleeves and Vanessa could barely rip her eyes away.

'Are you hungry? I thought I'd make a risotto.'

'Sounds delicious.'

She would have been happy to eat an old boot.

'You're not gluten-free, fructose- or lactose-intolerant, a vegan or on the paleo diet, are you?' Marcus asked with a grin. 'I should have checked earlier.'

'No, it's okay. I eat everything.' God, that made her sound like a pig. 'I mean, no special requirements. I'm pretty low maintenance.'

'You are, aren't you?' he said in a tone that she couldn't quite place, and he looked at her for so long that she started to wonder if there was something hanging out of her nose.

As she took out a tissue and blew it in case, he finally spoke. 'I know my way around a kitchen, but I can't pretend that my risotto Milanese will compete with your salmon patties.'

Her salmon patties? Was he pulling her leg?

'I'm serious, everything you gave me was delicious—thank you again, by the way. But those salmon patties were sublime.'

Sublime? Wow. 'Really?'

Marcus nodded. 'This is going to sound corny, but they were just like the ones my mum used to make.'

Vanessa glowed. 'Really?'

'Yeah, my brothers and I used to pester her for her salmon patties.'

'My boys love them too—I think I told you.'

'You did. They must be a perennial favourite.'

'Yeah.'

They shared a smile and she pictured him as a little boy running into a kitchen with grubby knees and eager eyes, saying, 'Mum, can we have salmon patties tonight?' It made her heart do a little flip.

'How many brothers have you got?'

Something about Marcus's smile changed. 'Two.'

'Are they close in age to you?'

'Pretty close.'

'Where do you come?'

'In the middle.'

'And do they live nearby?'

'No.'

'Oh, that's a shame. So your mum and dad aren't here either?'

Marcus shook his head.

'Where do they live?'

'They're all in WA. Kalgoorlie.' He picked up the Moët bottle. 'Top-up?'

Vanessa nodded. 'Thanks.'

'I'm glad you like it—it's my vice of choice.'

He was smiling, but she sensed that he'd just closed the subject. Had she been interrogating him? How gauche and inappropriate. Not everyone was like her, happy to blather on about their family until the cows came home. So she shut up, but she still felt curious—part of a writer's toolkit, after all. She looked around for family snaps or shots of Ivy Jones, but there were no photos in the room except for a couple of abstract black-and-white landscapes. And no knick-knacks or ornaments either.

'What about your boys?' he asked. 'How old are they?'

'Jackson's thirteen and Lachie's eleven.'

'Old enough for trouble, then.'

'Tell me about it.'

They shared a smile.

Vanessa showed him photos on her phone and spent the next ten minutes rabbiting on about her sons. Marcus seemed genuinely interested and was in no apparent hurry to start cooking.

'I can hear the love in your voice. You'd do anything for your kids, wouldn't you?'

'Of course—I'd die for them. But I'm hoping that won't be necessary.'

Marcus chuckled at her little joke and leaned back into the sofa. He pointed to a nearby pouf. 'Feel free to put your feet up.'

'Thanks, don't mind if I do,' Vanessa said, still riding the thrill of having made him laugh.

But as she lifted her bare feet, Marcus exclaimed in alarm, 'My God, your heels are bleeding.'

Vanessa's feet froze above the pouf. 'What?'

She looked down. Her heels were not only blistered but her pantyhose were stained with blood!

'Oh my gosh! I didn't realise. I could have got blood on your pouf.'

'Forget the pouf. What's happened to your poor feet?'

'I don't know,' Vanessa lied. But Marcus looked dubious and she felt compelled to provide a vaguely credible explanation. 'Actually, I suppose it could be my shoes. They're newish. This is only the, ah, fourth time I've worn them.'

She sounded as lame as her feet looked, but luckily Marcus had stopped listening.

He stood up. 'You need antiseptic. Come with me.'

He held out his hand. Vanessa took it, and she felt a shock of electricity so pronounced that she half wondered if it had singed her hair. He led her down the hall to his bathroom. Her palm felt so safe and dainty inside in his, and she prayed that he couldn't tell it was clammy. In the bathroom, he discreetly looked away as she peeled off her bloodstained pantyhose. She knew it should feel mortifying, which it did, but there was something strangely exciting about it too. He tossed the pantyhose into a stainless-steel bin, then guided her to the gleaming toilet seat.

'Sit,' he said softly.

Vanessa sat. Marcus was a man living alone, but the lid was still down, and she wished that she could take a photo to share with Jackson and Lachie. See? It's not that hard to remember. It was more evidence that Marcus was a class act, not that she needed any. She watched as he went to his marble-topped vanity and pulled out a first-aid kit. Then he ran a pristine face washer under warm water.

'Hold out your foot,' he said, bending to kneel in front of her.

Vanessa had a sudden flash of him making a marriage proposal. How would she respond? *It's way too soon, we barely know each other—but yes, yes, yes!*

'Let's do the left one first. That looks the worst.'

'You don't have to do this. I can—'

'I want to do it,' he said. 'So behave yourself.'

Marcus took her left foot in his hands and cleaned her wound with the warm face washer. It was just like the Pope washing prisoners' feet at Easter, except nothing like that at all. Then he applied some antiseptic. She winced, and his face creased empathetically.

'Are you okay?'

Are you kidding? I think I just died and went to heaven.

'I'm fine.'

Marcus applied two bandaids to her left heel and then repeated the process with her right. Vanessa was certain he must be able to hear her heart thumping like jungle tom-toms in her chest. You Tarzan, me Jane! She wanted to grab a handful of his silver-sprinkled hair and kiss him and never stop. Was Marcus feeling the chemistry too? The signs seemed to be pointing that way, but Vanessa couldn't allow herself to believe it. This was probably just an act of courtesy that he'd show any guest.

'Thank you,' she managed as he snapped the first-aid kit shut. 'That was really nice of . . .'

But now his hand was back on her ankle, and his fingers were softly tracing the curve of her calf . . . just like Dr Magnus Maddison had done to Georgie Sinclair on page 117. Oh my God, surely *this* couldn't be put down to hospitality?

'You've got freckles behind your knee,' he murmured.

'I know,' Vanessa squeaked, aiming for a rueful shrug. 'What can you do?'

'I like them.'

He stood up, took her hands and guided her to her feet, pulling her so close that Vanessa could no longer be in any doubt about his intentions. For a brief moment she actually thought she might die of happiness.

'Did I mention how beautiful you look tonight?'

'In a manner of speaking . . .'

Marcus laughed. 'That's not good enough. Should I try a different manner of speaking?' And he inclined his head and kissed her softly on the lips, and she was glad he had his arms around her because she was sure that otherwise she'd fall. She could feel his bristles rub against her soft skin and it was impossibly sexy. When he lifted his lips from hers, she was speechless.

'I love what you've done with your hair,' he whispered.

He reached up to run his fingers through her tresses, but Vanessa felt a sudden tug and realised to her horror that his fingers were stuck.

'Oh . . . I'm sorry.' He sounded nonplussed. 'I'm not sure . . .'

'It's the hairspray.' Her face felt hot enough to fry an egg, but she couldn't help chortling. 'Sorry, the stylist went a bit overboard. Here, let me—'

They both yanked at her coagulated helmet.

'Ow.'

'Sorry.'

'No, it's fine.'

They finally freed his fingers.

'What a relief!' Vanessa laughed, and Marcus silenced her mirth with his lips, kissing her more passionately and urgently this time. Her whole body shuddered with desire and she knew that her Mum had been right—she was going to go off like a firecracker.

With all the élan of Dr Magnus Maddison, Marcus unzipped her dress while still kissing her. It slid to the floor. He stood back to look at her and she reddened, acutely aware of her cellulite and post-baby stretch marks and those red plucked chook spots. But he put his hand under her chin and brought her gaze up to meet his.

'Don't be shy,' he whispered. 'You're beautiful.'

He pulled his own T-shirt off, and she nearly fainted at the sight of his tanned abs. Then he kissed her again and reached around to unclasp the black lacy bra . . . but as he pulled it free, Vanessa heard him chuckle. She looked at the bra dangling from his fingers and discovered that the sale tag was still attached! Marcus laughed softly and dropped it to the floor.

'Twenty-five per cent *off*.'

And it was on . . .

Four hours later, Vanessa pulled her Corolla into the driveway in a blissful haze. She climbed out and glided through the back door, stooping down to greet Daisy, whose normally piercing bark somehow sounded muted and far away. Before she could even make it through the laundry, Joy appeared.

'Well? How did it go?'

Vanessa caught herself in the mirror. Her chin was red raw from kissing and her hair looked like a bird's nest. She couldn't string a coherent response together, but luckily there was no need for words because Joy had already read the signals.

'Oh, Nessie . . .' She gazed at her daughter emotionally. 'Did you have a vaginal orgasm?'

'Mum!'

'I'm just curious—it is a lot easier said than done.'

Vanessa felt her smile widen—a feat that she wouldn't have thought possible.

Joy squealed with delight. 'What did I tell you?' she beamed. Then she reached over and touched Vanessa's chafed chin. 'I see a touch of beard rash. Come on, I've got just the thing.'

Chapter 27

DAVE

Dave patted his jacket pocket to make sure he hadn't forgotten the tickets. He'd been toying with the idea of casually whipping them out and saying, 'Vanessa, what do you know? I just found these two tickets to the Amnesty Trivia Night in my pocket,' but that was bound to be exposed for the lie it was when she found out he was one of the organisers. It looked like he'd have to grow a pair and ask her straight out. Everyone loved trivia, didn't they? The Amnesty Trivia Night was an annual tradition for Dave, and when he'd rung fellow committee member Jo Fry and requested two tickets, she'd barely been able to disguise her delight.

'Two this year?'

'Yeah, two.'

'And what's the name for the other ticket?' asked Jo, who was a notorious busybody.

'Vladimir Putin. I hope that won't be a problem?'

Jo gave the uneasy laugh of a politically correct person who knew that they shouldn't find something funny but couldn't help it.

'Oh, Dave. What's the real name? I'm doing place cards.'

'Vanessa Rooney.'

'Vanessa? What a pretty name. I'm so happy for you.'

'Thanks, Jo, but you're crossing bridges before they're even constructed. She's just a friend.'

'Of course she is,' Jo said, but Dave could almost hear her winking. He knew that as soon as she hung up she'd be dialling Katherine Bell, another committee member who seemed more interested in Dave's non-existent love life than the imprisonment of political dissidents. 'Dave's bringing someone to trivia!' Jo would tell Katherine, and the two of them would cluck with concern. 'Let's just pray she's not a lesbian.'

Dave shot a look at the clock. Vanessa would be here any minute. Would she say yes? He was optimistic, although God knows he'd never been an expert at interpreting women's feelings. Assailed by a sudden crisis of confidence he distracted himself by typing up a handwritten 'email' for one of his elderly clients, Mrs Zhang. Mrs Zhang's family were scattered all over the country and they sent her newsy emails to Dave's address because she didn't have a computer. He printed out the emails for her and then transcribed her replies. It was no bother. He'd been fond of Mrs Zhang ever since she and her husband Cheung employed him to draw up their wills ten years ago. Poor old Cheung was pushing up daisies now—Dave had done the probate last year—and most of the news he typed up for Mrs Zhang referred to upcoming medical appointments. As he squinted to decipher her spidery scrawl he noticed that she had the eye specialist next Thursday. He frowned. Already? He could have sworn that she was at the eye specialist two weeks ago.

'David.'

Dave turned to see his dour Bosnian PA Ms Izetbegovic in the doorway. He'd lost count of the times he'd invited Ms Izetbegovic to call him Dave but she insisted on sticking with the more formal David, which always made him feel like a kid who'd been caught wagging school. But looking at her now he was brought up short—was she smiling? No, on second viewing that was a smirk.

'Vanessa Rooney is here.'

'Ah, what's that?' Dave asked, even though he'd heard every word. He started fiddling with the papers on his desk for no apparent reason.

'I said Vanessa Rooney is here. You know, the author.'

As she said the word *author* she raised two fingers on each hand to indicate scornful quotation marks. Dave thought that was beyond the pale and was about to say so, but then he reminded himself that her superior attitude probably covered a deep insecurity that had its roots in the Bosnian War. So he bit his tongue and settled for, 'Thanks, Ms Izetbegovic. Show her in.'

She turned towards reception and called curtly, 'Come.'

Dave tried to pull himself together, but when Vanessa appeared in the doorway all his efforts came unravelled. She looked positively . . . what was the word? Luminous. Yeah. She always looked gorgeous, but today it was like she had a light shining inside her. Jeez, Dave, that's a bit poetic. It just showed the effect she was having on him; he'd become a poet and he didn't know it. Ha ha, etc. The only thing marring her perfection was an angry red rash around her jaw. Hay fever, perhaps?

'Hi.' He smiled, swallowing nerves.

'Hi, Dave.' She smiled back.

'Take a seat.' But then he remembered that Mrs Hipsley's half-built doll's house was on the spare chair. He picked it up and took it back to the coffee table.

'Thanks.' Vanessa sat.

Dave wondered whether he should mention her flaming chin. Maybe she was self-conscious about her allergies? But if he didn't mention it would he come across as a heartless bastard who didn't even notice?

'It's nice to see you,' she said.

'You too, but are you okay? What's happened to your chin?'

'This?' she replied with a weird-sounding laugh. Her hand flew to her face and her entire dial turned bright red. 'It's, er, just an allergy.' She was obviously embarrassed about it, because she changed the subject. 'It's so strange that I haven't been to your office before.'

'You're lucky; it's usually admission by ticket only.'

Vanessa laughed and Dave was filled with delight. He could feel the trivia tickets burning a hole in his pocket.

But then Vanessa's eyes came to rest on his bulging bookshelf. She leaned forward to read a couple of titles. '*The Last Utopia: Human Rights in History. Half the Sky: Turning Oppression into Opportunity for Women Worldwide.* Wow, you've got a lot of great books.'

'Thanks.' Dave experienced a familiar pall of despair even as he kept his voice breezy. 'I've always wanted to practise human rights law.'

'Really? That's so great. I love that Gandhi quote: "You must be the change you wish to see in the world." I think that's it?'

'Yeah, that's it. Actually, that was my mantra when I was at uni. I was going to enshrine Indigenous rights in the Constitution and put an end to discrimination against asylum seekers. Not sure what I would have done after lunch.'

Vanessa laughed.

'But when uni finished, I kind of got off track.' Cripes, how feeble could a bloke sound?

But Vanessa looked like she understood. 'Yeah, that can happen. What was your first job after uni?'

Dave gave an involuntary little flinch and she said hastily, 'That's okay, you don't have to say if—'

'No, it's all right. My mum was diagnosed with cancer and my sister had moved overseas, so when I finished uni I went back to Shepparton to nurse her.'

'Oh, I'm so sorry. That must have been tough.'

You don't know the half of it, thought Dave, and I'm not about to tell you. He remembered that wintry afternoon, champing at the bit to get out of the house because dying doesn't always bring out the best in the dying, and his mother's resentment was killing *him*. He walked the streets of Shep for half an hour with guilt nipping at his heels, and when he arrived home his mum, who was supposed to have a few weeks left, had died. What was the last thing his mum saw? Not her son's face. Probably the ceiling, riven with cracks in the ancient paint. And now was he blaming her for his career woes? Class act, Dave. He shook off the thought.

'Then after she died, my uncle offered to sell me this practice and I thought, Hey, why would I fight for Indigenous rights when I can do conveyancing for the good people of Preston?' It was a lame joke from a lame duck.

'But you volunteer on the NorMel advice line.'

'Yeah, and I'm on the Amnesty Committee, but . . .' Those tickets were making him itch.

'I so get it,' Vanessa said. 'The whole time I've been a dental assistant, I've really wanted to be a writer.'

'And now you are.' Dave regarded her with pride. 'Good for you.'

She smiled bashfully, and he thought, You've got more guts than me, and I love you. Crikey. Where had love come from? But hadn't love been waiting inside him all along? It just needed Vanessa to come and claim it. He was turning into a poet again.

He glanced at his watch and felt himself clench up. Stafford would be here any minute—it was now or never.

'Vanessa?'

'Yeah?'

His hands were shaking. He grabbed the *Vanessa Rooney vs Charlotte Lancaster and Wax Publishing Pty Ltd* file as a cover. 'Ah, I was wondering if . . .' But he fumbled with the file and it fell to the floor, spilling its contents all over the carpet. 'Shit!' Just what he needed—to look like an incompetent nong in front of Stafford again.

He crouched and started scooping up papers. Vanessa got up from her chair to help. 'I need Velcro implants on my fingers,' he joked.

She laughed. 'Yeah . . . Anyway, you were wondering if . . . ?'

But there was a crunching sound and she stopped mid-sentence. Dave looked down to see that she'd just trodden on the USB copy of *Lost and Found Heart* and broken it. She looked aghast. 'Oh no! My book.'

'It's all right,' he reassured her. 'It's not your fault. Ms Izetbegovic should have filed it by now . . . Ms Izetbegovic!' he called. 'Could you come in here, please?'

There was no response for what seemed like minutes.

'Ms Izetbegovic!' Dave called more loudly. 'Can I see you, please?'

Ms Izetbegovic appeared in the doorway with a hairbrush and a sullen expression.

'There's been an accident. I need you to make another USB copy of Vanessa's novel.'

'Why? It's already in the Cloud,' she replied, pointing up to the sky. She may as well have added: 'Idiot.'

'I know, but a back-up's essential. So please make another USB copy.'

Her lip curled disdainfully. 'Do I have to read it?'

'No, just copy it.'

'All right, then. As long as I don't have to read it, I'll do it.'

She turned and left. Poor Vanessa looked dumbstruck, and Dave was mortified by his PA's appalling manners.

'I'm sorry about that. I don't think she means to be rude—it's probably post-traumatic stress.'

Vanessa looked confused. 'Post-traumatic stress?'

'Bosnia.'

'Oh . . .'

Vanessa nodded politely but she didn't look any the wiser. Dave contemplated going into detail, but that would just be diving down another rabbit hole leading away from the trivia night. He decided that if he didn't act now, he deserved to be shot and put out of his misery. He cleared his throat and started patting his jacket pocket.

'Are you okay?' she asked. 'Your hands are shaking.'

Dave pulled out the tickets. 'What do you know? I just found these—'

But he was thrown off-message by a deep male voice out in reception, followed by a tinkle of girlish laughter. Was Stafford here already? Bugger. And who was the giggling schoolgirl? Good God, that couldn't be Ms Izetbegovic!

'That must be Marcus,' Vanessa said. Her whole face turned as red as her chin. Was her allergy flaring up?

Just do this, Dave.

'Anyway, as I was saying—'

The door flew open and Ms Izetbegovic appeared with a winsome smile. 'Marcus Stafford is here,' she said pleasantly.

Dave couldn't help staring. He'd seen Ms Izetbegovic's flat features soften around Nickie, but this was something else altogether. She looked, to use a colloquial term, hot to trot. For the first time ever, Dave thought of his PA as a sexual being, and he hoped it would never happen again.

'Thanks, Ms Izetbegovic.'

Stafford appeared and touched Ms Izetbegovic's shoulder lightly as he passed. She giggled for no apparent reason.

'Thanks, Trjkla. Vanessa, Dave. Good to see you both.'

'You too,' Vanessa said. 'Hhhmmm . . .' Her voice was suddenly hoarse. Her allergy must be worsening.

'G'day,' Dave said. 'Pull up a pew.'

As Stafford sat down beside Vanessa, Dave started looking through his desk drawer for antihistamines—he usually kept some for Nickie, who was prone to sinusitis.

'Coffee or tea?' Ms Izetbegovic asked Stafford warmly.

He shook his head. 'I'm fine thanks, Trjkla.'

Dave couldn't find antihistamines, and now poor Vanessa was clearing her throat and kind of coughing.

'Hhhm, Ms Iz . . . Ms Izet . . . could I have, hhhhm, a glass of water, please?'

'There's a tap in the kitchen,' Ms Izetbegovic replied shortly.

'It's okay,' Dave said hastily. 'I'll do it. I want to see if I've got some antihistamines, anyway.'

Vanessa smiled. 'Thanks, Dave.'

He got to his feet. Ms Izetbegovic rolled her eyes contemptuously and made her exit.

Dave knew he should have insisted that Ms Izetbegovic get the water, but he wanted to regroup before the meeting. He needed to be on the ball with Stafford, who could spot an underconfident legal practitioner at fifty paces. Hopefully, Vanessa would linger afterwards and he'd finally get to ask her out. What would she say? 'I thought you'd never ask!' No, women only said that on TV. A simple 'yes' would more than suffice. Dave poured her a glass of water and unearthed a packet of Telfast from under the sink. Sweet, as Nickie would say. Just what Vanessa needed.

But as he was heading back to his office, he saw something through the door that made him stop. Vanessa and Stafford's heads were close together—and was Stafford running his fingers over her raw chin? Dave blinked in shock. He must be seeing things . . . He moved closer. If they turned they'd probably see him, but they seemed engrossed in each other.

'This is all my fault,' Dave heard Stafford murmur with mock remorse. 'I'm sorry I gave you pash rash.'

Pash rash? Dave's world skidded sideways. Surely the bloke was joking? But Vanessa was looking up at him rapturously.

'It was worth it,' she whispered.

Dave almost staggered against the wall. He saw Stafford lean over to kiss Vanessa, but she playfully pushed him away. 'Shhh, not here. This is work, remember?' She stood up. 'I'm going to sit over there.'

'No, you're not.'

Stafford grabbed Vanessa and pulled her down onto his knee, ignoring her protests. It was a prick move and Dave was sure that she'd be pissed off, but bizarrely she seemed to love it.

'No, this is inappropriate!' she said between giggles. It was a protest that sure didn't sound like a protest. 'Listen to me . . .'

But instead of listening Stafford forced her into a kiss, and she instantly surrendered. He had her in the palm of his hand and all of Dave's hopes lay crushed on the grey carpet.

So much for her allergy. What a moron he was with his helpful search for antihistamines. Dave's cheeks burned with humiliation. Of course Vanessa wouldn't be into him—hadn't she written a romance novel about an arrogant prick who just takes whatever he wants? Grow a brain, Dave. He was just thankful that he hadn't actually asked her out.

He took a few deep breaths to rally then coughed loudly.

Vanessa and Stafford jumped apart.

He strode into the room, tossed the Telfast down on the desk and handed Vanessa the glass of water.

'Thanks, Dave . . .'

She looked flustered, but Stafford was cool as a cucumber. Those kinds of blokes always were.

'Right, will we get down to it?' Dave began briskly. He sat and opened the *Vanessa Rooney vs Charlotte Lancaster and Wax Publishing Pty Ltd* file, forcing himself to meet Stafford's eyes and feign a confidence he didn't feel. 'I've been researching the procedure for making discovery of the relevant documents. It appears that I can compel Charlotte's counsel to produce Amy Dunphy's computer and early drafts of *Love Transplant* that allegedly demonstrate Charlotte's authorship, plus the email trail between Vanessa and Amy . . .' He felt his confidence waver. 'Ah, is that correct?'

Stafford nodded. 'Yes.'

Dave felt glumly cheered. At least he was getting *something* right.

Chapter 28

Dave froze with the basketball in his hand and stared at the hoop like a sniper. Sweat beaded his forehead in spite of the arctic winter wind. He waited for the right moment and then hurled the ball like a missile. It slammed straight through the hoop and bounced hard onto the concrete driveway. Dave raised his arms in grim victory.

'Fifteen in a row,' he barked. 'That's a record. Your go.'

He hurled the ball at Nickie so hard that she almost doubled over. 'Dad!'

'Oh, sorry, sweetie! Are you okay?'

'What's up with you? You're acting like a psycho.'

Clarity slapped Dave in the chops. His daughter was right. He was taking his frustrations out on her, and he'd turned an innocent game of shooting hoops into lethal combat. 'Maybe I *am*. I'm sorry.' He gave her a hug. 'I'll chill out now.'

She wrinkled her nose and wriggled free. 'You stink, Dad. You're all sweaty.'

Dave chuckled. 'What's a bit of bodily perspiration? Come on, give your old dad a hug.'

Nickie giggled and tried to escape his grasp as he chased her around the driveway. 'No! Gross!' She laughed and squealed like the teenage girl she almost was. Her shrieks were so high-pitched that Dave had to stop himself from wincing. A mate of his with a fifteen-year-old daughter had warned him to get used to it—or, failing that, invest in a good set of earplugs.

'My goodness!' exclaimed an elderly lady who'd just appeared in the next garden. 'I thought someone was being murdered.'

'Oh, hi, Mrs Morgans. Sorry about that.'

'Yeah, sorry, Mrs Morgans,' said Nickie.

Dave checked for a can in Mrs Morgans's hand. She didn't have much strength left in her wrists and Dave was her official can opener—which was fine, except she kept pretty odd hours and she'd been known to wake him at 5 am with a tin of sardines. But today she was only carrying pruning shears.

She waved their apologies away. 'My girls sounded like banshees. You should have heard them.'

Dave was rather glad that he hadn't.

Mrs Morgans bent down to prune her wisteria and disappeared behind the fence.

Dave watched as Nickie lined up a shot. She'd make a handy basketballer if she chose to play. She'd undergone quite a growth spurt lately, and she now towered over all the other Redbacks, except for Tom McDonald, and according to Evanthe she was feeling self-conscious about her height. That was part of the deal at her age, of course, but still, poor kid. She just needed the benefits pointed out to her.

'You're lucky you're taller than the boys. Maybe you could play for Australia one day?'

But to Dave's surprise Nickie didn't look cheered. She looked the opposite, if anything. Without any of her usual gusto she threw the ball apathetically and it dropped to the ground well short of the hoop.

Dave blinked in surprise. 'Nick? Are you okay?'

'What if I don't stop growing? What if I end up like some kind of giant? I don't want to be as tall as you—I'm a girl.'

So Evanthe was right. She usually was.

'You won't grow as tall as me,' he assured her with more confidence than he felt. But her face was still clouded with worry and memories of his own puberty came flooding back. Hadn't he spent hours trying to get out of swimming lessons because he thought he was too skinny and bony? He found himself writing a cheque that he couldn't cash. 'I promise you won't grow as tall as me.'

'Thanks, Dad . . .'

But her smile was still listless and she made no attempt to resume the game. It seemed like there was something else on her mind. Dave thought he was probably supposed to guess what it was, but, as established multiple times, there was Buckley's chance of that.

'Is there something else, sweetie? What's up?'

She hesitated.

'Come on. You can tell me.'

'Do you think I'm pretty?' she asked finally.

'Of course you're pretty.'

'Pretty enough?'

'Enough for what?'

She looked down and twisted her foot on the ground self-consciously. 'Enough for boys to like me.'

And there it was, the burden borne by little girls all over the world who didn't look like Barbie dolls. The anger that Dave had so recently quashed rose and filled his chest again. 'No, don't fall for this. This is exactly why I wanted you to read *Snugglepot and Cuddlepie* instead of *Cinderella*.'

She looked up at him with a 'huh?' expression.

'Those stories are a conspiracy against little girls. Think about it, Nick—all these princes falling in love at first sight before they've exchanged so much as a word with the princess. Don't you think that's pretty shallow?'

Nickie looked like she'd never thought about it, but Dave had been thinking about it since the night he'd first read *Snow White* to her as a toddler. As soon as he'd tucked her in and turned out the light, he'd registered his protest with Evanthe.

'Doesn't it concern you that the prince falls head over heels for Snow White when she's in a coma? You can only assume that the bloke has no interest in her conversational abilities. What kind of message does that send to Nickie?'

'Oh, David, it's just a story—you're taking it too seriously,' Evanthe had chided him. And when he'd gone out and sourced little girls' books that focused on female independence, she'd accused him of being too politically correct.

He'd ceded to her superior knowledge as a woman, but even now his hackles rose. Why was the hero always a prince? There was probably some poor bloke with a heart of gold scraping up the horse's shit—but would Snow White notice him? Of course not! Resentment flared again. How many times had he heard women, both real and fictional, ask despairingly, 'Why can't I just find a nice man and settle down?' Because you don't want a nice man! Because nice men are always too tall or too short, or they're not rich enough or in the right job, or they don't have the right kind of laugh, or they're instantly dismissed as just 'not your type'. Because, given the choice, women who claim to want a nice guy will always go for the arsehole.

Dave took the ball and threw it with such force that the hoop rattled and shook. Nickie was looking confused and he struggled to calm himself, mustering a smile. 'I'm just saying, there's a lot more to life than appearances. You need to remember that, sweetie.'

Her eyes inexplicably filled with tears. 'You think I'm ugly.'

'What? No! You're beautiful.'

'You think I'm ugly and no one will ever like me.'

'Sweetie . . .'

Dave reached for her but she burst into sobs. 'I don't want to play anymore.' And she turned and flounced off.

Dave was floored. What just happened? 'Nickie, wait—'

But she'd already disappeared into the house, slamming the door behind her.

As Dave hovered helplessly, Mrs Morgans popped her head back up over the fence and regarded him with sympathy. 'You don't know much about women, do you?'

Clearly not.

Chapter 29

VANESSA

Vanessa was appalled by the parking rates. Forty-eight dollars for three hours! It was daylight robbery, but she couldn't reverse because there were other cars lined up behind her. And, besides, she would have paid two hundred bucks if she had to, because her boyfriend was waiting for her.

Marcus!

After three intimate dinners at Marcus's apartment, tonight was their first outing as a COUPLE. Yes, a C-O-U-P-L-E! Vanessa Rooney and Marcus Stafford were now boyfriend and girlfriend, lovers, partners, an item, a 'thing'. They were meeting at a gallery opening in Flinders Lane, and Vanessa was already twelve minutes late. She felt a peculiar mix of stress and elation as she took her ticket and sped through the gates.

'Why don't we grab something to eat first?' Marcus had suggested last night, when they were lying with their limbs entangled after making love.

'I wish I could, but I've got Lachie's parent–teacher interviews. Sorry.'

'Don't be sorry.' He smiled, running a finger down her back as softly as air. 'I love how you put your kids first. It's one of the things I find sexiest about you.' Then he whispered into her ear, 'Would you like me to list the other things?'

'I'd rather you showed me,' she replied, thrilled by her own boldness.

Even now, Vanessa felt a shiver ripple through her whole body. That first encounter had been no fluke. Her mum had predicted that Marcus was the kind of man who could drive his sports car straight to a woman's G spot—well, he pulled over and parked there! She wondered idly if Craig even knew that she had a G spot. It seemed too late to ask him now.

She manoeuvred the Corolla into a tight space between two huge urban tanks, opened the door and squeezed out, hurriedly throwing on her coat and tying her scarf around her neck in what she hoped was a flattering knot. It was still mind-boggling that Marcus would break up with a woman like Ivy Jones for her, but that was exactly what he'd done. Apparently, he'd told Ivy that they were 'on different paths', because he didn't want to rub Vanessa in her face. Vanessa would like to rub herself in his face! But she had to stop thinking about sex every second. It had almost got her into trouble at Lachie's parent–teacher interview.

When she'd arrived at Preston Primary School in the little black number from Zara, Craig had stared at her in surprise.

'You're pretty dressed up for a school thing.'

But then his face softened with pity and Vanessa could tell that he was thinking this was a big night out for her these days. If only he knew! But then Lachie's teacher, Mrs Murcell, called them in and announced that, in her opinion, Lachie had oppositional defiant disorder. Vanessa could remember a time when that was just called being naughty, but if promoting naughtiness to a disorder made parents feel less responsible, she was all for it.

'The poor kid's probably just acting out,' Craig explained, practising the counsellor-speak he'd so helpfully learned from Natalie. 'He's been through a lot with the marriage break-up, and he's trying his hardest to be a big boy and look after his mum at a very vulnerable time in her life.'

And then Mrs Murcell looked at her with pity too, and Vanessa wondered how they'd react if she said, 'Can we wrap this up, guys? I want to have sex with my hot new boyfriend.' She swallowed a little guffaw and Mrs Murcell and Craig exchanged concerned looks.

'Vanessa? Are you okay?' asked Craig.

'Yeah, I'm fine.'

But as Mrs Murcell rabbited on about NAPLAN, Vanessa found herself fantasising about Marcus and Craig having a duel. It would be somewhere picturesque, like the grounds of the grand Victorian mansion, Ripponlea. She'd beg Marcus not to go through with it, but he'd insist on defending her from Craig's relentless concern for her feelings. He'd look amazing in breeches and boots with one of those white frilly shirts undone to his chest, and on the twentieth pace he'd leap around and shoot Craig right through the heart—and Natalie would be jogging past with her ponytail swinging and find Craig exsanguinating near the duck pond. Vanessa shook her head, startled by her bloodthirsty fantasy. Exsanguinating? Woah. No wonder Lachie had oppositional defiant disorder.

She turned into funky Flinders Lane and gazed up at the translucent Adelphi Hotel pool that protruded from the building high above the footpath. Did swimming laps give the guests vertigo? But there was no time to ponder that so she hurried on, and as she wove her way through the chic passers-by she realised she was starting to feel a bit glamorous and European—until she collided with someone.

'Oh. I'm sorry.'

'It's okay,' the young woman said, but then their eyes met and they both recoiled. Of all the gin joints in all the towns! It was

Amy Dunphy, the commissioning editor from Wax who'd denied receiving *Lost and Found Heart*. What were the odds? But then Vanessa remembered that Wax's office was in Flinders Lane. She'd been so ecstatic about seeing Marcus that it hadn't even occurred to her that she was in enemy territory.

'What are you doing here?' Amy asked suspiciously. 'The office is closed.'

'Relax, I'm just passing,' Vanessa said coldly, but then she saw Amy wince and noticed that the editor's face was a deathly white, and her hands were reaching up to cup her conspicuously swollen jaw. Was the poor girl in the grip of a dental disaster? 'Keep walking,' Vanessa told herself. 'What has Amy Dunphy ever done for you?'

'Are you okay?' she heard herself asking.

Amy eyed her warily. 'I'm fine.'

'Toothache?'

Amy shrugged—she could hardly deny it. In spite of everything, Vanessa couldn't help sympathising. There was nothing worse than a bad toothache. It was amazing to think that such a tiny part of the anatomy could cause such unbearable pain, but Vanessa had seen burly blokes weeping in agony in the dental chair.

'Can I have a look?'

Amy hesitated but acquiesced, and Vanessa peered inside her mouth. The gum around her lower-right second molar was super-inflamed—no wonder she was in such pain.

'Have you been to a dentist?'

Amy shook her head. 'I'm on a deadline—I had to work late. I've got an appointment tomorrow.'

'Tomorrow?' Vanessa grimaced. It looked to her like an abscess that couldn't wait. 'Have you taken anything?'

When Amy shook her head, Vanessa reached into her handbag and pulled out some painkillers, popping a couple out of their packaging. 'Here, have these. It'll take the edge off—I'm not trying to poison you, I swear.'

As Amy swallowed the tablets, Vanessa rang West Melbourne 24/7 Dental and used her influence to get Amy squeezed in. 'Thanks a million, Greg.' She hung up. 'He'll see you in forty-five minutes.'

Amy seemed torn between gratitude and resentment. 'Why are you being so nice to me? It's not like I'm suddenly going to tell the—I mean, remember receiving a manuscript that I never received.'

Vanessa gave her what she hoped was a slyly confident smile. 'It's okay, you don't have to remember, but you do have to give us your computer records—and I'm sure your computer will remember.'

'I wouldn't bet on it,' Amy mumbled.

What did she mean? Was she bluffing?

'Well, thank you,' she said ungraciously before Vanessa could pursue it, and she scuttled off and was quickly submerged in a sea of passers-by.

Vanessa decided not to mention the encounter to Marcus—it might put a crimp on their first official date. But she needn't have worried; Amy had already flown from her mind by the time she reached the gallery. Shyness pounced as she stopped outside. What if Marcus's friends didn't like her? But why wouldn't they? She pictured herself laughing wittily at the centre of a sophisticated conversation and felt a cold clutch of terror. Who was she kidding? She'd be lucky if she could string a sentence together. What if she embarrassed Marcus by standing there like a tongue-tied twerp?

She peeked into the gallery. The place was packed with people wearing black, so at least she'd got that much right, although most of them looked a lot more eclectic than her. Was that the word, *eclectic*? She'd google it later when her fingers weren't shaking too much for the keypad.

She fixed a smile on her face and stepped into the gallery's warmth. She removed her coat and scarf and tried to check out the paintings, but she couldn't see them through all the people who seemed to be looking at each other instead of the walls.

A young waiter with a Clark Gable moustache proffered a tray.

'Thank you.' Vanessa took a glass of champagne, resisting the urge to scull it in one gulp as she scoured the room for Marcus. She heard the velvet baritone of his laughter first, and then she turned to see him holding court among a group of affluent arty types. Her heart did a reverse somersault in the pike position. To borrow from her mum's lexicon, Marcus was a big hunk of spunk. He couldn't possibly be hers—there must be some mistake. She felt an irrational need to flee and started squeezing her way back to the door, but the sensible little voice inside her said, 'What are you doing? Don't be an idiot.' 'I can be an idiot if I want to,' Vanessa snapped back, but she knew the sensible little voice was right, so she forced herself to turn around, and she almost collided with Marcus.

'Vanessa? Where were you going?'

'Oh, I was just . . . um . . .'

'You weren't planning to run out on me, were you?' He looked more amused than annoyed.

'I was thinking about it,' she admitted, 'but I changed my mind.'

Marcus laughed. 'I'm glad to hear it. Hello, by the way. You look beautiful.'

He reached down and kissed her cheek. Vanessa would have preferred a kiss on the lips, but even that chaste peck made her feel so flustered that she could barely speak.

'Come and meet Pollyanna, the gallery owner.'

With his hand at the small of her back, Marcus guided her through the crowd to an elegant woman in her late fifties whose clothes were so fashionably shapeless that Vanessa couldn't quite tell if she was wearing a dress or a jumpsuit. She was chatting to a tattooed brunette with an asymmetrical haircut and a middle-aged man with black-rimmed glasses and a morose expression, wearing what seemed to be a skirt.

Vanessa tried not to feel intimidated. What would her mum say? 'Just believe that you're not intimidated and you won't be.' Problem was, she didn't believe it.

'Vanessa, this is Pollyanna Street, Michaeley Duggan and, of course, Dante Boseley, whose brilliant works are adorning the walls.' Marcus smiled smoothly. 'Vanessa Rooney.'

'Hi,' Vanessa managed.

So far so good.

Pollyanna, Michaeley and Dante looked her up and down with bemused expressions, and then Pollyanna's face lit up. 'Oh, Vanessa Rooney. I recognise you. You're the woman who's suing Charlotte! Marcus's client.'

'Yeah, that's me.'

'One and the same,' Marcus confirmed.

Vanessa waited for him to tell his friends that she was more than a client, but he didn't elaborate. Meanwhile, she saw Pollyanna and Michaeley exchange glances and Dante waved at someone over her shoulder.

'Have you written anything before?' Pollyanna asked.

'Not really, just essays at school.'

'And you're a dental assistant, aren't you?'

'That's right.'

'And have you always been a dental assistant?'

'Yeah.'

'So you haven't studied literature at a tertiary level?'

'What is this, the Spanish Inquisition?' Marcus interjected. 'Can you give the poor woman a second to sip her champagne?'

'You're right,' said Pollyanna. 'I'm sorry, Vanessa. Do you mind if I steal Marcus away for a moment?'

Yes, I do! Don't leave me alone!

'No, of course not.'

Marcus winked at her as Pollyanna led him off into the crowd, leaving Vanessa alone with Michaeley and Dante. The awkwardness was excruciating—she had to say something.

'Um, how long have you been an artist?' she ventured.

'How long have I *been* an artist?' Dante repeated.

Was there something wrong with the question?

'It's not as if a person suddenly decides to become an artist,' Michaeley explained patiently. 'You just are an artist. Or you're not.'

Vanessa wasn't sure that was true. Hadn't she decided to become an artist when she decided to write her novel?

'Deciding that you want to be an artist doesn't make you one,' Michaeley continued as though she'd read Vanessa's mind. 'But I'm using "you" in the general sense, so please don't construe it as specific.'

Right, I'll just construe it as a general insult then, thought Vanessa.

'Dante! What can we tell you? It's transcendent.'

An elderly couple pushed past her and pounced on Dante, and Vanessa found herself edged out of the group.

Thank goodness.

She took the chance to go to the bathroom and do a wee—her bladder always felt more nervous than she did. When she emerged, she spotted Marcus and Pollyanna and headed over to join them, catching the tail end of an exchange.

'Do you really think it's fair to take advantage of someone like Vanessa Rooney just to put the screws on Lotts?'

'I'm not taking advantage. Vanessa has a very strong case. Lotts did breach her copyright, and I'm going to prove it.'

'I believe you,' Pollyanna said disbelievingly. 'And, regardless, it's kind of you to bring her out for the night.' She turned and saw

Vanessa. 'Oh, Vanessa! I didn't see you there. We were just chatting about Dante's work. Have you been to an art gallery before?'

'Of course she's been to a gallery!' Marcus snorted. 'Have you?'

'Of course,' said Vanessa, wishing the scrutiny away. Meanwhile Dante rejoined them, along with a guy in tartan pants who looked a bit like a mosquito. 'It's been a while though, you know, with the kids and everything. I think the last exhibition I went to was a Ken Done retrospective.'

A sudden silence descended on the group and Vanessa was acutely aware of the deafening chatter from everywhere else in the gallery. What had she said?

But then Marcus chuckled. 'I think you'll find she's being ironic.'

I think you'll find I'm not, thought Vanessa. Why were they all staring at her?

'I love *your* paintings,' she said to Dante, desperate to change the subject.

'Yes, Dante cites Ken Done as his primary inspiration,' chipped in the guy who resembled a mosquito.

Pollyanna laughed but Dante glowered, and Marcus looked distinctly unamused.

Pollyanna took Vanessa's hand. 'We shouldn't make fun. I'm sorry.'

'No, you shouldn't,' Dante said darkly. 'She has every right to execrable taste in art. If she wasn't a bogan you'd call it postmodern.'

A bogan? Vanessa bristled.

'And so what if she thinks she wrote that book? You're forgetting that I've struggled with mental illness too. It's not just the province of the great unwashed.'

Where did this guy get off?

'I'm not mentally ill,' she protested, but he turned his accusatory gaze on her.

'How are we going to conquer the stigma if the people who have it won't even own it?'

'Vanessa does not have a mental illness,' Marcus cut through, 'with all due deference to those who do. Those were just lies spread by Charlotte to distract attention from her own egregious behaviour.'

'Marcus!'

A woman with a pixie cut was tapping Marcus on the shoulder. Vanessa heaved a sigh of relief.

The woman's name was Lucia Something-or-Other. Apparently, she was a jewellery designer. Vanessa was feeling tongue-tied after the Ken Done incident, but luckily that wasn't an issue because Lucia Thingamabob was showing no interest in her whatsoever. She'd been chatting to Marcus for fifteen minutes and had barely registered Vanessa's presence. Marcus gallantly tried to bring Vanessa into the conversation, but it never stuck, until a woman called Alice joined them. Apparently, Alice was a 'foodie', but Vanessa thought she must only sniff the food because she looked like she hadn't eaten in months. Vanessa sucked in her tummy, feeling doubly self-conscious because Alice was wearing an original Alexander McQueen dress that had likely served as the inspiration for her own Zara knock-off. When Alice realised that Vanessa was wearing the Zara version, she was full of praise.

'More fool me, paying a fortune for the real thing,' she said with a sideways glance at Lucia. 'Good for you!'

'Thanks,' said Vanessa, though it sure didn't sound like a compliment.

They stayed so long that the crowd thinned, and Vanessa could actually see Dante's paintings. She was relieved to find that she liked them, which meant that technically she hadn't been lying.

'Shall we make a move?' Marcus suggested finally.

Thank God! thought Vanessa. They went to farewell Pollyanna, and the gallery owner pulled Vanessa into a hug.

'Good luck with the case. If anyone can convince a judge to ignore all logic, it's Marcus.'

Do your worst, Vanessa thought. I've been patronised by much bigger dickhids than you.

'Thank you,' she said aloud.

Pollyanna and Marcus kissed goodbye.

'Give Ivy my love.'

'Actually, Ivy and I have parted ways.'

Pollyanna raised her eyebrows. 'Really?'

'Don't look so excited, there's no intrigue—we were just on different paths.'

'Different paths? That's what they all say. Come on, spill. What happened?'

Vanessa waited for Marcus to explain that he'd broken up with Ivy for her, but he just gave Pollyanna another quick hug and said lightly, 'Wouldn't you like to know? Great show, congratulations,' and then he led Vanessa out of the gallery. She was hoping he might take her hand, but he guided her out by the small of her back again, exchanging farewells with glamorous stragglers who urged him to call them for a catch-up.

When they finally emerged onto Flinders Lane, Vanessa felt like she needed a shower. As she searched for words, Marcus spoke.

'You probably gathered they're full of shit.'

Her eyes shot to his face and found him smiling. She felt a rush of relief.

'I don't know what you're talking about,' she quipped. 'I've never met more down-to-earth people.'

Marcus laughed and Vanessa was thrilled by the conspiratorial moment.

'They're not such a bad bunch when you get to know them.' They turned the corner and he took her hand. 'Allow me to walk you back to your car.'

'Thanks. Would you like a lift home?'

'I thought you'd never ask.'

As Vanessa pulled up outside Marcus's apartment block twenty minutes later, her shyness came flooding back. What was the protocol? Should she keep the Corolla idling? If she turned it off would it seem presumptuous? But even as she angsted over her options, Marcus reached past her and turned the key, killing the engine. He pulled her into his arms and gave her a soft kiss that sent her world spinning. She kissed him back, and soon they were pashing like a couple of kids. Marcus took her hand and held it against his cheek, which felt surprisingly smooth.

'See? I shaved extra-close for you. No more pash rash.'

Vanessa giggled. They kissed hungrily.

'Come inside . . .'

'I can't—it's a school night. I have to be there for the boys in the morning.'

'Just five chaste minutes for a cup of tea; I won't touch you,' he promised, his hands expertly cupping her breasts.

'I can't,' she murmured, hoping he wouldn't be annoyed. 'I'm sorry.'

'No, don't be . . .' Marcus pulled away with a playful groan. 'I was just trying it on. But I'd better go inside before I take you hostage.'

Vanessa laughed, but even as he reached for the door she could already feel herself missing him, and despite his kisses she couldn't help fretting. Why hadn't he revealed that they were a couple? Unless they weren't actually a couple . . . Maybe she'd built this up into something it wasn't? Was it just a casual fling?

She'd almost convinced herself she was fine with that when Marcus said, 'You probably noticed that I didn't announce our relationship.'

'Kind of.'

'It's difficult.' Marcus frowned. 'It'd be construed as unethical because you're a client. And the media and online trolls would have a field day—which wouldn't be good for your case, obviously.'

No, of course not. Vanessa nodded glumly. She'd been so caught up in the lust and excitement, but Marcus was making perfect sense. She couldn't subject the boys or herself to that kind of scrutiny again.

'But . . .' he continued.

There was a but? Vanessa held her breath.

'It's probably selfish of me, but I can't stop thinking about you . . . So if you're happy we keep it under our hats, I'd like to pursue this regardless.'

Swoon!

Vanessa leaned over and kissed him.

'It's our secret.'

Chapter 30

DAVE

The August gathering of the Romance Readers' Club was underway in a tiny living room bathed in beige, and six elderly ladies were staring at Dave with eager anticipation.

'Well? What did you think?' asked Mrs Hipsley, who was clearly on tenterhooks. 'Did it answer your questions, love?'

Dave hesitated. A grandfather clock chimed in the corner and Mrs Hipsley's bald friend Myra seemed to have forgotten the lamington that was lifted halfway to her lips. How could he avoid hurting their feelings? They wanted so badly to help him—and, after all, it had been his idea to join the Romance Readers' Club. In a fit of desperation, he'd thought it might help him learn to finally understand women (i.e. Vanessa). The only thing he hadn't factored in was actually reading the novels, and now he'd lost five hours of his life consuming *Passion at Pasadena Ranch*, a tome about a rich horse rancher that read like a pile of equine excrement from start to finish.

'Yeah, some of them,' he said, choosing his words carefully. 'But the rancher, that Kurt Devereaux bloke, he's pretty arrogant, don't you reckon?'

The ladies exchanged indulgent glances and Dave discreetly wiped his brow. The heating was turned up so high that he thought he might expire.

'Of course Kurt's arrogant,' said Myra. 'Sexy men are always arrogant. That's what makes them so sexy.'

The others nodded enthusiastically. Mrs Turner, who must be eighty-five if she was a day, gave Dave a disconcertingly lascivious wink.

'So all you have to do is act like a prick?' Dave asked. 'Sorry, I mean a cad?'

'But they're not really cads,' Mrs Hipsley explained. 'They've got hearts of gold beneath their brash exteriors. And you've got a heart of gold, so you're halfway there.'

'I just have to work on my brash exterior.'

'And your bank balance!' chimed in Gwen, an octogenarian who resembled Humpty Dumpty with a perm. 'Romantic heroes are always rich.'

The other ladies nodded.

Dave suppressed a twitch of irritation. 'But that's not fair, we can't all be rich.'

'Of course not,' Mrs Hipsley assured him—without much conviction, in his opinion. 'A man doesn't have to be rich to be sexy.'

'Confidence is more important than money,' Myra declared.

They all turned to listen. As hostess and book club founder, it seemed she was deferred to as the expert.

'You just need to be confident, David. If you like a girl, just sweep her up into your arms and kiss her before she knows what's hit her.'

Bloody hell, thought Dave. Where had she been for the last fifty years?

'But if you don't ask first, it's sexual assault.'

'No, it's not. Only if the man who didn't ask isn't sexy.'

The other old dears nodded their agreement. Dave was appalled. So much for the post #MeToo era. He tried to reassure himself that these ladies were products of their generation—it's not like anyone under seventy shared their views. But then he remembered Dr Nob in Vanessa's book, and the ecstatic look on her face when Stafford had manhandled her in the office. He fought off a fog of despair.

'So that's what makes a man sexy? Sweeping a woman into his arms?'

'Yes, in spite of her protests.'

'In spite of her protests? So now you're saying that no means yes?'

'Oh yes.'

'Of course it does.'

'Absolutely.'

Then they all nodded sagely as Myra added, 'Depending on who the man is.'

What?

'Oh yes, it's very important who the man is,' Mrs Turner concurred. 'If the wrong man did it, I'd have him arrested.'

⁓

Dave was more confused than ever when he arrived back at the office. Ms Izetbegovic was engrossed in her computer screen. Was she actually working? It was possible, wasn't it? Dave wondered if she was writing a follow-up email after his fruitless attempts to make Charlotte Lancaster's lawyer Mike Schwartz comply with discovery. Of course she is, Dave. And that thing in the corner with a sparkly horn is a unicorn.

In profile Ms Izetbegovic's face looked even flatter than usual, but there was no denying that she was an attractive woman—albeit in a shit-scary kind of way. It was weird that after all this time he still didn't know if she had a boyfriend. He tried to imagine what he might be like. A broad, stoic Balkan who'd saved her during the Bosnian War? Or maybe she'd saved him? Get with the feminist program, Dave. Did they eat pickled cabbage together and carefully keep their chat to pleasantries, avoiding any references to their traumatic past? Or maybe there was no boyfriend? Maybe she was single and that was eHarmony on her computer? Dave wondered if she was typing in her requirements:

He must be rich and up himself, must race me off without asking permission.

But did Bosnian women want that too? Surely the elderly Anglo ladies didn't speak for every woman in the world.

'Ms Izetbegovic?' he said, against his better judgement.

She glanced up irritably. 'Yes?'

'If I swept you into my arms and kissed you, what would you do?'

'I'd call the police.'

Dave chuckled. 'Fair enough. I wouldn't blame you.'

He felt relieved. Of course not all women wanted to be manhandled. That was just a tiny subsection of the female community who were unhealthily obsessed with romance novels.

'But if someone else did it,' Ms Izetbegovic added, 'someone sexy, then that would be different.'

Dave grinned bleakly. He'd asked for that.

He slid some coins into the Seeing Eye Dog and headed for his office. As he passed Ms Izetbegovic's desk he saw that she was watching a lava lamp on eBay.

'It's two-thirty, Ms Izetbegovic. Your lunch break is over.'

'But the auction ends in eleven minutes.'

'I'm sorry, that's not my problem. I want you off eBay now.'

She ignored him.

'Ms Izetbegovic—'

The door opened, interrupting them, and Dave turned to see his ex-wife Evanthe. She was carrying Nickie's puffer jacket and looking stunning. He felt a flash of crankiness. Evanthe had decided that she was a lesbian, so the least she could do was look like one. Yes, of course he knew that lesbians came in all shapes and forms and some of the most glamorous women in the world were gay, blah blah blah, but did she have to turn up at his office with her hair hanging softly around her shoulders and wearing that black thing he'd always liked that hugged her Grecian curves? His ex-wife couldn't look more feminine, and frankly Dave thought that was unfair. It was high time she cut her hair short and invested in a pair of sensible sandals.

'David,' she greeted him pleasantly.

'Evanthe,' he pleasanted back.

Meanwhile, Ms Izetbegovic leaped to attention and clicked out of her eBay screen, but she wasn't quick enough to fox Evanthe, who was already standing behind her.

'Ms Izetbegovic. Still a diligent employee, I see.'

Ms Izetbegovic coloured, grabbing a file and opening it industriously.

Dave had often wondered why his PA was so scared of Evanthe when his own wrath had no effect on her. But, then, she'd never experienced his wrath, so that probably had something to do with it. He caught a small triumphant smile on Evanthe's lips and his ire rose. Who was she to tell Ms Izetbegovic off? His PA was none of her business anymore.

'Actually,' he said childishly, 'Ms Izetbegovic's watching a lava lamp on eBay and the auction's about to end. Log back in, Ms Izetbegovic.'

She looked at him like he was the most pitiful person on the planet.

'Go on. I'm your boss and I want you on eBay now.'

Ms Izetbegovic rolled her eyes but obliged.

Evanthe took the high ground, refraining from comment. She held out Nickie's puffer jacket. 'Nickie left this at home.'

'Thanks.'

He reached for the jacket but she didn't let go.

'Can I come in for a couple of minutes? I'd like a quick chat about the September holidays.'

Dave's brow darkened. 'All right.'

Evanthe followed him into his office, and as soon he'd moved some files so she could sit, she announced that she was speaking at a conference in Paris next month. Needless to say, she and Vicki thought it would be a wonderful opportunity to take Nickie with them and introduce her to the French capital, especially since she was doing so well in French at school. Of course, Nickie was technically scheduled to spend the September holidays with Dave, but they were hoping that he wouldn't mind swapping.

'But that's only six weeks away, and I've already booked the caravan park in Merimbula,' Dave heard himself say petulantly.

'We'll reimburse you for the deposit. I understand it's disappointing, but you can have two extra weeks with her at Christmas. That's fair, isn't it?'

Yeah, but Dave didn't feel inclined to admit it. He'd been planning to take Nickie to Paris himself next year, but trust Evanthe to get in first. She was a high-flying insurance broker but he'd never been threatened by her success until they'd divorced and she'd started using her jetsetting lifestyle like a weapon.

'Well?'

'Of course she can go,' he acquiesced ungraciously. 'As if I'd let her miss out.'

'Thank you, David.'

She smiled at him, secure in the knowledge that she'd won again. Evanthe, always Miss Smartypants. Sorry, Ms Smartypants. Dave wondered where he could take Nickie next year instead. Rome? New York? London? They were all good options, but they weren't Paris. Nickie was a budding Francophile and he'd pictured them strolling along the Left Bank in berets while munching baguettes, taking 'selfies' atop the Eiffel Tower, practising their French in chic cafes and yelling, 'Bravo!' at top-flight French football matches. But now Evanthe and Vicki were going to give his daughter that formative, once-in-a-lifetime experience, because Evanthe was still intent on punishing him.

'Why are you so determined to beat me? Is this still about the downpipe?'

Evanthe threw her hands in the air. 'Not the downpipe again. Don't you think that blaming a downpipe for our marriage break-up is a tad simplistic?'

'I'm not blaming the downpipe for everything, but it's emblematic, isn't it? How could we have spent hundreds of dollars on a romantic weekend when the gutters were clogged? It didn't make sense. We spent the weekend together at home anyway, and we got a new downpipe. Everyone won.'

'For goodness' sake! It was about so much more than that stupid downpipe!'

Dave did a double take. Evanthe rarely lost her cool. He watched as she carefully recomposed herself.

'Can we not get hung up on this?' she said, as though she were speaking to a preschooler. 'You were wrong for me on so many levels. I needed someone with . . . with a . . .' She paused as she searched for the word.

'Vagina?' Dave offered helpfully.

'Actually, I needed someone with balls.'

That stung. Advantage: Evanthe.

As Dave tried to regroup, she picked up a hand-knitted tea cosy from his desk. It was red with green leaves on top, a woollen strawberry, courtesy of client Mrs Kerslake.

'I see nothing's changed. Who made you this?'

Dave snatched it from her and put it in his drawer. 'Frankly, Evanthe, that's none of your business.'

So this was what his life had come to: hiding tea cosies. He wanted to hit his head on the desk.

'Whoever she was, did she pay you with money or just with the tea cosy?'

Dave didn't answer that question on the grounds that it might incriminate him, but Evanthe had already turned her attention to Mrs Hispley's doll's house. She raised her Smartypants eyebrows at him. And then, Murphy's law, a breeze wafted through the window and blew one of Mrs Zhang's handwritten letters right into her lap. Dave tried to grab it but she got there first. He squirmed as she read it but, surprisingly, she softened.

'David, I know how guilty you felt about your mum, but she's dead now. It wasn't your fault. You don't have to keep looking after her.'

Dave felt like a wrecking ball had just slammed into his stomach. 'I'm not trying to look after my dead mother.'

'Aren't you? Then what's happened to you? When we met you were going to save the world, but someone looks at you with sad little eyes and you save their guinea pig instead.'

It was vintage Evanthe, thinking she knew everything about him. Dave jumped up and snatched Mrs Zhang's letter back. 'I appreciate the helpful insights, but you seem to forget that the bulk of my clients are still in the workforce and pay me with actual currency. Now, if you don't mind, I'm busy.'

Evanthe nodded. She stood up and turned to leave, but she paused at the door. 'I know you fear change, David, but I read this very apt quote from George Eliot, who wrote *Middlemarch*. Actually, her real name was Mary Anne Evans,' she clarified, as if Dave gave a stuff. 'Anyway, she said, "It's never too late to be the person you might have been."'

'So many pearls of wisdom, Evanthe. You'll have enough for a necklace soon.'

Evanthe was too dignified to get into a childish slanging match, so she just gave him a weary look and walked out the door.

Dave paced around his office in agitation. His ex-wife had turned into such a snob. It was all very well for a corporate high flyer to be dismissive of elderly people at the bottom of the pecking order, but they deserved representation just as much as anyone else. And Evanthe thought she knew everything about him, but she knew nothing. Scared of change? What a load of crap! She'd been reading too many self-help books—or maybe it was Vicki's influence? Well, Vicki could take a flying leap off one of those cliffs she loved to abseil down.

He sat at his desk. And as for that stuff about still trying to look after his mum; well, he could do without the two-dollar psychoanalysis. He picked up a conveyancing file and opened it, but his eye caught something underneath—*Vanessa Rooney vs Charlotte Lancaster and Wax Publishing Pty Ltd*. He considered it for a moment and then snatched up the phone and rang Mike Schwartz's office. When Mike came on the line, Dave heard himself sounding like somebody else.

'Mike, I'm not putting up with this stalling any longer. I want Amy Dunphy's computer, Charlotte's early drafts of *Love Transplant*, all relevant email trails, text messages, Skype chats, and everything else I've asked for. If I don't receive them within the week, I'll file an injunction.'

It felt good.

Chapter 31

VANESSA

As Vanessa dipped the instruments into the ultrasonic tank, she was immersed in thoughts of Marcus. Today was 3 September, and that made it their 'twomonthiversary', if you bought into that silly kind of thing. Which she did. Last night she'd almost made him a funny little card, but then she'd decided against it. Not because he wouldn't laugh, but because she didn't want him to think that she was needy or expecting too much, even though she was both. She'd decided just to play it cool and see if Marcus brought up their twomonthiversary, which she knew he wouldn't.

Oh well.

It still blew her mind that she and Marcus were a bona fide couple. They had a shared history now—a short one, admittedly, but you had to start somewhere. They'd accumulated eight weeks and two days of happy memories, and they'd even weathered storms together. Tropical Cyclone Lachie mostly, but that was her fault—she'd pushed too hard in her desperation for Marcus and the boys to bond. It still made her cringe when she thought about the first time Marcus came over for lunch.

'Marcus, this is Jackson and Lachie! Boys, this is Marcus!' she'd shrieked.

'G'day, fellas.'

'Hi.'

'Hey.'

The intros were followed by a half-second lull in the conversation, and she'd pre-emptively over-compensated.

'Marcus is from WA!'

'Jackson plays soccer for the Redbacks!'

'Lachie got twenty-six out of thirty for his project on Australia's First People!'

'Marcus had a skateboard when he was a kid!'

'Jackson doesn't like broccoli either!'

'Lachie's best friend's dad is a lawyer!'

They were all staring at her like stunned mullets, and that was when she realised how uptight she was. Take a chill pill, she'd urged herself. This is hardly helping the situation. Hurry up and relax!

Over lunch, Marcus made a valiant effort with the boys, but he was rewarded with monosyllabic replies. Vanessa had expected as much from Jackson, but even chatterbox Lachie refused to contribute more than a grunt. Thank goodness Marcus's manners were impeccable. His attention drifted occasionally, but that was understandable for a man without kids, and he only checked his Twitter feed once.

'Hey, Mum said we weren't allowed to have our phones at the table 'cause it's bad manners,' Lachie said, scowling.

So now you come out of your shell? she thought.

'Lachie.'

'No, he's right. I stand corrected.' Marcus grinned and passed his phone to Vanessa. 'Here, I'll consider this confiscated.'

Vanessa laughed loudly and hoped the boys would join in, but they just looked at her like she'd lost the plot, and frankly she couldn't blame them. She found herself torn between wanting lunch to last forever and wishing she had a fast forward button so she could find out what they thought of Marcus.

She didn't have to wait long—the front door had barely closed when Lachie delivered his verdict: 'He's a tool.'

Vanessa's heart sank. 'A tool? Why would you say that?'

'Because he's a dick. He's up himself.'

'You can't tell over one lunch. You just haven't got to know him yet. Jackson, what do you think? Did you like him?'

'Yeah, he's awesome.'

Vanessa felt so grateful that she let the 'awesome' pass.

'See? You just have to give him a chance, Lachie. Please?'

'All right,' Lachie said sulkily.

'Thank you, sweetheart.'

She was sure they'd all hit it off the next time, but after two more outings things didn't improve, and when Marcus dropped them home from a tenpin bowling excursion, Vanessa heard a hushed altercation.

'You're a liar,' Lachie accused Jackson. 'Why do you pretend you like him?'

'Don't you want Mum to be happy?'

'But you said he's a wanker.'

'No, I said he *seems* like a wanker, but maybe he isn't. There must be some reason Mum likes the guy.'

Vanessa had fretted for days. Even if, as she hoped, the boys were motivated by loyalty to Craig, was she being selfish for pursuing this relationship with Marcus?

'That's crazy talk,' Joy said vehemently.

'But the boys don't like him. Maybe I should end it?'

Joy was aghast. 'You'll do no such thing! The boys have just got their noses out of joint because they don't have you all to themselves anymore. They'll come around.'

Vanessa desperately wanted to believe her. 'Do you really think so?'

'I know so.' And then Joy had grasped Vanessa's arms and stared intensely into her eyes. 'Nessie, you've been waiting your whole life for your knight in shining armour, and I will not allow you to throw this happiness away. Do you hear me?'

'Yes, Mum.'

Vanessa was relieved to be absolved of her guilt, and her mum's promise proved prophetic, because the next time Marcus dropped around, Lachie and Jackson appeared with a football.

'Hey, Marcus, want to have a kick?'

'You bet,' said Marcus.

'Sweet,' said Jackson.

Vanessa pretended it was no biggie, but as she watched the three men in her life kick the footy around her nondescript backyard, she was singing inside. It was just a shame that Marcus couldn't kick for long because he was wearing Christian Louboutin Oxfords.

'I'll come properly shod next time,' he promised the boys.

'Sweet.'

'Cool.'

Vanessa couldn't help wondering if her mum was behind her sons' change of heart, but Joy denied it, and Vanessa didn't press the point. She was hoping that the more Marcus stayed over, the more the boys would grow to like him, but his overnight visits hadn't panned out. Vanessa felt uncomfortable making love—they were only one thin wall away from Lachie—and even just flirty hi-jinks could prove tricky. Once, Marcus had bailed her up against the wall in a sexy 'I'm not taking no for an answer' way and silenced her laughing protests with a kiss, but when they came up for air they saw Jackson watching, which was embarrassing for all concerned.

And then there was Daisy. She resented having her place on Vanessa's bed usurped and she growled at poor Marcus constantly. He'd tried to bond with her at first, but he wasn't really a dog person, and Daisy refused to like him. When Vanessa started putting Daisy outside the bedroom door, she almost decided that she didn't like Vanessa either, and Vanessa was forced to bribe her with treats to win back her love the next morning.

Thank goodness things were blessedly uncomplicated with Joy. Her mum welcomed Marcus with open arms and Marcus humoured her saucy double entendres. 'Are you a *leg* man or a *breast* man?' Vanessa recalled Joy asking him as he carved a recent Sunday roast.

'Wouldn't *you* like to know?' Marcus chuckled.

'Would I ever.' Joy leaned forward provocatively until her breasts were brushing her dinner plate. Her new boyfriend Keith (Joy's nicest beau ever, in Vanessa's opinion) chuckled along amiably.

'What about you, Keith?' Marcus had asked. 'Are you a leg man or a breast man?'

'I'm a Joy man,' Keith said with unfiltered adoration.

He's so sweet, Vanessa thought, and Joy rewarded him with a kiss.

So although moments like that were lovely, they were rare, and soon Marcus was suggesting that they spend more time at his place. It made sense, but Vanessa pined for the boys and Daisy. Pets weren't allowed in the building and Jackson and Lachie said Marcus's apartment was boring without their Xbox—but when Vanessa offered to buy them a second Xbox, they demurred. Can kids demur? Is it possible to do something when you don't know what the word means? Regardless, the Xbox at Marcus' place never happened and, in truth, Marcus seemed relieved.

Vanessa reassured herself that introducing a new partner after a divorce was an emotional minefield—everyone knew that. She was sure it was nothing they wouldn't all work through in time, and the moments she spent alone with Marcus made all the challenges worthwhile. He was the smartest, funniest, most fascinating man she'd ever met, and his touch still inflamed her every time. She loved how he took her to intimate, out-of-the-way restaurants and they held hands in the dark at arthouse movies. The secrecy gave things extra spice, because even now no one in Marcus's world knew about her—except for his lovely mum, Shirley.

Vanessa had been nervous about meeting Shirley at first, but she needn't have worried, because they'd hit it off straight away. Shirley was a sweetheart who loved to tell adorable stories about Marcus as a little boy. It was touching to see how close mother and son were, but Vanessa was surprised that they spent so much of Shirley's visit cooped up in Marcus's apartment.

'Why don't you take your mum out on the town?' she'd suggested one night.

But Marcus shook his head with a little-boy smile. 'I'd rather keep her all to myself.'

Shirley beamed at Vanessa delightedly and Vanessa beamed back, but inwardly she felt bemused. It sounded like Marcus was making excuses not to go out with Shirley, but it wasn't like his mum was a secret too. Surely?

She glanced at her watch. Marcus should be calling her from the Federal Court at any minute—Charlotte's lawyers were dragging the chain and Dave had applied for an injunction to force them to comply with discovery. A wistful pang intruded at the thought of Dave. Something had changed in the past little while and he was no longer his warm and jokey self. At first, she'd wondered if he disapproved of her and Marcus blurring professional lines, but he didn't know they were dating, so it couldn't be that. It was a mystery—as if Dave had just woken up one day and decided, 'I'll be courteous to Vanessa, but nothing more.' She'd tried to convince herself that he was just preoccupied with work, but that didn't explain why he was still laughing it up with everyone else. The Redbacks' parents were elated right now because the team had made it to the semi-finals. Vanessa wished she could feel as pumped as everyone else, but Dave's new coolness was causing her surprising twinges of sadness.

As she pulled on her visor, Kiri appeared with a long-term patient. 'Hey, Niss, here's Cheryl.'

'Hi, Cheryl. How have you been? Come and take a seat on the Throne of Terror.'

Cheryl laughed as she lowered herself into the dental chair. She was a big lady and she only just managed to fit between the two armrests.

'I love your haircut.'

'Thanks.' Vanessa smiled, patting her sleek new bob. It was Marcus's idea, and he'd insisted on footing the bill for Jaymes at DisTressed.

'It looks fantastic, doesn't it?' Cheryl said to Kiri.

Kiri shrugged. 'I liked her curls better.'

She *would* say that, Vanessa thought as she fastened Cheryl's bib. Kiri had taken a set against Marcus right from the start, and Vanessa couldn't help resenting it. Kiri hated Craig's guts, so surely she should be happy that Vanessa had found somebody else—especially somebody so amazing and so generous. Not only had Marcus shouted her the haircut, he'd taken her shopping for new designer outfits that she could never have afforded herself. Of course, she'd refused at first. The sensible little voice inside her had said, 'What's wrong with the clothes you've already got?' But Marcus insisted that he just wanted to do something special for her, and she'd melted when he added, 'You're already gorgeous, but a bit of nice packaging never hurt.'

You couldn't argue with that.

Anthony entered in his surgical gear. 'Okay, ladies, let's get this party started.'

Vanessa shook herself out of her reverie and got stuck into the reconstruction of Cheryl's right bicuspid.

Chapter 32

DAVE

Dave glanced over at Stafford, who was heading for the Federal Court coffee shop with opposing counsel Graham Goetze. The two of them had just waved their dicks at each other in court like alpha teenagers in a playground, but Dave was prepared to give Goetze a pass because he'd won the village of Efoki in PNG millions of bucks in that famous case against Attwood Industries. So Graham Goetze had a social conscience. Did Stafford? Dave wasn't sure, but he supposed it didn't strictly matter. As they disappeared around a corner with their robes flapping behind them, Vanessa answered his call at the other end.

'Hello? Dave?'

'Hi, yeah, it's me,' he said politely. 'How are you, Vanessa?'

'I'm good, thanks. How about you? Are you at court?' She sounded anxious.

'Yeah.'

'Is it finished?'

'Yeah, that's why I'm calling.'

'Oh. Um, is Marcus there?'

Dave tried not to feel slapped. 'No, he's gone.'

'Oh.' She sounded crestfallen. 'I was kind of expecting *him* to ring.'

Of course she was. Why would she want Dave to call when Loverboy was in the vicinity? Bitterness bit at him. 'I think he's been called off on another case. But I knew you'd be waiting to hear, so I thought I'd ring.'

'Thanks, Dave, that's thoughtful of you.' Her tone shifted and he sensed that she'd decided to make the most of her consolation prize. 'How did it go?'

'We won. They have to hand over the documents.'

'Oh my God, that's great! So Marcus talked the judge into it?'

'Yeah.'

The truth was, Stafford had just spoken to Dave's exhaustive research and preparation. He'd spent about ten minutes skimming Dave's work before prancing around in front of Justice Haultain, but there was no doubt that he was a quick study and a brilliant courtroom operator.

'That's so fantastic! I knew he'd do it.'

Did she have to sound so personally invested in Stafford's performance?

'And thank you too, Dave. I really appreciate all your hard work.'

It was nice to get a crumb of praise, because Dave was actually feeling pretty pumped. He wanted to tell her how Justice Haultain had singled him out after proceedings and complimented him on his well-prepared brief, but the sound of her voice was messing with his head, so he wound up the call instead.

As he turned to leave, Charlotte Lancaster's lawyer Mike Schwartz sauntered over. They exchanged professional smiles; no dick-waving here.

'Dave.'

'Mike.'

They shook hands. Mike seemed like a good bloke—as obstructive as he'd been, Dave knew he was only following instructions, and he was pretty impressed with the way Mike conducted himself. It seemed the feeling was mutual.

'It's a pleasure to go into battle with someone so professional. When this is all over, let's have a beer.'

Dave was chuffed but he played it cool. 'You bet. Your shout.'

Mike laughed. 'We'll see. We're still going to wipe the floor with you.'

'In your dreams. You blokes are done like a dinner.'

Mike chuckled and headed off, leaving Dave alone outside Federal Courtroom 8F with a growing sense of accomplishment. If you took his feelings for Vanessa out of the equation, things were looking up. Not only had he steered her case towards this positive turn, he'd also steered the Redbacks into their first semi-final match in seven years. He felt a buzz of anticipation as he thought about Saturday. The kids had worked their arses off to get here, but their opponents—the Western Tigers—were a nifty little unit, so Dave was trying to manage the Redbacks' expectations.

'If we lose, it won't be the end of the world,' he was saying.

'There's always next year,' he kept pointing out.

'It's just a game,' he was trying to remind them.

But who was he kidding? This semi-final felt like life and death to the kids—and to some of their parents, he suspected. He was pretty sure that Vanessa wouldn't fall into that category, but he knew she'd be there, as supportive as ever. He imagined her laughing with Kiri on the sidelines and waving her GO REDBACKS! sign. Why hadn't Stafford thought to ring and fill her in before taking a coffee break? After all, she was both his client *and* his girlfriend. Not that Dave was supposed to know that because, apparently, they both thought he was an idiot.

Chapter 33

VANESSA

With just four minutes left on the clock the Redbacks were one goal in front—and even though it was only a semi, the parents were holding their collective breath. Vanessa turned to Marcus with crossed fingers, but he was checking his Twitter feed.

Hmm.

She found his lack of engagement disappointing, but was that really fair? He could hardly be expected to be as emotionally involved as she was. She was being too judgemental, a trait she deplored in other people.

He glanced up and caught her eye. 'Oops, busted.'

Marcus pocketed his iPhone and she laughed. He put his arm around her and she snuggled in, glowing with smugness (let's call a spade a spade) as the other mums shot them envious glances. Arriving with Marcus today had done wonders for her ego. All the parents' jaws had dropped to the ground—even Vicki Wong and Dave's intimidating ex-wife Evanthe looked impressed. But, best of all, Craig had gawped like a stunned mullet, and when Vanessa introduced him to Marcus he could barely string a sentence together.

And Natalie had taken her aside to congratulate her on finally finding the courage to move on, but she'd sounded more peeved than positive. Stick that in your pipe and smoke it, Natalie! They say that revenge is a dish best served cold, but Vanessa was willing to bet that nothing could beat serving up a piping hot Marcus.

But while having him here was a boon for her confidence, somehow it also put her on edge. She couldn't help wondering what Dave was thinking. He'd been priming the Redbacks when they arrived, but surely he must have clocked by now that she and Marcus were a 'thing'. And what did her friends think of Marcus? Did they like him? Could they see how funny he was? She heard herself laughing too loudly as if to underscore the point, until Kiri leaned over and hissed, '*Chill*, Niss.' It was just the circuit breaker she needed, and by the time the Redbacks took to the oval she felt ready to focus on the match.

It had been raining on and off since last night, and the playing field was a mass of puddles. Vanessa experienced a wistful moment thinking how Daisy would have loved to leap in the mud, but Marcus didn't allow dogs in his Mercedes, which was fair enough.

Something pointy poked into her ribs, bringing her back to the moment. 'Ouch.'

It was Keith, opening an umbrella. 'Sorry, love. Are you okay?'

'I'm fine, Keith. All good.'

Keith was such a sweetie. Vanessa watched him stifle a yawn as he gallantly held the umbrella over Joy's head. As a newsagent, Keith was up at 'sparrow's fart' every day and Joy kept him up late every night, but he never complained. Vanessa had noticed a new calmness in her mum since she'd been with Keith, and the boys loved him for his corny dad jokes. They already thought of him as a proxy granddad, having never met their actual maternal granddad, Jack Spriggs. Vanessa felt a tug of wistfulness as she thought of her beloved father.

Suddenly there was a communal gasp as Kiri and Anthony's son Sam, the Redbacks' goalkeeper, jumped sideways to block a goal shot from the Tigers but failed. The ball hit the back of the net and the Tigers had evened the score! The Tigers parents jumped up and down in jubilation. The Redbacks parents clutched their foreheads and let out jagged breaths. Poor Sam looked like he wanted to die, and Kiri and Anthony yelled out encouragement.

'Never mind, Sam!'

'Better luck next time!'

But Sam ignored his parents and looked to Dave, who was leaping up and down on the sidelines.

'Good try, mate!' Dave called warmly. 'Come on, we've still got time. We're all in this together! Go, Redbacks!'

Vanessa watched Dave's nylon tracksuit pants flapping around his calves. Somehow he'd wrangled this pubescent rabble of wooden spooners into a cohesive team—no wonder the parents loved him for it. One of the mums, Heather, a no-nonsense type who baked delicious cakes and raffled them for fundraising, had even started a collection to buy Dave a present, and Vanessa was surprised to find herself feeling a bit proprietorial.

'I'll choose the gift if you like,' she'd offered.

'Thanks,' said Heather, 'but I'll do it. Me and Dave are great mates, and you two don't really talk much.'

Which was true these days, Vanessa had to concede glumly.

'So close and yet so far; that nearly gave me a myocardial infarction,' Marcus joked about Sam's miss. Then he added for Joy and Keith's benefit, 'That's a heart attack.'

'Hon, believe me, I know what a myocardial infarction is.' Joy winked. 'I've caused a few of them.'

Keith chuckled adoringly. 'I hope you don't give me one.'

'If I do, I'll give you the kiss of life.'

'How about you give me a little kiss right now?'

Keith reached down for a modest peck, but Joy grabbed him by his coat collar and turned it into a tongue wrestle. If it wasn't for the onfield action, Vanessa wouldn't have known where to look. Beside her, Marcus was smiling at Joy's antics, but was there a hint of disdain in his eyes?

No, surely not.

He leaned down to murmur into Vanessa's ear, 'Just think, in a few hours we'll be on the slopes.'

Vanessa felt a tingle of anticipation. 'Yeah.'

In the adrenaline rush of the game, she'd almost forgotten that Marcus was about to whisk her away for a romantic weekend at Falls Creek. Winter had dragged on this year and there'd been a late season dumping of snow. She couldn't wait—it had been a tough few days. Just twenty-four hours after their victory with the injunction Charlotte had announced her engagement to Ned Kasch, and in the flurry of gushing on TV and social media, everyone seemed to have forgotten about her plagiarism and theft in New York.

'Their stalling with discovery has paid benefits,' Marcus told Vanessa through clenched teeth. 'It's months now since we leaked the news, and we've lost our moral advantage.'

Vanessa wondered if Marcus's stress was partly due to Charlotte's engagement—which would be completely normal, surely? Hadn't she spent two and a half years dreading the same announcement from Craig and Natalie? But Marcus insisted that he didn't care, and he made love to her so ardently that it almost quelled her doubts.

'I was worried about the case, that's all,' he said softly as they lay in the afterglow. 'I don't want to fail you.'

'You won't.'

But for the first time Vanessa had felt a few qualms—not about Marcus losing the case, but what if his emotional turmoil over Charlotte destroyed his relationship with Vanessa? But she assured herself that wouldn't happen. They just needed this romantic break to forget about Charlotte for a few days and focus purely on each other. She pictured them curled up together on a sofa, drinking cognac in front of a roaring log fire. Vanessa didn't much like the taste of cognac, but that didn't impair her fantasy. She'd be wearing stretch jeans and the new cable knit jumper she'd bought from the Country Road sale.

Her reverie was cut short by the referee's piercing whistle. With thirty seconds on the clock, Nickie had been awarded a shot at goal. The parents exchanged agonised looks as Dave called from the sidelines, 'You can do this, sweetie—ah, mate.'

Vanessa and Kiri clutched hands as Nickie lined up the shot . . . kicked . . . and—yes! The Redbacks were back in front! The parents went bananas—their little wooden spooners were seconds away from making it into the finals!

Dave jumped up and down and ran around in little circles but managed to keep his voice calm. 'Well done, Nickie! Go, Redbacks!'

There was a bit more cursory kicking and a few noble attempts by the Tigers to keep the game alive, but twenty seconds later the whistle blew, and the Redbacks had won! The kids jumped up and down and hugged each other as jubilant mums and dads swarmed onto the field. Vanessa suspected that it was a disproportionate reaction to a semi-final win, but most of these kids had been playing together for five years and had never come this close to victory.

Dave was the centre of celebrations, and after he led three cheers for the Redbacks, Anthony led three cheers for Dave, and then the Redbacks tried to heave Dave up onto their shoulders but only succeeded in dropping him into the mud, where he lay laughing that funny honking laugh of his.

Vanessa chortled and snapped a photo. Then she turned to take a shot of Jackson and found him shyly high-fiving Nickie, his freckled face ablaze. A penny dropped belatedly. Of course! Jackson was tongue-tied around Nickie because he had a crush on her. Der, she thought. That took me a while. But did Nickie reciprocate Jackson's feelings? Vanessa couldn't tell. She hoped that Jackson wouldn't get hurt. Underneath all the grunts and pimples he was still a fragile little boy—not that you'd know it right now, because he was following the captain Tom McDonald's lead and piling on top of Dave. The pile-on turned into an exuberant mud wrestle, but Dave eventually made it out alive. He was dripping with mud and looked like the Creature from the Black Lagoon.

'Hey, let's go back to my place for a party. I'll serve Coca-Cola intravenously!'

Cheers went up as everyone declared that an excellent idea.

Vanessa turned to Marcus. 'Can we go? Just for ten minutes?'

But Marcus's smile had taken on a new edge—was it impatience?

'If Falls Creek wasn't a four-hour drive,' he replied with regret that didn't quite ring true, 'I'd love to, but I think we need to get on the road.'

Jackson pushed through the throng towards them. 'Mum? You're coming, aren't you?'

Vanessa experienced a flash of resentment at Marcus, but quickly repressed the feeling. It was good of him to come to Jackson's semi-final in the first place—it's not like a kids' suburban soccer match was his natural habitat. And he'd gone to all the trouble of booking this weekend away—she shouldn't be ungrateful.

'I'd love to sweetheart,' she said apologetically, 'but Marcus and I have a long drive ahead of us.'

Chapter 34

DAVE

Dave was so elated when the Redbacks won that he'd even hugged Evanthe's partner Vicki, who'd stiffened like a fence paling. He knew in his heart that all this jubilation was over the top for a semis win, but the kids would be up against the all-conquering Parkdale Panthers in the finals, so this was probably as good as it would get. Hence his impromptu party. But now that he'd given everyone his address, he was starting to wonder if he'd been too hasty. He only had a card table and four chairs, and he wasn't too sure what was in his fridge. Not much without sugar or some kind of appalling additive probably, and mums were so fussy about that stuff these days. He'd have to stop off en route and get some carrot and celery sticks.

'Hey, Dave?'

Dave turned to see Josh Fitzpatrick's mum, Heather. He liked Heather. She was one of those down-to-earth, sensible types who you could tell would be good in a crisis.

'Heather. What can I do you for?'

'How's your catering situation? I've got some cupcakes and mini sausage rolls left over from Lucy's birthday party. Do you want me to stop off at home and get them?'

'Thanks! That'd be sensational.'

'No probs. What about chairs?'

Cripes, was she psychic?

'I *am* a bit light on for chairs, actually.'

'No worries. I've got ten plastic ones and a big fold-up table from Bunnings. I'll bring those too.'

Dave beamed at her. 'You're a lifesaver, Heather—that'd be awesome. Why don't I follow you home and help you?'

'No, no need.' She waved off his offer. 'Josh is a big boy—he can help. You just get home and wash that mud off.'

'Okay, great. Thanks.'

She smiled and headed off to her car, having just confirmed his assumption that she'd be good in a crisis. Go, Heather. But he'd still get those carrot and celery sticks.

Evanthe and Vicki passed hand in hand and waved goodbye. They'd begged out of the celebration party, pointing out that they'd be spending quality time with Nickie in Paris in a couple of weeks.

'Of course! I'd forgotten all about that,' Dave said, and they exchanged long-suffering glances. He wondered what they'd say if he added, 'And by the way, you still owe me for the deposit on that caravan park in Merimbula.'

It was a relief that Evanthe and Vicki weren't coming, but Vanessa would be missed. She'd clearly wanted to join the party, but Stafford had other ideas, and Vanessa had caved so quickly that Dave felt disappointed in her. Not that he had any right to be, he supposed.

'Come on, you lot, hop to it,' he called to Nickie and Jackson and Lachie, who were getting a lift back to his place. He noticed Jackson sneaking sidelong glances at Nickie. He was obviously still sweet on her—and Nickie thought that no boy would ever find her pretty. Even in victory she was doing her usual trick of slumping self-consciously. 'You don't have to slouch, sweetie,' he wanted to tell her. 'Can't you see that Jackson's crazy about you regardless of how tall you are?' But, apparently, she couldn't.

He opened the car boot and threw an old picnic rug over Mrs Hipsley's doll's house, which was finally fully constructed.

'Chuck your stuff in here.'

As the kids tossed their bags into the boot, Anthony and his kids passed en route to their car, with Kiri bringing up the rear. They all heard a toot—Vanessa and Stafford were passing in Stafford's mud-splattered Mercedes.

'Bye!' Vanessa called out the window, blowing kisses to Jackson and Lachie. 'Love you! I'll call you later. Have fun.'

Dave detected a wistfulness in her tone, but Stafford's smile seemed perfunctory. The kids called out their goodbyes and the Mercedes sped away.

'Your mum's boyfriend is cool,' Dave heard Nickie say.

'You reckon?' Jackson asked earnestly.

'Yeah. He's awesome.'

So Stafford's charm spanned generations. Dave wasn't sure why he found that so irksome until Kiri sidled up to him and whispered, 'No, he's not. He's a dickhid.'

Dave laughed as he realised just how true that was. It was an odd feeling, like experiencing a sudden revelation of something he'd actually known all along.

The kids clambered into the car and Dave allowed himself a small smile as he thunked the boot shut.

'Yeah. He's a dickhid.'

Chapter 35

VANESSA

The Mercedes was purring up icy Bogong High Plains Road with chains on its tyres. Lights twinkled in Falls Creek, snug at the bottom of snowy peaks. Vanessa was so excited that she'd forgotten her disappointment about missing the semi-finals party. She'd only been to the snow once before and she'd barely conquered the baby slopes, but Marcus came every year, and although he played it down she knew he'd be a whiz on skis.

She gazed out the window as they turned into the village, passing snow-covered lodges with skis and snowboards piled up outside and skiers swaddled against the cold. An impossibly cute little girl in a beanie and snowsuit waddled past hand in hand with her mum. Snow gums bowed down, laden with white.

'It's so beautiful . . .'

Marcus smiled across at her but he still seemed preoccupied. He'd been his usual chatty self for most of the journey but in the past hour he'd fallen silent. Vanessa wanted to say, 'A penny for your thoughts,' but she worried that might sound too intrusive. And was she really so needy that she had to know what was going on in his head every minute? Of course she was, but he didn't need to know that.

Marcus turned into the highest street in Falls Creek and came to a stop outside the picturesque Summit Ridge Alpine Lodge.

Vanessa was captivated. 'We're staying here?'

Marcus smiled indulgently. 'Only the best for my Vanessa.'

His Vanessa. Her heart did a star jump.

Marcus glanced around the car park as though he was looking for something, but if he was, he didn't find it. He turned back and gave her a kiss. 'Shall we?'

⟋⟍

The view from their suite reminded Vanessa of a Monet snowscape that hung in the Smile Clinic waiting room. She suddenly felt overwhelmed and for reasons she couldn't quite name, her eyes filled with tears.

'Are you okay?' Marcus asked.

Vanessa nodded but she couldn't speak. He laughed softly and took her into his arms, which only added to her emotion. In a wild moment she wondered if her heart might burst right out of her chest. She pictured Marcus down on his hands and knees, mopping up her splattered gizzards and saying with a reassuring smile, 'It's okay, darling, my heart almost did the same thing.' She really should ring the boys and let them know she'd arrived safely, but it was so lovely here in Marcus's arms.

He tossed her down onto the king-sized bed and she surrendered to his caresses. Their kisses intensified and he started to unbutton her cardigan, but she forced herself to push him away.

'Wait for a sec . . . I have to Facetime the boys and let them know we're safely here.'

'You can do that later,' Marcus murmured, his hands roaming over her tingling torso.

'No . . . I don't want them to worry,' she said.

Marcus groaned but he rolled off her and, for a brief moment, Vanessa mourned his loss. Then she sat up and refastened her buttons.

'Do you want to talk to them too?' Her voice sounded more plaintive than she'd intended.

'I've got a couple of emails to return. Tell them I said g'day.'

I guess that means no, thought Vanessa.

Marcus blew her a kiss and climbed the stairs to the mezzanine level of their luxury suite. She watched his bum disappear—he had a great bum. 'Prime rump,' she'd say to him as she squeezed his buttocks, and it always made him laugh.

But enough about Marcus's buttocks.

She dialled Jackson's number and, when he and Lachie answered, they were still at Dave's place. 'Wonderwall' by Oasis was blaring and it seemed like the party was in full swing.

'Are you having a good time?'

'Awesome!' Lachie yelled through the din. 'I can say awesome if I want to, Mum. I'm an individual with my own opinions.'

Aren't you what, thought Vanessa. She heard shrieks of laughter and saw someone falling over in the background.

'Goodness! What's going on?'

'Oh, that's the grown-ups,' Jackson said in a 'what can you do?' kind of tone. 'Dave found this old game called Twister. It's got coloured spots and—'

'Yeah, I know it,' Vanessa said, hearing envy creep into her voice. 'It sounds like they're having fun.'

'Have you got FOMO, Mum?'

Vanessa knew from previous conversations that this meant Fear of Missing Out. 'Maybe a bit,' she admitted, and she realised she actually had quite a lot of FOMO. She heard more howls of hilarity. 'What's happened now?'

'Dave and Heather just fell on top of each other.'

⟿

Vanessa was wearing a red beanie with a big pompom and a puffy snowsuit that made her look like the Michelin Man, but she was having way too much fun to care.

'Oh my God . . .'

She laughed hysterically as she tried to put Marcus's instructions into practice, but her legs slid further and further apart until she was in danger of doing the sideways splits.

'Plough position!' Marcus laughed. 'Pigeon toes!' But to no avail—she'd already tumbled into the snow again. It was lucky the first thing he'd taught her was how to fall without breaking any limbs.

'Are you okay?'

'I'm fine.'

He stood over her with his hand extended, and as Vanessa squinted up at him, the soft sun shining behind him gave him a halo. St Marcus.

'I'm going to do snow angels,' she announced, and she lay on her back making 'wings' with her arms in the snow.

'How old are you?' Marcus teased.

'Old enough to be an angel, so back off, buddy.'

Marcus chuckled and when she'd made her 'wings', he helped her up. Her snowsuit was soaked and the chilly air was freezing her face, but Vanessa could barely remember a time when she'd felt so exhilarated.

'Jackson and Lachie would love this. We'll have to bring them next time.'

Marcus's smile briefly faltered before he said, 'Absolutely.' It cast a shadow over the moment. Didn't he want the boys to come? Or had she been too presumptuous? Maybe there wouldn't be a next time. But seconds later he was tweaking her pompom, and all was right with the world again.

'You've been so patient,' she said as she caught him glancing longingly at the ski lift. 'I don't want to hold you back anymore. Go and do your thing. I'm happy to hang around here.'

'Are you sure?'

'Of course.'

'All right, I'll be back soon. Just try to stay in one piece in the meantime.'

He disappeared up into the mist on the ski lift and Vanessa pootled around on the baby slopes with the other beginners, taking lots of selfies and scenery pics to send to the boys and Joy. Then she gingerly made her way to the bottom of a black run and watched Marcus speeding down the slope, zigzagging from side to side and sending snow flying like a skier at the Winter Olympics. She found it incredibly sexy and Marcus seemed to appreciate her reaction, because before she knew it they were back in their suite taking up where they'd left off.

Censored!

⌐

Vanessa changed into her new stretch jeans and Country Road cable knit jumper, neither of which looked as flattering as they had in her fantasy—but nothing ever did, did it? She decided to expedite her make-up, because although Marcus was allegedly reading a book, he kept sneaking covert peeks at his watch. A man in a hurry to take it easy. It reminded her of Craig lounging on the couch before a night out. He'd watch the footy with a beer while she brought the washing in off the line and ironed his shirt and fed Daisy and made the boys dinner and bathed them and got them ready for bed and prepared the babysitter a snack and wrote a note about Lachie's peanut allergy before eventually making it into the shower and snatching a few moments for her hair and make-up. Five minutes before they were due to leave, Craig would switch off the TV, jump in the shower and throw on the shirt that she'd ironed for him, and then he'd stand in the doorway harrumphing, 'Hurry up.' Not that Marcus was in Craig's league—for one thing, he was smart enough to hide his impatience. When she emerged from the ensuite he smiled and said, 'You look beautiful.'

'You don't scrub up too badly yourself,' Vanessa said, but at second glance his smile seemed distant and she could tell he was preoccupied again.

As they walked downstairs he strode ahead and Vanessa thought, Great, I love a romantic stroll in single file. So she was taken completely by surprise when they walked into the lounge and he suddenly pulled her into his arms and kissed her in front of everyone. As he released her, she felt flushed and radiant—until she turned to see Charlotte Lancaster and Ned Kasch staring at them from a couch in front of the open fire.

Charlotte was looking stunning in designer jodhpurs and a long cashmere jumper that hugged her slim but curvy frame, and she was curled into Ned, who radiated handsome hipster. Vanessa nearly died. She instinctively sucked her tummy in—why was that her response to everything? Charlotte and Ned looked as shocked as she was, but Marcus seemed unperturbed.

'Hello, Charlotte,' he said coolly. 'And Neville, isn't it?'

'It's Ned,' Vanessa whispered—but, der, he already knew that.

'Hi, Marcus,' said Ned, who seemed to be attempting civility.

But Charlotte was blatantly laughing as she looked between Marcus and Vanessa. 'You and her? You've got to be kidding.'

If Charlotte was trying to make Vanessa feel like poo on the bottom of her shoe, it worked. Vanessa's eyes searched the room for something to hide behind. But then Marcus put his arm around her and she was buoyed by the thought that at least somebody liked her.

'I don't see the joke.'

But as he pointedly pulled her close, Vanessa started to feel like a weapon, which proved just as unpleasant as feeling like poo. Charlotte smiled derisively and, even as Vanessa fantasised about punching her in the mouth, she couldn't help marvelling at her teeth. Why did Americans always have class I occlusion? It was lucky Anthony wasn't in practice over there—he might not make a living.

'That's pathetic, not to mention unethical. Are you really that desperate to get back at me?'

'Charlie . . .' Ned said warningly, but she ignored him.

'And what are you doing here, anyway? You know I've been coming to Falls on the last weekend of the season for over twenty years.'

Vanessa's stomach clenched. Was that true?

'I won't answer your calls or emails so you've followed me here, haven't you?' she sneered at Marcus as the diamond on her engagement finger glinted in the lamplight. 'You're a very sad man. I'd almost feel sorry for you if you weren't such a vindictive arsehole.'

Vanessa saw Marcus's nostrils flare, but his voice remained cool. 'How do I know *you* haven't followed *me*?'

Charlotte scoffed in disgust, but then she glanced around the lounge and seemed to check herself. Vanessa followed her gaze and saw other guests watching discreetly. Charlotte smiled for their benefit and muttered to Ned through gritted teeth, 'Let's go. I can't bear the sight of him.'

'It was terrific to run into you too,' Marcus said with more sarcasm than even Vanessa thought strictly necessary. 'We'll look forward to receiving all those early drafts of *Love Transplant* that Justice Haultain has ordered. Of course, that could be a tad problematic since those early drafts don't actually exist.'

Vanessa watched the colour drain from Charlotte's face as though someone had just flicked a switch.

'Enjoy your weekend, *Charlie*. Oh, and congratulations on your engagement.'

She stopped and eyeballed him. 'Thank you, and congratulations on your new relationship—it's very appropriate. What do they say? You can take the boy out of Kalgoorlie, but you can't take Kalgoorlie out of the boy.'

Marcus looked apoplectic and Vanessa hoped it was about Kalgoorlie and not about her.

'Shhh,' Ned urged Charlotte. 'Don't stoop to his level.'

'See you at dinner,' Marcus called with a twisted smile as they disappeared out the door.

Vanessa felt distinctly unsettled. What just happened? Had Marcus really known that Charlotte would be here? And had he been calling and emailing her?

As she tried to wrangle her emotions into lucid questions, he spoke first. 'Well, that was unfortunate.'

'Is it true? Does Charlotte come to Falls Creek on the last weekend of the season every year?'

'Of course not. Lotts is completely chaotic—she doesn't do anything at the same time twice.'

'Really?'

'Really.'

'And have you been calling and emailing her?'

'Of course I haven't.'

'But why would she lie?'

'I have no idea. Why would she plagiarise your book? It's a mystery. The woman's a law unto herself—I'm starting to think that she's actually evil.'

Vanessa considered that for a second. She'd love to believe that Charlotte was evil, but in reality she was probably just venal. And deceitful. And egotistical. And lots of other things ending in 'l'—but not evil.

'I don't think so. Evil is a very big word.'

'And she fills the two syllables out nicely,' Marcus said in a clipped tone. 'But I don't want to talk about her.' He softened and pulled Vanessa close. 'The only thing I know for sure is that you're worth a hundred of her, and I'm glad I'm here with you this year.'

He kissed her lingeringly and Vanessa threw her doubts into the fire and watched them evaporate into ash. Then Marcus took her hand and led her to a leather couch and they curled up together, just as she'd pictured them doing.

He studied the cocktail list. 'What would you like? A Sex on the Beach? A Screaming Orgasm? A Slippery Nipple?'

Vanessa laughed. 'You're making those up.'

She snatched the menu and of course he was. Marcus chuckled and Vanessa relaxed into him, feeling the knot in her chest dissolve. There was nothing to feel uneasy about.

'Excuse me, Stafford?'

Vanessa looked up to see Ned Kasch in front of them, his man bun tilted slightly to one side. Ned had the air of a person who didn't need to pretend to be calm and reasonable because he actually was calm and reasonable. Vanessa saw Marcus's eyes dart over his shoulder in search of Charlotte, but she was nowhere to be seen.

'Could I have a word in private?'

Marcus leaned back and draped his arms along the back of the couch in a gesture that Vanessa recognised as a 'power position' from magazine articles about body language.

'Anything you have to say to me, you can say in front of Vanessa.'

'Okay . . .' Ned turned to Vanessa. 'We haven't officially met, have we? Apologies. I'm Ned Kasch.'

He held out his hand. Vanessa was impressed by his impeccable manners under trying circumstances. She shook his hand. 'Hi, Ned. Vanessa Rooney. It's nice to meet you.'

Marcus shot her a peeved look when she said 'nice', but what was she supposed to say? 'It's horrible to meet you'? Good manners didn't cost anything.

Ned turned back to Marcus. 'I'm sorry about what happened. I know you were devastated when Charlie—Charlotte—left you, but wouldn't it be healthier for everyone if you just moved on, instead of pursuing these bogus breach of copyright claims?'

'Bogus? I can understand that you're blinded by love, Neville—sorry, Ned—but I've known *Charlie* for a damned sight longer than you. I know she stole Vanessa's book, and I know exactly why.'

Vanessa felt herself flinch. What? But Marcus had just assured her that he didn't have a clue why. She could see that Ned was perplexed too.

'So why don't you ask *Charlie* about that? And while you're at it, tell her that by the time I've finished with her, the world will know that she's a lying, talentless thief.'

Marcus's bile hung in the air and stained it. The sensible little voice inside Vanessa's head said, 'Any idiot could see that he's more focused on destroying Charlotte than righting a wrong against *you*,' and Vanessa said back, 'You might have a point.'

'I'm not going to grace that with a response,' Ned replied calmly, and he turned and left the room.

Vanessa inched away from Marcus—she needed some distance in order to think. What had he meant when he said he knew exactly why Charlotte did it? And was this whole 'romantic weekend' just a set-up so he could see Charlotte?

'Hey, where are you going?' He slid across, closing the gap between them. 'I know this is ugly stuff and you shouldn't be tangled up in it. I'm sorry, Vanessa. Forgive me?'

I'm not quite sure, she thought.

'Why don't we go somewhere else for dinner?' she suggested. 'It'll be too uncomfortable here.'

But Marcus shook his head. 'Charlotte's not going to stop me from taking you to the best restaurant in Falls Creek. And, besides, I've already paid for dinner as part of our package.'

Vanessa acquiesced. She'd never advocated wasting money and she wasn't about to start.

Ned and Charlotte's table was on the other side of the restaurant, thank goodness, and Vanessa was almost managing to pretend that they weren't here. Marcus was being super-attentive, which certainly helped, and after a bottle of bubbles the evening took on a nice hazy feel and the whole thing didn't seem like such a big deal.

Until.

She went to the ladies after dessert, and was trying to wipe the mascara smudges from under her eyes when the door opened and Charlotte entered. Vanessa stiffened. She tried to bury her face in her handbag, but she could see Charlotte approaching her in the mirror. Oh God, what now?

'I'm so sorry about before,' Charlotte ventured unexpectedly.

Vanessa blinked at Charlotte's reflection. She looked contrite, but could she be trusted?

'I know I acted like a "mean girl", and I'm not proud of that . . . I guess I was lashing out because I feel so hurt. I don't get why you're doing this to me. You're a fan. I welcomed you into my home.'

Vanessa turned to face her. 'Only so you and your father could buy my silence.' She squashed down irrational guilt for being an ungrateful lunch guest.

'Dad wasn't trying to buy your silence—we've got nothing to hide. You wrote a novel inspired by my work and I wrote *Love Transplant* independently. Like Dad said, that's bad luck, and I feel for you, but don't you think it's natural that our books would be similar, seeing that I was your writing role model?'

Her beautiful face looked so troubled that for a brief moment Vanessa almost believed her.

'And maybe I'm overstepping the mark, but can I tell you something, woman to woman?'

No, thought Vanessa, but we both know you will anyway.

Charlotte touched her arm. 'I'm worried that Marcus is using you.'

Vanessa recoiled.

'You don't want to hear it, and God knows I don't want to say it, but have you considered that he might be using you as some kind of twisted revenge against me?'

Of course I have, thought Vanessa, but he swears that he isn't, and I'd rather believe him than you.

'I never thought he'd stoop this low. I'm really sorry you've got tangled up in this.'

Wow, everyone was so sorry she was tangled—you could knit a jumper with this much remorse. Or was that too cynical? She didn't know. The only thing Vanessa was sure of now was that she wasn't sure of anything. She had to get out of here. But Charlotte was reaching into her handbag and pulling out a packet of Nivea facial wipes.

'I saw you trying ... May I ... ?' Without waiting for a reply, she reached over and gently rubbed Vanessa's mascara smudges away. 'There, gone. That's always happens to me too. Panda eyes, it's such a pain.'

Vanessa was so disarmed that she didn't know what to do, so she looked in the mirror. No panda eyes.

'I've got an idea,' Charlotte said. 'You might think this is crazy, but would you consider writing a novel together?'

A novel? Together? Vanessa wondered if she'd heard right.

'I think we'd be unstoppable if we combined our talents. We could set it in a hospital, or on a cruise ship, or at a scientific station in the Antarctic—wherever you liked. By Charlotte Lancaster and Vanessa Rooney. Or by Vanessa Rooney and Charlotte Lancaster?'

'By *Mia Fontaine* and Charlotte Lancaster.'

'Absolutely! Mia Fontaine and Charlotte Lancaster.' Charlotte smiled into her eyes. 'Whatever you want.'

Vanessa was transported back twelve months, to when co-writing a novel with Charlotte would have been the stuff of her dreams. She pictured them at the computer together, laughing and exchanging confidences. 'Brilliant idea,' Charlotte would say as Vanessa came up with yet another gem. And Vanessa would sit in the audience at writers' festivals while Charlotte said from the stage, 'Working with Mia has made me a better writer.' And the fans all around Vanessa would call, 'Who *is* Mia Fontaine?' 'Spill the beans!' 'Please!' And Charlotte would say, 'I'll never tell,' and give her a secret wink. It was certainly tempting . . . And did she and Charlotte really need to be enemies when they could be co-creators? All of this unpleasantness would go away—the publicity and the acrimony that made her feel like a peeled onion. Vanessa felt herself teetering towards a 'yes' as Charlotte moved even closer still.

'Wouldn't it be awesome? All you need to do is drop the case.'

Of course! Cue the 'ba-boing' music, thought Vanessa, cursing herself for being so stupid. 'I'm not dropping anything. You copied my book.'

'I didn't. I've never seen your book.'

But Vanessa had stopped listening. She turned and left the ladies. Charlotte followed and they both collided with Marcus, who was lurking outside.

'Marcus?'

'I'm on my way to the men's room.'

'Bullshit,' Charlotte scoffed. 'You followed me out here.'

'Don't flatter yourself.' Marcus turned to Vanessa. 'What has she been saying to you?'

'That she's sorry I'm caught up in this—same thing as you, basically.'

Vanessa looked between Marcus and Charlotte and her unease escalated into anger.

Chapter 36

MARCUS

He'd never seen Vanessa like this. Her sunny face had iced over. Not that he could blame her—she had every right to be furious with him.

'I want the truth. Did you know that Charlotte would be here?'

Her tone reminded him of his mother in one of her rare moments of rebuke: 'I'm disappointed in you, Marcus.' He'd always hated disappointing Shirley, and it seemed he hated disappointing Vanessa too. He felt himself squirm.

'I'm sorry, you're right. It had occurred to me that she might be here, but I thought that with the stress of the case, it'd be unlikely.'

Of course, that wasn't the whole truth, but he could hardly tell Vanessa that when Lotts announced her engagement he'd been consumed by a need to hurt her in any way possible. When she wouldn't take his calls, all he could think of was turning up here and rubbing Vanessa in her face. But confessing that would hardly play to his advantage. Not that his pitiful plan had, either. But what had he really imagined would happen? 'Cop this, Lotts. I'm sleeping with the woman who's suing you and together we're going to destroy your gilded life.' And Lotts would . . . what? Fall sobbing at his feet?

Send Kasch packing? Go mad with jealousy over Vanessa? Perhaps he was hoping for all those reactions—but what he received instead was contemptuous laughter, which was entirely predictable if he'd been bothering to use his brain. Back upstairs he still felt searing humiliation, but at least Vanessa was accepting his word.

'Okay. I wish you'd told me she might be here, but I appreciate your honesty.'

Marcus pulled her into his arms, but she stepped free of him and frowned. 'What did you mean when you told Ned that you knew why Charlotte stole my book?'

He suppressed a twitch of irritation.

'I didn't mean anything. I was just trying to mess with the guy's head. Barrister games.'

She bit her lip and studied his face.

He held up two fingers. 'Scout's honour.'

Her features softened into a smile. 'That's all I wanted: the truth. Thank you.'

He felt a wave of relief, immediately followed by the sting of resentment. Who was Vanessa to absolve him of his sins? She wasn't his mother. He felt like one of her kids, bloody Jackson and Lachie. Sure, they were nice enough kids, but they were so damned ubiquitous. Would it kill her to forget them occasionally and put him first? Apparently. He even took second place to the damned dog sometimes. He probably should find it funny, but he was still smarting about going to the theatre alone last week because the dog had swallowed a Mars bar.

'So what?' he'd made the mistake of saying. 'Is it on a diet?'

'Chocolate's toxic to dogs!' Vanessa had cried in a flap. 'Daisy could die!'

So don't leave a Mars bar lying around. And, of course, the dog hadn't died, and Vanessa had missed out on a Pulitzer Prize-winning play. Whatever way you looked at it, her life was the full suburban nightmare.

His gaze fell on her faux leather handbag lying on the bed and his irascibility rose. He remembered how she'd held her knife like a pen at dinner tonight and then placed the curved edge facing outwards instead of inwards when she'd finished her meal. He'd had to restrain himself from reaching over and fixing it. He'd wondered if the waiters had noticed, and he'd found himself glad that Lotts was too far away from their table to see. Charlotte Lancaster, she of the perfectly aligned cutlery who'd been dining in exclusive restaurants her whole life. Charlotte, who'd gone out of her way to avoid spending one second alone with him tonight and had laughed when she learned about him and Vanessa. But, of course, she'd laughed. Vanessa's lack of sophistication might be refreshing to him, but to self-obsessed social piranhas like Lotts it was grounds for disdain. As was he, it seemed. Her words reverberated around in his brain: 'You can take the boy out of Kalgoorlie, but you can't take Kalgoorlie out of the boy.' Bitch.

It was as if she'd never rolled over and reached for him at night or walked into functions with her hand in his and a smile that said, 'Eat your hearts out.' She was trying to erase him with that limpet Ned Kasch, flashing that crassly oversized rock at so-called A-list events and on Instagram, Twitter, Facebook, TV. The woman's need for validation was pathological, and the sycophantic public seemed happy to oblige. Meanwhile, he was watching kids' soccer matches in the burbs and being sucked back into the working-class vortex that he'd fought so hard to escape. He felt a sudden clutch of panic followed by the bitter pill of relevance deprivation.

'Marcus? Vanessa was looking up at him, her face creased with concern. 'Are you okay?'

He wondered how many times Charlotte had asked him that question—he could probably count them on one hand. She never thought of anything beyond herself. It was like being married to a concept, not a flesh-and-blood person.

'I'm fine. Are *you* okay?'

Vanessa nodded. 'I am now that you've been honest.'

She smiled, and grace glowed out of her like light. Marcus felt his tension ease. She was so sweet and trusting, just the refuge he needed from the slings and arrows of post-marital life.

'You're beautiful,' he said, and he meant it.

She smiled and raised her rosebud lips for his kiss. Ardour grew and soon he forgot everything else and lost himself in her goodness.

Chapter 37

DAVE

Dave's Volvo pulled up outside the NorMel Community Legal Centre, across the road from Mrs Hipsley's high-rise government flats. The wind was whipping its way through the canyon between the buildings and a couple of women with shopping bags were clutching at their flapping burqas.

He and Nickie were here to deliver Mrs Hipsley's cumbersome doll's house. After yesterday's effort in the semi-final, Dave reckoned his daughter had earned the right to just flop around and commune with her iPhone, but she thought Mrs Hipsley was 'cute' so she'd wanted to help. Dave saw this as a sign of a nascent social conscience and he was pretty chuffed.

'Okay, sweetie?'

'Yep.'

'You're a star, Nicks.'

They climbed out of the car, and as Dave opened the boot he spotted Chris Tatarka through the NorMel window, working at his desk. That'd be right, thought Dave, the guy's a saint. He went over and tapped on the glass.

'Chris, g'day,' he called.

Chris looked up and waved cheerily. He got to his feet and opened the window. 'Dave, mate. What brings you to these parts?'

'Special delivery for a friend. You working on a Sunday?'

'Why would I have a fucking life when I can draft an affidavit?' Chris grinned. Then, spotting Nickie behind Dave, he called, 'G'day.'

Nickie waved.

'This is my daughter Nickie,' Dave said pointedly, hoping that Chris would curb his language.

'Nickie, good to meet you. Your old man's our best fucking volunteer—and I'm not bullshitting.'

Nickie giggled.

Chris watched as Dave and Nickie tried to lift the unwieldy doll's house out of the boot, then offered to lend them NorMel's document trolley, which made things a lot easier. They wheeled the doll's house across the road and into the building. Then they caught the lift up to the ninth floor and found Mrs Hipsley waiting in the drab corridor, atwitter with excitement about surprising her neighbour, Zafeera Kuoth, and her little twins.

'Oh, David, Nickie, thank you. I can't wait to see their faces!'

She rang their doorbell. Dave smiled. She was such a frail little thing, but her heart was bigger than Phar Lap's, to coin an exhausted phrase, and Dave thought this Zafeera Kuoth was pretty lucky that Mrs Hipsley had taken her under her wing.

The door was opened by a young woman with a big beaming smile. Dave felt his own smile widen. She was wearing a brightly patterned dress (in 'happy colours', as his mum used to say), and sparkling disco ball earrings were swinging above her shoulders. Dave wasn't normally the type of bloke who noticed earrings, but these were impossible to miss. Zafeera—that must be who she was—saw the doll's house and her eyes lit up.

'Mrs Hipsley! What's this?' she yelled.

'It's all right, Zafeera, I've got my hearing aids in,' said Mrs Hipsley, and then she proudly performed the introductions.

'Come in, come in,' Zafeera cried warmly. 'This is so awesome.'

As Dave squeezed through the door with his bulky cargo, she turned and called, 'Amira! Tahani! Come and see this, quickly!' She cleared some space on a table. 'You can put it here.'

As Nickie helped Dave to transfer the doll's house onto the table, two little girls in yellow dresses burst into the room.

'What, Mummy?'

'What is it?'

Dave's heart flipped. They looked like bright little bookends.

'Oooh, they're so gorgeous.' Nickie exclaimed.

'Hello, my little poppets!' said Mrs Hipsley.

Zafeera clapped her hands together. 'Amira, Tahani, look what Mrs Hipsley and her friends Dave and Nickie have made for you.'

The girls squealed with delight and pored over the doll's house, examining every nook and cranny and fingering the tiny furniture with awe. What was it about the sound of kids' laughter? Dave thought there was no better sound in the world.

'Isn't it beautiful?' said Zafeera. 'What do you say?'

The girls dutifully tore themselves away from the doll's house and trotted over to Mrs Hipsley. 'Thank you, Mrs Hipsley,' they said in thoroughly Aussie accents.

'You're welcome,' said Mrs Hispley, who was smiling so broadly that Dave thought her face might crack. 'Can I have a kiss?'

She proffered a papery cheek and the little girls pecked it.

Zafeera nudged them in Dave and Nickie's direction. 'And what do you say to Dave and Nickie?'

'Thank you,' they mumbled, bowing their braided heads bashfully.

Dave would have liked to pick them up and toss them into the air, but he didn't want to terrify them.

'Our pleasure,' he assured the girls.

He was impressed by Zafeera's insistence on manners, especially as so few people seemed to teach their kids common courtesy these days. That probably made him sound like one of those grumpy old blokes on *Sesame Street*, but as far as he could see it was true. 'Please' and 'thank you' seemed to have become optional even in the most middle-class of families, so good for Zafeera.

Glancing around the small flat, Dave noticed that nothing was new but everything was in an immaculate state. He was starting to sense that Zafeera was one of those incredibly capable people, and he wondered how much she really needed Mrs Hipsley 'looking after' her.

Zafeera made a pot of tea and gave them all a slice of *bishbosa*, which turned out to be a delicious semolina cake, and as Dave cadged a second slice, Nickie rearranged miniature furniture with Amira and Tahani.

'How can I ever thank you, Mrs Hipsley?' Zafeera said affectionately. 'I don't know what we'd do without you.'

Mrs Hipsley's concave chest swelled before Dave's eyes.

'Have you taken your warfarin today?'

'Oh, I think I forgot.'

Zafeera tore a strip of paper from a magnetic notepad on her fridge and wrote *Warfarin*. She put the note into Mrs Hipsley's hand. 'Try to do it as soon as you get home. This will help you remember.'

Mrs Hipsley nodded obediently. 'All right. Thank you, Zafeera.'

'Mummy, look,' called Amira or Tahani—Dave wasn't sure which. 'Come and see the baby toilet.'

Zafeera went over to join Nickie and her daughters, exclaiming over the doll's house. A ray of sunshine danced through the window and her disco ball earrings caught the light. There was something inexplicably cheering about it.

'Your earrings are awesome,' Nickie said.

'Thanks. My brother bought them for me. He's a DJ.'

'A DJ? Sweet.'

'Yeah, DJ Kariem. He wanted me to wear these so people will ask about them and it'll be free advertising for him. I told him he was an idiot, but it's starting to look like he was right.'

Dave laughed. 'That's very enterprising. You should write *DJ Kariem* on them.'

'No way. Don't give him any ideas.'

Dave turned to the little girls. 'Hey, what do you reckon? Would you like a disco ball for the doll's house?'

'A disco ball?'

'Yeah.'

Zafeera shook her head. 'I've only got one pair.'

'No, I meant I'll make a disco ball,' Dave said. He could already feel his creative juices flowing as he thought of potential raw materials.

'Dad's good at that kind of stuff,' Nickie said loyally. 'He once made me an awesome crocodile out of a sock.'

Dave beamed at her, touched that she still remembered the crocodile—it wasn't one of his better efforts. He spent the next fifteen thoroughly enjoyable minutes fashioning a disco ball out of Blu Tack and foil, and hanging it from the 'living room' ceiling with dental floss.

As they were leaving, Zafeera opened her freezer and pulled out a few home-cooked meals, handing them to Mrs Hipsley.

'Here's your *kajaik*, and your chicken pie.' She went to a cupboard and took out a tin of baked beans and a can of sardines. 'And here, take these too.'

Mrs Hipsley gave Zafeera a kiss. 'Thank you, love.'

Dave smiled to himself. In spite of what Mrs Hipsley thought, it was obvious who was being looked after.

He and Nickie shepherded Mrs Hipsley back down the corridor, and the poor old thing shuffled along so slowly that Dave was half tempted to pop her onto Chris's trolley. They deposited her in her poky flat, crammed with piles of romance novels. Dave found the sight oppressive, and the glumness he'd been trying to outrun since yesterday caught up with him. He attempted to shake it off.

'Mrs Hipsley, why don't you take your warfarin while we remember?'

He helped Mrs Hipsley with her medication and put her meals in her ancient freezer but, when he turned back, Nickie's nose was stuck in a book called *Bride for a Price*.

'Would you like to borrow that, love?'

'No, she wouldn't,' Dave snapped. He whipped it out of her hands and Nickie rolled her eyes in teen disgust.

'I'm going to, like, wait in the car. Bye, Mrs Hipsley.'

'Bye-bye, love. Thanks for everything.'

Dave was about to say, 'Wait, I'm coming too,' but Nickie had already flounced out the door. He turned back to find Mrs Hipsley regarding him sympathetically.

'How are things with you, David? Have you found yourself a nice lady yet?'

'Oh, you know,' replied Dave, but of course she didn't, and he didn't elaborate because there was nothing else to say. 'Well, I'd better head off in case Nickie decides to drive home alone.'

Mrs Hipsley laughed with such appreciation that Dave could have sworn he was Oscar Wilde.

'Oh, David!'

Chapter 38

VANESSA

'Ah-choo! Ah-choo!'

Vanessa grabbed a tissue and blew her flaky nostrils. She was in the grip of a heavy cold, and it felt like there were tiny workmen jackhammering inside her head and laying sandpaper carpet in her throat. She must have picked it up from those tumbles in the snow a few days ago, but it was worth it to have spent the weekend with Marcus. 'Was it? Really?' the sensible little voice inside her asked. 'Of course it was,' she snapped back. It was just a shame she'd spent part of it with Charlotte too.

She pushed thoughts of Charlotte out of her mind and returned to her ironing in front of *SBS World News*. She liked the way *SBS World News* made her feel. Brainy. Informed. Engaged. Although it also made her uncomfortably aware that the world was going to hell in a handbasket.

She coughed so hoarsely that Daisy cocked her head sideways. 'Sorry, Daise.'

Joy and Keith appeared from Joy's room, and Joy put a small glass bottle on the ironing board. 'Echinacea. Take plenty, Nessie.' She pecked her daughter on the cheek. 'We're off to Keith's place.'

'No rest for us newsagents,' Keith said genially. 'Got to get to bed early.'

'If you know what we mean.' Joy winked. 'Have you got any batteries?'

'Mum! That's way too much information.'

'For Keith's alarm clock!' Joy laughed. 'You've got to get your mind out of the gutter, Nessie.'

Keith chuckled.

'I think there's some in the bottom drawer in the kitchen. Ah-choo, ah-choo, ah-choo!'

'You make sure you get to bed early, love,' Keith said kindly as Joy rifled around in the drawer and unearthed a packet of batteries.

'You heard Keith. The boys are at Craig's place, so you've got no excuse not to rest. Off to bed early, or this thing might hang around all week.'

'Oh, I'm sure I'll sleep it off by the—' But Vanessa got no further because she was gripped by a coughing fit.

Joy switched the iron off at the wall and pointed towards Vanessa's room. 'Bed. Now.'

After a cursory protest, Vanessa padded off with a box of tissues. She wondered if it would occur to Joy to put the ironing board away, but she knew that was a long shot. She fell against the pillows and inserted a Vicks nasal inhaler so she could free up one nostril for breathing. Slumber beckoned. But, unfortunately, her hopes of sleeping the cold off overnight proved wildly optimistic—by the next morning she felt even worse. She dragged herself out of bed just long enough to give Daisy her breakfast and force a slice of toast down. She called Kiri to let her know that she wouldn't make it into work, and then she sat up in bed surrounded by cough lozenges and used tissues with Daisy curled up beside her, delighted to have her home for the day.

As Vanessa coughed into Daisy's woolly head she felt grateful that colds couldn't be transmitted from humans to canines. Which made her wonder if Marcus had picked this up too. Who knew? The poor man might be lying in bed coughing and sneezing just like her. She called him and he answered on the third ring—not that she was counting.

'Morning, you.' He sounded like he had a smile in his voice but nothing germ-related.

'Borning, Barcus,' Vanessa replied, surprised by how blocked up she sounded.

'Vanessa! You poor baby, you sound terrible.'

She coughed loudly into the phone. 'Sorry . . . I'm just glad that you haven't got it. You sound okay—do you feel okay?'

'I'm fine, but you're obviously not. Is there anything I can do for you?'

Vanessa blew her nose, touched by his boyfriendly offer of help. 'Actually, I don't think I'm well enough to go out. Would you bind dropping in some bread and bilk?'

'Some bread and bilk?'

'No, bilk. For cereal and coffee.'

'Oh, bilk.'

'Yes, bilk.'

'Of course. Anything else? Do you need buffins, or bargarine or barbalade?'

Vanessa chortled. 'No, thanks, just the bilk will be fine.'

But then she had another coughing fit and had to get off the phone.

⁓

Sheer boredom had driven Vanessa out of the bedroom and she was lying on the couch watching *Dr Phil*. A mother and daughter who were dating the same man were listening intently as Dr Phil condensed their decades-long dysfunctional relationship into a three-word slogan. The slogan contained a germ of good sense, but still. That's America, Vanessa thought, the only place in the world where you can make millions of bucks from stating the bleeding obvious. The doorbell rang and her spirits soared—that would be Marcus with the bread and milk.

Daisy started barking and jumping around in circles. 'The door! Oh my God, there's someone there! Come on, quick! Let's see who it is! Hurry!'

'Daisy, shhh!' Vanessa croaked as she shuffled down the hall in her ugg boots. 'Who is it?' she called through the door.

'It's a burderer.'

Vanessa laughed but Daisy didn't seem to appreciate the joke. When Vanessa threw the door open to reveal Marcus holding a huge bunch of exotic flowers, she growled.

'Oh, Marcus, they're beautiful. I love them. Ah-choo! Ah-choo!' Vanessa cried, her eyes welling with emotion. 'Daisy, shut up.'

Daisy finally fell silent and sat on the floor with her back legs splayed, eyeing Marcus warily.

'Thank you so much,' Vanessa said as she took the flowers, 'but I won't kiss you. I don't want you to catch anything.'

Something flashed across Marcus's face. Was it relief? She thought she saw him take a step backwards, but she'd probably imagined it.

'I'll store up all your kisses on credit and demand payment later,' he said playfully. 'With interest.'

Vanessa laughed but it mutated into a cough. A blade of spear grass was sticking up her nose, so she shifted the flowers.

'Well, come in.'

Marcus hesitated. 'I haven't seen those before,' he said, gesturing towards her pyjamas.

'Oh these? They're my old comfies.' Vanessa felt bad that she'd forgotten to change out of her flannelette PJs into one of the silky thingies he'd bought her, but her head was so woolly she wasn't thinking straight. 'Why? Don't you like them?'

'I'm just jealous of them,' he joked. 'Wrapped around your body like that.'

Vanessa suddenly felt like a frump. She must be quite a sight with her watery eyes and her red flaky nose—and was all this coughing giving her bad breath? She discreetly put a hand over her mouth.

'Come in,' she repeated from behind her hand. 'I'll put the flowers in water.'

Marcus hesitated again. 'I should let you rest.'

'No, don't be silly. I've been a bit bored.'

'But I've got a case conference. I can't get out of it.'

'Oh.' Vanessa wondered if he was lying but she quickly shooed the thought away. 'Well, can you stay long enough for a cup of tea?' She suddenly noticed that his hands were empty. 'Where's the bilk?'

'Damn, I forgot. I'm sorry.' He grimaced. 'I spent so long choosing the flowers that it flew out of by bind. Would you like me to go and get it now?'

She was about to say yes, but she saw him glance at his TAG Heuer watch and checked herself. Marcus was a very busy barrister—if she demanded even more of his time she might come across like one of those divas with ridiculous riders in their contract. Mariah Rooney. 'Where are my seventy-three bottles of Evian and my white Smarties?' she imagined herself barking. Which made her smile.

'What?' Marcus said quizzically, but she was too tired to share the joke.

'Oh, nothing. It's fine. I'll call Kiri about the bilk.'

He smiled. 'That's my girl. I'll call you later.' He blew her a kiss and left.

⁓

Vanessa spent the next twenty minutes sorting the washing, and by the time she'd finished, she felt exhausted. The couch called and she saw Joy's copy of Nancy DuPont's new romance, *The Bedouin Bride*, on the coffee table. Perfect! She lay back and started reading, but to her astonishment she had to put the book down after fifteen minutes because she wanted to punch the heroine in the head. And as for the hero—what a dickhid. It was unsettling—she'd never had that reaction to a romance before—but she was probably just irritable because she felt unwell.

She decided to start writing her own new novel instead, about a gutsy young TV reporter who clashes with the owner of a media empire. She'd come up with the idea a while ago but hadn't felt the need to write a romance because she was too busy living one. She opened her laptop and typed in her title: *Love on the Air*. And then she just sat and stared at the screen for what seemed like hours. She eventually managed a couple of paragraphs but found that she couldn't rouse the enthusiasm to keep going. But that was normal, wasn't it? She must have writer's block. Plus, she was feeling crappy with this cold, and she was in the middle of a stressful breach of copyright case. It was no wonder she'd lost her spark.

She turned the TV back on, and she was watching Judge Judy decimate a gormless young guy who owed his former best friend ninety-three dollars when Jackson and Lachie arrived home from school in a flurry of noise and testosterone.

Then Kiri dropped off a packet of Strepsils with some extra tissues and bread and milk.

'Bloody hell,' she said when she saw Vanessa. 'You look like shit.'

'I know.'

Kiri offered to buy takeaway but Vanessa knew that Anthony's parents were visiting and Kiri and Anthony were planning a 'date night' while they had the free babysitting. So she assured Kiri that she'd be fine, and soon afterwards she was frying sausages. Her head still throbbed and there was a buzzing sound in her ears, but that turned out to be a blessing because it meant she could only half hear the bombs exploding in the living room.

She'd banished her daffodils to the top of the fridge so Marcus's flowers could take pride of place on the kitchen table in her only crystal vase, a wedding present from her Aunty Julie. The vase hadn't been used since the day that Craig had dropped his bombshell about Natalie, and presented Vanessa with a bunch of brightly coloured gerberas, 'to cheer her up'. When Kiri heard she was incensed. She said that Vanessa should have told Craig to stick the gerberas up his arse—the stems were wired, it was doable—but Jackson and Lachie were in the vicinity, so what could Vanessa say but thank you? As she drank in Marcus's exotic blooms, she felt grateful that these circumstances were so much happier. If only Kiri could understand that, but she still had a set against Marcus.

'It's easy to buy a bunch of flowers,' she'd snorted. 'But why isn't he here helping you?'

Vanessa experienced a rare surge of annoyance. 'Why won't you give Marcus a chance? Shouldn't you be glad that he's making me happy?'

'If that's what he's doing,' Kiri replied tartly, but then she had the grace to look chastened. 'You're right. I'm being a shit frind.'

'You're never a shit frind. You're the best frind anyone could wish for and I don't know what I'd do without you, but can't you just give him a break?'

Kiri turned into her serious self then. 'Of course. I'm sorry, Niss,' she said gravely. 'I suppose I'm being too overprotective because I don't want you to get hurt again, but you're right. You're a big girl and it's your decision.'

Vanessa had hugged her gratefully.

The doorbell rang, startling her back to reality. Maybe this was Marcus returning to prove Kiri wrong? The thought cheered her, but she couldn't leave the sausages.

'Boys,' she croaked, 'can you get that? Jackson? Lachie? Can someone . . . ?'

But Jackson and Lachie couldn't hear her over the rat-a-tat-tat of machine-gun fire.

Vanessa shuffled past them and down the hall, cursing herself for not changing into a silk nightie just in case. But at least Daisy wouldn't hassle Marcus again—she was in the backyard getting her head messed with by the neighbour's cat Basil and clearly hadn't heard the doorbell. Vanessa stifled a coughing fit and opened the door to see Dave.

'Dave!'

She felt a rush of delight that slightly threw her. What did it mean? But did it have to mean anything? Dave was standing under the verandah light and the single hair that stuck out of his eyebrow was illuminated. Vanessa wondered why he'd never noticed it. Or maybe he had, and he just didn't care?

'Vanessa, hi,' he said in his new polite-but-distant voice, and her heart went plop at the friendship they'd lost. 'Just thought I'd drop in on my way home from work.' He pulled out a manila envelope. 'This is from Charlotte's lawyers. After the injunction some stuff's finally starting to trickle through—' He stopped as she erupted into sneezes.

'Ah-choo! Ah-choo! Ah-choo! Sorry.' She blew her nose.

Dave regarded her sympathetically. 'You sound terrible.'

'Yeah, I know. Come in.'

Dave stepped inside and she suddenly felt self-conscious about her old pyjamas. 'I'm sorry about these.'

Dave looked mystified. 'Why? What's wrong with them?'

Good question, she thought. She coughed again, and her face turned puce.

'Are you okay?'

'Yeah, I'm fine . . .' she rasped. 'But can you give me one sec? I just have to check on the thingummies, and then I can talk . . .'

She led Dave down the hall and into the living room, and, astonishingly, the boys looked up and engaged with a non-screen-based situation.

'Dave.'

'Hey, Dave.'

'Fellas.' Dave waved to them over the warfare. 'Not inflicting any collateral damage, I hope?'

He was so easy with the kids. Vanessa experienced a wave of relief. Did that mean she was glad he wasn't Marcus? Oh, who the hell knew?

Jackson craned his neck to look behind Dave and she saw her son's face colour beneath his freckles.

'Um, is Nickie . . . ?'

Dave shook his head. 'No, just me, mate.'

Jackson tried to feign indifference, but Vanessa could see he was crestfallen. She wanted to take him in her arms and say, 'It'll be okay, sweetheart, the first crush is always the hardest,' but, of course, that would be a disaster. So instead she said, 'How many times have I told you, Jackson? Take your filthy feet off the couch.'

Cough. Sneeze. Snot. Etc.

When she'd recovered, she remembered her manners. 'Can I get you anything, Dave? Tea?'

But Dave was lifting his nose in the air and sniffing. 'What's . . . ? Is that . . . ?'

'What?' Vanessa's nose was so blocked that she couldn't smell a thing—but as Dave sprinted towards the kitchen she followed and saw to her horror that there were flames leaping up out of the pan. 'Shit, the sausages!'

Quick as a flash Dave yanked Marcus's flowers out of the vase and tossed them onto the floor. Then he tipped the water into the frypan, dousing the flames with a loud hiss. The sausages looked like wizened black sticks and smoke billowed from the pan and set off the smoke alarm. Vanessa winced at the discordant high-decibel sound, but Dave reached up and disabled it within seconds, without even having to climb on a chair. Vanessa was still in shock as she opened the windows to let the smoke out.

'Oh my God . . . Thank you . . .'

She blinked at Marcus's magnificent blooms, strewn like pick-up sticks all over the floor.

Daisy appeared, drawn back inside by all the commotion. After giving Dave a friendly lick, she started chewing the flowers.

'I've heard of chargrilled, but this is ridiculous,' Dave joked.

Vanessa half laughed, half cried. She wished she could hurl herself into his arms and say, 'I need a hug,' but you can't always get what you want, as the Rolling Stones would say. Which was laughable, when you thought about it, because if Mick Jagger couldn't always get what he wanted, then who could?

'Thank you so much,' she repeated in lieu of a hug. 'I've got no sense of smell at the moment. The house could have burned down . . . Ah-choo!'

Dave stood looking down at her with his huge brown eyes. Her heart did a little springy thing as she watched his polite mask drop and he turned back into the warm Dave of old.

'What were you thinking? You're as sick as a dog. Get on that couch now.'

Vanessa tried to protest, but Dave led her back to the living room and flicked off the Xbox unannounced. Vanessa watched in awe as the boys barely made a whimper—if she did that she'd never hear the end of it.

'Okay, fellas, off your backsides. Your mum's sick, in case you hadn't noticed.'

Jackson and Lachie obediently jumped up and Dave settled Vanessa onto the sofa. She knew she must be below par, because when he tucked a throw rug around her, emotion engulfed her and she wanted to cry.

'Thank you, Dave.'

'You just lie there and make the snot—we'll make the dinner.'

Jackson and Lachie laughed and pulled faces.

'Gross, Dave.'

'Snot. That's disgusting!'

Vanessa found herself doing a mental inventory of the pantry and fridge.

'There's no more sausages,' she said hoarsely, 'but there's some lasagne in the freezer and some leftover shepherd's pie in the fridge and there's some mince in the meat drawer and a packet of peas and—'

'Hey, shut up,' said Dave. 'I'll work it out. Just leave everything in my culpable hands.'

She laughed at his little joke.

'Okay, fellas, into the breach.'

The boys happily followed him into the trenches.

Vanessa drank some water with a Strepsil chaser and sank back into the cushions, feeling she could almost weep with relief. She turned on *SBS World News*, but she barely registered the day's horrors—she was too distracted by the sounds of Dave and the boys clattering around in the kitchen and laughing.

But then her eyes fell on Dave's briefcase, and she remembered the documents from Charlotte's lawyers. She tensed. What now?

Was the case about to get even more combative? She opened the briefcase to grab the manila envelope and discovered two novels, *Passion at Pasadena Ranch* and *The Handmaiden's Revenge.* Her lips twitched. Dave was reading romance? How funny! As she pulled the books out of the briefcase, Dave reappeared from the kitchen.

'Lachie reckons he's allowed to skip peas. Is that true?' He stopped when he saw the novels. 'Oh, those.' He grinned sheepishly. 'I'm in a book club.'

Vanessa smiled. 'But they're romance. I thought you hated romance?'

Dave shrugged. 'I've always wanted to learn a new language. Same difference, I guess.'

She met his eyes and there was a weird moment in which neither of them seemed to know what to say. But then the oven alarm rang.

'The pie's ready,' said Dave, sounding relieved. 'But what about the peas?'

'The peas? Oh, Lachie. Okay, he can skip them.'

Dave nodded and headed back to the kitchen.

⟳

When dinner was over and the boys had been dispatched to their bedrooms, Dave joined Vanessa on the couch and reached for his briefcase.

'Right.'

He'd removed his jacket and she noticed that his shirt was badly ironed. She found that endearing, but she wasn't sure why.

'Ah-choo!'

'Bless you.'

'Thank you.'

He pulled out the manila envelope and she felt her innards twist into a nervous knot. 'Okay, hit me with it. What's the story?'

'Well, let's start with the bad news . . . Wax's computer system was upgraded a few months ago, and Amy Dunphy reckons her old computer was destroyed at the time and the records weren't brought forward.'

Vanessa felt a stab of dismay. 'But that can't be right, can it? Surely they'd bring her old records forward?'

'Of course they would,' Dave said, 'so I'm going to compel her to provide a statement to that effect under oath. Then she'll be tied to the story and she can't resile from it later when we prove her wrong.'

Vanessa felt herself relax. Dave was obviously on top of things, and he was sounding way more confident these days. He pulled a couple of pages out and handed them to her. 'Charlotte's lawyers reckon these are the initial story ideas she scribbled down—they tell me her more formal drafts are following.'

Vanessa scanned the pages covered in handwritten scribbles: *Love Transplant? Nurse discovers heart belongs to her fiancé mid-surgery? Faints and arrogant surgeon misinterprets?* Both pages were titled: *Initial Ideas for New Novel, April 2017.*

Vanessa freaked. 'April 2017. But that's before I sent *Lost and Found Heart* to Wax.'

'Yeah, I know, but she could have scribbled this yesterday and written any date on top,' Dave reminded her. 'This doesn't prove a thing—unlike that USB at my office that proves you finished *Lost and Found Heart* in September 2017.'

Vanessa felt awash with relief. 'You're right. I just panicked for a sec.'

'She can give us as many phony handwritten drafts as she likes and date them accordingly, but it proves nothing. And I was doing some digging around and I saw an interview she did at the Wheeler Centre last December, three months after those so-called 'Initial Notes' were written, and she said she never writes anything in longhand, not even sketchy ideas. So she's on the record.'

'You're right. I've heard her say that too.'

'Mike Schwartz must be just as aware of all this as us, so I wouldn't be surprised if you get a settlement offer soon.'

Hope flooded Vanessa's veins. 'You reckon?'

'Yeah, I reckon.'

They smiled at each other and things were in danger of getting a bit weird again, but Vanessa was gripped by a coughing fit.

Dave leaped to his feet. 'I'll get you some water.'

He disappeared into the kitchen and returned with a chipped glass.

'Thank you,' she croaked when she'd downed the water.

'All part of the service.'

His eyes crinkled in the corners when he smiled. Vanessa realised she was feeling all warm and calm and relaxed. It was a revelation—she just wasn't quite sure what it revealed.

'And thank you again for cooking dinner with the boys. It was really special.'

'Special? I'm not sure it deserves that accolade. We just reheated a pie and bunged some peas in the microwave.'

'Still, you saved my bacon. And you're so good with the boys.'

'They're good kids.'

'For you, maybe.' Vanessa laughed croakily. 'Nickie's a lucky girl to have a dad like you.' Dave's face flushed in response and she found herself biting back the words, 'Oh my gosh, you're so cute I could eat you.' Wow, where did that come from? Best change the subject. 'Jackson told me she's going to Paris with her mum. She must be excited.'

'She's jumping out of her skin. Only nine more sleeps.'

But Vanessa could hear sadness behind his smile.

'I guess you would have liked to take her yourself?'

'Nah, stuff her.'

Vanessa laughed, but Dave's mirth quickly evaporated.

'Christmas in Merimbula's going to feel like a bit of a letdown after Paris.'

'She won't care where she is as long she's with you.'

Dave looked doubtful. 'I don't know, I feel like boring old Dad sometimes. Evanthe's constantly jetting off to exotic locations and bringing back expensive presents. It's a bit hard to compete with that. Not that it's a competition—even though we all know it is.'

He was grinning, but for Vanessa the topic suddenly felt deadly serious.

'You know what? Having your dad around all the time is so much better than stupid presents,' she heard herself say. She was suddenly assailed by feelings clamouring to be freed—it was like a floodgate was swinging open that she'd never known was closed. 'My dad travelled a lot for work. When he was at home, he was so much fun that I kind of forgot that most of the time he wasn't there. But when I think about it now, he missed my birthdays, my first day of school, speech nights, all the important things . . .' She trailed off. Why had it taken her twenty-five years to admit that to herself, let alone to somebody else?

'That's tough,' Dave said sympathetically. 'Poor guy.'

'Poor guy?'

'Well, poor you too, of course, but he's the one who really missed out. He never got to see what a sensational woman you've become.'

Vanessa caught her breath. 'I'm not a sensational woman.'

'Yes, you are.'

Their gazes locked and she lost herself in his liquid brown eyes and realised how much they reminded her of a beloved and long-gone puppy, Boris.

'You're a beautiful mother, a caring friend and a talented author. And in spite of the fact that conflict terrifies you, you've got the courage to stand up for your rights in the public arena. I reckon that makes you pretty sensational.'

Vanessa's heart forgot its job. She tried to form words but they wouldn't come, and she wanted to look away but Dave's gaze had somehow become magnetic. He started moving his face towards hers and she felt her own face moving to meet it. Their lips were just millimetres apart when her mobile rang with its new sci-fi ringtone (courtesy of Lachie). They leaped apart. Vanessa checked her screen. It was Marcus.

'Oh, um . . . I'd better . . .' She pressed accept. 'Marcus? Hi . . .'

Why did she do that? A shutter slammed down over Dave's face, and she watched helplessly as he jumped to his feet.

'I'll see you later.'

Vanessa wanted to yell, 'No, wait,' but she nodded, feeling fuddled and horrible. Why hadn't she let Marcus's call go through to voicemail?

'Vanessa? Are you there? How are you feeling?' Marcus asked.

I don't know how I'm feeling—that's the whole problem, she thought.

'Oh, um, I'm feeling a bit better.' She watched Dave disappear down the hall. 'Ah-choo!'

Chapter 39

DAVE

Out in the hall, Dave hesitated. Was he being too hasty? He might be crap at reading women's signals, but he was sure that Vanessa had wanted to kiss him too. Maybe she'd only taken the call so she could give Stafford the flick? He was heading back to the living room when he heard her say into the phone, 'Who, that? Um, it was no one.'

Her words hit Dave like a train. He turned and walked out of the house, shutting the front door behind him. As he headed for the Volvo on autopilot, his mobile rang. He answered it through a fog.

'Hello?'

'Dave, hi. It's Heather Fitzpatrick.'

Dave tried to feign normality.

'Heather. G'day. How are you?'

'I'm good. I'm just ringing 'cause I left my sunnies at your place.'

'Bugger.'

'Yeah. I'm blind as a bat without them.'

Dave hadn't noticed any sunglasses, but there were still piles of stuff everywhere from Saturday, including a used piñata with

Donald Trump's battered-in face, which he couldn't quite bring himself to chuck out.

'Anyway,' Heather was saying, 'I was wondering if I could come over and pick them up?'

'Sure. Or I could drop them off at your work?'

'But I need them first thing. Can I come tonight?'

Dave was a bit surprised, but he was in too much disarray to argue.

'Okay. Sure, come on over.'

'I guess your sunnies must be prescription, if you needed them this urgently?' Dave said.

He and Heather were sipping wine in his living room and sharing the remains of a Sara Lee blueberry strudel that he'd found in his freezer.

Heather shook her head. 'I don't really need them,' she revelaed matter-of-factly. 'I only left them here so I'd have an excuse to come over again. I wanted to ask you out.'

For a second Dave thought that he'd misheard. Come again? Two hours ago he was a pariah and now he was an object of desire? That couldn't be right.

Heather smiled. 'It was pretty lame. I should have just asked you at the party.'

So he *hadn't* misheard. Dave found himself briefly lost for words.

'Am I freaking you out?' Heather asked.

'No,' he rallied. 'Not at all.'

Heather's honesty was refreshing and you'd have to be a goose not to find it flattering. Dave *was* a goose, but not quite that much of a goose, and let's face it, a bit of flattery wouldn't go astray right now.

'So would you like to have dinner with me?'

'Yeah. I would.'

'Cool.'

Talk about a reversal of fortune. They smiled at each other across his card table. Heather had an elfin face and a petite frame that made her look a bit like a fairy, but she was one of the more pragmatic Redback parents. 'You're not the best player in the team,' Dave once heard her tell her son Josh after he missed a goal, 'and you probably won't ever be, but that doesn't mean you can't work hard and make yourself valuable.' A couple of the other mothers had looked askance, but Heather was unapologetic. 'Josh is good at piano and I make sure he knows that,' she said to Dave, 'but there's too much kid adoration these days. I don't believe in blowing smoke up anyone's arse—not even my children's.' Dave thought that was pretty hard to argue with.

When she'd presented him with a new tracksuit on behalf of the parents he'd been touched by her efforts, but he'd never suspected she fancied him. But, then, why would he? He was the mug whose wife had dumped him for a woman and who'd then distinguished himself by falling for someone who thought he was 'no one'. Vanessa's words had cut him to the quick and, left to his own devices, he was sure he would have retired from the dating field wounded, but here was Heather not two hours later and she clearly had other ideas. As he noticed a cute little cleft in her chin, he made a conscious decision to go with the flow and see where this took him—he'd wasted way too much time already pining after Vanessa.

Heather put down her spoon and declared that she could make a better blueberry strudel herself.

'I love baking. It's so clean-cut. If you follow the recipe it works and if you don't, it doesn't. Simple. Do you like baking?'

'Haven't done much of it, but I'm an enthusiastic consumer.'

'Good.' Heather raised her glass. Dave raised his too. They clinked, and then conversation turned to their excess baggage. Apparently,

Heather's ex-husband Rob was a businessman who travelled a lot for work. 'He promised he'd get a non-travelling job so he could help me out more with the kids, but he never did, so I chucked him out,' she explained. 'He was always raving on about how we were the most important thing to him and I'd say, "Prove it, mate," but he didn't.' She shrugged. 'Actions speak louder than words.'

Amen, thought Dave. Why did so many people (i.e. women) find that concept so hard to grasp?

As Heather downed the last of her wine, Dave wondered what it would be like to kiss her. He was pretty sure he'd soon find out.

Chapter 40

VANESSA

It was 2 am and Vanessa hadn't slept a wink. Her throat still felt like sandpaper, and her chest was tight with an anxiety that she couldn't seem to specify. She was going crazy lying here, so she climbed out of bed and threw on her old dressing-gown. She padded out to the kitchen with Daisy trotting loyally behind her. As she poured herself a glass of water she heard the back door open, and a few moments later, Joy appeared.

'Nessie! You're sick. You should be in bed.'

'I can't sleep,' Vanessa croaked.

Joy was wearing a backless dress, and her post-winter pallor was peeking through a spot where she'd missed her fake tan. Oh, Mum, Vanessa thought. Like a bride insisting on a strapless gown in July, Joy always dressed for summer—and, for the first time ever, Vanessa found that faintly pathetic. The thought just made her feel more confused than she was already.

'Where's Keith?'

Her mother hesitated, and Vanessa noticed black lines of mascara streaking Joy's face.

'Mum? What's wrong? Are you okay?'

'Keith and I have broken up.'

Vanessa felt a stab of dismay. 'But why?'

Joy stepped past her. 'It's late,' she said wearily. 'You're not well. You should be asleep. Goodnight.'

No, you're not getting off that easy, Vanessa thought. She followed her mum to her room and watched as Joy removed her wedding ring and dropped it into the crystal bowl on her dresser that sat beside an eternal flame beneath a photo of Vanessa's father. Joy's dresser was like an altar to Jack—adorned with prosaic but precious keepsakes, like a rose he'd once given her pressed for posterity, a stuffed panda that he'd won her on the laughing clowns, and two tickets to *Fame—The Musical* that they'd never used. Vanessa and had often wondered how her mother's boyfriends felt about her makeshift shrine, but she'd never felt comfortable enough to ask, until one day a few weeks ago, when she'd found Keith relighting the candle.

'A breeze came through the window and snuffed it out. I know your mum likes everything on her dresser just so.'

Vanessa heard herself asking him, 'But doesn't all of this make you uncomfortable?'

Keith shook his head and said without a hint of bitterness, 'Your mum and me aren't spring chooks anymore, Nessie. Your dad was the love of her life, and I reckon I'm a lucky bloke to come second.'

Vanessa remembered wanting to hug him.

'But Keith's such a sweetheart,' she said now. 'What happened?'

Joy sighed regretfully. 'I wanted to go out dancing, but he had to go to bed early again. It's sad, but I just can't be with a newsagent.'

Vanessa stifled a scream of impatience. 'But so what if he's a newsagent? Keith's lovely.'

Joy looked taken aback. 'Yes, he's a lovely man,' she said defensively, 'but your father used to take me out dancing all night and then hold me in his arms until sunrise.'

'But he only saw you every few weeks!' Vanessa heard herself blurt. 'It's easy to be charming when you don't have to do the hard yards. Dad was never there—not when it counted. So why do we keep pretending?'

Her mother physically flinched, and then there was a horrible silence. Vanessa felt her chest rise and fall. She knew she'd just broken an unspoken covenant, but she couldn't turn back now.

'I'm sorry, Mum, but—'

'Your father was the most wonderful man who ever lived,' Joy cut across her.

But was he? For the first time, Vanessa thought that her mother's words sounded empty, and she wondered if Joy was trying to convince *herself*? She reached for her mother's hand. All the vitality had leached out of Joy and she seemed strangely hollow.

'Was he really, Mum?'

'Yes. He was.'

They both turned to look at her father's face smiling down at them from the wall. He looked so masterful, just like Marcus. The same square jaw, the same dark hair and self-assured twinkle. Yearning suddenly swamped Vanessa. Who *was* Jack Spriggs? And in that moment, she knew she was going to do something that she'd never quite found the courage to do before. Was it loyalty to her Mum that had stopped her, or just plain fear of what she might find? Tomorrow she was going to the Victorian State Library.

Chapter 41

Vanessa stifled a sneeze as her gaze travelled upwards and found the sky through a magnificent dome six storeys high. She'd read that when the State Library was built in 1913 its dome was the largest reinforced concrete structure in the world. Even now she found it awe-inspiring as it towered over the huge octagonal reading room, where long desks radiated out from the centre like points on a star. It was glorious, but she wasn't here for the architecture. She steeled herself as she opened a digital copy of *The Age* dated 25 January 1995. Her palms were moist and her heart was pounding so loudly in her ears that she half wondered whether the swotting students nearby could hear it. She didn't know what she was looking for and she wasn't even sure that this was a good idea, but maybe if she understood exactly how her father had died, she could somehow understand how he'd lived too? She took a deep breath and started scrolling through the paper.

There was nothing about Jack on the first few pages but plenty of news about the prosecution's opening arguments in the O.J. Simpson murder case. Huh, good luck with *that*, thought Vanessa. She scrolled down further, passing a large Harvey Norman ad—some things never changed. And then suddenly, on page 6, there he was: her beloved father, smiling with the unshakeable confidence of a man in complete control of his destiny. Except he wasn't. Poor Jack. And then Vanessa saw it: a separate photo of a pretty young blonde beside her father's.

TWO KILLED IN HORROR CRASH

She felt her stomach plummet.

A car lost control and veered off Harpsdale Road in outer Melbourne last night, colliding with a tree and killing the driver, dental instrument salesman John Edward Spriggs, 43, and his passenger, receptionist Tracey Joanne Winter, 28. The accident occurred on a remote stretch of road and the pair weren't discovered until the early hours of this morning.

Attending ambulance officer Jackie O'Brien reported that it appeared neither had been killed instantly because they were found holding hands.

'They died hand in hand,' Ms O'Brien said, 'and that must have given them both some comfort.'

Neither was reported missing because Miss Winter's family believed she was with an old school friend and Mr Spriggs's wife Joy wasn't expecting him back from a business trip to Queensland until the following day.

Vanessa sat frozen. So many emotions bombarded her that she didn't know what to do with them all. Shock competed with devastation. Betrayal jostled with humiliation. And then rage rose up and topped the lot. Vanessa sat quivering in the library, engulfed by a white-hot wrath directed squarely at her mother.

'How could you lie to me like that?'

Joy saw the printout in Vanessa's hand and her face went a deathly white.

'Yes, I've read it,' Vanessa barked shrilly. She closed Joy's door so the boys wouldn't hear. 'Dad was with another woman, and you never told me.'

Joy sank down onto her bed. 'How did you—?'

'Why didn't you tell me?'

'I was trying to protect you.'

'Bullshit. You were trying to protect yourself.'

Joy recoiled and Vanessa realised that wasn't strictly true. Her mother *had* been trying to protect her too, so why did it feel like such a betrayal?

'You let me think he was something he wasn't.'

'He was wonderful, Nessie.'

'But he cheated on you.' Vanessa fought tears as she waved the printout with a sudden flash of clarity. 'And I bet this . . . this Tracey Joanne Winter wasn't the first.'

Joy blanched. It was answer enough.

Vanessa sank down onto a chair before her legs buckled beneath her. It was as if everything she'd been taught to believe had been tossed up into the air and landed randomly all around her. Jack Spriggs, the ultimate romantic hero, was nothing but a horny salesman.

'So, there were others, and you turned a blind eye?'

Joy squirmed and Vanessa wanted to shake her.

'How could you do that? Where's your pride?'

'Pride's cold comfort at night.'

'So's a cheater who's not at home.'

Joy's face reddened with anger. 'I won't allow you to talk about your father like that.'

'It's too late, Mum. Why did you make me think he was perfect?'

'Every girl should think that her daddy's perfect.'

'No, she shouldn't!' Vanessa could hear herself shouting now, and she realised with a jolt that this was the first time she'd ever raised her voice with her mother. 'She should think he's a human being with whatever failings he actually had—' She stopped to suppress a coughing fit, then took a breath to calm herself. 'I get why you didn't want to tell me all the gory details, but why go the opposite way and propagate this myth?'

Joy's lips thinned into a ribbon. 'You're overreacting.'

'Don't tell me I'm overreacting. Pretending that someone's a certain way doesn't make it true, Mum. Did you think that if you lied to both of us, you could rewrite history? Is that it?'

Joy burst into tears, and a sudden wave of sorrow submerged Vanessa's rage. Despite everything, she couldn't help feeling desperately sad for her mother. She handed her some tissues from the bedside table and took the opportunity to blow her own congested nose.

'I'm sorry, Mum. I know you adored Dad and I can't imagine how devastating it was for you. And I know you've been trying to protect me, but I just . . . I can't be part of this anymore.'

Joy dabbed at her eyes with a tissue. 'It's easy for you to talk,' she said bitterly, 'when you've got a perfect man like Marcus.'

Her words hit Vanessa like a slap. Was Marcus perfect? She didn't know anymore. All she knew was she'd just lost her dad for the second time and that was almost more than she could absorb. She couldn't start thinking about Marcus as well. It was too much.

'Don't change the subject,' she said as kindly as she could. 'We're not talking about my relationship; we're talking about yours.'

'But I don't want to,' Joy said beseechingly. 'Why do we have to do this?' Please, Nessie—can't we just let things be?'

Vanessa couldn't bear to see her mother in such anguish, so she forced herself to drop the subject.

'Okay, Mum. Okay.'

Chapter 42

Anthony was drilling into Mr Ahmed's lower right incisor while Vanessa held the suction hose in his mouth. She was glad to finally be back at work—she'd been so sick that she'd even missed the Redbacks final against the Parkdale Panthers at the weekend. Sadly, the Redbacks had been thrashed, but it helped that Jackson and Lachie's team, the Collingwood Magpies, were playing in next Saturday's AFL grand final. Like virtually everyone else in Melbourne, Jackson and Lachie were in the grip of grand final fever, and Vanessa was observing her annual ritual of pretending to give a rat's.

Mr Ahmed was making polite noises while Anthony chatted about property prices.

'Vanessa and her ex did well in Preston, didn't you, Ness?'

Vanessa nodded, although that depended on how you looked at it. She'd had to buy Craig out when he left and now she owed three hundred thousand dollars on a single income—thank goodness for her mum's rent. But there was no point getting into all of that and, besides, she could feel a sneezing fit coming on.

'When did you buy it again?' asked Anthony as the suction hose latched onto Mr Ahmed's cheek and Vanessa pulled it off with a *thwock* sound. 'Five or six years ago? I should know, I helped you move in.'

But Vanessa's face was turning purple as she tried to suppress her sneeze.

Anthony glanced at her and frowned. 'Ness? Are you okay?'

'I'm just trying not to—' But she exploded into a sneezing fit. 'Ah-choo! Ah-choo!' Snot sprayed out of her nose and dripped down the inside of her visor. It was gross, and she could see the revulsion in Mr Ahmed's eyes even behind his protective goggles. Talk about a PR disaster. 'I'm so sorry, Mr Ahmed. Sorry, Anthony.'

Mr Ahmed mumbled graciously and Anthony raised his eyebrows over his mask. Vanessa removed her visor and sterilised it in the sink. Maybe she shouldn't have come in today? She was still at sixes and sevens about everything and finding it hard to concentrate. But it was too late to go home, so she put her visor back on and rehooked the suction hose into Mr Ahmed's mouth, just as Kiri appeared in the doorway. She was holding the phone.

'Excuse me, Niss? It's Jackson's school.'

'Jackson's school?' She felt a twinge of alarm. She'd never had a call from Jackson's school.

'Yis. They said it's important.'

Vanessa freaked and reached for the phone, taking the suction hose with her and pulling Mr Ahmed's mouth halfway across the room.

'Ergh!' said Mr Ahmed.

'I'm sorry,' Vanessa apologised, but frankly Mr Ahmed was the least of her worries. Had something terrible happened to Jackson? She grabbed the phone. 'Hello?'

Clunk!

It crashed against her visor.

Vanessa blinked in alarm at the principal, Mrs Hill, a mumsy type she'd always found inexplicably scary.

'Inappropriate behaviour? What do you mean?'

'Perhaps Jackson should be the one to tell you. Jackson?'

Vanessa tried to meet her son's eyes, but he was staring fixedly at the floor. Dave's daughter Nickie sat beside him, squirming. Dave was on Nickie's other side, but his ex-wife Evanthe had refused a chair and was prowling around Mrs Hill's utilitarian office like a caged tiger.

'Jackson? What did you do?'

Jackson kept staring at the floor, and Vanessa saw a teardrop fall and land with a silent plop on the carpet. She squeezed her son's knee and shot a bewildered look at Dave, but Dave was stony-faced. Was he furious about this 'inappropriate behaviour' too?

Evanthe made a loud huffing sound. 'Nicola, tell Jackson's mother what he did.'

'Mum, it's okay.'

The poor girl looked mortified, Vanessa thought. She could feel her anxiety escalating. What had Jackson done?

'It is not okay. You were distraught.'

'I was only crying a little bit . . . just 'cause he surprised me.'

'Exactly my point. Can we stop all this pussyfooting around?' Evanthe turned to Vanessa. 'Your son committed sexual assault.'

Something between a cry and a gasp formed in Vanessa's throat and lodged there as that awful phrase hung in the air. Sexual assault? Jackson? There must be some mistake. She looked entreatingly at her son, but his gaze remained fixed on the floor.

'Evanthe, that's enough,' Dave snapped. 'Will you bloody sit down?'

Evanthe ignored him.

Vanessa felt a rush of blood in her ears. None of this made sense. 'Jackson, is this true?' she asked.

'Yes, it's true. He sexually assaulted my daughter.'

Mrs Hill turned to Evanthe and addressed her in the kind of tone that Vanessa had heard her use to wrangle recalcitrant kids at assembly.

'This isn't helpful, Mrs Rendall.'

'Ms Politis.'

'Ms Politis. I appreciate that you're upset, but if we could try to take the emotion out of this . . .'

'I'm sorry, Nickie.' Jackson finally looked up, and his face was wretched with shame. 'I didn't mean to hurt you . . . I just . . . I like you.'

'And that's how you show it?' Evanthe glared at Vanessa. 'He pushed her up against a wall and shoved his tongue down her throat.'

Dear God.

Apparently, it had happened at recess. Nickie was on her way back from the canteen when she ran into Jackson outside the music room. He grabbed her and pushed her into the wall so her head was hard up against the corkboard—and then he stuck his tongue in her mouth and tried to kiss her. Nickie was understandably distressed, and her best friend Ava Bourke happened upon them and told the year seven coordinator.

Vanessa felt cold with shock. Jackson's shoulders were heaving up and down in a failed attempt not to cry, and she didn't know whether to hug him or shake him.

'Jackson, why? How could you do a thing like that? I'm so sorry, Nickie.'

'I'm sorry,' Jackson whimpered again.

'We know you're sorry, mate,' Dave said in a firm but not unkind tone.

'The question is, what are you going to do about it?' Evanthe demanded of Mrs Hill.

'Evanthe,' Dave said warningly.

Mrs Hill gave Evanthe a withering look that Vanessa would have enjoyed if she wasn't feeling so utterly awful. She wiped a bead of sweat from her forehead. Today was unusually humid for September, in spite of the fact that a week ago September had been unusually cold. Mrs Hill ignored Evanthe and addressed Jackson.

'I'm glad you understand the gravity of what you've done and that you've offered Nickie a sincere apology, but I'm afraid I have no choice—I'm suspending you for the rest of this week.'

Jackson nodded miserably. Snot was running out of his nose and dripping onto his lips and Vanessa scrabbled in her pockets for tissues.

'And, Vanessa, I'd also suggest that you seek some counselling to help Jackson understand appropriate behaviour with the female students.'

Vanessa nodded numbly, her face burning with self-reproach. This must be her fault. She'd left Jackson alone in his room too often with unsupervised screen time, and now he was a sexual predator.

As they left Mrs Hill's office, she had a bleak flash to a future filled with prison visits. She saw Jackson with tatts and missing teeth and greasy thin hair combed into a mullet, ranting about the 'screws' and asking her to sneak him in some ciggies.

On the drive home she managed to talk herself off that particular cliff but, still, this must be her responsibility. She should have sat Jackson down and talked about how to approach a girl in a gentlemanly fashion, as outmoded as that sounded—or she should at least have made sure that Craig did. But even given her sins of omission, it was baffling. Forcing himself on a girl was so out of character for her shy son. Was he aping something he'd seen on TV? But Jackson never watched TV. Was it YouTube? CoD? Facebook? Instagram? Snapchat? It could have been any one of those—but the buck ultimately stopped with her for not policing his online activities more strictly.

'*We* always supervise his screen time,' Craig said accusingly. He and Natalie had come over to discuss the crisis in a mature and mutually supportive fashion, but Craig seemed to have forgotten the brief. 'What were you thinking?'

Vanessa was feeling wretched with guilt and was barely equipped to argue—not that she was any good at arguing at the best of times.

'I tried, Craig.'

'Well, not hard enough.'

'Hey,' Natalie cut through calmly, 'this isn't about judgement, it's about solutions, okay?'

She gave them both a counsellor's smile, and Vanessa watched Craig morph from attack dog into submissive puppy. Bloody hell, she thought, he may as well roll over and ask Natalie to scratch his tummy. Natalie was wearing lycra running pants and a workout bra without a hint of a muffin top, and her sleek tresses were impervious to the humidity that made Vanessa's hair resemble a Steelo soap pad.

'You're right, Nat,' Craig said compliantly. 'I'm sorry, Ness.'

For what, exactly? Vanessa wondered. Lying to me? Cheating on me? Leaving me for our marriage counsellor and sending the kids' lives into a spin? Or just for the screen time thing?

'Can I speak frankly?' Natalie asked.

Just try and stop you, Vanessa thought.

'I think you both need to take responsibility.'

Whoa.

It was one of the few things Natalie had ever said that made sense. Vanessa wanted to put her thumb on her nose and waggle her fingers at Craig like a little kid. 'Na-na-nana-na, it's your fault too!' But this was such a serious matter that even entertaining fantasies like that didn't feel appropriate. She tried to give herself space to regroup by offering Craig and Natalie a lamington.

Natalie shook her head politely. 'No, thanks. I'm in training for a half-marathon.'

Vanessa resisted the urge to say, 'What, only half? Can't hack the whole thing?'

'Can I run something past you both,' Natalie asked without a question mark.

Of course, Natalie. Share your wisdom!

'It seems you guys haven't been entirely successful in guiding Jackson through puberty, so why don't I act as the counsellor Mrs Hill suggested? After all, Jackson and I are already great buddies.'

As if, Vanessa thought petulantly. She'd never heard Jackson say, 'Me and Natalie are great buddies.' But then, in all fairness, he was hardly likely to say it to *her*. She hated to admit it, but Natalie was probably making sense.

'That's the perfect solution,' Craig enthused slavishly. So Craig agreed. What a surprise!

They summoned Jackson to join them, and he slunk into the kitchen with his eyes downcast.

'Hey, buddy, take a seat,' said Natalie.

Jackson sat down at the wonky table, where Vanessa's daffodils were wilting in a vase. The poor kid still looked like he wanted to die, and it took everything Vanessa had not to hug him. How on earth had they ended up here?

'How are you feeling, buddy?' Natalie screeched like a wicked stepmother.

Not.

They waited for an answer, but Jackson just shrugged.

'You've had some time to think about your actions now, buddy,' Natalie persisted. 'It's perfectly normal to like Nickie, but why would you express it in that particular way?'

Jackson bit his lip. They waited some more.

'It's not on, mate,' Craig said sternly. Natalie shot him a warning look. 'But, ah, this is a safe space,' he qualified. 'There's no judgement here.'

Yeah, right.

'Jackson?' Natalie pressed. 'We're trying to understand, buddy.'

Vanessa thought Natalie was going a bit overboard with the 'buddy' stuff—but maybe it was some kind of counselling tool?

'I thought that's what girls liked,' Jackson muttered finally.

Vanessa felt a jolt of alarm, and she could see that Craig did too. Why would Jackson think a thing like that?

Ever the professional, Natalie remained neutral. 'But why would she like being forced? Where did you get that idea?'

Jackson turned to Vanessa, his face riven with confusion. He looked like he wanted to say something but didn't know how.

She took his hand. 'You can tell us, sweetheart. Why did you think that was okay?'

Their gazes remained locked for a moment longer, then he turned back to Natalie. 'I didn't mean to assault her,' he said in a tiny voice, and then he burst into tears again.

Natalie pushed some tissues across the table, but Vanessa couldn't bear it anymore.

'No, stop, he's been through too much today.' She sounded more assertive than she'd intended, and Natalie looked a tad disconcerted. Vanessa squeezed Jackson's hand. 'We know you didn't mean to assault her, but you must never touch a girl without her permission. All right?'

Jackson nodded. 'I'm sorry.'

He looked like he didn't know if he was Arthur or Martha, and Vanessa knew exactly how he felt.

Chapter 43

DAVE

Dave opened the door. Vanessa was standing on his front porch, silhouetted by a flickering streetlight that was on its last legs. He toyed with the idea of telling her to get lost, but he liked to think he wasn't that petty.

'Hi.' She sounded nervous, which Dave found grimly gratifying. 'Can I come in for a few minutes?'

He stepped aside to let her pass.

'Thank you.' She walked inside.

'Tea?' Dave asked curtly, and before she could answer he turned and headed to the kitchen. He would have liked to close a door and put some distance between them, but thanks to his townhouse's 'open-plan living', the kitchen was in the same room as the front door.

Vanessa followed. The place was a mess, with dirty dishes stacked in the sink and an ageing lettuce on the bench, but it's not like Dave was trying to impress her anymore. He took teabags out of the cupboard and filled the kettle without saying a word. He could tell his silence was unnerving her, but he didn't care.

Eventually she spoke again. 'I'm so sorry about what happened.'

He turned to meet her remorseful eyes and almost felt sorry for her—but not quite.

'How's Nickie?'

He shrugged coolly. 'She's okay. She was convinced that no boy would ever like her, so I suppose it's not all bad.'

After the imbroglio in Mrs Hill's office, he and Evanthe had taken Nickie out for lunch. She was a good kid with her head screwed on straight, and she'd managed to get things into perspective by the time her fish and chips had arrived. Of course, the fact that she was going to Paris on Saturday helped, and for the first time Dave had felt glad about her trip. He knew that Nickie would bounce back quickly, but he wasn't so sure about Jackson. The kid shouldn't have done what he did, but he was good at heart and Dave didn't blame him. As for Vanessa, that was another matter. He didn't know if he was more disappointed or angry with her, but then he decided he was both. He flicked on the kettle.

'I've got no idea why Jackson would do that.' she said.

It was disingenuous, to say the least.

'No idea?'

'None. Unless it was, I don't know, YouTube?'

'Vanessa. It was *your* fault.'

He was expecting defensiveness, but to his surprise she nodded ruefully.

'You're right. I've let him have too much unsupervised screen time. But from now on—'

'Screen time?' Dave scoffed harshly.

She looked startled.

'Screen time's not the issue here. The kid lives in a house full of romance books where arrogant pricks do whatever they want with women.' Her face went pale and he rammed the point home. 'His mother even *wrote one*.'

301

Vanessa looked like she was clutching for words. 'But I never . . . I . . . I didn't . . . You really think this is my fault?'

'Not entirely. Let's not let Stafford off the hook.'

'Marcus?'

She seemed genuinely confused, and Dave marvelled at how such a smart woman could be so stupid.

'What's Marcus got to do with—?'

'Oh, give me a break. How many times has Jackson seen Mr Master of the Universe manhandle *you*?'

She reeled back as though he'd punched her. 'He doesn't manhandle . . .' She trailed off limply. 'I mean, maybe sometimes . . . but that's got nothing to do with—'

'Wake up!' Dave shouted. 'Kids are like sponges.'

She leaned against the benchtop in shock, and Dave felt bad for losing his temper. Was he motivated more by concern for Jackson or bitterness at Vanessa's rejection? He hoped it was the former, but he couldn't be sure. Back off, Dave, he told himself. Give the woman a break.

'Do you want some cake with your tea?'

'What?' Vanessa took a second to switch gears. 'Oh, uh, yeah. Thanks.'

Dave opened the fridge and pulled out Heather's latest cake.

'Is that a pineapple upside-down cake?'

'Yeah, a friend baked it for me.'

'Oh.'

He didn't elaborate. Why should he? Vanessa was looking at the cake with an odd expression and Dave wasn't sure why she found it so fascinating, but at least it had eased the tension a little. The kettle whistled. He poured the water into the mugs and added milk.

'Strong or weak?'

'Just normal,' she said meekly. 'Thank you.'

Dave handed her a cup of tea and noticed that her hands were shaking, but he could see that she was already steeling herself to get back on message.

'Okay,' she said. 'I take your point about the romance novels—but I don't think it's fair to bring Marcus into—'

'The guy's a dickhid, as Kiri would say.'

'He's not a dickhid.'

Dave snorted. 'You have to believe that, don't you? Otherwise you'd be forced to admit that you've wasted your life waiting to be "saved" by some wanker.'

Her body seemed to react before she did. It gave a little jolt. 'He's not a wanker.'

'His hand would have to be surgically removed.'

'That's crap! Marcus is *not* a wanker.'

Dave wondered if she was protesting too much.

'He's so bloody transparent,' he persisted, 'with his fancy flowers and his shit-hot car and his hollow gestures.'

'Just because *you* don't have a romantic bone in your body.'

'You know what? You can take an empty box and wrap it in shiny paper and put ribbons and bows on it and make it look like the best present in the world, but inside it's still empty.'

She looked like she wanted to throw something—Dave just hoped it wouldn't be her hot tea. But when she spoke again, she was disconcertingly calm. 'At least I've got the guts to follow my dreams, which is more than I can say for you.'

Her words hit him like a body blow.

'It's easier to talk about saving the world than to actually do it, isn't it? Sure, you volunteer on the advice line, but what happened to your human rights career? Too hard—is that it?'

Yeah, that's it. It was like she'd found all the fear and self-loathing lodged in his heart and dredged it up into his throat.

'I told you: my clients . . .' He could hear how pathetic he sounded.

'Oh, save it. You use your clients as an excuse not to try because you're so petrified of failing. Is it fun staying safe in your comfort zone, passing judgement on everyone else?'

'I'm not doing that.'

But he knew he was. So much for the moral high ground. Dave Rendall, gutless wonder. As he stood there like a goose, his phone started buzzing in his pocket.

Vanessa put her tea down. 'Goodbye, Dave. I'll see myself out.'

She marched from the room and Dave fell into a pit of despair. Then he remembered the buzzing phone and pulled it out. He didn't recognise the number but he answered it anyway. What the hell? It wasn't as if things could get any worse.

'Hello?'

Chapter 44

VANESSA

Vanessa closed Dave's front door, shaken. She'd never seen him angry before, let alone been the object of his anger, and she was surprised by how distraught she felt to know that he thought poorly of her.

She hated to think Dave might be right. Had Jackson really been aping Marcus? Surely not? 'Oh, give me a break,' snapped the sensible little voice inside her head. 'Of course he was.' The realisation landed like lead. Jackson was a victim of her poor modelling. How could she have let him down so badly? As she stood there paralysed by guilt, the front door flew open and Dave strode out.

'Dave?'

'There's been a robbery at the office. Some bastard threw a rock through the window.'

He was stalking past her and out the front gate, ignoring the Volvo in the driveway. In the flickering streetlight Vanessa noticed that underneath *Wash me!* someone else had now scratched: *Please!!!*

'What are you doing? Aren't you driving?'

'The Volvo's on the fritz. I'm going to hail a taxi on St Georges Road.'

'Don't be silly. I'll take you.'

Dave hesitated for a moment and then he nodded. 'Okay, thanks.'

And so they found themselves driving along in Vanessa's car while Dave called his PA, Ms Thingie, and asked her to meet him at the office so they could give the police an inventory of what had been stolen. As Vanessa half listened to his conversation she found her mind drifting back to that cake. Who'd baked Dave a pineapple upside-down cake? It must have been a woman, surely, but what woman? Her mind was filling with pictures of a nubile young thing wearing nothing but an apron when she suddenly remembered his elderly clients. Of course, it would be one of Dave's lovely old ladies. The thought relieved her more than it probably should have.

Meanwhile Dave was promising to pay Ms Thingie triple time with a three-hour minimum for inconveniencing her.

When he ended the call, Vanessa couldn't resist commenting. 'Triple time with a three-hour minimum?'

'I know.' Dave grimaced. 'But she probably needs all the money she can get for counselling.'

'Counselling? Why?'

'I think she's got PTSD from the Bosnian War.'

Vanessa felt a rush of sympathy. 'Oh my goodness, that's awful. Is that why she's so . . . ?'

'Horrible? I hope so.' There was a nonplussed silence as they both realised that hadn't come out quite right. 'I mean I'd hate to think she was just born that way.'

Vanessa nodded politely. It occurred to her that they would have chortled together about this before, but now they'd become polite strangers.

⁓

A young cop was waiting outside Dave's office while an emergency repair guy fixed the window. The cop was polishing off a kebab from Ali's Kebabs across the road.

'Place is a mess,' he said, wiping garlic and yoghurt sauce from his mouth. 'Youse might want to brace yourselves.'

Vanessa held her breath as they followed him into reception. Ms Thingie's desk drawers were flung open with their contents strewn all over the floor, and the Seeing Eye Dog collection box was lying plaintively on its side with the slot at the top jimmied open. Vanessa saw the colour leach from Dave's face and she wanted to wring the perpetrators' necks—what kind of lowlife would violate his workplace like this? A sudden wild thought leaped into her head. Had Charlotte and Chip paid someone to ransack Dave's office? It seemed far-fetched, but she still felt a lurch of dread. Were they about to find Dave's filing cabinet jimmied open and all her evidence stolen?

'We know who it was,' the young cop said, knocking her conspiracy theory on the head. 'There's a bunch of young scrotes around here who've got form. They did over a couple of places on Murray Road tonight too.'

Oh, thought Vanessa, it was young 'scrotes'. She felt relieved, but was that selfish? Dave's office had still been pillaged.

'I'll be paying 'em a visit as soon as I've finished here,' the young cop assured Dave. 'I just need to know what I'm looking for.'

Dave nodded and led the cop into his office.

Vanessa lingered and propped the Seeing Eye Dog back upright, patting its head. 'Poor thing . . . you'll be okay.'

'It's not a real dog,' someone said behind her, and she turned to see Ms Thingie regarding her with a smirk. 'It's an inanimate object. They don't have feelings.'

'Yes, I'm aware of that,' said Vanessa, even as she felt herself turn pink. No wonder Dave was prepared to pay Ms Thingie extra for counselling—clearly it couldn't start soon enough. Vanessa wondered if she'd found a counsellor yet. She'd be happy to recommend Natalie!

She and Ms Thingie joined Dave and the cop in Dave's office, where Dave and Ms Thingie compiled an inventory. Vanessa looked at Dave's precious human rights books lying all over the floor—she would have liked to pick them up for him but she wasn't allowed to because of fingerprints—and she wished that she could hug him in comfort. But imagine what Ms Thingie would make of that. Not to mention what Dave would make of it; she wasn't exactly his favourite person right now.

She shrugged off a shroud of sadness and focused. Apparently, things weren't as bad as they looked, so that was some consolation. Apart from the Seeing Eye Dog money, the 'scrotes' had only got away with sixty-one dollars in petty cash, Dave's laptop, a World's Greatest Dad mug and three tea cosies. Vanessa wondered aloud what they'd want with Dave's mug and the tea cosies and the young cop said they probably pinched them as gifts for their parents.

'Oh, how sweet,' Vanessa said with mock emotion.

'Now wouldn't you be proud of a kid like that?' Dave joked humourlessly.

Vanessa watched as he unlocked his filing cabinet.

'I'm glad this is all under lock and key, but we might make some more back-up copies regardless.' He flipped through the *Vanessa Rooney vs Charlotte Lancaster and Wax Publishing Pty Ltd* file and suddenly stopped. Vanessa saw his brow furrow. 'Ms Izetbegovic, where's the USB with the second back-up copy of Vanessa's novel?'

Vanessa felt a twinge of alarm.

Ms Thingie looked back at Dave with a 'what are you talking about?' expression.

'Remember I asked you to make a second back-up of Vanessa's novel?'

Suddenly she looked a bit shifty. 'It's not there? It must have been stolen too.'

'But why would they steal a USB?'

'Do I look psychic?'

Vanessa studied Ms Thingie's flat impassive face. She was sure the woman was lying and she'd never actually made the copy. Why was Dave letting his PA take advantage of him? Well, because of Bosnia of course, but that was hardly his fault—it's not like Dave had personally mobilised forces in Herzegovina. Ms Izetbegovic was frightening, there was no denying it, but Vanessa felt something had to be said.

'Did you really copy it?' she asked.

Ms Thingie shrugged defiantly. 'I can't remember.'

Dave snapped to attention. 'Does that mean you didn't?'

'I personally heard Dave ask you to copy it,' Vanessa persisted. 'I asked you several times. Why didn't you do it?'

'I've been busy.'

'Doing what, exactly?' Vanessa demanded.

Ms Thingie pulled a face at the young cop as if to say, 'She's a loony.'

'I'll get back to the station and write this up,' the young cop said, clearly reluctant to get involved in some kind of quasi-domestic.

'Thank you, Constable,' said Dave.

'I'll see you out,' Ms Thingie offered with uncharacteristic courtesy.

As Dave's PA made her escape with the young cop, Vanessa felt panic take hold. 'We need that USB.'

'Not technically,' Dave reassured her. 'Don't forget, your book's still stored in the Cloud—but I'll make another USB copy myself right now.'

Phew, thought Vanessa. She followed him out to reception and once again marvelled at his height. There was something about a man who could touch the ceiling without even standing on tippy-toes. She wasn't sure what that something was, but she liked it.

Dave sat down at Ms Thingie's desk as Ms Thingie closed the front door behind the cop. She turned and registered Dave's presence with annoyance. 'What are you doing at my desk?'

'I'm going to make another USB copy from the Cloud.'

'It's not in the Cloud.'

'What?!'

'Pooff! It's gone from the Cloud. I needed extra storage.'

#$@&%#?>*!

Vanessa freaked. Dear God, please let Ms Pain-in-the-Bum be joking. But, of course, she wasn't joking—you needed a sense of humour for that.

'So you deleted vital evidence?' Dave yelled.

Ms Thingie winced. 'You drag me down here in the dead of night and then you scream at me for being efficient?'

'Efficient?!' Vanessa cried. 'What have you done?'

She felt like someone was wringing her insides dry. Thanks to Ms Thingie they'd just lost all the evidence that proved she'd written *Lost and Found Heart* and had submitted it to Wax before Charlotte wrote *Love Transplant*. Not to put too fine a point on it, she was rooted. Her mind raced with catastrophic thoughts. She'd have to withdraw from the case and sell the house to pay for Charlotte's legal fees. She and the boys would end up begging on the streets with Daisy sitting on a threadbare blanket beside them like some kind of forlorn drawcard. But were dogs allowed in homeless shelters? They couldn't leave Daisy alone on the street at night . . . but wait, Ms Thingie was talking to her.

'You should think of this as a blessing.'

'A blessing?'

'It's time somebody told you the truth,' Ms Thingie continued, and her face took on an unfamiliar expression that Vanessa could almost have sworn was sympathy. 'Nobody else is going to tell you, but you're making a fool of yourself. Your story is rubbish. You can't write. You need to stick with dental nursing.'

Vanessa felt like she'd just been kicked in the teeth by Ms Thingie's pointy ankle boots.

'Ms Izetbegovic!' Dave barked. 'That's enough! You owe Vanessa an apology.'

'All right, I'm sorry,' she said tartly. 'I'm sorry that you're a laughing-stock.'

And with that she took her handbag and swept out of the office, leaving Vanessa feeling like a little girl who'd just been bullied at a birthday party. Was Ms Thingie right about *Lost and Found Heart*? Was she a laughing-stock?

'That's bullshit,' Dave said. Vanessa could tell that he was mortified, but bloody hell, he ought to be. 'Since when is she a literary critic? Would one of the genre's most successful authors really copy your work if it was crap?'

Vanessa felt slightly cheered, but the point was moot seeing as all her evidence had gone up in smoke.

'And don't forget, this isn't a total disaster. You've still got a USB copy at home, remember?'

Actually, Vanessa had forgotten. She sagged with relief.

⁓

Vanessa's whole body went rigid with horror. 'What did you say?'

Lachie was standing before her and Dave, wearing his Antman pyjamas and an expression that read, 'Oh, shit.'

'Just tell us exactly what happened, sweetheart,' she said. 'You're not in trouble.'

But we sure are.

Vanessa threw Dave a dread-filled look as Lachie fidgeted and stared at the floor.

'The Xbox hard drive wouldn't save my progress on CoD,' he mumbled, 'so I needed a USB. And by the time I realised it had your story on it, the Xbox had already reformatted it and the story was gone.'

Vanessa seriously contemplated fainting, and poor Dave looked like someone had just sucked all his blood out with a vacuum cleaner.

'Mate, please say that didn't happen,' he said.

Lachie burst into tears. 'I'm sorry.'

On autopilot, Vanessa reached out and patted his shoulder. 'It's okay, sweetheart.'

But it wasn't. Nothing was okay right now—not this, not her mum's lies about her dad, and especially not Jackson forcing himself on poor Nickie because Vanessa had set such an appalling example. But at least that crisis was resolvable—or so she fervently hoped.

After Dave had made his shell-shocked retreat, she headed into Jackson's room. Jackson was pretending to read Libby Gleeson's *Refuge*, a novel about a brother and sister's plan to shelter an illegal East Timorese immigrant, but Vanessa could see *Peter Parker, the Spectacular Spider-Man Volume 1* poking out from under his Magpies doona.

She sat down on the edge of his bed and felt guilt gnaw at her like fangs. 'Jackson, sweetheart, I owe you an apology.'

He looked up at her in surprise. 'Huh?'

'I'm sorry I let you see Marcus grabbing me and kissing me without my permission. It was selfish and thoughtless—I couldn't expect you to understand the context. It's my fault that you didn't know how to behave with Nickie, not yours.'

Her eyes welled. She tried to blink back the tears, but dismay was already clouding Jackson's face. He patted her arm awkwardly.

'It's okay, Mum. Don't get upset. It wasn't because of you and Marcus. I thought of it all by myself.'

Vanessa would have loved to believe him, but she knew he was trying to console her because, just like her, he couldn't bear to see his mum in distress. 'It's kind of you to say that—'

But now Jackson was looking over her shoulder. 'Hey, Nan.'

Vanessa turned to see Joy in the doorway. In the past few days her mum's effervescence seemed to have ebbed away, and Vanessa felt another tug at her heart. For a moment it seemed that Joy was going to join them, but then she just said, 'Well, goodnight,' and disappeared down the hall. Vanessa suspected she should still be angry with her mum, but Joy was so much more fragile than she pretended that all Vanessa could feel was love. She adored her houseful of flawed humans—and Daisy, who'd yet to reveal any flaws.

She turned back to Jackson. 'I'm not sure I believe it was your idea but, regardless, Marcus and I shouldn't have been carrying on like that.'

'I never noticed,' Jackson lied.

'Oh, sweetheart, give me a cuddle.'

Before he could object she pulled him into her arms, and time stood still as she breathed in his pubescent boy scent of hormones and acne and heartache. In that moment, Vanessa resigned herself to losing the house. It wouldn't be so bad. It was only bricks and mortar after all, and she knew they wouldn't really end up homeless. She and Joy could rent something cheap, and as long as they were all together, who cared about the rest? She'd done her best to fight the honourable fight and now she was going to show the boys how to lose honourably.

Chapter 45

'I admit it's not ideal,' Marcus said the next morning as the sounds of the raucous AFL Grand Final Parade filtered through from several streets away. 'But we can still work with this.'

Vanessa was floored, and she could tell that Dave was too.

'But how?' he asked. 'We haven't got a leg left to stand on.'

Poor Dave looked like he'd had about ten minutes' sleep. Vanessa knew he was blaming himself for her lost evidence, but it's not like he could have guessed that Ms Thingie would be twice as incompetent as usual. As much as Vanessa would love to punch the woman's lights out, in Lachie's parlance, that wouldn't achieve anything except huge satisfaction—and possibly a suspended sentence.

She just wished Dave could see things that way, but he looked so miserable sitting with his ungainly limbs overhanging his chair while Marcus leaned back comfortably behind his desk like something out of an Ideal Man catalogue. *'I'll have that one on page two, thanks. Azure-blue eyes, I think. Paediatrician or barrister? Hmm . . . think I'll take the barrister.'* But it occurred to Vanessa that there was something about perfection that was just too . . . perfect. She'd always had a soft spot for seconds stores—it was the flaws that made things interesting.

Marcus smiled. 'You might have to trust me.'

Dave's phone started buzzing in his briefcase. He hesitated.

'Go ahead.'

As Dave rummaged around for his phone, Marcus blew Vanessa a discreet kiss and she stifled a sudden surge of rage. *Now* he chooses to be discreet? Marcus was the other guilty party in poor Jackson's misadventure and she needed to have strong words with him, but she found herself baulking at the idea. For some reason she didn't feel inclined to share Jackson's private business with Marcus.

Dave unearthed his phone and checked the screen. 'It's Mike Schwartz.'

Vanessa tensed.

'Mike. G'day, mate . . . Yep?'

As Dave listened to Mike he suddenly sat up straighter and a big smile lit up his dial. Vanessa found herself thinking what a lovely warm face he had.

'Well, I'm glad to hear common sense has prevailed . . . Okay, mate, thanks for the call. I'll discuss it with my client and get back to you.' Dave hung up and leaped to his feet, his head almost hitting the ceiling. 'Yes!'

Vanessa held her breath. 'What did they say?'

'Well?' said Marcus.

'Charlotte and Wax want to settle. They're offering you two hundred and fifty thousand dollars plus the cost of your legal fees.'

'Oh my God!' Vanessa jumped up and she and Dave hugged for a millisecond before they awkwardly pulled apart. A quarter of a million dollars plus legal fees! She turned to Marcus with a smile so wide that she felt like her face might split in half. 'How's that for timing?'

'I think we should knock it back.'

Huh?

Vanessa blinked. She must have misheard him.

'Knock it back?' Dave said incredulously.

'Yes.'

Vanessa could almost hear the whooshing sound as all the joy was sucked from the room.

'I strongly advise that we continue to trial. I'll be able to get you twice that much.'

'What? But that's impossible,' Dave protested. 'We've lost all our evidence.'

'Not all of it. We still have Kiri and Joy as witnesses.'

Vanessa's head was spinning. But hadn't Marcus said that Kiri and Joy would be laughed out of court?

'But you're the one who said they'd be discredited,' Dave pointed out. 'We all know that everything hinges on proving the date Vanessa finished the document, which we can no longer do. Eventually Schwartz and co. are going to work that out, and two hundred and fifty grand is a lot of money—it could change Vanessa's life.'

Vanessa nodded eagerly. 'It'd make a huge hole my mortgage.'

'It's a no-brainer,' said Dave. 'You have to accept this offer.'

'No,' said Marcus decisively.

Vanessa stared at him in bewilderment. Those full lips that she'd kissed so often were set in a thin cold line.

'Dave, let's clarify something here. I'm a national leader in IP litigation and you'd be lucky to aspire to Legal Aid.'

'Marcus!' Vanessa snapped. It was one thing to demolish a professional rival with an incisive argument, but launching a personal attack on someone as sweet as Dave? 'Play the ball, not the man.' Wow, a pretty apt metaphor for footy grand final season.

She saw surprise flit across Marcus's face. 'Quite right. I apologise, Dave.'

Dave nodded guardedly. Marcus stood up and came around to lean against his desk in front of Vanessa. When he'd done that the first time they'd met she'd swooned, but now that sensible little voice inside her said, 'Hey, mate, you're crowding my space.' She felt distinctly unsettled. Why was he telling her to reject the offer?

'I've been here before,' he said as though he'd just read her mind. 'Of course, our case is compromised—there's no doubt about that. But we've still got cross-examination. Once I get Charlotte in the witness box, I'll prove that she stole your book.'

'How exactly? With a magic wand?'

Marcus gave Dave a withering look. 'I know her buttons—I'll force a confession.'

'Oh, I get it.' Dave shook his head. 'This is just about some sick game between you and Charlotte. You're so consumed with the need to humiliate her in the witness box that you're deluding yourself into thinking you can win this without any actual evidence.'

Vanessa's breath caught in her throat. Was Dave right?

'Mate, you're good in a courtroom, but not that good.' Dave turned back to Vanessa. 'As soon as Mike Schwartz finds out that we've lost our evidence, they'll withdraw their offer. I strongly advise you to accept it immediately.'

She nodded. Of course. It made perfect sense.

'And I advise that you reject it.'

Oh God!

Marcus moved closer and sat on the arm of her chair. Vanessa caught that familiar scent of cinnamon and the sea and wondered why she'd forgotten that cinnamon gave her indigestion.

'Of course, winning against Charlotte will give me some personal satisfaction—I'm only human. But do you really think I'd be where I am if I based my professional decisions on emotion? That's ludicrous. With all due respect to Dave, I'm the expert here.'

Vanessa bit her lip. She turned to Dave, and it was like watching one of those inflatable pencil-shaped men being injected with a sudden burst of air and leaping up tall in the sky.

'And I'm the one who's done all the work. I've done all the research, gathered the facts, handled discovery and liaised with opposing counsel. I'm the one making you look good.'

Go, Dave! Vanessa thought proudly.

But Marcus just threw back his head and laughed. 'That's a joke. You're a hack.'

'No, I'm a bloody good lawyer, and I should never have let myself forget that.' Dave turned back to Vanessa. 'Are you accepting the offer?'

'Of course she's not.'

'Vanessa? Are you?'

What to do? Vanessa felt gnarly hands tying a knot in her chest as she looked between Dave and Marcus. Agonising seconds ticked past.

'Surely you're not considering this?' Marcus's voice took on an intimate timbre. 'Ness, who won *Network Ten versus Channel Nine*? *Wilson versus Sony Computer Entertainment*? *The Grain Association of Victoria versus the Commonwealth*? Need I go on?'

Not really. It was undeniable that Marcus was a nationally renowned IP barrister with countless wins on the board. And what was it Dr Phil always said? 'The best predictor of future behaviour is past behaviour.' Just because Dr Phil was an idiot, it didn't stop him making sense. Marcus was the obvious and only choice—so why did she want to go with Dave? Was she just looking for an excuse to chicken out?

'You think you could get me twice as much?'

Marcus nodded. 'Trust me.'

His gaze locked on hers, and Vanessa thought there was something calculating about his eyes that she'd never noticed before. But surely all the best barristers had calculating eyes?

She turned back to Dave regretfully. 'I'm sorry, Dave, but I'll have to defer to Marcus's experience.'

Dave nodded, and that same shutter she'd seen before slammed down over his face.

'Fair enough. But I can't in all conscience support that position, so I'm proffering my resignation.'

WHAT?! NO!

Dave turned to Marcus. 'Obviously I'll liaise with you to brief an experienced IP solicitor to take over immediately.'

Marcus nodded. He held out his hand. 'It's been a pleasure working with you, Dave.'

Dave shook Marcus's hand and Vanessa felt like the floor was swaying. How would she cope now? She couldn't go through this without Dave by her side. He was . . . well, he was Dave.

'Please,' she entreated him. 'Don't resign.'

'It's for the best.' He shook her hand too. 'Good luck, Vanessa.'

Marcus put his arm around her shoulder as they watched Dave gather up his papers and leave. She couldn't speak. An awful emptiness crept into her tummy, and a tickle in her throat erupted into a cough. Marcus poured her a glass of water and she sipped it forlornly.

'Poor baby,' he said, stroking her back. 'You're still not well.'

'I'm okay,' she managed from the depths of her despair.

He squeezed her fondly. 'You're an angel. I think the choice you just made speaks volumes about your loyalty to me.'

She met his eyes. Something in his expression seemed familiar, and then she realised that he was looking at her in the same way she looked at Daisy. Dear old faithful Vanessa. Give that girl a pat on the head. He leaned in to kiss her, but she turned her cheek.

'No,' she murmured.

Ignoring her protest Marcus chuckled and pulled her close—but a wall of wrath slammed into her. She jerked away and jumped to her feet. 'I said *no!*'

Marcus recoiled in shock. 'What the hell?'

Chapter 46

DAVE

Dave climbed off the tram across from the two-dollar shop and paused to ponder his office. The 'D' in David Rendall LLB was peeling off. He should have had that fixed months ago instead of just thinking each time he passed, I must get that fixed, but now his inaction seemed prescient.

He wondered how his clients would cope. The probate and conveyancing lot would be okay, but what about dear old Mrs Hipsley, and dotty Mrs Zhang and her emails? What about Mr Maboud with his halal snack packs and Mrs Kerslake and her tea cosies? He sighed pensively. Why did his least financially rewarding clients always weigh on him the heaviest? Had Evanthe been right when she'd accused him of not being able to let go of his mum? Probably. Dave looked up at the sky.

'Goodbye.'

A woman at the tram stop sidestepped him, taking him for a crazy person, which Dave found pretty ironic, because right now he felt saner than he ever had. Shit scared, but sane nonetheless. He took a deep breath and straightened his shoulders, silently geeing himself up as he'd done with the Redbacks. 'You can do this, Rendall. It's time.' He crossed the road and walked into his office.

Ms Izetbegovic was on YouTube and barely glanced up when he entered. He paused to slide some coins into the violated Seeing Eye Dog and then he went and stood next to her desk. She was watching a make-up tutorial.

'Ms Izetbegovic?'

She ignored him.

'Ms Izetbegovic!'

Her face twitched with irritation. She looked up. 'Is yelling necessary?'

'Apparently it is. I need to talk to you. I'm afraid I have some bad news.'

For the first time in fifteen years, Ms Izetbegovic looked interested. 'You've got cancer?'

'What? No.'

She looked disappointed. 'Then what?'

Dave hesitated.

She looked up at him, her moon-shaped face tight with impatience.

'There's no easy way to say this. I've decided to close the practice.'

'What?'

She looked astonished. Dave felt a pang of guilt. With her PTSD, would this news throw her over the edge?

'I'm sorry. I'm giving you four weeks' notice, and I'll do everything I can to help you find another job in the meantime.'

He almost felt guiltier about her potential employers. Could he really in all conscience recommend her?

She was looking at him like he was speaking gibberish. 'What are you talking about?'

'I told you: I've decided to close the practice.'

'I heard that!' she snapped. 'But why?'

Dave could have done with a bit more courtesy, but as his only employee, it was her right to know.

'I'm going to try to make the move into human rights law.'

Ms Izetbegovic's lips twitched. 'You?'

'Yes, me.'

She raised her immaculately pencilled eyebrows, and Dave heard himself rise to the bait.

'What's so funny?'

'You'll never make it.'

His hackles rose, but he urged himself to stay professional. 'Ms Izetbegovic, I understand that you're shocked and you might want to lash out, but can't we try to have a civilised conversation?'

'But you've got a good thing going with the probate and the oldies,' she said. 'They're stupid, it's easy. Why don't you stick with what you know?'

'First, my clients are not stupid and, second, I want to work in human rights.'

She snorted. 'You've been hanging around with the "author" for too long—she's made you delusional too.'

Her hair was bunched up in a ponytail thing and Dave wanted to reach out and yank it.

'I'll let that pass that because of the circumstances, but this conversation is over. I'm going to go and start sourcing other solicitors for the clients.'

He started for his office, but he'd barely reached the door when she said, 'I'm going to sue you for sexual harassment.'

Dave span around. 'Sexual harassment?'

Ms Izetbegovic nodded, her flat face tilted defiantly. 'I felt threatened in my workplace when you asked what I'd do if you grabbed me and kissed me,' she said, clearly improvising. 'I was traumatised and emotionally distressed. I was terrified that you'd sexually assault me. I'm going to sue.'

'Do your darnedest,' Dave said with disgust.

'I will—and I'll make sure I get a better lawyer than you.'

A dam burst inside Dave and washed the last of his illusions away. He'd tried so hard to be sensitive to his PA's emotional landscape, but he couldn't deny it any longer—Bosnian War or not, Ms Izetbegovic was an odious human being.

'On second thoughts, you can leave today,' he told her coldly. 'I'll pay all your entitlements, of course, but I want you gone by five-thirty.'

She swore at him in Croatian. 'I'll get you for this. I always get my own back, you can count on that.' Her eyes glinted threateningly, and in spite of his better judgement, Dave felt another small twinge of remorse.

'I'm sorry it's had to come to this. Perhaps if you'd sought the right help after the war . . .'

She looked blank. 'The war? What war?'

'The Bosnian War.'

Ms Izetbegovic made a 'phttt' sound. 'That? I was nowhere near it. I was working as an artist's model in Paris.'

Chapter 47

VANESSA

Vanessa was fighting an urge to run around in small circles, screaming. Why had she decided to go with Marcus? But what else could she have done? He was a recognised authority in intellectual property.

'Vanessa?' Anthony said brusquely.

'Sorry.'

She handed him the curing light, and he gave her a 'get it together' look over his mask. She'd been like this all afternoon, preoccupied and stuffing things up. She'd even advised an eleven-year-old patient, Liam, to brush his teeth twice a week.

She passed Anthony the bite silk. This was the only decision she could have made, so why did she feel like someone had scraped her insides out with an ice-cream scoop? And why couldn't she stop thinking about Dave's disappointed but dignified face and the finality of his 'Good luck'? Did that mean 'Good luck with the case' or 'Good luck with your life'? It probably meant 'Good luck with your life', because without the breach of copyright case or the soccer season, there was no need for their paths ever to cross again.

Her heart did a swan dive into her tummy and she almost dropped the drill on the floor.

'Vanessa!'

'Sorry.'

She was driving herself and everyone around her bananas. She had to get a grip. She forced herself to focus on work and made it through the remaining patients without incident, but as soon as the waiting room had emptied, she found herself angsting at Kiri's desk.

'Marcus is a recognised authority on IP law, and he took on my case for no win, no fee,' she reminded Kiri. 'I had to go with him, didn't I?'

Kiri snorted. 'If you say so.'

'Kiri, please. Can't you put your prejudices aside and help me to look at this objectively?'

Kiri clicked out of Quickbooks and gave Vanessa her full attention. She frowned thoughtfully. 'Well, looking at this purely from the perspective of your legal case and keeping the personal out of it, I'd say you've got a few things to consider.'

'Like?'

'Like, do you really believe that Marcus is thinking purely of *your* best interests?'

Vanessa nodded. 'Yes.'

'And do you trust that his ego isn't a factor in his advice?'

'Yes.'

'And do you accept his word that's he's not obsessed with revenge?'

'Yes.'

Kiri sighed. 'Then yis, I suppose you've made the right decision.'

'Shit,' said Vanessa. 'I've stuffed up big time.'

Kiri nodded emphatically. 'Yis.'

It was 7.30 pm and the light was fading as Vanessa stopped at the entrance to the NorMel Community Legal Centre. Across the road, boisterous boys were riding bikes with tiny wheels in the skate park outside the government flats. Vanessa took a deep breath to calm her nerves. She'd contemplated calling Dave first, but she couldn't risk him saying no—she had to see him as soon as possible. Butterflies the size of small bats were flapping their wings in her chest, and she realised that she felt even more jittery than she had on the first day she'd met Marcus. Goodness, what did that mean? 'What do you think?' said the sensible little voice. 'Do I always have to explain the subtext?'

The NorMel door opened, and the friendly guy with the shaggy grey hair whom she'd met outside Marcus's chambers appeared. He was wearing a North Melbourne Kangaroos jersey, which would make him a mortal foe in her boys' eyes—the Roos were up against the Magpies in tomorrow's grand final.

'G'day,' he said.

'Hi, I'm Vanessa Rooney. We met a few months ago.'

'Yeah, I remember. Chris Tatarka. How are you?'

'Good, thanks. How are you?'

'Can't complain. If I did, no one would fucking listen.' He grinned and Vanessa grinned back, although she was so on edge that she was sure her grin must look like a scowl. 'You after Dave?'

'If that's okay. I won't keep him long; I know he's on the advice line.'

'It's pretty quiet tonight. Go for it.'

He held the door open for her.

'Thanks.'

'You bet.'

Chris headed off whistling. Vanessa ventured nervously into the office. It was a jumble of messy desks with boxes of files on the floor and a GO ROOS! banner strung across a wall above community-related posters. There was no sign of Dave.

'Dave?' she called, and thought how strained her voice sounded.

There was no answer—but then she heard the whistle of a kettle and followed it into a small kitchen. Dave had his head stuck in the fridge and she found it strangely touching that he was so tall he was almost doubled over. There was a sign on the wall that read KEEP THE FUCKING KITCHEN CLEAN, but there was dirty crockery everywhere and the bin looked like Mount Vesuvius mid-eruption. Dave closed the fridge and turned to see her, and Vanessa was suddenly overwhelmed by emotions she couldn't name.

'Vanessa? What are you doing here?'

'I'm sorry,' she blurted. 'I made a mistake this morning—I shouldn't have gone with Marcus. He just, you know, the experience thing. But you were right. I want to accept the offer.'

Dave regarded her in silence.

Say something, she thought.

'Then you need to tell Marcus.'

It wasn't what she'd been hoping for.

'But I want to tell *you*.' She'd thought he'd be pleased. Why wasn't he pleased? 'Will you come back to the case?'

Dave shook his head. 'I'm sorry—I don't think that's a good idea. And, besides, I'm out of the running. I'm closing my practice.'

Vanessa gaped. 'Closing your practice?'

'Yeah. I'm going to live on my savings while I do full-time volunteer work here and at Amnesty and the Human Rights Law Council.'

'Really?'

'Yeah. If I want to move into human rights law before it's too late, I'll need this kind of experience.'

Vanessa wanted to throw her arms around him and say, 'I'm so proud of you,' but instead she just stood there grinning like a nincompoop.

'Oh, Dave, that's wonderful. So you're going to follow your dreams?'

'Yeah, finally. Nothing ventured, nothing gained, eh?'

Vanessa nodded. She opened her mouth but now words refused to come out. She and Dave stood in a long and excruciating silence and she could hear the low buzzing of the fridge.

'Well . . .' he said. *I'm working, you should leave*, he meant. What was it with all the subtext tonight?

Vanessa nodded tensely. 'I should get going.'

But she found herself frozen to the spot. Why couldn't she take that first step towards the door and out of Dave's life? And then it hit her like a thunderbolt—because she loved him. 'Der!' said the sensible little voice, and her cheeks burned with sudden shame. She'd been an unmitigated fool, obsessed with status and appearance. She'd been as shallow as . . . well, as shallow as Marcus, and the whole time Dave had been a hundred times the man he was. Dave with the food stains on his tie and the eyebrow at a perpendicular angle and the biggest heart of anyone she'd ever met. She wanted to curl up on the couch with him, to take Daisy for long walks with him, to make a blended family with him and, yes, to make love with him. And, ideally, she'd like the making love part to start tonight.

'Vanessa? Are you okay?'

No. Yes. I think so. I love you.

'Dave, I don't know why I didn't realise before, but I—'

The buzz of the front door interrupted her.

'Sorry,' said Dave. 'That'll be my dinner.'

Oh, he's ordered takeaway, thought Vanessa. How sweet! Not that ordering takeaway was intrinsically sweet, but the fact was anything Dave did at this point would be sweet. She pictured them nibbling on the same slice of pizza and meeting in the middle for a cheesy kiss.

'What did you get? Pizza?'

'Lasagne.'

Lasagne? That could present more of a challenge for nibbling on the same slice together. She followed Dave out of the kitchen. He pressed a button and the front door opened. Vanessa was expecting

Uber Eats, but instead Heather Fitzpatrick entered with a Tupperware container, and Vanessa's heart came loose from its moorings.

'Home delivery fresh from the oven.' Heather saw Vanessa and stopped. 'Oh. Vanessa. Hi.'

'Hi, Heather.'

In a pointedly territorial move, Heather kissed Dave on the lips. 'Hey, you.'

'G'day.'

Dave looked pink but pleased and Vanessa felt herself pale. Dave and Heather. Heather and Dave. While Vanessa had been obsessing about Marcus, Dave had found love somewhere else—and didn't she just deserve it? She feigned a bright smile that she hoped was convincing.

'I just dropped in to talk to Dave about the copyright case,' she told Heather shrilly.

'He's closing his practice.'

'Yes, I heard.' Vanessa turned back to Dave, willing her voice not to crack. 'Well, I'll be off. Make sure you send me your bank account details so I can pay you.'

Dave gave her a subdued smile. 'I don't want your money. All the best, Vanessa.'

It sounded so final. But, then, it was.

'And to you too,' she said shakily. 'Nice to see you, Heather.'

'You too. See ya.'

Vanessa turned blindly and walked outside. She climbed into her car and sat staring into the middle distance as she tried to rally. Time passed. Was it five minutes? It felt like an hour. Her mobile rang. She was tempted to ignore it, but what if it was one of the boys? No, the screen said it was Marcus. She was about to toss the phone back into her bag, but somehow, through her slough of despair, she remembered the settlement. She wanted this awful business behind her, and the sooner the better. She pressed accept.

'Marcus.'

'Vanessa,' he said, sounding all energised. 'I've got something to—'

'I want to accept the offer,' she interrupted.

'What? But I just had a—'

'I appreciate all your experience,' she ploughed on, 'but I just want this whole thing to end with some financial security for me and the boys. I don't have a new solicitor yet and I'm not allowed to do it myself, so I'm instructing you to accept the offer.'

'The offer's been withdrawn.'

No, please tell me I didn't hear that, she thought.

'What did you say?'

'It's been withdrawn, regrettably,' Marcus confirmed, although he didn't sound at all perturbed. 'I would have called sooner but I had that Bar Council thing tonight. Mike Schwartz called me—we're off to court.'

Vanessa felt her whole body seize.

'But why would they withdraw the offer? They only made it this morning!'

'Who knows?' Marcus said airily. 'Although Schwartz did allude to the goalposts having shifted.'

'The goalposts? But the goalposts could only have shifted if they know we've lost our evidence. Nobody knows we've lost our evidence except you, me, Dave and Ms—' Ms Thingie's contemptuous smile flashed in front of her. 'I bet it was Ms Izet . . . Ms Iz . . .' How the hell did you pronounce that woman's name? 'I bet it was her!'

'Who?'

'Dave's PA.'

'Are you sure about that? Maybe it was Dave. He was pretty unhappy with me before. He might have thought a well-timed leak to opposing counsel was a good way to get back at me.'

'Dave would never do that,' Vanessa bit back heatedly. 'And believe it or not, everything isn't about you.'

She heard a sharp intake of breath, then Marcus said in a teasing tone, 'Uppity today, aren't you? Have you been taking feisty pills?'

Vanessa attempted a chuckle but it came out sounding like a snort.

'What are you doing?' he asked. 'Want to come over and be feisty at my place?'

The voice that Vanessa had once found so sexy now just sounded smarmy.

'Of course, with the boys at Craig's place I'd come to yours, but I'm too—'

'Too selfish to inconvenience yourself?'

In the stunned silence that followed, she suddenly realised that she was overcome with boredom.

'Actually, Marcus—I'm sorry, but I don't think it's going to work out between us on a personal level.'

'What?'

'I think it's best we don't see each other outside the case anymore. It's nothing to do with you, it's just . . . we're on different paths.' She winced and held her breath.

Marcus's voice came back laced with ice. 'I see. *Different paths.* Am I correct in assuming that you're breaking up with me over the phone?'

'Yes,' said Vanessa, shrugging off a tiny soupçon of guilt. 'I'm sorry, but I can't be bothered making a special trip.'

Chapter 48

Vanessa arrived home to her daily standing ovation from Daisy and, in spite of everything, she found herself smiling. Daisy was so easily pleased. All Vanessa had to do was turn up and give her a bit of food and attention, and it was pure devotion twenty-four seven. She was a fluffy ray of sunshine, and Vanessa had no idea what she'd do without her.

Jackson and Lachie were in the living room playing *AFL Evolution* on the Xbox. It was after 9.30 pm but school holidays were starting tomorrow and they were too excited about the grand final to sleep anyway, so Vanessa let it slide. At least with *AFL Evolution* there was no warfare or car theft involved—although there was still plenty of conflict.

'Free kick!'

'That sucks!'

'*You* suck!'

'Shut up!'

'Hi, boys.'

'Hey, Mum.'

'Hi, Mum.'

'And he kicks a screamer!'

'Ha, that was a *clanger*!'

'Was not!'

'Was so!'

As Vanessa watched Jackson cuff his younger brother, guilt stabbed at her like a knife again. Poor pubescent Jackson and his misguided 'move' on Nickie—no matter what he said, she knew it was her responsibility. Had her shenanigans with Marcus damaged his future love life irreparably? Hopefully not but, still, the sooner she gave him the good news the better.

'Boys, can you turn that off for a sec? I've got something to tell you.'

'Ball!'

'Bull!'

'Boys!' Vanessa yelled. 'I've got something to tell you.'

Jackson switched off the XBox.

'Hey!' Lachie protested.

'Mum's got something to tell us, idiot.'

'What is it?'

They looked up at her with their grubby boy faces and her heart overflowed.

'I just wanted you to know that I've broken up with Marcus.'

Lachie whooped with delight. 'You've broken up? Sweet! Marcus is a tool.'

Jackson thumped him. 'Shut up.'

'It's okay, Jackson—Lachie's right.' Vanessa looked into Jackson's soulful grey eyes, determined to drive her point home. 'Marcus is a big fat arsehole wanker.'

Jackson's jaw dropped. 'Mum!'

Lachie laughed his head off. 'You swore!'

'I know. And you know what else? He's a nob.'

Both boys burst into guffaws and Vanessa chuckled along before she found herself sobering. It wasn't fair to hang everything on Marcus.

'But seriously, like I told you last night, it's my fault too. No means no, and men should never ignore that word and women should never allow them to.' She added for good measure, 'If you want to know how to treat a woman, follow Dave's example instead.'

Yes, watch how Dave treats Heather. Her eyes welled and she threw her arms wide. 'Group hug?'

The boys shuffled into the embrace and Daisy jumped around their ankles, keen to be part of the love-in.

Lachie snickered. 'Mum said nob.'

'And wanker.' Jackson sniggered.

'And don't forget arsehole,' said Vanessa.

They all laughed together, and Vanessa had a sudden image of Dave sharing the moment. She pictured the two of them exchanging loving looks over the boys' heads, and bleakness rushed at her like a wave. That ship had sailed. She tried to drag her head above water.

'Love you, guys.'

'Love you too, Mum . . .' they mumbled in boyish embarrassment.

As Vanessa opened the kitchen bin to empty the vacuum cleaner, she glanced at the oven clock. It was 10.41 pm. She wasn't quite sure why she'd started vacuuming at this hour. Maybe she'd been hoping that the noise of the vacuum cleaner would drown out her thoughts?

No such luck.

All night she'd been assailed by images of Dave and Heather holding hands at the movies and gazing at each other across candlelit tables. It was torture. She wished she could be big enough to feel happy for them, but it would probably take a few more lives before she became quite that evolved. Not that she believed in reincarnation, but still.

She bent to empty the vacuum cleaner, and was stunned to discover Joy's tatty old panda discarded in the vegetable peelings. She leaned down for a closer look and found the *Fame* tickets ripped into pieces and her mother's cherished pressed rose obscured beneath a snotty tissue.

Vanessa was aghast. Was this her fault? She hated to think her mum felt forced to throw out her most precious keepsakes. Vanessa took the panda out of the bin and brushed it off gently, and then she padded down the hall to Joy's room. As she stopped in the doorway she caught her breath. Jack's photograph was gone from the wall, his makeshift shrine had been dismantled, and Joy was blowing out the eternal candle. Her face was almost make-up free and the hair extensions she usually wore were lying like a dead ferret on the bed.

She turned and saw Vanessa. Their eyes met for a long, still moment, and then Joy smiled sadly. 'You think I don't know how ridiculous I've been?'

Vanessa's heart broke for her. 'Don't say that. You're not ridiculous.'

'It's all right . . .'

Vanessa gestured towards the dresser. 'Mum, you don't have to do this because of me. I'm a big girl, I chose to buy into it.'

'No,' Joy said gravely. 'I should have done this a long time ago.' She put the candle in her bottom drawer and closed it. 'I heard you and Jackson talking last night, and I thought, what have I done? It's rippling down the generations.'

'Oh, Mum. Don't say that.'

But Joy was clearly stricken. 'I'm so sorry I lied about your father . . . I suppose the truth was too hard to bear.'

She sank down onto the bed. Vanessa sat beside her and took her hand and, for a moment, the only sound was silence.

'I thought that if I could turn myself into the sexiest woman he knew, he'd stop looking elsewhere,' Joy confessed out of the blue. 'I bought every copy of *Cleo* and I devoured all those articles about how to keep your man happy in bed. I tried so hard, but it still didn't work.'

Vanessa was lost for words. Was Joy's whole 'sex bomb' persona a construct designed to keep a man who didn't deserve her? A ludicrous picture popped into her head of her mother dressed like a straitlaced librarian. Was that the real Joy? Surely not.

'And then, after Jack died, I suppose I didn't know how to stop playing the sex kitten. Not that I haven't enjoyed the attention.' Joy allowed herself the ghost of a wicked smile. 'But it wasn't the attention I wanted.'

'Dad didn't deserve you,' Vanessa heard herself say fiercely. 'Where did he get off, cheating like that?'

'It was my fault too—I turned a blind eye. If I was stronger I would have sent him packing.'

'That's victim blaming, Mum. He's the one who was unfaithful.'

Joy smiled wearily. 'But I'm the one who invented the fairytale, and now I've not only ruined my life but yours and Jackson's too.'

'No, you haven't.'

But Vanessa could see that Joy didn't believe her.

'Are you happy, Nessie?'

Vanessa hesitated a fraction too long, and Joy dissolved into tears. 'I'm sorry.'

'It's not your fault.'

'But I pushed you to be with Marcus when my gut was telling me all along that Dave Rendall was the man for you.'

Vanessa was gobsmacked. But, then, why should she be surprised? Hadn't her own gut been telling her the same thing, while she'd been consumed with trying to mould herself into the kind of woman that Marcus wanted? She and her mum were peas in a pod.

'Dave? Really?'

Joy nodded. 'Oh, I tried to deny it—he doesn't quite fit the picture, does he? But Marcus hasn't made you happy and I've lost my darling Keith, and now poor Jackson's in trouble over Nickie. We're a romantically dysfunctional family, and it's all my doing.'

But Vanessa knew that wasn't true.

'I'm an adult, Mum, and I'm the one who's been carrying on with Marcus in front of the kids. And don't worry too much about Jackson—we've had a chat and I've set him straight. He'll be fine.'

'Really?'

Vanessa nodded. 'I promise.'

Joy exhaled with relief, then said anxiously, 'But what about you?'

'Marcus and I have broken up.'

Joy clutched at that news like a lifeline. 'Then run to Dave! I think he loves you.'

'It's too late. He's with somebody else.'

As despair settled over Joy's face, Vanessa squeezed her hand. 'It's all right—I'll be okay. We both will.'

But would they?

Vanessa and Joy sat hand in hand, surveying the bare dresser in silence. Their delusions had led them to a lonely future, and they had no one to blame but themselves.

Chapter 49

DAVE

Dave squinted as he proofread page 11 of the NorMel Community Legal Centre's submission to the Victorian Law Reform Commission Police Accountability Review. He was wearing those thirteen-dollar magnifying glasses from the chemist because he'd left his own glasses at home. Good one, Dave. But the document was only thirty-one pages, so it shouldn't take too long. By the time he finished it'd be about 5 pm and he could duck out for noodles before coming back to do his shift on the advice line.

Sometimes he found it hard to believe that it was two months since he'd closed his practice, but in other ways it felt like years. Between NorMel, Amnesty and the HRLC, he was witnessing brilliant but largely unsung work around domestic violence, youth detainees and refugee family reunions. It wasn't the lofty heights of The Hague that he'd dreamed about, but these lawyers were at the coalface of social inequities in the communities where they worked. They were thinking globally and acting locally, and Dave found that inspiring.

'How are you going with that fucking thing?' Chris asked as he passed Dave's desk in the cramped cubicle he time-shared with another volunteer. 'Your eyesight fucked yet?'

Dave grinned. 'Not yet.'

'Good man.'

Chris sauntered off. As a volunteer Dave was mostly doing menial stuff, like this proofreading. He was champing at the bit to dive into a case, but Chris had a phalanx of idealistic young full-time lawyers, so the ageing volunteer would have to wait, unless he poisoned one of the millennials—although, judging by the state of the kitchen, that could happen anyway. They might be gung-ho about social justice but they were all still resolutely ignoring Chris's KEEP THE FUCKING KITCHEN CLEAN sign.

Dave was no neat freak by a long stretch, but he'd started tidying up a couple of times, until Chris had seen him and said, 'Fuck off out of here, you're already doing too much for no fucking money.' But Dave could honestly say that the money didn't bother him. His savings would stretch for another few months, and after that he'd work something out—he was just so happy to be here. He still got a buzz when he thought about Nickie calling him a 'legend', and even Evanthe had praised his life change. He'd been a bit pissed off to realise how much Evanthe's approval mattered—although, of course, he'd made a point of hiding that from her.

He smiled as he headed into the kitchen to risk a cuppa and a slice of Thanksgiving pie made by one of the lawyers' American mum. Life was pretty good right now. Social justice was where he wanted to be, and Heather was great . . . maybe a bit prone to earnestness and not quite as quick to laugh as he'd like, but since when was he Jerry Seinfeld? The sound of Vanessa's cute chortle invaded his brain and he tried to quash the memory.

'Look at this fucking kitchen,' Chris said behind him. 'It's a wonder we don't all have fucking salmonella.'

Dave grinned, but he was distracted by thoughts of Vanessa now. He'd heard she was continuing to court, and he wondered why she'd changed her mind for a second time—she was obviously still in Stafford's thrall.

'Fuck! There's an empty fucking biscuit packet in the fridge,' said Chris. He pulled out the empty packet to show Dave and then promptly put it back in the fridge. 'Can you fucking believe that?'

He closed the fridge door and walked out. Dave laughed. As he turned on the kettle the receptionist, June, popped her head in the door.

'Dave, there's some people here to see you.'

'Me?'

'Yeah. Zafeera and Kariem Kuoth?'

'Oh, Zafeera? Yeah, we've met.' But who was Kariem? It rang a bell. That's right—the DJ brother. 'Thanks, June. Why don't you send them through to my well-appointed office.'

⁓

'I don't want to sound like I'm up myself, but my DJ business is going gangbusters', Kariem said, as he juggled one adorable niece on each knee. Dave thought he seemed like a good bloke, with a big gap-toothed grin that lit up his face like Christmas.

'It's because of the earrings,' Zafeera joked, and Kariem punched her like brothers do.

Dave felt a moment of wistfulness for the relationship he'd never really had with his much older sister Debbie, who'd moved to England when he was ten. He shrugged it off. 'I get the sense there's a but.'

Kariem nodded. 'A big one. A few weeks ago my business partner Brett Cummings booked LightZone nightclub for a function this coming Saturday night and they accepted the booking—but today I rang to confirm some details, and when they found out that it was an African party, they cancelled.'

Dave felt himself bristle. 'Cancelled?'

'Yeah, and it's only five days away. They said they'd need to liaise with police and hire extra security they can't afford because if it was an African party, there'd be violence.'

Dave immediately started jotting notes. 'They can't just cancel a booking because of the attendees' race,' he said. 'That's discrimination.'

'That's what we reckon.'

Zafeera nodded. 'Kariem's done lots of white parties, and no one's ever cancelled those.'

Of course not, thought Dave. This was clearly a case of a whole community being blamed for the sins of a few bad apples—a microcosm of the vilification of Muslims around the world. He felt his adrenaline pumping. A DJ function might seem frivolous at first glance, but this kind of thinking was dangerous and needed to be nipped in the bud.

'This should go to VCAT—that's the Victorian Civil and Administrative Tribunal,' he said. 'You deserve compensation for discrimination against yourself and your patrons, and someone needs to put all Melbourne venues on notice that their entrance policies cannot discriminate on the basis of race.'

Kariem and Zafeera exchanged jubilant looks.

'Sweet.' said Kariem. 'We've got to fight the fight, so things will be different when my nieces grow up.'

They all looked down at Amira and Tahani, who were now busily pulling stuff out of Dave's briefcase.

'I hear you, but I'm just a volunteer, as I think you know. I'll take this to the lawyers, but I should caution you that they're pretty flat chat, so it might take a while.' Kariem and Zafeera looked disappointed, and Dave kicked himself for sounding defeatist. 'But I'll do everything I can—that's a promise.'

As soon as Kariem and Zafeera had left, Dave went to Chris's office and briefed him on the situation.

Chris frowned at him over the piles of paperwork on his desk. 'They've definitely got a case, but we're all up to pussy's fucking bow.'

Dave felt his temperature rise. 'I understand that, but we can't let this kind of ingrained discrimination go unchallenged. It's a slippery slope, Chris. Let *me* run with it.'

Chris shook his head. 'No fucking way. It'll be a shitload of work, and we can't fucking pay you.'

'I don't fucking care.'

Chris leaned back and regarded him for a moment before breaking into a grin. 'Then fucking get on with it,' he said.

Chapter 50

VANESSA

Vanessa's mobile said 11.13 pm, Monday, 6 February. She tried to refocus on the task at hand, but anxiety kept intruding.

She was going to court in two days, and she was petrified.

Had she made a mistake? Would she lose the house? Regardless, it was too late to pull the plug—she'd made her final decision four months ago.

'If you withdraw now, the court will definitely order you to pay Charlotte and Wax's legal fees,' her new lawyer Marianne Winton had advised her back in October. 'But if we proceed to court we might get a compassionate judge who'll sympathise with your David versus Goliath situation and not compel you to pay their fees.'

It was a straw that Vanessa had clutched at eagerly.

'And you do have an excellent advocate in Marcus Stafford.'

Oh yeah. Him.

Vanessa had toyed with the idea of sacking Marcus, but that would probably fall into the cutting-off-your-nose-to-spite-your-face basket, and Marianne made a persuasive point. So she'd decided that proceeding was worth the risk, although it didn't stop her from freaking out. She loved this place. The boys had spent most of their lives here, and losing their home at the start of a new school year would be quite a blow.

Her eyes swept around the kitchen and everything took on a sentimental glow—the cupboard she'd painted lime green at Lachie's request; the boys' initials scratched into the windowsill; even the scuff marks on the lino under the wonky table where Daisy was now lying with her head on her paws. Vanessa had a sudden flashback to Dave sitting at the table on the day they'd first met ten months ago, when Daisy had plonked her head on his feet uninvited.

'Is Daisy bothering you?' she remembered asking.

'She's better than ugg boots, aren't you, mate?' Dave had said.

Vanessa fought rising desolation. She wondered if Heather had a dog and if Dave liked it better than Daisy. And had Dave spent Christmas at Heather's place, stealing kisses under the mistletoe? (Vanessa had once been surprised to read that Australia had seventy native species.) Had they shared an intimate New Year's toast to their future while Vanessa was at Kiri and Anthony's hangi, trying to hold herself together? Had they frolicked in the surf and sand on a romantic summer getaway?

She knew that Dave and Heather were still a couple because Jackson and Nickie were friends again (thank goodness), and she'd been shamelessly pumping her son for intel. 'Did Nickie mention her dad?' she'd ask, or, in a slight variation, 'What are Dave and Heather up to?' Jackson usually shrugged and grunted, 'Dunno,' but after the first day back at school he'd mentioned that Nickie thought Heather's profession, podiatry, was 'gross', and Vanessa had felt pathetically grateful for a victory even as puny as that.

It was four months since she'd seen Dave, but he was proving impossible to forget—partly because he was her inspiration for sitting here in front of her laptop at 11.15 pm on a weeknight. As her New Year's resolution, Vanessa had started writing *Laws of Love*, a novel about a down-to-earth veterinary nurse who grows to love a suburban solicitor she meets at the bus stop. The solicitor's name is Dane Campbell. He's tall and lanky, with liquid brown eyes and a recalcitrant eyebrow . . .

Daisy scratched at Vanessa's knee, and she reached down to ruffle her fluffy ears. She knew that canine experts said you were supposed to ignore attention-seeking behaviour, but clearly they didn't have a dog as irresistible as Daisy.

The doorbell rang. She jumped, her reflex reaction panic. At this hour? Where were the boys?

She relaxed as she remembered that Jackson and Lachie were asleep in their rooms and Joy was safely ensconced at her book club. Phew. But, who'd be ringing her doorbell at 10.40 pm? She walked warily down the hall, wishing she had a peephole.

'Who is it?' she called through the door.

'It's Amy Dunphy.'

Amy Dunphy?!

Vanessa flung the door open and was assailed by the sound of cicadas. Amy Dunphy stood on the threshold in a little sundress, looking a wreck. Her face was much paler than Vanessa remembered and her hands were visibly shaking as she clutched a large Crumpler backpack. Vanessa almost felt sorry for her until she remembered that Amy's lies about not receiving *Lost and Found Heart* had got her into this God-awful mess.

'Amy?' There was no need to add the rest: *What the hell are you doing here?* Subtext!

'Hi. I'm sorry for turning up so late.' Amy's voice was reedy with stress, and for a second Vanessa wondered if she might collapse. 'I've got something important to tell you. Can I come in?'

'What is it?'

'Can I come in first? Please?'

Curiosity might have killed the cat, but not knowing why Amy was here was much more likely to kill Vanessa, so she led Amy into the living room and offered her a seat. Amy sat and fidgeted silently for what seemed like hours.

'Well? What did you want to tell me?' Vanessa prompted.

Amy grimaced and fiddled with her black-rimmed glasses and Vanessa thought, If you don't tell me soon I'm going to rip those glasses right off your head and let Daisy wee on them.

'Well?'

Amy took a deep breath. 'I did receive *Lost and Found Heart*, just like you've always said.'

Vanessa felt a jolt of adrenaline.

'You *did*?'

'Yes.'

'So you're admitting the breach of copyright?'

'Yes,' said Amy, and Vanessa could see she was genuinely remorseful. 'But it wasn't my idea, I swear.'

'But . . . how?'

'I was new at Wax and I was so in awe of Charlotte . . . you know how that is . . .'

Do I ever, thought Vanessa.

'Anyway, Charlotte got writer's block and we already had her next novel scheduled for release, so I forwarded her a few manuscripts for inspiration, including yours. But then Charlotte delivered *Love Transplant* and I realised what she'd done and I was like, holy shit, and then she told me to delete *Lost and Found Heart* from Wax's system, and I didn't know what to do, because she was Charlotte Lancaster and I was just me . . . so I did it. But I've felt like shit about it ever since.' Amy's eyes were so teary that her glasses had fogged up and she took them off to clean them. 'And then you were so nice about my tooth that time we ran into each other. And I know you're going to court the day after tomorrow, and I just . . . I can't live with myself anymore. I know it's going to cost me my job, but I think you deserve the truth.' She looked at Vanessa beseechingly. 'Do you hate me?'

Yes!

No, not really. Well, only a bit. Props to Amy for coming clean, but her timing left a lot to be desired.

'Well, thank you for your honesty,' Vanessa said, resisting the urge to yell, 'But a fat lot of good it's going to do me now.' She took a moment to check herself. 'But, unfortunately, I think you'd just be discredited in the witness box as a "disgruntled former employee".'

'I know. That's why I wanted to see you in person.'

Amy reached into her satchel and pulled out a manuscript. Vanessa's eyes boggled.

'This is a hard copy of *Lost and Found Heart*, stamped and dated six months before Charlotte delivered *Love Transplant*, and this is the email correspondence between you and me.' Amy held her treasure out to Vanessa. 'It's yours.'

Chapter 51

A siren wailed its way through the city streets below as Charlotte Lancaster and her father Chip stared at the manuscript in horror.

'Oh, and I should mention,' Vanessa added, 'I also have a copy of the email correspondence between myself and Amy Dunphy.'

Mike Schwartz exchanged an alarmed glance with Charlotte's barrister, Graham Goetze. Alan McManus, the publisher at Wax, looked apoplectic. And as for Charlotte—that was the most gratifying part of all—she looked like she'd just bungee-jumped off a bridge and someone had called out after her, 'Oops, the elastic broke.'

'Amy! That little bitch. What are we going to do?'

'Shut up,' Chip barked.

'Can we see that?' Mike asked Vanessa.

She could tell his smile was masking panic, and she thought, I know the feeling.

She handed Mike the manuscript, and as he and the others pored over it, she took the time to rally. Her heart was pounding in her chest as she wiped her clammy palms on her best summer dress. Marianne Winton was interstate and wouldn't be back until late tonight, so with the trial due to start at 9 am tomorrow, Vanessa had convened this meeting in Graham Goetze's chambers solo. Glancing around his immaculate office she saw a miniature thatched hut on his desk with a plaque that read: WITH APPRECIATION FROM EFOKI VILLAGE. It rang a bell. Had Marcus mentioned something once? But she couldn't ask Marcus because he wasn't here—she hadn't bothered calling him. He was hardly an objective negotiator and, besides, she didn't need him. The realisation had empowered her, but it didn't mean she wasn't petrified. It was five against one.

'I want a settlement,' she demanded, cursing the quiver in her voice.

'Let's wait for your counsel before we discuss this,' Graham suggested pleasantly. He was short and stumpy with ears that seemed strangely out of proportion—but he exuded an air of authority. 'My PA's just called Stafford, and he's right across the road.'

'No. You shouldn't have made that call. I told you, I'm handling this myself.'

They all exchanged shifty glances, and then Chip gave Vanessa a dazzling smile. She could see his evil corporate negotiating skills kicking in.

'I underestimated you, didn't I, Ness? More fool me. You're obviously the kind of smart operator who'd prove an asset in a high-paying executive role in my company.'

'You can't bribe me with a job,' Vanessa told him disgustedly. 'You just said you'd underestimated me, but apparently you still think I'm stupid.'

She was quite pleased with that riposte. There was a nonplussed silence, and then Alan McManus exhaled loudly. His bald head was bright red.

'How much do you want?'

'Alan . . .' Mike Schwartz said warningly.

'She's got the evidence—it's over. Well? How much do you want?'

Vanessa quailed inwardly. 'Feel the fear and do it anyway,' she heard her mum say.

'I want three hundred and fifty thousand dollars.'

'Three hundred and fifty thousand dollars!?!'

'Yes. I want three hundred and fifty thousand dollars, plus my legal fees and a guarantee that Amy Dunphy will keep her job. Or I'll go to Buzzfeed and Facebook and Twitter—and I'll see you in court.'

At this, Charlotte flipped out. 'For God's sake, just give it to her! If this comes out, I'll lose the TV deal.'

The TV deal? What TV deal?

'Charlotte, shut up.' Chip roared.

Looking mutinous, Charlotte obeyed.

Vanessa turned back to see Mike Schwartz and Graham Goetze exchanging shrewd glances.

'Three hundred and fifty thousand seems like a reasonable starting point,' Mike said equably.

Graham nodded. 'I agree. I'm sure we can come to an equitable arrangement with a bit more discussion.'

'I'm not discussing anything,' Vanessa said firmly. 'I've told you my terms.'

She was proud of how 'badass' she sounded, and she wished the boys were here to see it. Meanwhile, Charlotte was making panicky noises.

Alan rounded on her. 'Be quiet,' he snarled. 'This is all your fault.' He turned to Vanessa. 'All right, you can have it: three hundred and fifty grand, and Amy keeps her job.'

'Oh, thank God!' Charlotte exclaimed. 'But we need a confidentiality clause—'

'I'm not a fool,' Alan cut across her. 'Of course, we'll only pay out on the strict condition of confidentiality.'

Vanessa's heart did a victorious little leap. 'Done.'

'But we're not paying your legal fees.'

The door burst open and Marcus appeared, looking tanned and astonishingly handsome in an artfully crumpled linen suit.

'What the fuck's going on?'

'I've just settled,' Vanessa informed him.

She couldn't help thinking how gratifying it was to see one of the legal profession's most articulate practitioners gawp like a constipated goldfish. She showed him the manuscript and waved the emails.

'How did you get all this?' he demanded. 'When did—'

'It doesn't matter. It's over.'

'Like hell it is.' Marcus's face was fuchsia with fury. 'You can't cut me out of the loop.'

'I just did.'

Marcus looked to Graham and Mike. They nodded in confirmation, and it seemed to Vanessa that Graham Goetze was hiding a smirk.

'Poor Marcus. There goes your chance to destroy me in the witness box,' Charlotte said maliciously, and Vanessa wondered how she'd ever held such a loathsome woman in such high esteem.

Chip marched over to Marcus and, even though Marcus was at least a head taller, for a second Vanessa thought that Chip was going to punch him.

'God knows, I felt sorry for you with all of Charlotte's goddamned shenanigans, but you've behaved reprehensibly,' he bellowed at Marcus. 'Why couldn't you just take it like a man instead of trying to destroy all the success that Charlotte's earned for herself?'

'That she's earned for herself?' Marcus scoffed. 'Lotts owes all her success to *me*.'

Vanessa was no fan of Charlotte's anymore, but she thought that was a bit of a stretch, and Marcus must have too, because he quickly qualified: 'What I meant to say is, ah, what I meant was, ah . . . I meant, obviously, as Charlotte's spouse I offered her moral support and, ah . . .'

'Will I tell them what you really meant, Marcus?' Charlotte said with a sneer as he trailed off.

They stared at each other with such intensity that Vanessa could almost see the steam rising.

'You wouldn't dare.'

But Charlotte just smiled blithely. She crossed her long honey-tanned legs and Vanessa noticed for the first time that she was knock-kneed.

'I'm moving on to greener pastures, so what do I care?' She turned to the room at large and announced, 'Marcus co-wrote six of my novels.'

Come again?!

Vanessa and the others gaped at Marcus as he attempted a derisive snort, but there was no stopping Charlotte now. She was clearly having the time of her life as she twisted the knife. *'Isabelle's nipples hardened like pink cherries at his brutish touch.'* She turned to Vanessa. 'Sound familiar?'

'That's from *A Healing Heart.*'

'He wrote it.'

'You're a fantasist!' Marcus said, throwing his head back and roaring with unconvincing laughter. He turned to Graham. 'Surely you're not going to take the word of a plagiarist?'

But Graham and Mike were openly snickering now, and Alan McManus looked like someone had slapped him across the face with a wet mullet.

'What the hell?'

'I'm sorry, Alan,' Charlotte said, with an apologetic expression that Vanessa thought was transparently fake, 'but Marcus wouldn't let me tell you. We couldn't risk his precious reputation as a cutting-edge intellect, could we, Marcus? But it does seem a shame that you've never been able to take a bow for your superlative prose. *Her back arched like a cat in the sunlight as she gasped in ecstasy.* A personal favourite.'

Vanessa recognised that sentence from *Emergency Love*, Charlotte's third novel. And Marcus had written it? This was hilarious. She found herself stifling giggles.

'Well, Marcus, your florid turn of phrase in the courtroom's got nothing on that,' Graham said, when he'd stopped laughing long enough to speak.

Marcus's head looked in danger of exploding. Mike was trying to rein in his mirth, but Chip seemed more perplexed than amused.

'What are you talking about?' he demanded of Charlotte. 'How did this happen?'

Charlotte shrugged. 'I'm sorry, Dad, I know I should have told you, but I was too scared to defy Marcus.'

Yeah, right, thought Vanessa. The only thing you'd ever be scared of is a compact without a mirror.

'I wrote *Intensive Caring* solo, but then I met Marcus and we wrote the next six books together. But Marcus was so obsessed with his reputation as an erudite intellectual that he insisted I take the sole credit.'

'She's lying,' Marcus interjected limply, but no one was listening to him anymore.

'The six novels we co-wrote were bestsellers, as we all know, but on a personal level I was starting to struggle with Marcus's control issues . . .'

Vanessa felt a flash of solidarity. I hear you, sister, she thought, before remembering that Charlotte was no friend of hers.

'And then I met Ned, and I tried to fight it, but we fell in love, so I left Marcus. And I thought, Well, I'll just have to write by myself again. How hard can it be? But then I discovered that I was so cowed by Marcus's bullying that I'd forgotten how. I had writer's block. It was devastating. I was terrified of letting my readers down . . . there's so much pressure.' Her bottom lip wobbled 'vulnerably', and every man in the room except for Marcus rushed to offer her

a hanky. She took them all. 'Thank you ... So in desperation ...'
She dabbed at eyes that looked suspiciously dry to Vanessa. 'Well,
you all know the rest.'

The men nodded fawningly and Chip patted her back. Vanessa
was suddenly overcome with revulsion. She'd had enough of this
venal self-serving lot to last her a lifetime.

'I'm leaving. I need a shower.' She stood and walked to the door.

'I'll get the settlement drafted today and send it to Marianne,'
Mike said.

'Oh, and you can also expect my invoice, Vanessa,' Marcus added
coldly. 'For one hundred thousand dollars.'

A hundred grand?! Vanessa felt the blood drain from her face,
but before she could say anything, Graham stepped in.

'Aren't you forgetting something, Marcus? Vanessa negotiated
this settlement, not you. And it might elicit some interesting reactions if our fellow members of the bar were to find out about your
tumescent prose.'

Marcus's humiliation was complete. It was like he was literally
deflating in front of Vanessa's eyes.

'All right,' he spat ungraciously. 'I'll forgo my fee.'

'Thank you,' Vanessa replied, and then she turned to Graham.
'And thank you too.' It seemed only polite, even though blind Freddy
could see that Graham had only intervened to spite Marcus.

Head high, Vanessa took her leave of the nest of vipers and walked
out to the marble-lined foyer. She stopped at the lift and pressed
the down button.

'Wait!'

She turned to see Alan McManus behind her. Oh, great.
What now?

'Just for the record, I didn't know about Charlotte's plagiarism
until after *Love Transplant* was published.'

Vanessa believed him, but so what? 'You still perpetuated the lie.'

'I was in an invidious position.'

Weren't we all, mate, she thought.

Alan scratched at his fulsome beard that seemed at odds with his bald head. 'But I'd like to talk about something else,' he transitioned smoothly. 'I want to offer you a contract with Wax.'

A contract? Really?

'*Love Transplant*'s sales were modest by Charlotte's standards, but for a novice author they warrant a second book. And we'd give you an advance—a generous one, obviously, because of this bloody mess. Are you interested?'

Was she interested?! Adrenaline coursed through Vanessa's veins, but she feigned nonchalance. 'Actually, I'm already working on my new romance.'

'Terrific! Fortuitous timing, then.'

'Yeah. It's about a veterinary nurse who falls in love with a suburban solicitor who catches her bus and—'

'Stop right there,' Alan interrupted. 'No suburban solicitors.'

Vanessa frowned. 'Why not?'

'Women read romance *because* they're married to suburban solicitors. The brief's simple—an obscenely rich bloke with an attitude to match. And for Christ's sake, forget the bus, Wax's heroes have got their own helicopters.'

'But I don't want to write about that kind of man,' Vanessa protested.

'Of course you do—you're a *romance* writer.'

'But who says that ordinary men like suburban solicitors can't be romantic heroes?'

'*I* do. The offer of a contract is still open, but the hero has to be an alpha male with a bulging wallet. Take it or leave it.'

Vanessa weighed this up for a millisecond. 'Thanks very much, but I'll leave it.'

Ping!

The lift arrived. Vanessa stepped inside and saw Alan McManus's astounded face reflected in the mirror. The lift doors closed and her heart thumped against her ribs all the way down to the ground floor.

Ping!

As she stepped out of the lift, she was overcome by an urge to ring Dave and share her news. After all, he'd been her lawyer until four months ago—he'd laid all the groundwork, surely he had a right to know? She rehearsed a casual tone in her mind. 'Oh, Dave, hey, just thought I'd give you a quick call to let you know that I've negotiated a settlement solo. Three hundred and fifty thousand. Not bad, eh?' She pictured Dave's smile and heard his warm voice glowing with pride. 'Good for you, Vanessa! Why don't I go and get some bubbles and we'll celebrate?'

She was so lost in the fantasy that she accidentally did two loops of the revolving door at the entrance, and it brought her back to reality. She couldn't call Dave. He'd made it clear that he didn't want to be involved in the case and, besides, he and Heather were probably engaged by now. She wondered if they'd have a church wedding. Unlikely; Dave was an atheist and Heather was the unsentimental type. Did that mean she wouldn't go too bridal? Maybe they'd toss convention aside and elope? Vanessa pictured Dave and Heather hand in hand under a palm tree, exchanging funny but heartfelt vows against a burnished sunset. It was torture. She had to stop doing this to herself.

She took out her phone and, before she could change her mind, she deleted Dave from her address book. She told herself she should feel relieved but, of course, she just felt like crap. To distract herself, she left a message for Marianne Winton, and then she headed home to share the good news.

Chapter 52

Lachie jumped up and down in the parched backyard. 'Three hundred and fifty thousand bucks?!'

Jackson punched the air. 'We're rich!'

'Well, not exactly.' Vanessa laughed. She still owed two hundred and ninety-three thousand dollars on the mortgage, and then she'd have Marianne's fees on top of that—and regardless of what Dave had said, she was planning to send him a cheque. Plus, she really should get a new car—the Corolla was on its last legs. 'Most of it's accounted for, but I reckon there'll be enough left over for an Easter holiday in Hawaii.'

'Hawaii? Sweet!'

As the boys excitedly speculated about surfing lessons and live volcanoes, Daisy leaped in the air and barked. Vanessa felt a flash of sadness that Daisy couldn't come to Hawaii with them, but she resolved to send her to one of those posh 'pet resorts' she'd heard about, where dogs could stay in studio rooms with lounge suites and TVs that opened out onto grassy grounds. It would probably be exorbitantly expensive, but so what? Daisy deserved a special holiday just as much as the rest of them.

Joy's car pulled into the driveway and the boys ran to meet her, clamouring around her window.

'Nan, Mum got three hundred and fifty thousand bucks!'

'Mum won, Nan!'

'Oh, Nessie, that's wonderful!' Joy cried as she climbed from the car with her knee joints clicking. 'Congratulations! I'm so proud of you.'

'Thanks, Mum.'

They shared a hug. Vanessa felt radiant. She really had negotiated a three-hundred-and-fifty-thousand-dollar settlement with hardened professionals all by herself.

'I knew you'd do it.' Joy released her, and Vanessa noticed her mother's breasts straining against her plunging neckline. Since her epiphany about Jack, Joy had lowered the volume on her more provocative outfits, but her cleavage was still as non-negotiable as her fingers or toes.

'Mum?'

Vanessa felt a hand on her shoulder and turned. It was Jackson. He'd shot up in the past few months and now he was slightly taller than her. She felt a lump in her throat—he was growing up.

'How are you feeling?' he asked in his new squeaky deep voice that didn't quite fit yet. He patted her self-consciously. 'Are you glad it's all over?'

'I'm very glad it's all over. Thank you for asking, sweetheart.' She squeezed his hand and he reddened.

'Hey, Mum?' Lachie interrupted. 'Will there be enough left over for a PS5 Pro?'

Vanessa grinned. 'There might be.'

'Yes!' Lachie shouted, jumping high. 'Sweet!'

'That's sick!' said Jackson.

'Woof woof!' said Daisy.

'G'day,' said Craig.

Vanessa spun around to see her ex-husband. He was wearing loafers without socks. You're kidding.

'Craig. I didn't hear the car.'

'Hey, Dad, Mum got a settlement!'

'Three hundred and fifty thousand bucks!'

'Really?' Craig looked impressed—as well he might, thought Vanessa. 'That's brilliant, Ness. Congratulations.'

'Thanks.'

His loafers had little tassels on top and they made him look like an idiot.

'Okay, fellas, hop to it,' he said. 'We're picking Nat up from work in twenty minutes.'

'Sweet,' said Jackson.

'Awesome,' said Lachie.

'That's a dollar,' said Vanessa.

'Why does Nat need a lift?' asked Joy. 'Is her broomstick in for a service?'

'Mum. Shhh.' Vanessa stifled a laugh, but the boys were heading for the back door and hadn't heard.

Craig scowled at Joy. 'That's supposed to be funny, is it?'

'Only for those with a sense of humour.' Joy winked and followed the boys into the house. Vanessa was about to say, 'Sorry about Mum, don't take any notice,' but then she thought, No, why should I? So she didn't. Craig looked like he was waiting, but when she didn't say anything he let it go.

'Three hundred and fifty grand, eh? Marcus must be pretty cluey to negotiate that much dough.'

'Actually, Marcus wasn't even there. I did the negotiating.'

He grinned as if she'd just cracked a cute joke. 'If only, eh?'

Vanessa felt a rush of rage and drew herself up to her full height. 'Craig,' she said icily, 'you might like to think that I'm an ineffectual person who warrants pity, but I'm actually a beautiful mother, a caring friend and a talented author with the courage to stand up for my rights in the public arena.' She realised she was quoting Dave and almost toppled over a cliff of despair, but she managed to bring herself back from the brink. 'And another thing—' she held out her hand '—I want my key back.'

Tap! Tap! Vanessa stirred from a fitful sleep and blinked at her bedside clock. It was 5.14 am. Tap! Tap! What was that? She looked outside. It was pitch-black. And then she heard a window open. Vanessa felt a cold clutch of fear. She jumped out of bed and grabbed a baseball bat that she kept nearby for just this eventuality. Daisy woke. Vanessa made a 'shhh' gesture and then silently tiptoed down the hall as Daisy followed.

Joy's bedroom door was ajar. Vanessa stopped as she heard the murmur of voices. She raised the bat in readiness and peered around the door—only to exhale with relief when she saw Joy helping Keith through her window. Sweet, gorgeous Keith! He was carrying the *Herald Sun*.

'I'm sorry to wake you up,' he was saying, 'but the early edition's just come in, and I was tickled pink to read about Nessie's settlement. I thought you might want to see the article?'

Vanessa caught her mother's expression in a sliver of moonlight. She was wearing an old polyester nightie and her hair was scraped back from a face devoid of make-up, and Vanessa thought that she'd never looked so beautiful.

'Oh, Keith, I've missed you so much . . .'

'Not as much as I've missed *you*.'

And they reached for each other in the moonlight.

Misty-eyed with happiness for her mum, Vanessa smiled and closed the door. She made her way to the kitchen. No point going back to bed, she was wide awake now. She'd give Daisy a chicken neck and make herself a cup of tea and check out the news sites, and then she'd . . . what? A sense of hopelessness descended as she thought of her future stretching long and lonely before her. But that was crazy, she told herself. She had so much to look forward to—paying off her mortgage, the holiday with the boys in Hawaii, self-publishing her second novel. Vanessa cheered at the thought of her novel. Yes, that's what she'd do—she'd get back to work on *Laws of Love*. She went to her room and grabbed her laptop, and then she made herself a cup of tea and started typing at the wonky table.

Rosie's head was lying on Dane's feet as he sat at Virginia's kitchen table.

'I'm sorry, I hope you don't mind,' Virginia said, but Dane reached down and patted Rosie's woolly head.

'She's better than ugg boots, aren't you, mate?'

Vanessa felt a small sense of comfort. She may have lost Dave Rendall forever, but she'd always have Dane Campbell.

Chapter 53

DAVE

Dave was on edge. The commissioner of the Victorian Civil and Administrative Tribunal was handing down his ruling on Kariem's discrimination case today, and it was due to land in Dave's inbox at any moment. Kariem was pacing in tiny circles behind him.

'What's taking so long?'

'Any second now,' Dave assured him, hoping he sounded more confident than he felt. He winked at Zafeera in her *Team Kariem* T-shirt and tweaked Mrs Hipsley's disco ball earring as it swung to and fro.

'Oh, David,' Mrs Hipsley giggled. She was such an old trooper, Dave thought fondly. She'd been a bit crook lately and really should be at home, but she'd insisted on seeing this through. 'I'm on Team Kariem too,' she'd said, swimming in a T-shirt that would have been a tight fit for a kid. Dave just hoped he wouldn't let Team Kariem down, but at least he could say hand on heart that he'd given it his all. LightZone nightclub had refused to acknowledge any discrimination, so mediation had failed and they'd proceeded to a final hearing on the VCAT Human Rights List, where he'd advocated for Kariem with such conviction and clarity that he'd even surprised himself.

'You were awesome, man,' Kariem declared.

'Amazing,' Zafeera agreed.

'You were wonderful, David,' Mrs Hipsley had trilled as she stood on tiptoe and planted a kiss on his cheek. Her coral-coloured lipstick had left an imprint that he hadn't noticed until he'd arrived home and Nickie had demanded, 'Who have you been kissing? Not the podiatrist?'

Nickie had been leery of Dave dating Heather from the start.

'You can't go out with someone who removes old people's ingrown toenails for a living,' she'd said with her face screwed up in revulsion.

'Of course I can. You're discriminating against podiatrists—that's exactly the kind of ingrained discrimination that I'm fighting against at VCAT.'

'You're a dork, Dad,' Nickie had said, laughing.

'Yes, but I'm a dork who doesn't discriminate.'

But as it turned out Nickie needn't have worried, because things between Dave and Heather had fizzled. Her pragmatism and no-nonsense attitude, so refreshing at the beginning, had started to seem like a lack of imagination. Where was the laughter? The hopes? The dreams? In truth, he found Heather a bit joyless, especially when he compared her to—Don't go there, Dave. He'd worried about hurting Heather's feelings, but she'd faced their January break-up with the same brisk attitude she brought to everything else.

'If it's not going to work, there's nothing I can do about it. New year, new start.'

Heather was in his past, but he was sure going to miss her cakes.

He tried to distract himself and Team Kariem by teaching Mrs Hipsley to surf the internet. She'd barely seen a computer, let alone experienced the worldwide web, and it was a treat to see her rheumy eyes light up with wonder. She asked him to take her to Myra's website for the Romance Book Club. Cripes! Dave was wincing at Myra's tortured prose and inexplicable design choices when *blop!* a new email arrived. They all jumped. Dave held his breath and checked the sender.

'It's from VCAT.'

'Quick, open it, man!'

Dave vaguely registered Kariem, Zafeera and Mrs Hipsley clutching hands as he opened the email and scanned it. Oh, thank Christ.

'We won! VCAT has ruled that you and your patrons were discriminated against, and they've awarded you twelve thousand dollars in compensation.'

Everyone cheered.

'Group hug!' said Kariem, and they all huddled together happily. 'Say it loud and say it proud—Team Kariem!'

Chris appeared around the side of the cubicle. 'What's all the fucking ruckus?'

Mrs Hipsley looked shocked at his language.

'We won!' Dave said. 'We won the fucking discrimination case. Oops, sorry, Mrs Hipsley.'

The poor old dear seemed a bit perturbed, but Dave thought to himself, She'll get over it.

'That'll fucking learn 'em, eh?' Chris said to Kariem. 'Good for you, and good for this bloke.' He gestured towards Dave with his thumb.

'Yeah, Dave's a legend,' said Kariem.

It was becoming a recurring theme, Dave noted with a touch of hubris. Dave Rendall, legend. But just as quickly as he puffed himself up, he reminded himself that it was the outcome, not the advocate, that mattered. Although he couldn't deny he was pretty stoked to have a win in front of Chris.

'Can I borrow this bloke for a second?' Chris asked.

'Of course,' said Zafeera. 'Go on Dave. We might check out the dark web while you're gone, eh, Mrs Hipsley?'

Everyone laughed, including Mrs Hipsley, who had no idea what Zafeera was talking about.

Chris led Dave to his office and plonked himself down behind his chaotic desk.

'So, good fucking work.'

'Thanks.'

Dave could feel the smile refusing to leave his face, as if someone had stuck it there with superglue. He looked around for somewhere to sit but all of Chris's chairs were covered in files, so he leaned against a cabinet.

'Actually, I was planning to talk to you about something else,' Chris said intriguingly.

'Yeah?'

'Yeah. Fucking Steph's decided to move to fucking Newcastle.'

'Fuck!'

Steph was one of NorMel's best lawyers.

'Yeah. Her partner's going, so she wants to go too. Fucking selfish, eh?' Chris grinned. 'So what do you reckon? You want her job?'

Dave's heart stopped. 'Ah, sorry . . . what did you say?'

'You heard me, you fucking plonker. Do you want Steph's fucking job or not?'

Dave beamed so widely that his face hurt. 'Fuck, yeah.'

———◡———

Dave walked out of Chris's office. He'd actually done it, he'd achieved his dream of a career in social justice, so why was his elation fading so fast? It was a strictly rhetorical question. Not being able to share this moment with Vanessa somehow diminished it, and that pissed him off. Wake up to yourself, Rendall, stop wallowing. Life had moved on and he had to move with it. He resolved to leave all thoughts of Vanessa behind—but when he arrived back at his cubicle, he was confronted by Charlotte Lancaster's website.

'David, guess what?' said Mrs Hispley. 'Charlotte Lancaster's going to host a new book show on TV. It's just been announced.'

That'd be right, thought Dave. If you're rich and famous, you can count on being rewarded for appalling behaviour.

'I think it's so lovely,' Mrs Hipsley rhapsodised. She was a rusted-on fan, no doubt about it. 'I know you were on that other girl's side, but I could never bring myself to believe that Charlotte would copy somebody else's book.' Dave bristled on Vanessa's behalf, but if he hadn't convinced Mrs Hipsley yet, he never would. 'I'm just so glad for Charlotte that all that ugly business is over.'

'It's not quite over yet,' he pointed out. 'They're probably in court as we speak.'

'No, they didn't go to court.'

'Yes, they did.'

'No, they didn't.'

Dave frowned. Was Mrs Hipsley getting confused?

'They settled yesterday,' Zafeera confirmed. 'I saw it online this morning.'

Dave was surprised. So Stafford had settled at the eleventh hour? How had he managed that in the absence of evidence? And how much had he settled for? Curiosity got the better of Dave, and he sat beside Mrs Hipsley and googled *Vanessa Rooney settlement Marcus Stafford*. The first link that came up was a *Daily Mail* headline:

RED FACE FOR GLAMOUR BARRISTER

Dave's eyes goggled. He clicked on the link.

As if Marcus Stafford's year hasn't been bad enough with his celebrity wife Charlotte Lancaster shutting him out of her life, now he's been shut out by client Vanessa Rooney, who's negotiated a confidential settlement in her breach of copyright case against Lancaster and Wax Publishing Pty Ltd without involving Stafford, her high-profile counsel. Sources close to the negotiations say that Ms Rooney deliberately excluded Stafford and negotiated the terms solo. And in the words of our confidential source, the dental assistant 'played hardball'.

Dave's heart swelled with pride in Vanessa, but what had prompted her rebellion? He read on.

Reached by phone, Ms Rooney's mother Joy Spriggs confirmed that Ms Rooney also rejected Wax Publishing's offer to publish her new novel, *Laws of Love*, 'because this second book is so very special to her'. Mrs Spriggs said that Ms Rooney plans to self-publish the new tome, featuring a love affair between a veterinary nurse called Virginia Clooney and a suburban solicitor called Dane Campbell who, in Mrs Spriggs's words 'is modelled on the real-life man of Vanessa's dreams'.

'See, David? I told you: they've settled.'
'How much do you think she got?'
'Yes, how much do you think?'
'Dave?'
'David?'
'He looks a million miles away.'
'David?'

'Dave?'

Dave turned and blinked. Zafeera and Mrs Hipsley were looking at him expectantly, but it's a bit hard to hold up your end of a conversation when your heart is exploding with sunshine.

Chapter 54

VANESSA

Vanessa was wiping saliva from a bikie's beard. It was a long grey scraggly beard that went all the way down to his chest, and it occurred to her that every time he made love to his wife, it must tickle her cleavage.

'Thanks, darl,' he said gruffly.

'You're welcome, Spike,' she replied, smiling at him through her full-face visor. She chucked his soggy bib in the bin and replaced it, and then Anthony handed her the triplex syringe. He was shaking his head at Spike's mouth.

'Mate, this isn't good.'

'What can I say, doc? I love me lollies.'

'You've got to get over that. You still need another six fillings— that's three more appointments.'

Spike grimaced in horror.

Anthony resumed drilling and he and Vanessa bent over Spike's mouth.

Bzzzzzzzzz!

Vanessa had a faint sense that she could hear a voice beneath the buzz of the drill, but she decided she must have imagined it. She focused on Spike's sepia-coloured teeth and wondered how he'd managed to eat anything, let alone sugary lollies, with so many cavities.

Anthony briefly turned off the drill.

'Vanessa!' a voice yelled into the sudden silence.

Vanessa jumped in shock and turned, squirting Dave in the eye with water.

He reeled backwards.

'Dave?! I'm so sorry!'

'It's okay,' he said, squinting at her. 'I love you.'

Vanessa almost fainted, but instead she fell into his arms and he pressed his lips against her visor. She kissed him back from the other side of the plastic. Fireworks shot into the sky. Angels serenaded them. Please dear God, she thought, please let this really be happening. She was terrified to open her eyes in case Dave was a mirage—but then he pulled her foggy visor up and their lips met properly for the first time and all her doubts were dispelled.

'Oh, Dave, I love you too.'

His breath tasted minty fresh and she could tell that he'd brushed his teeth especially. It was so typically thoughtful. Somehow Dave's kiss managed to be transcendent and feel like home at the same time, and Vanessa would have loved for it to go on forever, but eventually reality intruded and she forced herself to pull away.

'Umm, we shouldn't . . . sorry Anthony . . .' she said, wondering if she looked as flustered she sounded. 'I know this is inappropriate in the workplace . . .'

Anthony shook his head with a smile she could only describe as sardonic. 'You reckon?'

'Yeah, sorry, mate . . .' Dave's ears were bright pink, and Vanessa thought it was the most adorable thing she'd ever seen. 'And sorry to interrupt your appointment,' he said to Spike. 'I was going to wait for Vanessa's tea-break, but Kiri said—'

'About bloody time.'

Vanessa turned to see Kiri smiling smugly in the doorway.

'I thought you two would never get your act together.'

Was there ever a better frind in the world? If there was, Vanessa would like to meet her—but only briefly, because no one could ever replace Kiri.

'Oh, Kiri,' she said emotionally.

Anthony shook his head at his wife.

Kiri marched into the room and grabbed the triplex syringe out of Vanessa's hand. 'I'm taking over. No arguments, Niss.'

Vanessa wondered how Kiri could possibly think that she'd argue. All she wanted in the world right now was to be alone with Dave.

'Thank you . . .' She wanted to cry, but in the best way possible.

'Yeah, thanks,' added Dave, and Vanessa noticed that his voice sounded wobbly too. 'And sorry for the interruption, fellas.'

'Yeah, sorry.'

Spike and Anthony waved their apologies away.

'Just get out of here,' ordered Kiri.

Vanessa and Dave walked out to the empty waiting room hand in hand. Vanessa's heart was overflowing with a joy that seemed to have swallowed her vocabulary.

'Oh, Dave,' was all she could manage.

'That's me,' he said with a chuckle. He looked as flushed as she felt, and she was transfixed by his long thick lashes, worthy of an alpaca. He reached behind Kiri's reception desk and produced a dozen long-stemmed red roses. 'For you.'

Oh my goodness, thought Vanessa, what exquisite torture. She would have loved to accept these sublime roses—she could already picture them dignifying Aunty Julie's crystal vase. But she reminded herself that she'd almost lost Dave because of her obsession with hollow romantic gestures, and she wanted him to know that she'd learned her lesson.

'Thank you, but I don't want them.'

She threw the roses into the bin, hoping that Kiri would rescue them later. She was expecting Dave to be delighted, so she was a bit surprised when he seemed bewildered.

'Oh.'

He stood uncertainly for a moment, and then he reached behind the desk again and pulled out a box of handmade chocolates. Dark chocolate and ginger, her favourite! Trust Dave to remember.

He held them out tentatively. 'Um, do you want . . . ?'

'No, I don't want those either,' Vanessa lied. She put them back on Kiri's desk, because she couldn't quite face the thought of throwing them into the bin. She reached up to put her arms around him. 'I'm prioritising life's true values, Dave. I don't need empty romantic gestures, I just need you—you're a full box, even if you are wrapped in brown paper.'

She hugged him and rested her head against his chest. There was a little dark mark on his tie and she sniffed it—soy sauce.

But Dave was gently disengaging from her embrace. 'Okay, now I'm confused. Should I cancel it?'

'Cancel what?'

'I've booked us into the Park Hyatt. Anthony's giving you twenty-four hours off.'

'Oh my gosh! Does Anthony know that?'

'I don't know, but I'm sure Kiri will tell him soon.' Vanessa chuckled, but Dave still looked confused. 'I've booked us a private spa and couple's massage for six o'clock, but if you think that's a hollow gesture . . . ?'

Every fibre of Vanessa's being longed to be in that warm bubbly water with him, but she couldn't abandon her new principles so quickly. She had to prove to Dave and herself that she'd grown as a woman and a human being.

'Yeah, pretty hollow,' she said, hoping she sounded more convinced than she felt. 'Why don't we spend the money on something more useful?'

'More useful?'

'Yeah. Like, um . . .' She racked her brain in search of a sensible household product. 'Like a compost bin. Or a whipper snipper.'

Dave regarded her silently for a moment. Then he grinned. 'You're a dickhid.'

The Ind

Acknowledgements

Jo Bell has given me invaluable feedback and brilliant ideas right from this story's inception. I can't thank you enough, Jo. Ali Lavau is the editor of my dreams. Thank you, Ali. I'd also like to thank Annette Barlow at Allen & Unwin for placing her confidence in my novel, and editor Christa Munns for her wonderful work and support. And a big thank you to my agent Anthony Blair and my former agent, Jo Butler, both of whom took the time to read my manuscript more than once.

Michael Wise QC very generously led me though the litigation process step by step. Any inadvertent legal inaccuracies are mine, not his. Dr C. Andrew McAliece kindly acted as my dental consultant, and any inadvertent dental inaccuracies are his. Just kidding.

Many thanks to Lynne Haultain for giving me rigorous and extremely helpful feedback, and to Lou Ryan for spurring me on to get cracking. Ray Boseley went above and beyond the call of duty to help a Luddite like me with the latest games technology, so thanks Ray. Jesse Blackadder and Fiona Wood offered moral support and advice, and Jesse even took time out to format my early manuscript. (Told you I was a Luddite.)

Emma Cornall, Anne Chehebar and Ariane Vrisakis helped me with early legal queries, and Angela Christa, Stephanie Coleman, June Coleman and Jane Lee-Stewart read early excerpts for me. Thank you all, but an extra special thanks to Angela for coming up with the title, *Losing the Plot*.

And, of course, I have to thank Hazel, the model for Daisy, who sat loyally under my desk for every minute I spent writing this book. And thanks also to beautiful Tori, and most of all to Alan, who shares me with the characters in my head without complaint (mostly!). Love youse all.